PENGUIN B

BOOK OF E

Esther David writes about Jewish life in India and personally illustrates her books. She is the author of the highly acclaimed *The Walled City, Book of Rachel, Man with Enormous Wings* and *Ahmedabad: City with a Past,* among others. She has also written a collection of short stories, *By the Sabarmati,* a children's book, *My Father's Zoo,* and co-authored *India's Jewish Heritage: Ritual, Art and Life-cycle.* Her books have been translated into several languages, including French, Gujarati and Marathi. Her work is included in the library of modern Jewish literature, Syracuse University Press, New York.

Esther received the Sahitya Akademi Award for English literature in 2010 and the Hadassah-Brandeis Institute Research Award, USA, for documenting the Bene Israel Jews of Gujarat and the study of Indo-Jewish cuisine. The French translation of *Book of Rachel* received the Prix Eugénie Brazier. Esther belongs to the Bene Israel Jewish community of Ahmedabad.

PRAISE FOR THE BOOK

'This book is a celebration of colours, fragrances, rituals, textures and variously coded emotions of a vanished milieu. A living archive, it is a visit to the childhood museum'—Ranjit Hoskote, *Gentleman*

'There is just one word to describe *Book of Esther*: gutsy. Deeply personal and unflinchingly honest, Esther David chronicles the lives of a prodigiously talented Jewish family, sweeping across places, generations and times with a deft and sure hand . . . Esther [is] a gifted storyteller'—Subashree Krishnaswamy, former editor of *Indian Review of Books*

'A Jewish woman traces her ancestry. The result is a vivacious Indian story . . . delicately woven between memory and fiction'—*Sunday Express*

'The tale sweeps across generations, times, cities with panache'—*Deccan Chronicle*

'Jewish literature has down the ages displayed a unique ability to flow in continuity like an underground river. Esther David's first novel catches mystical and magical rhythms of life with an individual voice, which enriches the novel'—Randhir Khare, *Indian Review of Books*

'Few can write with Esther David's subtlety and depth and tell a good story'—*Book Review*

'*Book of Esther* is East of Esther's Persia, a full-scale Indian Jewish novel of the unique Bene Israel community in India'—Shalva Weil, *Jerusalem Post*

'A potent groundbreaking powerful novel, which is brutally honest'—Amy Kazmin, *Jerusalem Report*

'Esther David evokes a world of colourful Indian Jewish characters, bringing to mind Isaac Bashevis Singer's evocation of the Shetetls in Poland and the Dybukks haunting them'—Marie-France Calle, *Le Figaro*

BOOK *of*
ESTHER

Esther David

PENGUIN BOOKS

An imprint of Penguin Random House

PENGUIN BOOKS

USA | Canada | UK | Ireland | Australia
New Zealand | India | South Africa | China

Penguin Books Books is part of the Penguin Random House group of companies
whose addresses can be found at global.penguinrandomhouse.com

Published by Penguin Random House India Pvt. Ltd
4th Floor, Capital Tower 1, MG Road,
Gurugram 122 002, Haryana, India

Penguin
Random House
India

First published in Viking by Penguin Books India 2002
Published in Penguin Books by Penguin Random House India 2018

10 9 8 7 6 5 4 3 2

This is a work of fiction. Names, characters, places and incidents are either the
product of the author's imagination or are used fictitiously and any resemblance to
any actual person, living or dead, events or locales is entirely coincidental.

ISBN 9780143444541

Typeset in Sabon Roman by SÜRYA, New Delhi

Printed at Repro India Limited

www.penguin.co.in

For Kiran-Amos,
my first grandchild

Contents

Contents

Acknowledgements

Four years back, when I was in New Delhi, David Davidar of Penguin spoke to me about this project. I agreed. I had no idea where it was going to lead me. The only clarity was the title—*Book of Esther*. After discussions with Krishan Chopra, my editor, I started writing. His continuous support and Mala Dayal's, née Singh, editing made this novel possible.

Book of Esther is based loosely around my family. As I began to work on it, I found that old family photographs were inspiring. I opened boxes containing notes, diaries, documents, paper clippings and every possible written material besides to help me along. To add to this, my cousins Sybil and Elizabeth gave me some rare material. And I already had the memory of my grandmother's narratives of the family history and my observations of the lives led by various family members.

I also had my own experience of growing up in a zoo, which my father Reuben David had made in Ahmedabad, to which Babu—Mohmedbhai Rasoolbhai Shaikh—my father's aide at the zoo, provided further inputs.

Namrata Dwivedi worked as my research assistant. She organized manuscripts, books, photographs, sheafs of papers, letters. Her mere presence in the house was of great help. While Lilabehn looked after the kitchen, Piyush Desai helped me with my computers and Villoo Mirza helped simply by believing in me.

I took lessons on the Torah from Johny Pingle, the cantor of the Magen Abhraham synagogue, Ahmedabad. His wife Julie introduced me to Jewish cuisine and rituals. On the initiative of Dr Shalva Weil of Jerusalem University, the study of Jewish costumes helped me describe my characters in detail.

My son Robin and daughter Amrita helped me with the editing and were critical but supportive when necessary. My son-in-law Nathaniel's idea of continuity with my first novel *The Walled City* has given more body to the text, yet the part on Joshua is about my father Reuben David, who set up a zoo in Ahmedabad. For the analysis of my drawings, I would like to thank Dr Paulette le Tarte and Dr D.M. Rao.

Halfway through the book, I also experienced a writer's block. I went on a yatra to Alibaug, where my ancestors had landed after a shipwreck. For this trip I am thankful to Irene and Abhraham Rohekar and Samson David Wakrulkar. The landscape around Alibaug gave a new dimension to my work. The story really took shape from this point. Charged, I returned back to Ahmedabad to give the final touches to *Book of Esther*.

Author's Note

BOOK OF ESTHER is a work of fiction inspired by a real event, the arrival of my ancestors on the Konkan coast. I am named after Queen Esther from the Megillat and *Book of Esther* in the Bible.

As the only child of working parents, I was left with my grandmother in the ancestral house where she stayed with her oldest son and his family. Here in the Delhi Darwaza house, where relatives visited us during vacations and sometimes stayed on for long periods, I heard all the family stories. That was before their exodus to Israel or England or America or Canada. Yet, the house remained the focal point which received all those stories, through letters, telephonic talks or as the nostalgic recollections of those who were left behind.

With my own deep desire to run away from the family, it so happened that I stayed the longest in Ahmedabad. The elders passed away and the others started losing contact. Till I found myself alone, with just my own children and a large collection of photographs and stories I wanted to tell them. This became the fertile ground for *Book of Esther.*

But, before that, *The Walled City* was born. It was created from a torn photograph of my mother's family. A family I had never known. This was the period after the death of my father.

I needed the comfort of the large extended Jewish family I had lost. Some characters, which took shape there, have found their way in the later part of *Book of Esther*.

The ancestors have now become very real to me. I feel their presence around me. Sometimes they bind me, sometimes they comfort me. When I left them in safe custody with my editors, I felt strangely lost without them.

This feeling was accentuated when I heard that the old house at Delhi Darwaza had been reconstructed and the ladder made of Burma teak leading to the upstairs rooms, specially the mysterious storeroom, had been sold. On my last visit there, I had felt the touch of all my ancestors in the grain of the old wood and I brought back an old terracotta tile from the kitchen.

During the writing of *Book of Esther*, Gujarat experienced the worst earthquake of the century and saw a communal riot which has shaken the very roots of our existence. *Book of Esther* proved to be a salvation and helped me to keep going through these enormously difficult periods.

Lastly, I had assumed *Book of Esther* would be a historical novel. But as I journeyed with the patriarchs and matriarchs, I decided that I did not want to write a historical book.

I wanted to rewrite *Book of Esther*.

1

Bathsheba

Bathsheba

1

Every afternoon, after a bath, Bathsheba closed the door of her room and sat on the floor oiling her hair, facing Solomon's portrait on the wall. That was the only time that she felt in total communion with him and knew that he was alive.

The portrait showed Solomon sitting erect on a gilded chair, dressed in his best blue angarkha and a white dhoti with a gold border. He was holding a jewelled sword in his hand and wearing a red turban. He looked an impressive man with his bushy eyebrows and small but expressive eyes, and under the long thick nose was a huge black moustache whose ends were spread out like pointed daggers. At his feet sat a panther; the patterns on Solomon's clothes and dots on the panther's body were both in gold. The background was a flat green with a sprinkling of red flowers and gold dots.

Solomon was very fond of animals. He would bring home any little animal—or bird—he found in Danda, Revdanda or Nandgaon. Solomon had found the panther cub alone and dying in a ber bush on the hillock behind their house. He had brought it home and fed it warm milk soaked in cotton.

This is how Chitta had grown up in the house, and for

company he had the hounds which Abraham had bought from a travelling trader. It was a common sight to see Chitta sitting at Solomon's feet. In the house Chitta behaved like a domestic cat. Solomon had taught him to retract his claws and to eat mincemeat and chapatis like the dogs. During the day, Chitta was kept on a leash. Nights he spent with the dogs on the veranda.

One night Solomon had woken up with the barking of the hounds. He had sensed that there was something dangerous lurking outside. Opening the window, he saw two eyes shining in the darkness. Perhaps Chitta's mother had not died, as they had assumed, and had come looking for her son. Solomon understood that there was a link between Chitta and the animal which stood staring at the house. Chitta was standing still, and not growling as he normally did when he saw strangers. Then Solomon heard him moan. There was a welcome in his call. Solomon was certain that the panthers belonged to the same family.

At some point, the dogs stopped barking and he saw that the other animal had disappeared into the night. The next day, the men combed the entire Dandekar estate and the surrounding area armed with swords, sticks and whatever else they had in the house. But there was no trace of the other animal, and he was relieved to find its pugs disappearing into the forest beyond the fields.

The following night, Solomon kept the dogs indoors and left Chitta unchained on the veranda. He waited at the window with a sturdy stick. Around midnight the dogs started growling, and he heard the soft paws of a big animal moving on the veranda.

Not sure about the intentions of the stranger, he stood ready with the stick but relaxed when he saw the animals touch noses and lick each other's necks. That night Chitta disappeared into the forest.

Sometimes, on silent nights, they heard his familiar call from the distant hills. Solomon knew that Chitta was better off in the forest with his own kind.

Soon after, Solomon himself left.

2

IT WAS VERY hard on Bathsheba not to speak about her husband or ask somebody to go to the army headquarters in Bombay for the latest news. She wanted to tell the women of the house that she missed her husband and feared for his life. There was news that there would be another battle with the formidable Tipu Sultan, the last and final battle, it was said. She would have liked to cry and speak about her fears. But the house maintained its calm routine, and Bathsheba controlled herself.

In his absence, day after day, Bathsheba had watched the curving road which would bring him back to Danda. In the evening light, it looked like a serpent—glistening and dangerous. Would it lead Solomon home or would it become a symbol of their separation?

Whenever Bathsheba returned from her lonely vigil on the hillock behind the house, she saw Abraham sitting on the chair with the lion legs. From here he kept watch on the entire property, the badee which he had inherited from his father. Every day, he sat on the veranda worrying about the future of the estate. With just Sombhau in charge of everything, the maintenance was no easy matter.

Since Solomon had left, Abraham was finding it hard to cope with the house and the baadee. It was a common sight to see him banging his walking stick on the floor and cursing his youngest son. 'Enoch, stop flying kites and learn something from Sombhau,' Bathsheba and Shlumith would hear him scream, as they made poha-papads in the courtyard.

Abraham's second son, Menashe, worked as a teacher and was married to Bathsheba's niece Shlumith. He was disappointed that none of his sons took an interest in farming.

Bathsheba understood Abraham's feelings and often discussed this matter with Elisheba. 'Enoch is like my son. He is far too young to take up the responsibility of the baadee.'

Bathsheba hoped Elisheba would explain to Abraham that it was not good to push Enoch too hard. But Elisheba always took Abraham's side. 'Don't you see that none of our sons are interested in the baadee? This includes your own husband. Could you stop him from joining the army? It is necessary to train Enoch in such matters from a young age. Eventually he must shoulder the responsibility of the Dandekars.'

3

WHEN SHLUMITH AND Menashe closed their bedroom door at night, Bathsheba could not help feeling jealous. She missed Solomon. The beauty of a closed bedroom door was lost on her.

Bathsheba touched her quilt with deep longing. She remembered Solomon's massive chest and the comfort of his arms. She scolded herself for grudging Shlumith the pleasures of love. 'Perhaps Shlumith is pregnant,' thought Bathsheba. 'She has not entered the Rajodarshan room for the last two months.' Shlumith was much younger than her, and Bathsheba decided that she would look after her like a daughter.

Solomon would surely return and they would sleep under the quilt together. She inhaled the smell of the old quilt and it comforted her with the fragrance of happy memories which were stitched within its folds. She decided to make a new quilt to celebrate Solomon's return.

She looked into her box of old clothes and began putting aside pieces of cloth. At the end of the day, she realized that they looked grey and old. Perhaps it was the evening light playing tricks on her eyes. Then she realized that it was her sense of gloom that had made her choose a range of greys. She did not hear Shlumith come in. 'Tai, shall I help you?' she asked.

Bathsheba did not answer. She rushed out of the room and threw the bundle of cloth into the kitchen fire.

Shlumith was taken aback. She had never seen Bathsheba act in such a way before. 'Why did you do that?' she asked Bathsheba tentatively. Bathsheba shook her head and did not reply. Sitting next to Bathsheba, Shlumith whispered, 'We will make a quilt together. It would be good to mix and match patterns. Look at this orange and green, they look good together, don't they?'

Bathsheba saw the younger woman's bright face in the half light. She raised the wick of the lantern and said, 'You have a good eye for colours. You know I wanted to make a happy quilt for my husband's return with bright colours and all sorts of patterns. Tell me, how does one begin?'

'My aunt taught me quilting, embroidery and bead work. She always said that when one works with cloth, it is always good to have a plan in mind. Let me suggest a design. If you do not like my idea, we can think of something else. I feel you would like the pattern of a beautiful night.' Shlumith smiled mischievously. She saw that Bathsheba liked what she was saying because her cheeks were flushed. 'So the quilt will have a sprinkling of stars. But then stars have a silver colour, so we would have to use brocade, and that is not nice to have near the skin. Instead we could make the stars with the colours of the rainbow, in red, green, purple, blue, orange . . . . They will give the quilt a feeling of light and brightness. The stars will form the centre of the quilt. But just stars can be boring, so I will teach you some embroidery and we will make borders of flowers.'

When Shlumith saw that there was a broad smile on Bathsheba's face, she said, 'Let us start making it right now, why wait for tomorrow?'

Shlumith's mood was infectious and both women started planning like young girls. Elisheba peeped into the room to see what had made Bathsheba laugh. She felt relieved that Bathsheba was feeling better, as the whole house had a smell of burning cloth. If it meant making a quilt for Solomon—her first born—she sighed, she would give them her box of cloth pieces she had collected through the years.

Under the light of the lanterns, the three women sorted out the box of coloured cloth, prints, borders and embroidery. The starry night pattern would be made for Solomon, and the design of green leaves would be for Shlumith's first born.

As they made the base of the quilt, Bathsheba told Shlumith that she could not spend her Saturdays doing nothing. It depressed and troubled her. She only thought about death. In fact she had started dreading the shabath.

Shlumith said to Elisheba, 'Tai is becoming very depressed, she scares me when I see her sitting in her room. Could we not make a concession for her? She could at least make her quilt on the shabath?'

'I cannot take a decision on my own. I must ask my

husband. After all it is a religious matter,' replied Elisheba.

The shabath was the only day that work stopped on the farm. All other days they woke to the cranking of the oil press that would stop only when the bullocks were led to the village pond in the evening. That and, of course, the sound of the sea as the waves broke upon the shore.

The shabath, which actually began from sundown on Friday itself and continued till sundown the next day, was special for the family. Friday night they lit two clay lamps and said some prayers in Hebrew. Dinner followed with chicken curry, rice, vegetables and the choicest fruit from their orchard. They sang songs, as Enoch strummed a tune on the sarangi. Then they played games in which the old and the young joined in. The shabath meant festivity extending into the night. They did not work on Saturdays and ate leftover food during the day. At sunset, on Saturdays when the shabath ended, the women made a quick dinner of moong dal khichdi and bombil-batata, Bombay duck with potatoes.

When she asked Abraham, he had a ready solution. 'Bathsheba does everything in accordance with the law. So there is no harm if she does something for herself in the house. The most I can allow her is that she can work on the quilt, but nothing else. I am taking this decision based on the story of prophet Abraham. When the Jews were making the pyramids, was there any proof that they did not work on Saturdays?' With this, for the first time, a tradition was broken in the Dandekar house. Many more were to be broken in the years to come.

4

'IT IS IMPOSSIBLE for Enoch to discuss details about the harvest with Sombhau,' argued Bathsheba. But Elisheba was adamant.

'Enoch must stop behaving like a child,' she said.

Bathsheba and Shlumith were grinding the flaked rice, kneading it into a dough with flour, then rolling and drying the papads on an old sari. Bathsheba's thoughts were moving in circles, like her hands. When Elisheba left them alone and returned to the kitchen, Bathsheba confided in Shlumith. 'Our baadee needs somebody from the family to look after the accounts, the storage and payments. Your husband's elder brother was never interested in these matters. The property exasperated him. And now our father-in-law is forcing Enoch to take the responsibility. He is still a child, and more interested in gilli-danda. Remember, he was born when I came here as a bride. And although I was just a girl, I helped our mother-in-law with his birth.

'I have always been interested in the baadee. It attracts me. I would like to learn everything about paddy and supari from Sombhau . . . My mother always said that I had a bossy streak in me. She never liked it. She tried to change me, saying that only men had a right to behave like masters. Why can't we take their place in their absence?'

Shlumith did not know how to react. She was afraid that her elder sister-in-law would go too far with her notions and throw the house into turmoil. But without Solomon, Bathsheba was bored. He was the centre of her life. Without him, she compared her life to the oxen which turned the oil press.

Elisheba had her own life in the kitchen. It was her domain. Like a hawk, she saw to it that Shantabai, the maid, did everything in the proper way. And it was Abraham's duty to cut the birds and animals according to the laws of kosher he had learnt from his grandfather. It was a common sight to see him cutting the meat on the chopping board in the courtyard, his hands smeared with blood.

Bathsheba and Shlumith had both come to the family as young girls and their role in the kitchen was that of helpers. They were given only limited tasks, besides which it was their duty every day to clean the shabath room or the courtyard where they ate together. The artistic Shlumith decorated the house, changing the position of things and objects. In the afternoon she embroidered bedsheets and made quilts, skills she had learnt from her aunt who lived in Surat.

For the shabath and other rituals, the women prepared the wine with black currants and prepared a thali with a bowl of salt and bhakri, on the special shabath carpet. Carpets of all sizes, colours and designs were stacked in the storeroom for different occasions and rituals.

5

IT TOOK COURAGE for Bathsheba to speak to her father-in-law about her desire to be in charge of the property. She wanted to help Sombhau, who was almost as old as Abraham—the two had grown up together on the farm—and also learn in the process.

Bathsheba was aware that none of the women of their family had ever taken an interest in what was supposed to be the domain of men. It was always the men who were in charge of everything. The women were expected to stay indoors, look after the house and bring up the children. She was certain that her decision to step outside the house would bring a lot of opposition from her own family and other Bene Israel families from Revdanda and Nandgaon.

When Bathsheba decided to speak to Abraham, he was taking his afternoon nap. 'How can he sleep in a chair,' she wondered. She noticed that the pillow behind his neck was dirty and faded, and made a mental note to ask Shlumith to make him a new one. Nervously, Bathsheba framed and reframed the sentence several times in her mind.

When Abraham woke up, he saw Bathsheba sitting on the steps staring at him. He did not like the intensity of her eyes. So he yawned and asked, 'Has something happened?' Bathsheba was surprised that he had read her thoughts.

A little shaken, she stood up and said that she would get some kheer for him. He surprised her further. 'Elisheba is already bringing it, so tell me, what is bothering you?'

Taking a deep breath she spoke so softly that Abraham had to remind her, 'Arre, have you forgotten that I am going deaf.'

'This is about Enoch,' Bathsheba said loudly and saw Abraham bristle. He had become very sensitive about Enoch. Enoch had started playing hide-and-seek with his father because Abraham started a volley of abuses as soon as he saw him. Everybody dreaded the moment when father and son confronted each other. Bathsheba continued, 'Enoch is still young. I have been listening to all the exchanges you have with Enoch. Since my husband joined the army, it is very clear that nobody is interested in the baadee. Excuse me if it sounds as though I am interfering in family matters. I know that women should not discuss matters which concern men. But I feel Enoch is being forced to do something he does not like. He is still a child and needs to play and study. You know he is doing very well at the missionary school in Nandgaon.'

Here she had to stop as she was interrupted by Abraham's snigger, 'Child, huh! I was married and running this place at his age.'

Bathsheba did not react and continued speaking, 'I am not taking his side but times are changing. And if you see life from his eyes, you will understand what I mean. I am the eldest daughter-in-law of the house, and in the absence of my husband, I would like to take his place. I want to take the responsibility which you want to give Enoch . . . or else, the family will fall upon bad days. We may have to sell the property, move to a smaller place.'

When she finished speaking, her face was flushed. Abraham had closed his eyes. There was no expression on his face and she was afraid that he was angry. Not knowing what to do next, she fumbled over her words. 'I do not know what to do. I know I should not ask such a question—but can you tell me whether my husband is dead or alive?'

'Keep faith in the Lord.' Abraham's hand was trembling. Bathsheba could not decide whether it was a blessing, refusal or consent.

That night, as Bathsheba slept on her faded quilt with her youngest snuggling in the curve of her body, she thought, 'He is as old as my sorrow. His father left just after his circumcision.' She sat up and told herself that Solomon would return. She would teach her youngest to sleep on another quilt and she would keep the new quilt ready to celebrate Solomon's return.

Watching the night sky and listening to the spotted owlets which lived in the neem tree near her window, she asked herself, 'Why did I have to ask for Abraham's permission? Does the opinion of the other Jewish families of Danda really matter? Will anybody support us if we become poor? Abraham is too old to work. There is no news of Solomon. The other two brothers have chosen to lead their own lives. Who else is there to look after the house? I am the only one willing to take responsibility. What is stopping me from doing what I want to do?'

The next day, Bathsheba woke up early. As she stepped

out of the house, Abraham asked from his chair, 'Did our Parmeshwar show you the path?'

Bathsheba's first experience with the baadee started with heavy rains. The Dandekar house seemed to be standing in a vast lake. Bathsheba found an exquisite bamboo umbrella in the storeroom. She carried it with her wherever she went. She was not sure how the umbrella had found its way into the house. She liked it so much that she also carried it to the market.

With her new-found freedom, Bathsheba's days were full of small pleasures—collecting freshly laid eggs, milking cows, feeding young calves, tending goats, collecting supari, tamarind, coconuts, pots of tadi-badi, jars of oil, and preparing home-grown vegetables and fruit for the market. At the end of which, the quilt was there to go back to. Every Saturday, new forms and stitches emerged on the fabric. Each stitch seemed to instil hope in Bathsheba.

6

THE DANDEKAR HOUSE stood amidst a cluster of coconut, supari, neem, mango, chikoo, guava, papaya, banana and banyan trees. The house had a fencing of wild cactus and a web of dry palm fronds. A large gate led to a pathway covered with red earth and lined with mehendi bushes. Halfway there was a diversion which had the terracotta sculpture of a dwarpal, who protected the fields and orchards. From here, a small gate led the labourers to the fields. All along the path there were bird baths which the birds and squirrels shared.

The house was a huge structure with a high A-shaped roof covered with red tiles which almost touched the ground and a long veranda which extended along its entire front. One entered the house by opening a heavy wooden door which had an ornate marble mezuzah, brass knockers and floral carvings on the lintel. The veranda served all sorts of purposes. Abraham spent the whole day on his chair there. And after the hounds had had a free run of the grounds, they kept watch over the house by sitting on their colourful cushions placed on the western end of the veranda.

The veranda was used for cleaning wheat, rice and dals of all types. It was also the perfect place to chat and to chop vegetables. According to the season, the veranda floors were covered with coconut, supari, tamarind, toddy fruits, red chillies, turmeric, cumin, coriander and mangoes. Bathsheba particularly loved the dry, tangy odour of the spices, which permeated the veranda and seeped indoors.

For herself, Bathsheba had reserved the steps which led to the main gate. From here she had a clear view of the road. The house was on a hillock and from the veranda, they could see the entire baadee. And the sea was at their doorstep.

They often spent their evenings playing there on the golden beach, clean but craggy. The children made castles in the sand, and the women hitched up their saris and splashed in the water like young girls. Sometimes the men organized the monthly oxcart race on the beach at Danda. Or soon after the monsoon, on full-moon nights, they had boxing matches with gloves made of empty coconut shells.

From the beach, they could see the silhouette of the historic Janjira fort which had changed hands many times. The citadel stood on a rocky island at the entrance of the creek. It had a commanding view of the terrain all around.

Danda was smaller than most Konkani villages and the Dandekars owned most of the land there. They were the only Bene Israel family in Danda. The other houses on the hillock belonged to Sombhau and some of the farmhands. A few kilometres away, in Revdanda and Navgaon, there were many more Jewish families. Once a month the Bene Israel of all the neighbouring villages organized community get-togethers at the prayer hall in Nandgaon. They would eventually build a synagogue here.

The front room of the house was used to receive guests. During summer, the room was covered with straw and served as a bed for mangoes—ratnagiri and alphonso. When the mangoes were not there, the floor was covered with a Persian carpet, mattresses were spread out and embroidered gol takias were placed along the walls. There were hookahs, bowls of seasonal fruit and a silver paan box. When necessary, a cloth punkah was installed and the mali's son deputed to pull the cord to keep the room cool.

This room led into the central courtyard of the house. Twice a year the women of the house plastered it with a mixture of pili mitti, ash and cow dung. On Fridays it was cleaned properly and durries were spread out on the floor for the shabath prayers. Around the courtyard there were rooms for sons, daughters, parents, guests and relatives. The grinding stone for making wet masalas and the wooden pounding bowl with its pestle for dry spices were placed here in a corner, close to the kitchen door.

A thatched hut behind the house, next to a well, was used as a bathroom, outside which water was heated in huge black pots on clay stoves during the winter months. Another hut next to it was used as an isolation chamber for women when they had their monthly cycle—the Rajodarshan room. It was also a sort of labour room, where the women stayed after delivery as they were considered unclean for forty days.

The rooms nearer to the kitchen were used for lunch,

dinner and the shabath prayers during the monsoon months—although everybody preferred the open courtyard for family dinners. There was also a storeroom, where there were huge terracotta containers full of grains, clay pots of rice flour marinating in toddy, ceramic bottles full of chik or dry wheat cakes which they used to make the new year halwa, mounds of dry Bombay duck, and huge baskets of vegetables, jackfruit, coconut and toddy.

The firewood used for the huge clay stoves was kept in a shed behind the kitchen with the larger vessels which were used for weddings, circumcisions and funerals.

The courtyard was the main hub of activity, where Gangaram the parrot watched everything from his brass cage. The courtyard filled the house with light and air. In summer, everybody slept there.

Across the courtyard was the kitchen. The kitchen was attached to the house, but had a lower roof. Inside the kitchen, clay pots full of drinking water were placed on a wooden platform. This was Elisheba's domain, and the shelves were arranged with shining brass and copper utensils which were her pride. She had special dishes for the meat and the milk, and the two sets were never mixed.

From the courtyard, a wooden staircase led to a room on the roof. This was where valuables were stored in boxes locked with huge brass locks or were kept hidden in the flooring with a secret catch door. This room was often used by young couples seeking privacy or by elders when they had a serious topic to discuss.

Behind the kitchen was the vegetable garden, where they had canopies of tindla and grew everything from mint, coriander, green chillies, brinjals, pumpkins, drumsticks, pumpkins, marrow, bhindi, tomatoes to watermelons. Nearby was a pond of water lilies beside which were coops for the poultry, geese and ducks.

Bathsheba learnt about crops, oil, the maintenance of poultry, harvesting and everything about the earth from Sombhau. But account keeping was difficult for her. Not having learnt to read and write, she had to memorize everything. Bathsheba decided to overcome this hurdle, and learnt the basics of mathematics from Enoch. He saw that she was a serious student. For him teaching her was more interesting than being a caretaker of the property.

7

WHEN WORD SPREAD in Danda that Bathsheba had taken over the management of the Dandekar property, the other Bene Israel families were not pleased. When the women of Nandgaon and Revdanda saw her with her umbrella, they said, 'Why is she trying to attract attention this way? She should be indoors, praying for her husband's return, not flaunting her best saris and going about with an umbrella like an Englishwoman. It looks like she has got a swollen head.'

'Swollen head,' Bathsheba would repeat to herself. She knew that it was not true. She was always polite and friendly with everybody. She tried to hide her misery from other women, as she did not want them to pity her. And if she wore bright saris, it was only because she wanted to convince herself that she was not a widow. For this very reason, she also wore the string of chrysanthemum flowers in her hair and bought new green bangles. She did not want to feel wretched and widowed in old dull saris.

But the gossip affected Bathsheba. The words, 'swollen head' hurt her so much that by the time she reached home her temples began to throb. It was the beginning of a migraine which would trouble her often in later years. When it became unbearable, she would close the doors and windows of her room, draw the chicks and sleep on the floor with a wet cloth on her forehead.

To try and mend relations, she invited the Bene Israel women from Nandgaon, Murud-Janzira and Revdanda to her house. She spread out colourful rugs in the courtyard and was at the door to welcome them.

When the women entered the Dandekar house, there was a festive air all around. The entrance was decorated with strings of mango leaves and marigold flowers. Bead festoons with intricate designs were strung on the front door. Shlumith brought out her precious embroidered cushion covers and tablecloths from her box for the occasion.

As they settled down, Shlumith offered them bowls of cool sonkadhi made with coconut milk, semolina laddus, freshly made coconut chikki and poha-papads.

Bathsheba sat in the centre and the ordinary chit-chat became serious when the eldest of them sitting next to Elisheba asked Bathsheba whether she had news from her husband. The women stopped talking among themselves and turned towards Bathsheba. Bathsheba said in a rather loud, hysterical voice, 'Nako, I have no news of my husband. But today I have not invited you for a celebration. God willing I will do that when my husband returns. I do not even know where my husband is. With this we are faced with another problem in our house. Our baadee was not giving enough produce. We all know that we need our baadees to sustain us. So I decided to take the responsibility. I know I should not say such things, but if something happens to my husband . . .' Bathsheba felt sobs rising in her throat and stopped speaking. She did not want the women to see her tears.

The elderly woman sitting next to Elisheba was critical. 'I still do not understand. You would not have to work in the baadee if Abraham had been strict with his sons. It is their duty, not yours,' she said.

Flushed and angry, Bathsheba tried to explain. 'We have to accept the fact that the other sons are individuals. They have a right to choose their profession, in the same way that my husband decided to join the army. None of them have an interest in the property. I do not understand why we should force them into doing something they do not want to do. I am free and willing to see to the well-being of my family. In no way am I doing anything wrong or going against the law. The people who work here respect me, and you all know Sombhau.'

Then she hesitated and blurted out, 'I enjoy working in the baadee.' Her eyes brimming with tears, she asked, 'If you were in my place, perhaps you would have done the same?' The women saw the look of determination on Bathsheba's face and they accepted her decision. They would convince their men.

8

BATHSHEBA HAD STARTED depending on Abraham. In the evening, after she had given the children a bath and had one herself, she would sit on the veranda steps and discuss the day's activities with her father-in-law. If there was a problem, she found, she could always depend on him for a solution. She confided in Shlumith, 'Earlier, when I stayed at home, I always thought our father-in-law was just a cranky old man. He used to irritate me by tapping his stick on the floor all day. But since I have started having these long conversations with him, I have discovered that he is a man of wisdom. He has become my guru. I now understand why he was so worried about the property. It is a lot of work and needs personal supervision.

'You know why he gave me the permission? Because he realizes that Sombhau and the farmhands need the presence of someone from the family. He knows how to handle a sudden crisis or a problem after the years he has spent handling the estate, but he needs support. It is sad that none of his sons are interested in the land. He dreads the day we will not be able to live by our land. He is afraid that some day he will have to sell the property. The family would then disintegrate.'

One day, as Bathsheba was returning from the farm, she almost slipped. She felt a soft touch on her heel. It was a snake. When it pulled back its hood, she saw that it was a cobra. She had a sudden vision of her death.

As she ran towards the house, she felt that the cobra had changed into a winged ogre and was chasing her. Then she remembered what her grandmother had taught her about misleading snakes. She pulled out a red handkerchief tucked into her waist and threw it in the direction of the snake. It followed the red cloth and left her alone.

Bathsheba slumped down on the veranda, and Abraham tapped his stick on the floor and called out to Enoch who was flying a kite nearby. The kite fell on the ground like a dead bird as Enoch came running.

As Elisheba caressed her burning forehead, Bathsheba asked her in a trembling voice if she was turning blue because she had stepped on a cobra. Parmeshwar was punishing her for breaking the law.

Enoch was frozen with fear. Abraham felt old and disabled. He listened to Bathsheba's story about the cobra. He did not want to lose Bathsheba, nor did he believe that she was weak and vulnerable. She was their pillar of strength.

When Vinayak Vaid came and checked Bathsheba's pulse he told Abraham that there was no need to panic. She was just in a state of shock. He prescribed a concoction of some herbs.

The next morning, she looked like a corpse wrapped in an old sari. Shlumith, who had slept next to her all night, gave her a bowl of milk and cajoled her to take a bath and eat something. She would feel better. Bathsheba felt comforted.

Sombhau stood silently at the door, watching the fear in her eyes. He consoled her, 'Nagdev is the guardian of our fields. He will never harm us as you have dedicated your life to Gauri—the goddess of fertility. The one who gives us an abundant harvest.'

Later, sitting on the veranda step, he asked, 'If you will give me permission, I would like to make a vow at the shrine of our village deity. If your elder son returns unharmed, I will light a lamp and offer a bowl of milk.'

Abraham did not answer. Sombhau was sure his silence meant disapproval. He knew the Dandekars never prayed at the village shrine or the temple. But Abraham respected Sombhau's sentiments. He said, 'Our religion does not accept certain things, but please yourself.' Sombhau smiled when he saw that there was some expression in Bathsheba's eyes. She had been following the conversation closely.

That evening Abraham asked Elisheba to light a lamp, as he was thankful to the Lord that Bathsheba was alive. Bathsheba's heart warmed to see that the white-and-gold embroidered cloth had been spread out with the offerings of a thanksgiving. Her eyes filled with love for the family which needed her as much as she needed them. She had often thought of death, but when she had faced danger, she had wanted life.

Bathsheba's grandmother had told her that before the

parting of the waters and the escape from Egypt, Parmeshwar had told Moses and Aharon when the Pharaoh speaks to you, saying show a miracle, you shall take your rod and cast it before the Pharaoh and it shall become a serpent. When the Pharaoh called his court magicians, their rods also became serpents. But the serpent created from the staff of Moses was so powerful that it swallowed the serpents of the Pharaoh.

The stories of the serpents, specially in her depressed state worrying about Solomon, obsessed Bathsheba's mind and whenever she reached the main door of the house, the threshold became a serpent. Bathsheba could not cross it. It worsened to such an extent that she confided in Pramila.

This continued for more than fifteen days. Bathsheba did not leave the house. Indoors, she worked all day long on the quilt which was taking a different shape from what Shlumith had planned. It had taken the shape of a peacock. The stars had moved to the borders and were embellished with geometric designs.

One day Pramila, Sombhau's wife, told her a surprising thing. She said that when Bathsheba was ill she had visited the shrine and offered a coconut. When she told her she would be going there again, Bathsheba offered to accompany her.

There was a soft early morning glow around the shrine. Under the square stone chhatri, the idol of Shesh Nag was placed on a raised platform. He stood erect on his coiled tail and his seven hoods were coloured with vermilion. The light was such that the bright beads imbedded in the eyes seemed to stare at the women.

Pramila touched her head to the pedestal. Lighting a lamp, she offered flowers, broke the coconut on the floor, closed her eyes and prayed. Bathsheba watched her. Staring into the shining eyes of the serpent, she also made a silent wish. If

Solomon returned safely, she would offer five coconuts and light a lamp at the shrine. Mysteriously she was drawn to the deity, who was compelling her to make a wish.

9

THAT YEAR, THEY had a good crop of rice. After she had put away a year's stock for the house, she sent the rest to the traders of Revdanda and Nandgaon.

Shlumith gave birth to a daughter. It was a difficult delivery. It had been an oppressively hot night, and the house resounded with Shlumith's screams. She, who never spoke above a whisper, was unable to bear the agony of childbirth. Bathsheba asked her to hold on to her hands and give as much pressure as she could. All the women helped. Elisheba rubbed her feet and prayed.

Looking down at Shlumith, Bathsheba thought how slim and pale she was. Just a young girl. She remembered her first menstruation. Shlumith had been terrified. Holding Shlumith's hands, she ached for her husband.

But when Solomon did return, Bathsheba was overcome with shyness. Bathsheba saw how big and handsome he was. His actual presence was vastly different than anything she could recreate in memory.

As a thanksgiving for Solomon's return there was a blessing, a baraka, followed by a ceremony of wish fulfilment prepared for the prophet Elijah, a malida in the open courtyard. Under a new moon, dressed in new clothes, Abraham said, 'Praise be the Lord, Baruk ata Adonai . . .' Everybody was charged with emotion. This baraka was different from the one they did after a good harvest, a newborn child, lamb, calf or bird, perhaps a new job, or for the recovery from an illness. This blessing was for Solomon because he had returned home unharmed. They did not know what had happened to him and how he had returned. That was for later. He would tell them at leisure.

Abraham had learnt the baraka from his father. It had come down over generations like the recitation of Eliyahu Hannabi for the prophet Elijah, the circumcision of their sons, the dietary laws they followed. Nobody remembered from where all these traditions had come down to them, but the Dandekar family followed the law like the rest of the Jewish families of the Konkan.

Solomon saw that there were two new arrivals in the house. One, Amiel, belonged to him and the other, Shegulla, was Menashe's. His youngest had never seen him, as Solomon had left after the circumcision, and when Bathsheba told him to meet his father, the child refused. He whispered to his mother that he was scared of the man with the big moustaches. He watched him from a distance, but when Solomon sat down cross-legged on the floor, he slowly crept into his lap.

All evening Bathsheba was looking for a reason to go closer to Solomon. When she saw her youngest was already sitting in Solomon's lap, she picked up Shlumith's daughter from the cradle, changed her dress, applied kohl in her eyes, stuck two red roses behind her ears and offered her to Solomon. She saw that his eyes were wet.

She went to her room, washed, changed into a new sari, wore silver armlets, new anklets, a diamond nosering and tied a string of jasmine flowers in her hair. Then she spread the quilt on the floor. On second thoughts, she opened her jewellery box and looked for a small silver box which had four small bottles of ittar—champa, rose, hina and mitti. She chose mitti—the earth after the first rains. She daubed it between her breasts and decided that the children would sleep with Elisheba.

'You could have waited for me to reach the house. Didn't you see me?' he asked that night while holding her in his arms.

Bathsheba could feel the disappointment in her husband's voice when he continued, 'I felt that you did not want to see me.' There was a question in his voice. 'Are you not happy to see me?'

Earlier when he said something like that, she would cling to him. But this new Bathsheba gave him a long look before she gave her answer, 'I thought it was a British soldier coming to the house with bad news about you.'

'You mean my death?' asked Solomon.

Bathsheba did not want him to talk about death under the night sky. Her mother had always stopped her from talking about death after sunset. 'Twilight words sometimes become a reality,' her mother had told her. Bathsheba did not want to tell Solomon that from a distance he had looked like the messenger of death. 'I was so frightened that I rushed into the kitchen and stepped on the pomfret. Aai had never seen me so hysterical. She was certain that we had received the message of your death. Holding each other, we cried and waited for the worst. Then we heard Gangaram's happy screams. The banjara hounds were also yelping with joy. We were certain it was you.'

She hesitated to tell him how much she missed him, and used to count the trees that dotted the landscape as she waited for him in the evenings. They were cousins and had grown up together. Earlier he had been almost like a brother. The separation had changed that. She understood the meaning of love and longing. She looked forward to their nights, when she hastily pulled off her sari and offered him her breasts. He took her with a hunger, born of long absence, that she had never known before.

The next morning, half asleep, Solomon's hands searched for Bathsheba. He was immediately wide awake when he realized that she was not there. The door was open, so his youngest sneaked in and snuggled close to him. Later the other children came and slept next to him. They wanted to know where he had been. He told them a tale about kings, horses, lions, tigers and slaves. They were happy.

That Bathsheba had changed was certain and that night he had seen a new woman emerge from the girl he had known. He missed her giggles. This Bathsheba was a serious woman. He sensed that she had become an elder of the house.

Having shooed the children away, Solomon got up, washed his face, tied his dhoti, and wore a vest. Abraham was waiting in the courtyard to have breakfast with him. There were fresh eggs—half fried, as he liked them—with warm chapatis, potatoes cooked in til, a bowl of papaya and bananas from the farm, and milk which had the fragrance of crushed cardamoms.

As he ate leisurely, talking to Abraham and Elisheba, he heard what they had to say about Bathsheba and her expertise as a manager of the baadee. 'But for her,' they said, 'the house would have been reduced to penury.'

Solomon's feelings were mixed. He didn't know whether to be angry or pleased. He was angry with his brothers for their lack of interest in the farm. In fact, though he did not say it, he thought them rather incompetent. If she had not done what she was doing now, they would have had to sell the property. He was also uncertain as to just how others in the community had reacted to Bathsheba's behaviour. It seemed so much at variance with how she appeared to him earlier, as she did indeed now, when he turned around and saw her at the door.

She stood in the doorway, looking fresh and happy in the morning sun, holding a huge green watermelon in her arms.

Solomon smiled at her and offered her a sip from his bowl of milk.

10

FOR HER HUSBAND'S safe return she had taken many vows which she would have to fulfil at different times in different places.

She had visited the shrine of Nagdeva to fulfil her vow, with a lamp, five coconuts and some flowers. She knew that she would have to take some of the coconut back to her house as prasad. But if she did, the family would become suspicious. So she ate some, left the rest for the ants and brought back a few pieces for the people who worked in the fields.

She was also aware that if the word spread, the Bene Israel Jews would brand her a kala or black Jew. The Jew with the mixed blood. Bathsheba always saw signs of danger when they started discussing such matters. The kala and gora Jew stories always circulated as a vicious undercurrent in their lives. Those who appeared to have a darker colour with typical Konkani features were branded black as they were suspected of having mixed blood, and the others considered themselves white or gora because they had only married their cousins and looked exactly like each other.

As an apology to her own Parmeshwar, she had taken another vow. For that she would have to make a journey to Sagav, near Kandala, where there was a stone which had a relic of Eliyahu Hannabi cha tapa—the hoof mark of Prophet Elijah's chariot. It had stopped there before departing for heaven. According to legend, he had come to Alibaug from the land of Mount Sinai and Yerushalayem—Israel—the land they had left behind. How and why were questions which remained unanswered.

The arrival of the Bene Israel in the Konkan was associated with a shipwreck in Navgaon. The oral tradition had come down to them from generation to generation. In the process some stories were added, some were deleted. Bathsheba's great-grandfather had told her: 'We were running away from the Greek ruler Antioch. He wanted to destroy us. We fled in a ship with our families and belongings. For months we were at sea. One stormy night, we were sure we would drown and the fish would eat us up. Suddenly the ship rocked dangerously and crashed on the islands of Chanderi and Underi. Some of us swam to the shore, some died, but we lost our ark and the books.

'We do not know detailed prayers or stories about our religion or prophets. The little we know has come down to us from our ancestors. We try to remember and follow the code of law set by them. Although we do not know the meaning of the Hebrew words, we recite them regularly. These words keep us together and protect us from other influences. Yet some rituals from other religions have seeped into ours.'

Whenever the men of the Jewish community collected in the thatched prayer house in Nandgaon, they discussed their lineage. The women prepared snacks in the next room and the children went back and forth with bowls of food. In bits and pieces, the women heard all that was being said.

Some Bene Israel believed that there were seven couples when their ship had crashed on the Konkan coast. They said, 'The shipwreck was known to have taken place near Chaul, the port near Navgaon. It is mentioned in the Puranas that while Parshuram circled the earth to exterminate the Kshatriyas and give more power to the Brahmins, he had seen fourteen corpses on the Konkan coast. The bodies were burnt and charred. They appeared to be foreigners. He realized that they belonged to an ancient race. Parshuram brought them back to life by chanting some mantras. These were supposed to be the Bene Israel. It is surprising that the Chitpavan Brahmins have a similar story! Perhaps we adopted a similar story so that we would find acceptance in the communities around us.'

Bathsheba often asked Elisheba, 'If there were only seven couples who survived how did the tribe increase? How did we multiply into such large numbers? Perhaps the survivors understood that if they did not mix with the local population, they would disappear from the face of the earth?'

11

SOLOMON HAD RETURNED to Danda from the fourth Mysore War, disheartened after the death of Tipu Sultan. The subedar of his regiment, the 16th regiment of the Bombay native infantry of the East India Company, had been honoured with a bronze medal with a figure of the British lion subduing the Indian tiger. Tipu Sultan had granted life to his brethren like Subedar Major Samuel Ezekiel Divekar, belonging to a company in the 6th battalion which had fought the second Mysore war, and Solomon experienced a certain undefinable guilt that he had been party to the Tiger's death. He was disturbed by the way the Sultan had died, cornered and betrayed. After the victory of Mysore, on the way back to Bombay and. then Danda, Solomon was not sure whether he wanted to continue as a sepoy. The shabath of Solomon's return was memorable with Elisheba's beetroot wine, chicken cooked in a bright red coconut curry, rice flour chapatis, fried slices of aubergine garnished with til seeds and rice. There was laughter and love. In such an atmosphere Solomon and Abraham retold Divekar's story.

Subedar Major Samuel Ezekiel Divekar had fought the second Mysore War and had been captured by Tipu. Later Tipu had granted life to Divekar and his company of Bene Israel soldiers.

Tipu Sultan's second Mysore war with the British lasted two years. Death was certain. It had been a long march from Bombay to Bednur.

Tipu had planned an aggressive strategy and every day British soldiers lay dead in pools of blood. From the battlefield of Bednur, it appeared impossible to come back alive. Divekar became a prisoner of war when Tipu captured soldiers from the Sixth Bombay Regiment. Among them were fourteen Bene Israel soldiers. The captain of the regiment was Subedar Major Samuel Ezekiel Divekar. He did not lose hope. He had heard that Tipu Sultan was a fair ruler and he had faith in his god.

News had reached Tipu Sultan's court that certain captives behaved strangely on Friday evenings. They said prayers in an incomprehensible language. They did not pray like the Hindus, Christians, Parsis or Muslims. This news had also reached the Sultan's mother.

The queen mother was kindly and godfearing. She was also curious. She sent the eunuchs who guarded her palace to investigate. They came back with stories which fascinated her. Sensing that there was more to these prisoners than met the eye, she spoke to her son and requested that he find out who they were. She did not want him to commit a crime in the eyes of God.

The Sultan agreed to give his captives a hearing in the presence of the queen mother. Divekar did not know why the Bene Israel were being separated from the rest by the guards. They did not know what was in store for them, nor where they were being taken. Perhaps they were being led to the gallows.

Their thoughts went out to their families.

Tipu Sultan was no ordinary man. He had superhuman powers. How else could one man stand alone against the regiments of the British East India Company?

When they reached the steps of the palace, the prisoners were transported to a fairy tale world of white marble inlaid with intricate designs of trees and flowers, and fountains spouting scented water. Huge chained tigers stood guard at the gate. Elephants with elaborate howdahs stood swaying their trunks in the courtyard. And when they were led into the court, they were awestruck: huge shining chandeliers, silver chairs upholstered in velvet, carved arches, high pillars and artefacts in gold. Everything from cushions, pillars to drapes and carpets had a pattern of stripes. The entire palace appeared to be covered with tiger skins. Amidst all this splendour, the Sultan sat erect on his gem-studded throne. He was sitting like a tiger about to attack his prey. His kohl-lined eyes were large and terrifying. His left hand rested on his knee and the right hand was on the hilt of his magnificent sword that, it was said, needed five men to carry it.

A huge gem-studded turban shaped like an umbrella covered his head. They noticed that he was wearing rings with precious gems and a gold disc with his insignia on his waistband. Yet, he was not a very big man; he looked smaller than they had imagined. Since their capture, in their imagination he had taken the form of a gigantic demon.

Divekar was observing his surroundings and preparing himself for the confrontation with Tipu Sultan. He had closed his eyes and was reciting the Shema Israel, so that the Lord would give him strength.

When the chief minister of Tipu Sultan's court asked them to identify their leader, Divekar acknowledged he was the

Subedar Major of the Sixth Bombay Regiment.

All eyes turned to Divekar, who stood with bent head. Tipu Sultan picked up a toy-like object from a side table and started playing with it. He glanced at Divekar with bored eyes.

Divekar was cross-examined by the chief minister. How many soldiers were there in the Bombay regiment? How many had died? How many were left behind? How many were alive? What was their religion? And why did he have such a strange name, which was neither Hindu, Muslim nor Christian? Divekar was taken aback. He said he belonged to a community called Bene Israel. He did not have too many details about his religion, as they had been shipwrecked off the Konkan coast, and lost their books in the sea. All they had was an oral tradition and a strict code of conduct.

As soon as he said that, there was a slight change of expression in Tipu Sultan's eyes and he looked in the direction of a silk curtain. Divekar and his men sensed that somebody important was sitting behind the curtain. Perhaps the queen mother was watching the trial. The atmosphere was charged with tension. Nobody could predict what the Sultan's next move would be.

The queen mother sent a message to the Sultan through one of the eunuchs. Divekar feared that the jewelled sword of the Sultan, which looked like an ornament, could become a weapon of destruction in a split second. Or that the tiger at his feet, which looked like a pet dog, would pounce upon them with the flick of the Sultan's little finger. Divekar prayed silently, evoking all the Hebrew words he knew. He vowed that if by some miracle their lives were spared, he would build a house of prayer in Bombay, perhaps one as beautiful as the synagogue in Cochin he had heard about, where there were also religious books—the Sefer Torah.

After Tipu had listened to his mother's message, and sent back his answer through the eunuch, he gestured to the chief minister to continue with the questioning. He asked Divekar whether they were Banu Israel, as mentioned in the Koran and the Hijaz? Were they really the chosen people of God?

Divekar was confused. The word Banu or Bani seemed to fall into place, as his Muslim friends sometimes referred to him as the Banu Israel, meaning literally the children of Israel. He was sure that they were the children of Israel according to the texts of Moses Maimonides—the Egyptian philosopher and traveller who had visited the Konkan sometime in 1100 B. C.

When Divekar said, 'Yes,' he did not know what would happen next. Divekar's eyes were closed and he had broken into a cold sweat.

Then, to the amazement of the Bene Israel prisoners, Tipu Sultan made a gesture of pardon. The movement of his hand also said that they were to be released. Later they came to know that they had been released because of the queen mother. The chief minister said that she had read about them in the religious texts and did not want her son to kill them. They were the sons of the prophet Ibrahim.

The queen mother had saved their lives. The captives glanced gratefully in the direction of the white silk curtain—the only place in the entire palace which was not covered with tiger stripes.

12

SOLOMON WAS WATCHING Bathsheba. It was a Saturday, the shabath. They were alone in their room. Bathsheba was standing in the middle of the room with her thick black hair cascading down her back and her nine-yard sari floating around her. Her bright pink blouse was tied in a knot under her breasts, showing a deep and sensuous cleavage. One end of the bright blue sari was tied around her waist in a kela or small banana— a good hiding place for money, jewels or documents. In a quick movement she threw the long pallav over her shoulder and with three quick twists, the rest of the sari was draped around her hips. Then, parting her legs, she passed the lower end of the sari between her thighs and fixed the border of the lower end in the waistline over her hips. This exposed her waist, breasts and the roundness of her buttocks. Making small pleats with her pallav, she covered her head and breasts.

Unaware of Solomon's close scrutiny from the bed, Bathsheba stood in front of the mirror and applied kohl to her eyes. Solomon could see the curve of her waist—the skin there was lighter than her face. Bathsheba's face was a soft oval, her dark eyes slanted upwards, she had full lips and a large mango-shaped nosering covered part of her face. Solomon felt aroused, as his eyes strayed to her rounded calves. He leaned forward and pulled her down towards him.

They were happy, but there was one disagreement between them. Bathsheba had become superstitious in many matters and Solomon's practical mind did not accept this. Bathsheba was an intelligent woman and there was no reason for her to start shivering if she broke something, or a black cat crossed her path. At these moments he became impatient with her.

Time and again Solomon would find Bathsheba discussing black threads and sadhus with Shantabai. Sometimes a black string was tied on Bathsheba's toe, or a red thread around her wrist for her migraine. He reasoned with her, at first with love, then with anger. She exasperated him when she told him that she was sure that the bullock which had died in his absence had died because of snake bite. She said the shadow of the snake was upon their house. It had tried to entice her. She saw the look of disapproval in Solomon's eyes when he reminded her that it was an old bullock.

Somehow she had to convince Solomon to go with her to the graves of their ancestors. She used guile, tricks, love, intelligence and emotional blackmail—all the ploys that a woman could muster—to get around her husband. It worked.

To make it easier for Bathsheba, one morning, a three-horned bullock stood at the gate of the baadee. The animal belonged to Vithoba, a mendicant. He was taking it to the butcher's, and had met Sombhau on the way. Sombhau was instantly struck by the bull's three horns, which resembled a trishul, so when Vithoba told him that the animal was for sale, Sombhau decided that he would persuade Bathsheba to buy it. Surely it was a divine creature, and besides they were short of a bullock, and the production of oil had come to a standstill.

When Bathsheba saw the bullock and heard what Sombhau had to say, she decided to buy it. Solomon smiled as he sat on the veranda reading a local newsletter. Earlier Bathsheba always asked his advice on small matters. But now she took her own decisions. She was familiar with the accounts and knew that there was enough to buy a new bullock.

Sombhau named the bullock Shiva. Shiva was born on Vithoba's father's farm in Rajpur. Shiva's routine existence changed when the women of the village decided that he was a divine animal with his crown of three horns and began to worship him as an incarnation of Shiva. They applied kumkum on his extra horn and fed him fresh marigold flowers.

Vithoba did not like to work, and spent his time lazing about. This made his father very angry. So his mother suggested that Shiva help Vithoba make a living. They could travel from village to village with Vithoba dressed as a mendicant. The villagers would worship the animal and shower them with food and money.

Vithoba agreed to his mother's suggestion. He wanted to get away from his father's wrath.

The idea worked. On his travels, Vithoba made friends with sadhus and picked up their way of talking and beguiling audiences. Vithoba had a good following wherever he went. When he returned home, he had a big purse to offer his mother.

Vithoba also taught Shiva a simple tricks. The main part of the performance consisted of Shiva answering questions about the future. Devotees could never resist asking these. Vithoba would phrase their question suitably and Shiva would answer with a shake of his head. Downwards meant yes, sideways no. Or Vithoba would throw a silk cloth on the ground and if Shiva picked it up, it was supposed to be a boon from the gods. If not, it meant that the gods were not in a beneficent mood. He would then extract more money from his devotees. To provide a lighter touch, say if there was a cynic in the crowd, Vithoba would ask Shiva if there was a godless one among the crowd, or a troublemaker, and Shiva was to point out the person, sometimes by going right up to him. Shiva got this trick right often enough too to make his subsequent answers appear convincing.

The partnership worked well for a few years. But it was a lonely life for Vithoba. Loneliness, in fact, was something that tormented all the sadhus. They had found ways around it—an energetic kirtan at the end of the day was one of them—but the most popular cure they had was opium. Vithoba saw them grinding the small black seeds of opium with water and swallowing the concoction in one gulp. Once it took effect their eyes became bloodshot, and they appeared to float in another world.

Vithoba was initiated into this ritual, and soon became an addict. The small black seed ate into his earnings, and often he did not have enough to feed Shiva. In a few months, Shiva was nothing but skin and bone. The mild-tempered animal followed his master wanly from place to place, going through the motions of divination. One afternoon he fell on the ground in the middle of the road. Vithoba wanted to leave him to the vultures. But when he saw his brimming eyes, he stopped. They had been together for more years than he could count.

With the help of his opium buddies, he dragged the half-dead Shiva to the shade of a tree and fed him small quantities of grass. In a week, Shiva could sit up, but he could not travel long distances, and Rajpur was far away. Vithoba was in a dilemma. He wanted to get rid of the animal and join the sangh of the sadhus. But he had to have his father's approval.

So he left Shiva with a local farmer and returned to Rajpur.

He told his parents that Shiva was dying and if they wanted to recover some of what they had invested in the animal it was necessary to sell him to a butcher, as he had decided to join a sect of sadhus. His father agreed, but his mother wept, as she felt the foreboding of misfortune with such an action. She offered to look after Shiva, but neither father nor son would listen to her.

Vithoba avoided Shiva's eyes during the journey. With that strange sense that animals have, the bullock seemed to know what lay in store for him. That was when Vithoba had met Sombhau. He had stopped him to ask for directions to a butcher's house. It turned out to be journey's end for Shiva when Bathsheba bought him for the oil press.

Vithoba was happy as he rolled the money in the knot of his dhoti around his waist. He left without a backward glance.

Bathsheba decided that she would restore Shiva to health and then leave for Navgaon. Shiva was her good omen.

13

BATHSHEBA LOOKED AFTER Shiva diligently, and after he had regained his strength she persuaded Solomon to accompany her to Navgaon. He warned her that this was the first and last time he would indulge her whims and fancies.

Bathsheba started her preparations with the decoration of the animals. But first she had to make sure that the two animals accepted each other. Bathsheba saw the look of fear in Shiva's eyes when she yoked him and Mahesh, the other bullock, to the cart. She caressed Shiva's neck and offered him fresh grass to chew on. When Bathsheba was sure that Shiva and Mahesh were comfortable with each other, she took a long ride in the bullock-cart with Shlumith and the children around the baadee. Their laughter filled Shiva with energy, and Bathsheba was sure that she would make the journey to Navgaon.

The day before Bathsheba and Solomon were to leave, there was great activity in the house. Shlumith brought out the best collection of embroidered animal trappings and Elisheba prepared mountains of food. Besides snacks, dry fruit, vadas, coconut chiki, semolina ladoos, fruit and leather bags full of water, they had kept aside cloth bags full of grain, flour and vegetables in case provisions ran out. Solomon was amused. Instead of a week, there was enough food for a month. Fodder for Shiva and Mahesh was also tied below the cart. Bathsheba had not forgotten the seven coconuts which she was to offer at the shrine of Eliyahu Hannabi.

There was a sense of romance and adventure as they set

off. They had not been alone like this since they were married.

As they rode through villages, people stopped to look at Shiva. They praised Solomon for having given asylum to the three-horned animal, and said that his presence would bestow upon them the blessings of the gods.

When they saw the swaying palms amidst the sands of a golden untouched beach, Bathsheba knew they had reached Navgaon. As soon as her feet touched the earth, she felt transported into another world—the world of her ancestors.

The landscape was entirely different from what she had imagined. In her imagination, the earth was golden, the trees studded with rubies, the sun a diamond and the moon a huge pearl. Instead the earth was brown, grey and stony with dry trees and jagged rocks. Ancient coconut trees stood tall with their fronds growing around them like outstretched arms trapped in the aerial roots of the banyan trees which stood next to them. In the strong whistling wind of the sea, they could hear the sound of the ship dashing against the rocks and breaking into a thousand pieces. The screeching gulls seemed to echo the screams of their ancestors fighting against the forces of nature.

Navgaon was a small town with winding lanes which led to the sea. It had a mixed population of all communities, and it was not difficult to find their cousin Abigayail's house with its traditional oil press and mezuzah at the door.

Abigayail and her husband received them warmly. After Solomon and Bathsheba had taken a bath, Abigayail laid out a lunch of rice and drumsticks cooked in besan with beans picked from her garden and garnished with fresh coconut. She then went indoors to change her sari and took them to the graves.

Abigayail was a small, bright-eyed woman. Her face lit up

when she laughed. Much to Solomon's annoyance, she told
Bathsheba how their ancestors had heard her prayers and
fulfilled her wishes. She told Bathsheba that in the early days
of her marriage, each pregnancy had ended in a miscarriage.
This happened for five years. Then she had a dream in which
she saw enormous fishes, silver in colour and as large as their
house, swimming towards her. They were five or seven in
number, she was not sure. At first she had been afraid, and
tried to run away from them. Until she realized that she was
at the water's edge, and one wrong movement and she would
fall into the sea. So she stood still and waited. When they came
closer, she felt a curtain fall between her and the fish. When it
disappeared, the fish had been transformed into women. To
Abigayail's surprise, each one was pregnant, and dressed in
bright red robes with gold girdles. Walking in a line, they led
her to the graves.

Abigayail had woken up at this point. Sitting up in her bed,
she had tried to remember each detail of her dream. That night
she had taken a vow—if she received the gift of a child from
them, she would look after the graves as long as she lived.

That year Abigayail had become pregnant and the child
had survived. Since then Abigayail believed that the ancestors
were watching over them. Bathsheba was reassured in her
belief about the ancestors and their power. She was sure that
they had brought back Solomon from certain death. But she
kept her silence. She knew that Solomon did not like such talk.
Bathsheba did not tell Abigayail the reason for her visit to the
graves and Abigayail did not ask. She knew that some vows
were secrets.

Now, as they stood at the graves, heads covered, they fell
silent, thinking back to that day long ago when the survivors
had landed on the shore, and thanking Parmeshwar that they

were the children of the survivors.

At the spot where they stood, there were seven covered wells in a circle. The mounds on the wells, overgrown with needle-sharp weeds, concealed the secret of their ancestry.

Chanting the Shema Israel, Solomon and Bathsheba covered the graves with red roses, and lit diyas and joss sticks. They could feel their spirits soaring, as they placed one diya facing west in the circle of the graves—the direction of their homeland.

Bathsheba then broke seven coconuts on a rock, at the feet of the ancestors, and sprinkled the water from their belly over the graves. Then leaving half of each coconut on each mound, she offered some to Solomon and Abigayail, ate some herself and gave small pieces to Shiva and Mahesh. The rest she put away in a basket to take back to Danda for the family and farmhands. They washed their hands and left the scene of the wreck without looking backwards—one had to leave the dead alone without a backward glance.

After spending the night in Navgaon, Bathsheba and Solomon journeyed towards Kandala and then on to Sagav—a small sleepy hamlet near Alibaug where Prophet Elijah had appeared.

It was hard to believe that his chariot of gold had landed in such a faraway place. Was it possible that he was guiding the ship which was on its way to an unknown destination? Perhaps he had seen the ship crash on the rocks and disappear into the Arabian Sea. He must have tried to land, diving into space. The hoof of his white stallion must have touched the rock with such intensity that it had left a long scratch there. Elijah must have then flown upwards and over the rocking ship, creating a huge wave which washed some of the living and dying passengers to the shore.

There was a white haze around them. They sensed that

they were part of something which was beyond comprehension. The rock which the prophet's chariot must have touched stood in a tree-lined bowl which was obviously carved by an unseen hand. There was a sparkling blue pond on the left with purple water lilies. The turquoise wings of a kingfisher hovering above were reflected in the water. To add to the effect, a tall and thorny flame of the forest guarded the jagged rock edict which jutted out of the landscape, as if reaching out to the sky. Solomon and Bathsheba looked with awe at the hoof mark which cut through the rock. There was a certain aura around the rock, as the light played on the water, the trees, the bright red flowers and the hoof mark.

Solomon unyoked the bullocks so that they could drink at the pond. Bathsheba watched in wonder as a bright yellow butterfly alighted on the hoof mark which someone had filled with sindoor. It looked like a flower sprouting out of the rock. The sindoor was proof that some Konkani Hindus also worshipped there, as they believed that it was the relic of Ghodakdev, the horse-headed divinity, who was still to appear on earth as Kalki, the tenth avatar of Vishnu.

They washed their feet in the clear water of the pond and walked around Eliyahu Hannabi cha tapa as one did in a temple. Abigayail had whispered to Bathsheba that Eliyahu Hannabi was their Ganesha. All auspicious occasions started with the Eliyahu Hannabi, in the same way that the Hindus started everything with the Ganesha sthapan. In the land of idols, the relic was an image which helped the Bene Israel relate to their prophet. Abigayail had told Bathsheba that Muslims also offered flowers at the site. For them, it was possibly the hoof mark of a burakh, the human-headed winged horse. She was certain that the hoof mark was special because it linked together the people of various communities.

Bathsheba had a clear picture of the prophet in her imagination. She credited this to the painting Menashe had made on the walls of his room. That was before he had taken an interest in Ayurveda. The painter who had painted Solomon's portrait had been staying in Revdanda for a few months. Menashe had become his apprentice, paying him a guru-dakshina of rice, fruit, vegetables and coconuts.

Menashe had learnt many techniques from him, and one of them had been fresco painting. Many well-to-do Konkani families commissioned artists to paint the walls of their houses with mythological subjects. Sometimes they also bought printed landscapes from French and Dutch traders.

Abraham had been very upset that his son wanted to become a travelling painter—a low caste according to the varnas of Indian tradition. Why couldn't he take an interest in the baadee or take up some other profession? Abraham had told him that he could not give him permission to become a painter because the Bene Israel did not make idols and images— that was the law.

Menashe opposed his father with a hunger-strike. For four days he abstained from food and water. Elisheba and the women of the house wept all day and ate just a little out of fear of Abraham's rage. Abraham sat expressionless in his usual place on the veranda, caressing his beard. He told himself that a fast would not kill Menashe. When they had been wanderers in the desert, their ancestors spent innumerable days without food and water. Yet he warned the family that Menashe's fast had to be kept a secret. Nobody was to spread the news in Danda, Nandgaon or Revdanda that there was conflict in the family. Even Shantabai had been instructed by Abraham that she was not to speak about the tension in the house.

Solomon did not interfere when Abraham was in his

furiously religious moods, or had problems with one of the children. It was best to keep away from him. But in this case, as the elder son, he thought it necessary to take a stand. He convinced Abraham that painting was not a sin. Didn't they get their portraits painted? If Menashe had talent, why should he not do what he liked? By merely painting scenes of nature or portraits, he was not going against their religion. As a beginning, they could allow him to paint a wall in his own room. But it would be a secret from the Bene Israel community.

Finally Abraham agreed.

Behind closed doors, Menashe removed the old paint from the walls, rubbed the surface clean and applied a layer of specially prepared lime. When it was dry, he made a line drawing with a stylus. Then he started filling in the colours. Every morning, he would prepare the pigments, mix them with glue and paint a certain area. Menashe was so secretive about what he was doing that he did not allow anybody to enter his room, nor clean it. He lived in his own world of colours.

Menashe took a month to finish his painting. Then he invited the family to see his work. Menashe cleaned his room, dressed in new clothes and decorated the doorway with a string of mango leaves. Elisheba stood at the entrance and spontaneously sang the chant to Eliyahu Hannabi. The family stood spellbound in front of the painting.

Menashe had painted the scene of the prophet descending on the rock near Kandala. Parting a mountain of clouds and racing through the sky, the prophet was riding a chariot of gold, drawn by white stallions. The stallions had gold trappings and the chariot was studded with gems. The sky was an azure blue which showed the glory of the heavens. A winged angel dressed in a deep blue toga was flying with the horses. Another, with a sword of fire, was piloting the chariot. There was a golden ray of light falling like a halo around the bearded prophet, who was dressed in a purple cloak and dhoti with an orange waistband. His cloak was flying behind him like a pair of wings. Winged cherubs were playing flutes, drums and stringed instruments. One of them was carrying a scroll— symbolic of the religious texts they had lost in the shipwreck.

The chariot was flying over Eliyahu Hannabi cha tapa.

Not aware that Abraham was standing behind them, Solomon made everybody laugh by saying that the prophet resembled their father. When they heard the tap of his stick, all eyes suddenly turned towards Abraham. Menashe stood frozen and afraid, as he waited for his father's verdict. Fear turned to surprise when Abraham began weeping like a child.

14

WITH HIS FATHER'S permission, Menashe converted his room into a studio. Here he painted portraits and landscapes, till one day, he came down with whooping cough. It was impossible to bring the cough under control. For five days the house resounded with Menashe's cough. His face became red, his throat was painfully sore, he could not swallow and he began to rapidly lose weight.

Menashe could not sit, stand or sleep. Dattabhau Vaid said that he had whooping cough because of some allergy, and gave him some powdered herbs. Abraham was sure that by making images he had brought upon himself the wrath of the gods.

Menashe remained confined to his room, trying the concoctions people suggested. But nothing seemed to work. He thought his intestines were going to fall out from his mouth. He was tired of coughing and was sure that if he did not get the right medication, he would die. Then the mali's son told him to drink camel urine as a remedy. Menashe took note of this strange suggestion.

Once a week, a trader from Nandgaon supplied fodder for the animals of the estate. He came in a camel cart, and waited till the fodder was unloaded and he had been given lunch.

That week when he arrived and had settled down to gossip with Sombhau, he was shocked to see Menashe standing under the camel. He was coughing and his mouth was open. He was obviously waiting for the cascade of urine. Sombhau, who had been watching the drama, told Menashe that he should not believe such stories because there was a cure for whooping cough. He quickly yoked the bullocks and took Menashe to a pandit who was visiting Revdanda and was staying with a local landowner.

The pandit gave Menashe some powdered roots. The cough continued, but on the third day, Menashe fell into a deep sleep while resting in the courtyard with his back to the wall. He slept for two days. When he woke up, he waited for the dreaded cough, but nothing happened.

His throat just felt sore. For the first time in days, he had a quiet meal with the family. After Abraham and Elisheba retired for their afternoon nap, and the children ran out to play, Menashe whispered to Solomon that he wanted to speak to him. Bathsheba spread out a carpet in their room and left them alone.

Before his illness, Menashe had been certain that he wanted to become a painter, but since he had been cured by the pandit, he had become interested in medicine. More so, after he had met the pandit. He had decided to become his disciple. Menashe was not interested in the baadee. If he had not come across the pandit, he would have definitely been a painter.

That night, Solomon informed Abraham that Menashe had

decided to leave Danda for a year and stay with the pandit in Alibaug. Abraham raged and stormed but could do nothing to change his decision.

15

SOLOMON HAD NOT shown much interest in the baadee after his return. He had already announced his plan to Bathsheba. Despite his reservations, he would be going back to the army. The regimental spirit and the camaraderie of his fellow sepoys was too strong a draw, even though the money they were paid was not much.

The day before Solomon's departure, he refused to eat and was irritable with the children. Everybody left him alone. Late that afternoon, Bathsheba entered the room with his bowl of milk brewed with freshly crushed cardamoms, which he loved. She knew that that was the one thing he missed in the army. When he smiled, she felt confident. She wanted to speak to him. Once he left, they would not see each other for long. It could be a year or even much longer. And if something happened, they would never see each other again.

Bathsheba placed the milk on a low stool, closed the windows and doors and sat down next to Solomon. His eyes were closed as she kissed him tenderly. There was understanding in her silence when Solomon told her that he did not know whether he wanted to return to the regiment. She did not want to spoil the delicate moment when he was confiding in her. However much she wanted him to stay, she did not want to force him. He told her that even if he left the army, he did not want to look after the baadee. She was free to continue looking after the estate. Bathsheba was shocked. She had never expected that Solomon would want to forsake the baadee.

When Solomon left, a great silence descended upon the house. Even the children were subdued. Bathsheba stood behind the door. She did not want to see her husband leave. Only Gangaram had the audacity to scream, 'Has Solomon returned?' Bathsheba wanted to wring his neck.

Little did she realize that Gangaram knew what the future held. A month later, at midnight, above the friendly yelping of the banjara hounds, they heard a familiar knock at the door and Gangaram flapped his wings and announced that Solomon had returned. Bathsheba rushed to the door. The days of waiting were over.

Solomon told Bathsheba, 'On my way to Bombay, I stopped at the seashore. Here I made a fire, cooked some food, swam and slept under the stars. On clear nights the stars appear closer and seem to form a dome over the earth. The stars seemed so close that I felt I could stretch out my hand and touch them. Perhaps even catch a few, lock them in a box and bring them back for you,' he said with sudden tenderness. Drawing her closer he said, 'That night I had a strange dream. I saw a jewelled ladder of diamonds hanging over my head. Winged angels in silver togas were flying around the ladder. There was a glow as though I was surrounded by a thousand fireflies. The sword was emitting red flames and flying towards me. It was shaped like a human being. When it came closer, it transformed into a lion. The lion's head vanished and the body of the animal became a human head, which was neither male nor female. I was sure that I had seen the face before. I woke up. I realized that it was the sword of Tipu Sultan. It had a strange resemblance to the sword of the angel which protects the prophet Elijah.

'I sat listening to the sea and thinking about the meaning of the dream. Unlike you, I do not believe in omens or portents. But this was like a real experience. It was surely not a dream. Perhaps it was telling me to return to Danda. I could feel the presence of the Lord around me.

'When I went to the regiment headquarters and spoke to my officers about leaving, they tried to tempt me with more money. But I refused and decided to follow my heart. At the barracks at the army headquarters, I removed my uniform and all signs of the regiment. I felt free and weightless.'

16

ABRAHAM WORRIED ABOUT his son Solomon. He was a grown-up man and the father of three children. Abraham started getting irritated when Solomon took a nap in the courtyard, while Bathsheba was away at the baadee.

Moreover, Elisheba had told him that both Bathsheba and Shlumith were pregnant. This news bothered Abraham. He did not know what they would do once Bathsheba was laid up for a couple of months. Abraham was amazed that the family was not worried about the future of the property. He could foresee that the day was coming closer when they would have to sell it. Although he felt a certain relief when he saw Sombhau. As long as Sombhau was there next to Bathsheba, they were in safe hands. Abraham had become immobile, but Sombhau was still active.

Bathsheba wanted a daughter. She would take pleasure in dressing her and making pretty things for her. She would share her jewellery with her and comb her long tresses and tie them with colourful tassels.

Bathsheba imagined that her daughter would have dark eyes and long hair. She prayed for a fair skin for her daughter, like Solomon's. Being dark bothered her. Whenever she had time, she stitched clothes for the new arrival. Shlumith teased her that there was no use making so many clothes for a girl; what if she again gave birth to a son? Shlumith was afraid that Bathsheba would be disappointed if she had a son, so she persuaded her to make colourful quilts for the child. Girl or boy, the quilts would do for either.

It had become difficult for Bathsheba to move about. But besides looking after the baadee, Bathsheba had other things to worry about. She felt ashamed that her husband did not know what to do with his life, though, annoyed with his father's snide remarks, Solomon started taking a halfhearted interest in the baadee, helping Bathsheba with accounts, storage, marketing and transporting the produce. Once in a while he also lent a hand at grooming and washing the farm animals. And, being good at carpentry, he spent a large part of his afternoons repairing anything that had broken down.

17

THAT YEAR THEIR daughter Tamara was born. When she was about ten or eleven the summer they had a drought. The water level in the wells fell, lakes and ponds dried up, the earth was parched and cracked, cattle died and vultures hovering over the bloated carcasses of cattle were a common sight. There were havans and prayers. But the gods did not answer.

To make things worse, one afternoon they saw a huge cloud moving towards Danda. It looked like a monsoon cloud, but its shape was strange. It resembled a huge flying fox. It changed its form as it approached Danda. It was a swarm of locusts.

By late afternoon they were everywhere. There was not a single place where there were no locusts.

Within seconds they devoured everything. Bathsheba sat

transfixed in her room with Tamara in her lap. She had closed the door when she had seen the locusts falling in the open courtyard. Though they were harmless, she shivered with fear.

When the locusts disappeared, Bathsheba ventured out in the baadee and saw the damage caused by the insects. The landscape seemed stripped of green. As she was returning home she happened to look into a dried pond. As its bottom she saw a snake lying immobile. The memory of her own brush with a cobra was fresh in her memory. Perhaps it was dead, perhaps alive. Its wet eyes seemed to be staring at her. She wanted to make sure it was dead. She looked around hoping to catch sight of Sombhau or a farmhand, but there was nobody there. When she turned around, there was no sign of the snake. The dying cobra disturbed Bathsheba so much that when she reached the house, she was running a high fever.

That night, in a delirium, she heard a tap at her door. Tall and black like a granite pillar, the serpent stood there, staring at her. Bathsheba fainted.

Bathsheba had missed her periods, and knew that she was pregnant again. She was afraid that the snake had entered her womb when she had fainted. Perhaps she would give birth to a cobra instead of a human child. She conjured up the image of the village deity, the Nagdeva, and asked for his protection.

The thought of another pregnancy did not please her. The baadee demanded a lot of work. During those months everything seemed to go wrong and Bathsheba was always ill with something or the other. She needed Solomon, but he was busy with his own problems. Giving up the idea of joining the army, he was now trying to be inducted as a medical assistant, if his efforts with the oil press failed.

Bathsheba had become pale and thin. She often sat on the steps of the veranda next to Abraham. There was a strong bond between them.

He told her the story of the seven plagues which the Lord had brought upon Egypt, before parting the sea. In her imagination she saw a serpentine river of blood—the blood of the birds and animals who had died in the last few days. Shiva and Mahesh too had become thin. Their bones rattled like their bells.

When the water dried, frogs started appearing all over the baadee, panting and dying. They were migrating closer to the sea. The monsoon was a distant dream.

18

THIS WAS WHEN Tamara's hair was swarming with lice. All day long she scratched her head. Bathsheba was furious. She tied her hands with a rope. Tamara's screams filled the house. Shlumith reprimanded Bathsheba, 'Tamara is just a child and she has lice in her hair due to no fault of hers.'

Tamara hid behind Shlumith and did not allow her mother to touch her. Finally, it was Shlumith who tried to get rid of the lice from her hair. Tamara had confided in her that all the children at the missionary school had hair swarming with lice. Shlumith used neem oil and combed Tamara's hair five times a day but could not remove the lice. She then started all over again and washed her hair till Tamara developed a cold. She was miserable, scratching, coughing and wiping her running nose. Tamara and Shlumith were both tired of the hair and Tamara whispered in Shlumith's ear that she wanted to have her head tonsured.

To relieve her of the lice torture, Menashe prepared an oil with some bitter fruit of the neem tree, which he mixed with coconut, marrow and gooseberry oil. First he experimented on a stray dog with tick fever. When the ticks fell off the dog's body, Menashe knew that it would work.

When Shlumith started rubbing the mixture in Tamara's hair, Bathsheba was watching. Her own daughter would not allow her to touch her, but was sleeping in Shlumith's arms. Bathsheba was jealous. She realized that she had been wrong in punishing the child.

The lice fell off like dry husk. Shlumith did not want to disturb Tamara, so she requested Bathsheba to ask Shantabai to boil a mixture of soap-nut water to wash her hair. Although Shlumith had been very careful in not making her request sound like an order, Bathsheba resented that Shlumith was asking her to do something. So far it had always been Bathsheba who had given orders.

The news of Menashe's miraculous lice oil spread in the neighbouring villages. Everybody wanted it for their children. Menashe did brisk business. On Bathsheba's insistence, he bottled the mixture, naming it Sinha Tel, and asked Solomon to print labels for him with the design of a lion charging at a louse. This worked well. Pandubhau also carried a story about the hair of young virgins being infested with lice and mentioned that Menashe Dandekar's lice oil had been effective in eradicating this malady.

Bathsheba had persuaded Menashe to give a small advertisement for the oil without Solomon's knowledge. When Solomon discovered that it was Bathsheba's idea, he was annoyed. He did not like such publicity. When he reprimanded Bathsheba, she shot back, 'Why not?' and Solomon slapped her. Bathsheba was stunned that her husband could hit her. She was sure that Solomon hated her.

In times of difficulty everybody always looked to Bathsheba. But with the slap, Solomon had proved that he had more power than her. He was the lord and master of the house.

In protest, Bathsheba stopped speaking to Solomon. Solomon had regretted his action the very next moment. The sound of the slap, appeared to have woken up his heart. It had fallen asleep in the press. He felt a surge of love for Bathsheba and suffered from guilt. He had never slapped her before. That night Solomon took her hands in his, and asked her to forgive him. Bathsheba turned her back to him. She said, 'If you wanted to prove to me that I am just your wife and a woman, you could have taken my place in the baadee and become master of everything. I will recede into the recesses of the kitchen, like the rest of the women of the house.'

Bathsheba was unhappy. The pregnancy was bothering her. She did not know for how many more years she could keep on increasing the tribe. Each successive pregnancy was more difficult.

As if this were not enough, the stench of dying creatures attracted the scavengers—hyenas, wolves and vultures. They also occasionally saw huge monitor lizards disappearing into the deep burrows which were formed by the dry earth. People were scared of them when they saw them scavenging around the outskirts of the village, and sometimes even in the streets. They looked like miniature dinosaurs, walking on all fours, their slimy bodies raised above the ground, balancing on their tails. They were sure that wild beasts were coming closer to human habitation, and would eventually devour them.

Things came to a flashpoint when a two-year-old child disappeared. After a search, its body was found deep in the dying forest. From the marks on the body, the child appeared to have been attacked by wolves. There was panic and children were confined indoors.

A week later, someone saw four wolf cubs near a burrow.

The villagers were convinced that a she-wolf had carried away the child, to feed her cubs. Infuriated, a group of young men torched the burrow. When two cubs ran out, they clubbed them to death.

In the melée, the wolf returned and fell on the men, who were more than a match for her, and hit her on the head. The wolf collapsed. They left her there but were not sure whether they had killed her.

Solomon knew that an injured animal was dangerous and warned others to stay indoors after sundown. He had a feeling that the wolf would again attack. The wolf carried away three more children. The villagers were terrified. Solomon tried to pacify them and explained that the animal had become revengeful. Much against Solomon's advice, the young men of the village killed the wolf.

Solomon felt a premonition of even worse to come. Even Gangaram had become silent.

There was not a breath of air. There was an eerie silence. It was a common sight to see birds dropping dead from dry trees, sometimes straight into the mouths of monitors, stray dogs, wolves or a fox.

Suddenly the climate changed. Currents of hot air and black clouds drifted inland from the sea. Everyone was certain that it would rain, and life would become normal again.

But that was not to be. The clouds collected over Danda like a block of iron but stood frozen over Danda, Revdanda, Nandgaon and Murud-Janzira. The atmosphere became oppressive. Everybody was faint with the heat. After fifteen days of this terrible humidity, there was a community yagna to appease the rain gods. But nothing happened. Then the witch doctors were called. When they had done their rituals to locate the source of nature's fury, they claimed that all indications pointed towards the Dandekar estate.

Aharon the oil merchant, who was known as Hiran Teli and was an accomplished astrologer, was present and heard what was being discussed. He immediately called a meeting of the Bene Israel elders. Hiran Teli told them that the witch doctor had suggested that all their troubles stemmed from a house in Danda where there was a pregnant woman with hypnotic evil eyes, and a tremendous power over nature. She had the power to multiply fish, fowl and paddy. With her vile powers she could parch the earth and swallow the waters which made the earth fertile.

There was silence in the prayer hall. The Dandekars were a much loved and respected family. When Solomon asked whether his wife was being held responsible for the calamity, Hiran Teli nodded his head and advised Solomon that Bathsheba be kept indoors. Although the Bene Israel did not believe in black magic or the verdict of the witch doctor, they were afraid, and did not know how to handle a situation like this.

Solomon was frightened for the first time, an emotion he had not experienced even when he was in the army. This fear was beyond human control. The elders advised Solomon to protect his wife.

Hiran Teli was sure that somebody was jealous of the prosperous Dandekar house. Perhaps this particular person had a grudge against Bathsheba, and also suspected her of inspiring other women to become independent. Some people felt that Bathsheba was a bad influence on other women.

After much discussion it was decided that Hiran Teli would inform the witch doctor that the Bene Israel leaders had made the pregnant woman powerless. They had taken away the freedom her father-in-law had bestowed upon her.

Solomon was in tears as he requested the Bene Israel elders

not to be so hard on his wife. She was well meaning and pure of mind. It was finally decided that the women of the Dandekar house would be told about the episode by Hiran Teli. They would pray together to guard the Dandekar family against harm.

When the proceedings started, Abraham was in his chair, as usual. Abraham felt helpless and angry. He could not protest, as the situation had become dangerous for the women of his family. Bathsheba had a premonition of the worst, from the way Solomon was avoiding her from the night before. Her heart missed a beat when he called the women of the house to take their place in the western end of the veranda.

Hiran Teli was a compassionate man. He began his discourse by describing the climatic changes in Danda. He said, 'I will start today's proceedings with a prayer for good weather, so that our solar divinity will reduce his fire and shower us with pleasant times. It is a prayer I learnt from a Cochini trader. We can recite this prayer once in twenty-eight years. Either on a Tuesday or Wednesday. But as we have never recited this prayer, this is the best time to read it and request the Lord for our well being and for protection of the community.' He adjusted his skullcap and the married women covered their heads as he chanted in Marathi: 'This is the Tuesday's song for rain—Aho Eeshwar, we depend on you and look up to your throne and at the cluster of graves of our ancestors. And when we are surrounded by enemies, you appear like fire around us and destroy all that is harmful to us. That is the time you appear like lightning and the entire universe is illuminated—so much so that the earth trembles and mountains melt like wax. When we see this light, it keeps us away from all form of idol worship and we chant prayers in the Lord's praise and seek refuge in Mount Sion.

. . . And may our young girls rejoice in your glory. Because hear Oh Israel the Lord the God is one. Aho Parmeshwar destroy the evil forces around us, and preserve the lives of your devotees. Release us from the clutches of evil and show us the path of light and satisfaction. And, you who follow the laws of the Lord, rejoice in the name of the Lord. Remember his purity and grace and be grateful to your Deva for what he has given you.'

Then Hiran Teli brought out his sarangi and sang a bhajan to the lord. The men joined in the song to the lord. It was a Marathi kirtan which he changed into a Jewish song which was simple and easy to follow: 'Offer new songs to the Lord, because he showers us with well-being and surprises us with miracles which he performs on the earth. He has created us and led us out of difficulties. And he has compassion for the house of Israel. He has shown us the path of truth. Let us pray and rejoice in the Lord. And let us chant our words of prayer together, so that the sounds echo all over the universe. With this let the sea join in with the sound of her waves, may the rivers flow with the name of the lord, and the mountains echo with praise for the Lord, because he is lawful and truthful and will protect us forever. Our Deva, our lord and master, you make our enemies tremble with your aura. You, Eeshwar who resides on Mount Sion, you are above everything and higher than everybody else. When your devotees Moses, Aharon and Samuel called upon you, you revealed yourself from a pillar of clouds and taught us the law. And you destroyed our enemies, because you are Aho Deva our Lord—you are the only one.'

Everybody was deeply moved. They were sure Eeshwar would be pleased with their kirtan and would shower them with good rainfall. But this was not just a pleasant get-together like the one they had at the Prathnalaya or prayer hall. There were many serious matters to be discussed.

In an expressionless voice, Hiran Teli spoke about the rumours. He also announced that from that day there would be certain restrictions on the women of the Dandekar house. Like the rest of the Bene Israel women of the Konkan, they were not to step beyond the threshold alone. And if there was something important to do, they could leave the house in the company of other women or men of the family.

The women, sitting with their heads covered, understood everything. They looked like frozen sculptures. Then slowly they seemed to come to life, and disappeared inside the house.

19

THAT NIGHT BATHSHEBA lay inert and bleeding. She had had a miscarriage. She did not call for help. She knew that if she did not tell anybody, she would bleed to death. She felt the quilt becoming wet under her and turning deep red. That night she had decided to sleep alone on an old quilt, as she felt a strange throbbing in her womb.

At midnight, Solomon heard noises outside their window. He thought it was a wolf or a monitor lizard or a man trying to break in through the open veranda.

He got up to check the doors and windows, and saw that Bathsheba was sleeping between him and the door. When he stepped on her quilt to reach the door, he stepped on something wet. For a moment he stood immobile. He could not decide what it was. Was it water which had spilled from the jug? As his eyes got accustomed to the darkness, he saw that the water jug was on the window sill, and this was a different sort of wetness. It was sticky and thick. He panicked when he realized that he was standing in a pool of blood. Bathsheba's blood. It was the blood of their child. Bathsheba's eyes were shining in the dying light of the lantern. She was awake, but she was not asking him for help. Solomon called out to Menashe.

Shlumith was the first to hear Solomon. She rushed to their room and saw Bathsheba.

The women rushed with bowls of warm water and cloth to help Menashe stop the bleeding. Bathsheba was in pain, but was relieved. She did not want another child. She was sure that it would have a serpent's head and a human body.

In a delirium she recounted the story Abigayail had told her at Navgaon. Bathsheba could see the seven enormous fishes swimming towards her. The one in the middle was bleeding, and the other fish were swimming around her. They kept moving in circles, as they transformed into women. Bathsheba tried hard to keep her eyes open so that she could see what was happening to them, but she felt a numbing darkness overcome her . . .

Tamara woke up when everybody started running around with pans of hot water. Then, standing in the doorway, she saw her mother lying as though she were dead. Tamara hated her mother, but when she thought of life without her, she was frightened.

Tamara was thin and tall, long faced, with small eyes and beetle brows which Bathsheba had tried to rub off when she was a baby, saying that girls with beetle brows were not considered beautiful. A girl's eyebrows should be shaped like arches. But Bathsheba could not control Tamara's stubborn hair growth.

Tamara stood exactly as her mother had taught her not to—legs spread out and her feet with their long toes and silver toerings turned outwards. Bathsheba had always been strong and domineering but spread out on the floor, she appeared helpless and defeated. After many years Tamara felt a certain love for her mother and the bitterness seemed to melt.

At that very moment, a strange cramp gripped her stomach, and something wet slid over her thighs and dripped to her feet. She could not control it.

Tamara looked down at the rim of her skirt which touched her thick silver anklets. To her horror she saw that she was bleeding. Petrified she wondered how her mother's blood had entered her body.

Shlumith was massaging Bathsheba's stomach. She looked up and realized that it was the beginning of Tamara's first menstrual cycle. Soon they would have to start looking for a groom for her. Perhaps she would be the perfect wife for her son. Shlumith made a sign to Elisheba that Tamara needed help.

That night was endless. Elisheba taught Tamara to wear the cloth to hold the blood which would eventually increase the tribe, while Menashe struggled to stop the blood from Bathsheba's womb. They could not send a bullock-cart to fetch the vaid, as nobody had the courage to venture out and face the hyenas and the wolves.

Solomon sat all night in the veranda. He did not want Bathsheba to die. Only she had the capability to hold the house together. He had never imagined that one day he would lose her. She had always been full of life. He felt guilty. He had often been impatient with her. He would make an effort to be affectionate and spend more time with her. As the morning light touched the veranda, he felt Menashe's reassuring hand on his shoulder, telling him that Bathsheba was out of danger.

The next morning, when the bulbul called at Bathsheba's window, her bleeding was under control, but she was pale and a shadow of her old self. She would never be the same again. The bulbul would never herald the beginning of a new day.

20

IT DID NOT rain, but the villagers said that Bathsheba could not be blamed for the natural calamity as she had sacrificed her unborn child as an offering to that which was turning everything to dust.

Bathsheba seldom left her room and Enoch was forced to look after the baadee. She sat at the threshold of her room with vacant eyes. But Sombhau insisted on seeing her every morning before he left for work. For him she had become the incarnation of Jagatmata Gauri.

The baadee was no longer the same. The produce went down. The land did not give an abundant harvest and Sombhau could not work like before. He only gave instructions and maintained the accounts.

They sold some of their land and Abraham divided the rest between his sons. The only thing common between them was the kitchen and the oil press. It appeared to be a timeless machine, which filled the oil pitchers of the house.

Solomon wrote to his old unit of the Sixth British Regiment of the East India Company, to admit him in their medical wing. He had decided finally to leave the struggling oil business and become a licensed medical assistant. The licence would open the world for him. He was sent for training to the Bombay medical college for two years after which he received a licence that gave him the status of a regular medical practitioner. Considering the financial situation of the Dandekars, he was forced to work as a medical assistant for the East India Company.

21

ON HIS WAY to Bombay Divekar's youngest brother Essaji often stopped at Danda. Divekar himself was dead after fulfilling his ambition to build a synagogue in Bombay. On his latest visit, he was shocked by the changes he saw. He had many things to talk about.

That night, he regaled the Dandekar family with stories about the Cochini Jews. The temple of the Lord in Cochin was the most beautiful place he had seen in his life. It glowed with light and beautiful objects. When he described the temple, even Bathsheba had a spark of interest in her eyes.

Seeing the Cochin synagogue, Divekar had decided that he too would make a synagogue, his brother recounted.

Essaji said, 'The Jews of Cochin arrived on the shores of Cranganore or Shingly, perhaps from Marjoca in Spain or from North Africa. Till the fifteenth century they had their own little kingdom in India and the Rabban family presided over them like a royal family. In the olden days Shingly was the only Indian port known to the outside world. Perhaps the Jews came here looking for ivory, peacock feathers, gold and monkeys.

'There are some indications of their arrival such as a hillock named Judah Kunnu and a tank called Judah Kulam. They are the ancient shrines of the Jews, and a copper plate has the signatures of four Jewish witnesses. The language on the copper plate is in Vattezhuthu characters, an ancient Tamil script, and the meaning of the writing is: . . . the following gift of land has been given by His Majesty Sri Parkran Iravi Vanmar whose ancestors have been welding the sceptre for many hundred thousand years. In the thirty-sixth year after the second day, when he dwelt in Muvricote, he was pleased to make the following gifts: We have granted to Joseph Rabban the village of Anjuvannam together with seventy-two propriety rights, the revenue, land tax, weight tax, tolls, boats, carts, and the title of Anjuvannam—the lamp of the day. A cloth should be spread out wherever he walks. He shall have a palanquin, a parasol, a drum, a trumpet, a gateway, and a garland. He need not pay the dues which the inhabitants of other cities pay to the royal palace, and he may enjoy the benefits which they enjoy. To Joseph Rabban the prince of Anjuvannam and to his descendants, sons and daughters, and to his nephews and sons-in-law who married his daughters in natural succession, so long as the world, sun and moon exist, Anjuvannam shall have his hereditary possession. It is signed by Goverthan Marathandan, Kodaj Chirikandan, Manavepala Manavian, Kodai Iravi, Moorkan Chathan, Vandalcheri Kandan.

'Before the Christian era and afterwards many travellers had noted the presence of Jews in Cochin, and they described it as a Jewish kingdom of India. It is said that the Jews lived here in peace with many communities.

'In the fourteenth century, things changed. The vicious seed of black and white Jew was planted amongst the Jews. The fair-skinned Jews had a superior status, the blacks were inferior. In 1686, the Jewish Dutch traveller Moses de Pavia referred to the black Jews as Malabarese and the white Jews as Blancos.

'The dark skin could have been due to many reasons, as it was well known that there were many migrations. Or were the dark-skinned Jews converted slaves of the fair-skinned merchants?

'Moses de Pavia noted that although the Malabarese were dark, they were Jewish in every way—in fact much more traditional. Yet the Blancos tended to treat them like slaves, called them Meshuarim and gave them separate synagogues. The Rabban family was trying to remove all differences between white and black.'

With a sigh Essaji commented that even the Bene Israel suffered from this malady of colour. The pure and impure.

Gora-kala. White and black.

Essaji continued his story: 'It is said that during these years there was also a power struggle in the Rabban family. The younger brother escaped to Cochin by swimming across the backwaters, carrying his wife on his back. During those difficult days the Zamorim of Calicut and the Portuguese took over the flourishing pepper and spice trade of the Jews. They attacked the Jews and burnt their houses.

'The Raja of Cochin had always respected the Jews and admired their integrity. He granted them Mattancheri, next to the royal temple. He even gave special permission to his Jewish soldiers to observe the shabath. For this compassionate gesture, he was known as the King of Jews. This is how Jew-town came into being and a synagogue was built. Yet the Zamorim and the Portuguese were a constant cause of worry. With their sudden raids, the Jews lost some of their most important documents and artefacts. It was only when the Dutch came to their rescue that they could live in peace. The Dutch East India Company helped them reconstruct the edicts of their religion. When the Jews of Denmark received information about the Cochini Jews, they also helped them with books and religious artefacts.

'The Cochin Jews were known to have come to India before the Christian era. Perhaps it was an exodus from Persia which brought them here. Moses de Pavia wrote that there were eighty thousand Jews in Cochin. His theory was that after the destruction of the Second Temple, ten thousand Jews had come to Cochin and they were received graciously by the Hindu ruler who allowed them to settle in different parts of Cochin. Yet there are no definite dates, as it is said that some more came from Spain and the tribe increased. But one thing is certain—unlike us, they retained the memory of King

Solomon's Temple, and with that image in mind, they built the
first synagogue. Habban was the architect of the synagogue. A
lake and hillock were named Jooda, after Rabbi Judah who
was held in high esteem by the Cochin Jews. He was well
versed in the Jewish rituals. The Cochin Jews have something
which we do not have—the Sefer Torah. These silver steepled
caskets with delicate engravings, geometric designs and tassels
are things of great beauty. The parchments inside are inscribed
by hand with squid ink. They guard the text of the first five
books of the Old Testament. The scrolls are written in Hebrew—
our ancient language. When I held the Sefer Torah for the
shabath prayers on Saturday morning at the Pardesi Synagogue
in Cochin, I was in tears. Once I build the synagogue in
Bombay, I will have to make another journey in search of the
Sefer Torah, or else my synagogue will not be complete. The
house of God needs its 'books.'

When Essaji finished his story, his face was glowing. Till
then their knowledge about their religion was limited—saying
the Shema Israel in Hebrew, circumcising the male child,
singing a few lines of the Eliyahu Hannabi, following the
dietary laws, and being fiercely aware that they were Bene
Israel Jews.

22

ESSAJI NOTICED THAT Bathsheba had not stirred. Her head was
hidden between her knees. And nobody could believe that she
had spoken when she asked Essaji, 'Bhau, tell us about the
Pardesi Synagogue.'

His face lit up as he described the synagogue. 'It is like a
jewel. The copper plates there bind us to India. Seven gold
plated Sefer Torahs are placed in an alcove in the western wall.

They are covered with a silk curtain. The Teva or altar in the centre is shaped like a half circle. There is a separate gallery for women. The glittering chandeliers and lanterns are so ornate and beautifully crafted that when the oil lamps are lit they shine like stars. The entire floor is covered with blue tiles, which have come from Canton in China. They say there is a Jewish community in China, and just as we look like Indians, they look Chinese. And if you think that each tile is the same, you are wrong. Each tile has a different design, flower, leaf, plant, tree and landscape. Each tile is an artistic marvel. Almost everybody there knows how to recite our prayers in Hebrew. The Rabban family has promised to send us the learned people of their community to teach us the law. Their hazans will officiate at our prayers and translate our books in Marathi.

'Solomon Rabban has brought back to us the religion of our forefathers. He has broken the barrier between us and the Jews of the world.'

And Essaji opened a silk-lined bag and brought out the karna or the shofar. The spiral horn of a ram.

'It is to be blown on the morning of the Rosh ha shanah, the new year.' He had started practising on the horn. He touched the karna to his lips, blew air into it and played the four tunes he had been taught, the tekiya, the teruba, the tekhiya and the long wail-like note which brought tears to his eyes.

In 1796 Shaar'ha-Rahamin—the Gate of Mercy Synagogue—was built in Bombay by Divekar, as a symbol of the liberation of the Bene Israel Jews from Tipu Sultan's prison and sure death. Soon after, Aka Samuel Ezekiel Divekar, commonly known as Abraham Hasaji Divekar, died in Cochin. He was looking for a Sefer Torah for the synagogue. Yet he made the Hekal, or altar, to place the holy Torah. Someone was to later get them for the synagogue. He had also made the chairs for the prophet Elijah. They were covered with a blue brocade star on a velvet cover. One of them was used for the circumcision of the male child. There was also the brass-encased decorative Tamid for Elijah's batti. During Simhat Torah, there was bidding to buy oil for this particular lamp.

If Divekar had lived to participate in the new year prayers, the Selihot, he would have heard the hazan call out to him at five o'clock in the morning—Samaji Divekar, Se-Li-Hot . . .' But that was not to be.

If you look hard, you will come across Samuel Street and Divekar's grave in Cochin. And at Masjid Bunder in Bombay, look out for Samuel Street where Divekar built the synagogue. In the crowded street, Hindu and Muslim shopkeepers bow their head in respect as they pass the six-spoked Star of David on the wooden door of the synagogue.

To all appearances it looks like a residential house. The door opens into a small courtyard, with a tree and a washing place. The hazan lives on the second floor and the main prayer hall is small with shining chandeliers and polished wood. An old wooden building with carvings of Krishna, Ganesha and Laxmi on its facade, stands next to the synagogue.

23

THAT YEAR TAMARA returned to Danda from Navgaon, and refused to go back to her in-laws house. She was unhappy, she wanted to leave her husband. There was a crisis in the family. Marriages were forever. While her husband was alive, a married daughter returning to her parents' house was a sacrilege—the breaking of a law.

Tamara was married to Aharon, Abigayail's son. Bathsheba

had met Abigayail when she had visited the graves of the ancestors with Solomon. She had been tempted to give her daughter to Abigayail because the ancestors had appeared to her in the form of marine creatures.

Bathsheba and Abigayail had become friends and met often in Danda, Navgaon or Alibaug. During these visits Bathsheba had noticed that Abigayail's family had received religious education from the Cochini hazans. They followed the Marathi texts which gave detailed instructions about the observance of traditions. Bathsheba had not realized that Abigayail's family observed the rites and rituals with a certain rigidity.

When Tamara was seven years old, Bathsheba and Abigayail had decided that they would seal their friendship with the marriage of their children. Yet, sometimes, after she returned from Navgaon, Bathsheba found that she was uneasy about the atmosphere in Abigayail's house. In her own house, it was more relaxed. The Dandekars were flexible where the law was concerned. She herself had broken the law by working on a quilt during those endless shabath days when she had been waiting for Solomon's return. She had also been allowed to take responsibility for the baadee in Solomon's absence. Tamara had grown up in such a home. Yet a promise was a promise. Bathsheba asked Shlumith to inform Tamara about the various aspects of marriage because Tamara hardly spoke to her mother.

Shlumith knew that Tamara would not be happy in Abigayail's house and had often broached the subject with Bathsheba. But she received a stock reply that Bathsheba had given her word to Abigayail. After all, the girls of the Dandekar family had to be married into other families, and would have to learn the ways of other houses. Shlumith had tried to tell

Bathsheba that Tamara was in love with her own son, Moses. Her words tell on deaf ears.

Tamara's affection was obvious from the way she looked after Moses and his needs. Bathsheba had also noticed the attachment between them, and instructed Shlumith that she should not leave them alone or allow them to get too close. This was the beginning of the rift between Bathsheba and Shlumith.

Tamara and Moses often sat on the swing in the veranda while Abraham dozed. He was happy hearing their youthful laughter, and smiled in his sleep. Then he was awakened by Bathsheba scolding Tamara and telling her to stop laughing like a child. She was a grown-up woman, and should know how to behave with a boy. Quietly Moses slipped away. He could not handle complicated situations.

Tamara stared at Bathsheba defiantly. She told her mother that there was nothing wrong in sitting on a swing. There was an angry exchange of words. Bathsheba told Tamara that she was Aharon's fiancee, and could no longer speak to Moses. This infuriated Tamara so much that she became hysterical. She said that if she was forced to marry Aharon, she would run away from the house. She started running towards the sea, where there was high tide.

Her purple skirt swaying around her, Tamara plunged into the sea. Shlumith heard the commotion and rushed out. She shouted at Moses for disappearing into the house like a rat. When he appeared looking sheepish, she ordered him to bring back Tamara. She knew that only he could stop Tamara.

That night, Tamara slept next to Shlumith. Tears streaming down her face, she whispered, 'I do not like Aharon. When he looks at me, there is no feeling. I was very upset when Aunt Abigayail made a comment about my eyebrows. She advised me to rub a rough cloth on them and wash my face with gramflour and milk. She does not like me. I can never be happy with Aharon.'

With eyes lowered, she asked Shlumith, 'If you send a proposal, a manga for me, you can save me from aunt Abigayail. I would be happy to be your daughter-in-law. You could speak to my mother and at least complete the ful-bharni ceremony with flowers. That would seal our relationship. We could have the engagement later, just before the wedding. Please, please speak to my mother.'

Shlumith explained to Tamara that Abigayail had already sent a manga for her, so it was legally incorrect to interfere. She would have liked to have her as a daughter-in-law but once a manga was fixed, nothing could break it. A broken engagement meant sure death for the girl. She saw the shadow of fear in Tamara's eyes. 'Does it mean that if I break the engagement, the family will kill me? Is the family's honour more important than my life?' Shlumith did not answer but caressed her head till she fell asleep.

The next morning, Shlumith saw Moses with Tamara's eyes and realized that he had grown up. He was studying to be an architect. Moses was very tall and thin, with large eyes and dark curled eyelashes. He had an intense look. He sported a French beard and his lower lip was pink and full. Tamara was ready for marriage, and it was natural that she was in love with him. Bathsheba had not foreseen the consequences when she had formally accepted Abigayail's manga.

Besides, Tamara kept breaking the law and was careless about everything, including her appearance. Much to Abigayail's dismay, she refused to wear any gold jewellery on the pretext that it gave her an allergy. Abigayail was embarrassed that her elder daughter-in-law was dressed like a widow at every festival or celebration in the house. Abigayail was desperate that her son have children. She suspected that they did not sleep in the same bed. Aharon refused to discuss the matter with his mother.

Years later, when the family left for Ahmedabad, Tamara also returned to the city, but she did not tell anybody what had happened. She wanted to speak to Moses but that was no longer possible, as he was married to their cousin, the small and frail Sarah. They appeared to be happy and had a five-year-old daughter. Whenever he was at home, the child was always on his lap. Tamara kept her distance. She did not want any misunderstandings. Moses avoided being alone with her and did not want to know why she had returned to Ahmedabad. When they were alone in the clinic room, he whispered, 'Why don't you go back to Aharon?' Tamara was hurt. Moses, whom she had loved, behaved like her enemy.

Tamara returned to Navgaon, and again tried to settle down. She even wore gold bangles and the colourful saris her mother had given her. She realized that she had been so depressed that she had been wearing the same two saris day after day. One was olive green, the other ash grey. She also wove a string of flowers in her hair. And, while cooking with Abigayail, she realized that her mother-in-law was not the devil she had made her out to be. So she started talking to her and asked her how she had met her mother. In some strange way, Abigayail became a link between the two women.

Abigayail took this as an opportunity to speak to Tamara about making a vow to Eliyahu Hannabi, for the blessing of a child. She told her how she had dreamt about the marine ancestors who had given her Aharon.

That evening as Tamara served dinner, she saw that Aharon was not another Moses, nor was he like the men of her family. He was a simple farmer, who had grown up with the religious constraints of his family. He was older than her and had his limitations. Bathsheba had not taken this into consideration when she had decided to give Tamara in marriage to Abigayail's family.

Bathsheba had the romantic belief that Aharon was a boon from their ancestors. She wanted to thank the ancestors in her own way for bringing back Solomon. Much later she realized that she had not gifted her daughter to the ancestors but sacrificed her.

24

ABIGAYAIL INSISTED THAT Tamara follow the rules of menstruation according to the law. Tamara was told that as soon as her periods started, she had to move to the Rajodarshan room. She was treated like an impure animal for five days, eating from separate plates for the monthly periods.

All by herself, Tamara felt suffocated in the seclusion room. Once in a while some woman from the family would sit at a distance and talk to her about mundane matters. Tamara would become depressed and experience the vacuum of not having children. At least, her own children would have sat around her and kept her amused. She had seen the children of other women chattering away with their mothers. However much she tried, she could not be intimate with the children of the house. She kept away from them. And, although she was the elder daughter-in-law, she had never helped her younger sisters-in-law with their pregnancies. Nor had she held their infants in her arms or offered to watch over their children while their mothers were busy with household chores.

She behaved like an observer. She was certain she could

never have a child. Somewhere deep within her, the memory of her mother's miscarriage, and the shock of her first menstruation, had made her hate pregnancies and children. When her blood had mixed with her mother's, she had assumed that she had lost her fertility.

She hated the Rajodarshan room. It depressed her, yet she had to stay there for long periods. Unlike the other women, she bled for ten days. Around the tenth day, every evening, after sunset she had to often check that the bleeding had stopped. Then she had to take the long traditional bath.

According to the Marathi books of the law which Abigayail followed strictly, this was no ordinary bath. It was the mikwah. For this they had built a tank which stored 160 gallons of water in their outhouse. Like the rest of the women of the family, Tamara was expected to fast on the day of purification. Then with a sharp blade she had to clean her nails. Thereafter, she had to remove all her jewellery and wash it with warm water. At sundown she had to enter the tank with a cloth wrapped around her body and take a dip. For total purification, she had to go underwater for a second. Her body had to be immersed from head to toe. Only then was she considered clean. She could then step out of the water, remove her wet sari, and wear fresh clothes and jewellery. After the completion of this elaborate ritual, she was allowed to take part in daily affairs, and enter the room she shared with her husband.

Other women performed this ritual as a duty, but Tamara rebelled against it. She often cheated by pouring a iota of water over herself and not staying in the mikwah as long as she was expected to. During a heavy monsoon or during winter, she hated taking a dip in the water. Every time she stepped into the water she was certain she was going to die. And she almost did.

25

TAMARA COULD FEEL something was wrong. Aharon had become very distant. He did not even pick a quarrel with her. Although she was not supposed to sleep with her husband before her periods, she felt the desire to embrace him. She had worn a bright pink sari which Shlumith had given her, tied a string of flowers in her hair, and applied rose ittar behind her ears. With this she wore all the jewellery she was supposed to wear, including the silver armlets she hated.

Looking into the mirror she felt something was missing. She opened her jewellery box and, looking into the mirror fixed in the box, she wore a small diamond nosering. Its sparkle gave her face a happy glow. Abigayail complimented her and gave her son a knowing smile. Tamara was unnerved that Aharon had not smiled back at his mother. Brusquely he told his mother that he wanted to sleep by eight. Tamara did not take this seriously. She was sure that she would seduce him that night.

When the women were cleaning the kitchen and putting away the dishes for the night, Abigayail asked Tamara to wait for her in the courtyard. She wanted to speak to her.

Tamara was happy with herself. She told herself that this was the beginning of her love for Aharon. She wanted to rush to her room and hold him in her arms, but she waited for her mother-in-law. Abigayail was pleased that her elder daughter-in-law was at last behaving like a normal woman. Abigayail asked Tamara whether she was willing to make a vow for the boon of a child. Heady with the fragrance of the jasmine flowers in her hair, Tamara nooded. If she became pregnant she would offer a malida to Eliyahu Hannabi. Besides that, every Sunday she would offer flowers at the graves of the ancestors. For the first time in years, Abigayail took her in her arms. Tamara rested her head on her shoulder, and remembered Shlumith and her mother. For the first time she felt close to her.

That night, when Tamara entered her bedroom she could see Aharon in the darkness. From the sound of his breathing, she knew he was awake. She lay next to him and touched his shoulder. Holding his face in her hands, she kissed him. At first he did not respond. Then he held and kissed her with surprising passion. After they had made love, however, he seemed to withdraw again. He got up and dressed without a word. Bemused, she stared at him as he lit the lantern and sat down on a chair next to the window. He said, 'Why don't you sit up, I wish to speak to you.'

They stayed awake all night. Aharon told her that he was leaving for Rangoon. He had joined the British army as a soldier. Tamara sat frozen. She could hear her heartbeats as she crushed the jasmine flowers which lay strewn on the pillow. Perhaps she could have handled the situation better.

Now that she had come to terms with her marriage, fate was playing tricks with her. Aharon had made separate plans for his life. He said, 'I am leaving tomorrow afternoon.'

Tamara felt her head spin, and anger suffused her. Her voice shaking with emotion she asked, 'Does your mother know?' When he said, 'Yes,' Tamara felt deeply betrayed. The beautiful night became a nightmare.

He asked in a deadpan voice, 'Why are you upset? You do not love me. You have never loved me. So what difference will it make to you?'

Tamara wept soundlessly as Aharon stared at her without emotion. Tamara was thinking about their ancestors and the tricks they were playing on her.

The next day, when Aharon left, Tamara hid in the Rajodarshan room and did not see him. She had chosen the Rajodarshan room as an escape from the scene of farewell. She did not feel part of the family.

For fifteen days she stayed in the room, pretending that she was menstruating longer than usual. She drank endless glasses of water, slept all day, and walked restlessly all night. When Abigayail tried to cajole her to eat something and offered to get some medication from the vaid, she refused.

On the fifteenth day, she went into the mikwah and lost consciousness. When she did not emerge, Abigayail rushed in and, with the help of the other women of the family, pulled out Tamara's naked body from the water. Placing her on the floor, they pumped the water out of her lungs.

When she woke up, Tamara was like a corpse—like the dead date tree which stood next to the Rajodarshan room. She did not leave her bed, but she knew that she was pregnant.

When Abigayail was certain that Tamara was pregnant, she made sweet pancakes and rejoiced. But Tamara did not look at her. She lay near the window, staring at the sky.

When Solomon heard that Tamara had almost died because of the mikwah he was enraged. He did not want any daughter of his family to drown, or come to a tragic end because of tradition. He instructed the women not to observe the laws of Rajodarshan. They would continue with their lives as they had done before the books of law were translated into Marathi. Menstruation did not make women impure. They need not purify themselves at the cost of their life.

My grandmother Shebabeth belonged to the family of Tamara and Aharon. Tamara was her grandmother from her mother's side of the family. Shebabeth sometimes referred to her beetle brows and depressive moods. They also remembered her as the one who made the best quilts, an art she had learnt from her Aunt Shlumith. Shebabeth always said though Tamara could infuse so much happiness in her quilts, she could not weave it into her own life.

26

AFTER ABRAHAM'S DEATH some years later, the Dandekar family began to shift to Ahmedabad. The first to move was Menashe.

One afternoon Abraham did not wake up from his nap. His empty chair stood on the veranda. Solomon liked to believe that Abraham's soul was sitting there and watching over the house while he was away. He often regretted that he had not taken his father Abraham's advice, and shown an interest in the baadee. Bathsheba was the only one who had understood Abraham's wisdom. But Solomon realized that it was too late for regrets.

The house in Danda had begun to resemble a house of ghosts. Only Gangaram's whistles and the barks of the banjara hounds broke the silence that had fallen over the house. Those who had stayed behind were waiting for death. Elisheba was bedridden with a stroke. Bathsheba and Yacobeth looked after her. They had sold their fields, and all they had was the fruit orchard, a vegetable patch and the oil press. They were living off the oil press and Solomon's earnings as a doctor. Solomon had left the army and had a small clinic where he treated patients from the surrounding villages. He was well known for his mixture for fever and people from Revdanda, Nandgaon and Alibaug came to him for treatment.

He had also made a business of breeding dogs. He had bred a rare mixture of the banjara hounds and a wolf. This breed, that he called Banjru, had the characteristics of both dog and wolf and was a very ferocious watch dog with grey-brown eyes. It had long straight wolf-like legs and silver-grey fur. That was exactly what the British, Dutch and some Konkani landowners were looking for for their estates.

Menashe found a house in Salatwada, a street next to Delhi Darwaza. It reminded Solomon of the house in Danda when he visited him. Its prominent feature was a huge wooden doorway and brass knockers with a small wicket gate. The main door was almost never opened except on special occasions, such as weddings and religious ceremonies.

Salatwada was the area where Muslim artisans made stone tiles. Near the house there was a huge neem tree which was always full of birds. The toilets and the stables for horses and carriages were outside the house, as was common in those times. On entering, there was a huge courtyard. Solomon knew that this would be used by the women and their guests. On hot summer nights they would sleep there, as they had in the courtyard at Danda.

It was here that Solomon, who had finally left Danda to come and live with Menashe died in 1865, at a very ripe old age.

I shall add a small story about Solomon's burial. Menashe had made the arrangements for the burial in the Jewish graveyard, near the British cantonment. The women were stitching the shroud. Cloth was being cut into pieces for the pantaloons, a shirt, and an overcoat.

The Bene Israel were discussing the burial. The graveyard was full but they had managed to find a place for Solomon. But Menashe objected that it was too close to the gate and Solomon would be hemmed in between the other graves. Then Parbhatbhai, the milkman, held his hands and pleaded, 'Bury my brother on my land.'

Joseph did not know what to do. The Bene Israel of Ahmedabad were of the opinion that they had to bury Solomon before the shabath. Solomon was dressed and ready for the final journey, but nobody knew where to take him.

Then Parbhatbhai showed the land to Joseph. It was in a small plot, halfway between Dilli Darwaza and the cantonment. There were neem, banyan, acacia and tamarind trees. The cluster of trees reminded Joseph of Danda, and when he saw the banyan tree, he knew he would lay his grandfather to rest under its shadows.

Joseph offered to pay for the land. Parbhatbhai was offended.

Solomon was buried under the banyan tree.

Joseph persuaded Parbhatbhai to accept a token amount of eleven rupees.

After ten months Joseph built a marble grave for his grandfather. The headstone was marked by the Hebrew words which said: Buried here, Solomon Jacob Dandekar, may his soul rest in paradise. After which, he dedicated the graveyard to the Bene Israel community of Ahmedabad.

2

David

27

BATHSHEBA WAS VERY fond of Simha, because she was devoted to Joseph, her grandson, only child of her son Jacob. Jacob was often away, as a sepoy in the Anglo-Sind war with the 3rd regiment Bombay Light Infantry. He had passed through Gujarat and on his last visit home had regaled the family with stories of the walled city of Ahmedabad, its fourteen gates and the prosperous houses made in carved wood. Solomon and Bathsheba brought up Joseph as though he was their own child. Joseph had taken years to realize that they were his grandparents, not parents, as he was very young when both his parents died, for reasons I cannot determine.

Joseph had studied in the English missionary school and at one point he became interested in forestry and forest products. He went for long treks with his teachers and learnt to birdwatch and to identify animals and reptiles. When Solomon and Enoch voiced their worries about his interests, he remained silent. But he had long discussions with young Simha. He did not know how much she understood, but he told her everything.

Simha, Enoch's youngest daughter, was closest to Bathsheba, as there was still some tension between Bathsheba and Tamara.

Joseph and Simha made a handsome couple. Simha was tall and slim, with a clear skin and a smile which spread from ear to ear. She had soft, warm hands which Joseph liked to hold when telling her his secrets.

When they were in their teens, Joseph was shorter than Simha, and she looked older than him in her bright ghaghras and long frilled blouses. He had learnt to recognize her by the sound of her anklets, which had a different tinkle to those of the other women of the house. Or perhaps it was the way she walked. Somehow, without looking up, Joseph always knew when Simha was near him. Or perhaps it was because of the jasmine flowers in her long braids. But, he argued with himself, every woman in the house wore jasmine flowers, so what was different about Simha's fragrance? He concluded that there was a special feel about her, to which he responded. Perhaps she recognized and accepted the wild streak in him.

There was already some dissent in the family as he refused to wear dhotis, angarkhas and turbans. He had taken to the dress usually worn by Muslims and Parsis—loose, flared pants, a long-sleeved shirt and a long, flowing coat. He wore a fez, and sometimes changed it for a tall conical hat. For a festival or celebration, however, he agreed to wear a turban but was stubborn about the choice of colours. If everybody wore greys, whites or maroons, he wore a striped turban of bright colours. When he was not wearing any other headgear, he wore a small skullcap which Simha had made for him of red velvet that was embroidered with silver threads and the Star of David.

Fine thin hair had begun sprouting on Joseph's upper lip, yet he did not look his age. His voice was still soft and not hoarse as expected. Following Menashe's prescription, Bathsheba forced him to eat the roasted scrotum of goat. He hated it. He would poke around the pieces of meat and keep his eyes glued to his plate, wondering how the scrotum of goat could make him a man.

The men laughed at him and he suffered their bawdy jokes. For relief, he would sneak a look at Simha. He would find her looking intently at him. Her eyes would calm him.

Enoch was an office manager in one of the missionary schools. He wanted Joseph to become a teacher because he was good at mathematics and science. Joseph could not understand why everybody wanted him to become a teacher or join the services, like most other Bene Israel men were doing. Joseph had his own dreams.

It was a hard life for Joseph. Solomon woke him up at five in the morning to recite the prayers for his bar mitzvah. He was just twelve, and on the thirteenth day of his thirteenth birthday they would give him his prayer shawl, or tsisith as they pronounced it in Marathi. He would then become a man and could participate in the prayers at the synagogue or the prayer hall and he could officiate as one of the ten men necessary for a minyan. Ten men had to be present for all Jewish rituals.

At that point Marathi had become their mother tongue, though they sometimes still spoke Konkani amongst themselves. As they had lived close to the farming communities of the Konkan like the Kolis and the Agaris, their Marathi had words typical of these communities. To this day the Marathi spoken by some Bene Israel Jews has a touch of the Konkan.

As the younger generation began going to English-medium missionary schools, the Dandekars started speaking in English. And, when Joseph went to the American missionary school in Bombay, he learnt both English and Hebrew. When he was in Danda for his vacations, he conducted the shabath prayers in Hebrew and explained the meaning of the words. He also taught the women and children Hebrew and English.

Preparations for the bar mitzvah were on. The women had started storing grain and dry coconuts. Joseph was certain that he would look ridiculous reciting the prayers in the presence of their relatives from Surat and Ahmedabad and Bene Israel neighbours from Revdanda, Nandgaon and Murud-Janzira. He was also irritated. There were too many people in the house and it was impossible to be alone with Simha. He had to be satisfied with the sound of her anklets.

On the day appointed for his bar mitzvah, Joseph dressed in black trousers, a white undershirt and an elaborately embroidered purple silk overcoat and Pathani leather mojdis. Simha had embroidered the Star of David with silver threads on a blue silk kippa she had made for the occasion. It matched well with his clothes.

It was Saturday, the shabath morning, a perfect day to include a young boy in the community of men. At the prayer hall in Nandgaon, in the presence of family and guests, the hazanbaba blessed him and chanted the baraka for the wearing of a new cloth. With this prayer, hazanbaba covered his shoulders with the rectangular silk tsitsit or prayer shawl which had come from Amsterdam. The four corners of the tsitsith had a hundred and eight knots. The entire congregation chanted the Saturday morning prayers in praise of the boy who had become a man. With the tsitsit around his shoulders, Joseph no longer felt awkward or irritated. He felt grown up. He was no longer worried that he would forget the words and embarrass himself and the family.

With only a slight tremor in his voice he sang loudly, 'Parmeshwar, I lift my eyes to you on this great and solemn day. I re-enter the community of Israel. From now on, it is my duty to keep the Ten Commandments—the Daha Agnya. From now on I have become responsible for my own actions and I am answerable to you. Hé Deva, pour on me the bounty of your blessings, so that all my days may be fruitful with the rich spiritual blessings you shower upon me. Save me from evil, so that I may love you and revere you. Teach me the way to the Ten Commandments and help me to follow the path of the law. Take me by your hand and uphold me, lest I stumble when I take my first steps. Give me strength to keep the holy Torah and your commandments—so that I may be happy and fearless as I proclaim the Shema Israel ha shem elehenu ha shem akhad.'

The ceremony was followed by a malida and an elaborate lunch. Bathsheba was pleased that Joseph had conducted himself with confidence, but she felt a little uncomfortable with his baby face. He looked like a small boy dressed up like a man. She wanted him to grow up fast, so that she could discuss with Enoch and his wife Yacobeth the possibility of his marriage with Simha. Joseph understood the look in her eyes and smiled.

He was sitting in the courtyard on a specially decorated chair and could not help noticing Simha. She was covered with jewels from head to toe, and was dressed in a bright pink ghaghra. The green blouse showed her small tight breasts to advantage over her pencil-thin waist. He was amused that her nosering looked larger than her face and he wanted to tweak her nose.

Swinging her skirt provocatively, she went back and forth, carrying dishes and mats. Joseph felt a stirring within him that was new. And when they looked at each other and smiled, he wondered whether she felt the same. He looked down at her long toenails and he was annoyed that she was not wearing the anklets she normally wore. These were new, large and heavy.

They did not have the tinkle of the old ones.

He knew that he should not stare at Simha so brazenly. Nor was it possible to speak to her, as the guests had started coming in. It took a lot of control to keep his eyes away from her.

Joseph knew that he would have to wait many years to get married to Simha. Suddenly he was anxious. What if they arranged her marriage to somebody else? Joseph wanted to reserve Simha for himself but did not know how. He had read that girls grew up faster than boys. And he worried that soon Simha would start looking like a woman and her parents would want to get her married. He felt uncomfortable when Simha's grandmother taunted her, 'If you keep growing so fast, as tall as a toddy tree, you will never find a husband.' She would stop teasing her daughter only when Joseph's face became red with anger. She was not unkind, but Joseph's height bothered her. Perhaps they would not make a fine pair like the other couples of the house. She suspected that Joseph and Simha were already in love with each other. When she tried to question Simha, she was greeted with stony silence.

When he was sent to Bombay to the missionary school, he was constantly worried about Simha. He dreaded the mail. He would first check whether there was a wedding invitation.

He regretted that she had not gone to school and so they could not communicate while he was away. Whenever he returned to Danda for the vacations, he was relieved to see her still there, although he often heard discussions about possible grooms for her. He knew he had to keep silent, till the time his grandfather sent a formal manga for Simha.

Simha was restless. Joseph had not returned home for a year. He was preparing for his exams. The koel heralded an early monsoon and the mangoes were ripe on the trees.

Simha heard somebody approaching the house. From the sound of the footsteps she knew it was Joseph. She rushed to open the door. To her disappointment, a tall man with broad shoulders and enormous whiskers stood there. It took her just a second to recognize his familiar smile. It was Joseph. Spontaneously she threw her arms around his neck and laughed. Her mother scolded her. 'Behave yourself,' she said sternly.

Bathsheba did not interfere but from her expression, Joseph understood that she had manipulated to keep Simha for him. Shlumith had told him that Bathsheba held herself responsible for Tamara's unhappy marriage. The young couple had many differences, though Tamara never confided in her grandmother. That was one of the reasons that Bathsheba wanted Simha to stay within the family.

That year, Joseph and Simha were married. Joseph continued his studies in Bombay. When he came back he was armed with a licence to practice medicine and an appointment letter to work as a doctor in the British army hospital at Poona.

28

WHILE JOSEPH WAS studying in Bombay, Simha had become Solomon's disciple. She loved to take care of the birds and animals on the baadee. She fed the birds, cleaned their cages and saw to it that they had food and water.

She had also learnt to paint from Menashe. He had given her sheets of paper and a box of colours. She made sketches of the birds she saw around the house. When Menashe had time, he taught her various painting techniques. While it was common for daughters of the family to learn embroidery, crotchet work and quilt-making, Simha learnt painting.

Her sketchbook was like a guidebook to the birds of Danda and the surrounding areas. There were paintings of peacocks, mynahs, bulbuls, doves, robins, brahminy mynahs, sunbirds, flycatchers, green bee-eaters, tailorbirds, golden orioles, crows, sarus cranes, seagulls, pelicans, herons, egrets.

She painted what she saw. Then she would collect the children of the house and tell them stories about birds and animals. She had observed their food habits and spent her mornings feeding them grain and fruit.

She had also befriended a peacock.

He was a lone bird, and did not mix with the other peafowl who had a free run of the territory and their own feeding beats. Like Shiva, he was at a disadvantage, in his case a twisted foot. Simha had named him Keya.

The monsoon was the mating season for peacocks and Simha had observed that Keya was attracted to a certain female. She belonged to a large group which had a magnificent male as the leader. Keya would have to defeat him to win the bird of his heart. When Keya tried to approach the female, he was always driven away by the younger males of the brood who had an eye on her.

Eventually Keya and the big male had a fight. Simha watched helplessly as they flew in the air and attacked each other with open claws, their green-blue trains spread out like a shivering quiver of arrows. Keya could not withstand the onslaught of the stronger bird. He fled and disappeared into the foliage. Simha wanted to run after him and check on his wounds, but she could not find him. She spent the afternoon painting the peacock fight instead. She would send the drawing to Joseph.

Simha did not see Keya for a week and was certain that he

was dead. The victorious male strutted past the house with his magnificent train, and Simha hated him. She dreaded the moment when somebody would find his mauled body in the cactus around the house. She sat at the window brooding and refused to eat.

A fortnight later, in the evening, Simha heard a strange sound and rushed to the closed kitchen window. She had heard Keya calling out to her. Normally, he preferred the front of the house, where Simha kept a bowl of grain for him. The bigger group kept their distance and stayed under the pipal tree. To avoid another confrontation, Keya had chosen the backyard.

She saw his silhouette. She grabbed a malpuva from the kitchen and gave it to him. He ate it quickly and disappeared into the dark. Simha was moved. Keya had called out to her in his time of need.

The next morning, Simha opened the back door and inspected the ground. The women threw stale food, garbage and dirty water there. The ground was always slushy. Simha saw Keya's twisted footprint in the soft mud. She took a flat pan from the kitchen and picked up the footprint on it. She would dry it in the sun and bake it in the big clay oven. The footprint would become a memento.

Keya changed the timings of his beat around the house. The kitchen window and the backyard became his domain. He felt safe with Simha. Meanwhile, the day of Simha's departure for Poona was approaching. She would miss the attention in the big house.

Suddenly Simha announced that she would not leave with Joseph. She could not leave Keya behind, alone in Danda. She announced her decision with such determination that everybody was taken aback. Even Joseph could not persuade her. She refused to believe that Keya would survive without her. And if they took him to Poona, they could not keep him in the crowded Shivajipeth house which Joseph had rented for them.

Joseph was furious. He told the family that Simha could stay back in Danda with Keya. 'If necessary, I will take another wife,' he said. Sensing that this was no simple argument, Solomon asked Joseph to delay Simha's departure. He would escort her to Poona with Keya. He would capture the bird, clip his wings and put him in a cage so that they could transport him there. Seeing Simha soften, Joseph suggested that she leave with him and Solomon would follow with Keya. But Simha was adamant. She did not trust anyone with Keya.

A month later, Simha, Solomon and Keya reached Poona. Simha was in for a surprise. Joseph took them to a bungalow with a garden on the outskirts of Poona. He had put in a request for a small house in the cantonment area, as his wife was bringing her pet peacock and he needed a bigger house.

The quartermaster was at first a little surprised by the reason for the request but then, impressed by the attachment, arranged for the kind of house Joseph had asked for.

The next day, Joseph invited ten Bene Israel men from Poona and consecrated the house with a silver mezuzah, according to the law. Under the mezuzah, Simha cemented Keya's footprint in an alcove. Dr Joseph Solomon's house was known to be the house with the mark of Saraswati's vehicle— the swan. It was here that Simha lived in the company of Keya and her eleven children who were born to her in the years to come.

Simha was quick to learn and when the children studied she picked up history and geography from them. But when they spoke in English, though she understood everything they were saying, she answered them in Marathi.

One thing they learnt from her, which was the rites and

rituals of their faith. Many synagogues were coming up in Poona and Simha had learnt the Hebrew prayers and their meaning. This knowledge she passed on to her children.

Whenever he had time, Joseph indulged in his old hobby of taking long rides into the forests around Poona. He often did not come home for days. It bothered Simha at first, but when he returned he looked happy and rejuvenated, and had many stories to tell.

Lately, however, Simha had noticed that Joseph looked disturbed. There was something he was keeping from her. She asked him, 'Tell me what is bothering you.'

'You remember the time I returned home after five days. A very strange thing happened to me. I was following a herd of barking deer and had taken the path which led to the hamlet where I had befriended a Koli chief.

'This part of the forest is dark and dense. Sunlight filters down in small patches through the foliage. The Kolis live on a high mountain. You feel you could stretch your hand and touch the sky. When I rode into their territory the first time, I was afraid they would kill me. There was no way of communicating with them. They speak a strange sounding Marathi. The words seem to tumble down from their lips at such speed that it is hard to understand their meaning. Sometimes, they confuse me as their R's sound like D's and their A's sound like O's. That changes the meaning of words. Slowly, I trained my ears to understand their language. I was on my horse when a group of small, muscular men carrying spears and dressed in short dhotis tied tightly around their loins surrounded me. The colour of their skin was like granite and they looked ferocious.

'I alighted from the horse and greeted them but they did not respond. I could hear wild screams from a hut. The chieftain, whom I named Raghoji, was smaller than the rest. He raised his hand and made a sign that nobody should touch me. He then rushed into the hut from where the screams came and returned with a naked child in his arms. Raghoji put down the child, and showed me a huge scorpion which he had skewered with a spear. The scorpion had stung the child. I have never seen a scorpion of that size. The child's hand was swollen like a balloon. I took out my medicine box and made a sign that I could save the child. Raghoji stopped me. I could not touch the child without his permission.

'This was a good opportunity to befriend the tribals. But I knew that I should not rush things because I had to win their confidence. I waited.

'When he was certain that I meant no harm, he made a sign that I could look at the child. I rubbed the wound with an ointment, and gave the child some medicine. After some time the child stopped screaming.

'When Raghoji was sure that the child was better, he offered me a gourd filled to the brim with some intoxicating liquor. I hesitated, but I knew that if I wanted to make friends with him, I had to accept the drink.

'The drink relaxed me. I felt I was floating and asked for more. This pleased Raghoji, and he invited me into his hut. We sat on a reed mat and communicated with words and gestures.

'It was the beginning of a long friendship. Raghoji is the most powerful man in that area. He is also some sort of magicman of nature. He can read the stars and planets and make predictions. He taught me his brand of astronomy. He has his own names for the stars and planets. His witch doctor is very accomplished and I wish Menashe Uncle could meet him. He makes medicines with leaves and herbs for all kinds of ailments. They may not be fully effective, but they do make some difference. He has also told me about the various species of wildlife living in this forest.

'Together we saw panthers, a tiger, hyenas, wolves, pythons, all types of deer and antelope. Raghoji made me wait for hours to see the paradise flycatcher. It was worth the wait.' Simha smiled and made a mental note that she would paint the bird for Joseph, which was not so uncommon really.

Joseph continued with his story: 'I started going deeper into the forest, gradually becoming more familiar with it. Till, one day, I got a real scare. It was mid-day, and there was the normal sort of light that one sees deep in the forest. I decided to rest in an opening near a stream. Suddenly I heard a rustle behind me. At first I thought it was a herd of barasingha which abound there, or I had disturbed a panther which had dragged its kill onto a tree. Looking behind me to locate the source of the sound, I was blinded by a sudden light. In the still, dark shadows of the forest, it was like a flash of lightning.

'My horse neighed loudly and bolted. He galloped at such speed on the steep hillock that I thought he would break his legs and my head. But he brought me safely to Raghoji's hut. I was perspiring as though we had been racing in the Thar desert.

'That night, sitting with Raghoji on a rock, I told him about the light. "You are blessed by the divine god of the universe. Tomorrow you must return to the same spot," he told me. He knew something which I did not.

'I must admit I was afraid. And, much against his advice, I returned to Poona. I felt stupid getting carried away by Raghoji's superstitions and felt guilty that I was unfaithful to our Eeshwar. I was also trying to understand what I had seen.

'Since then I have been restless. I am drawn to this strange light. It fills my dreams. It is like a waterfall of light. It has hypnotized me. I cannot think straight, nor can I work. All I want to do is return to the forest and find its source. I am curious and also afraid. Am I being unfaithful to our Lord?'

Simha was frightened but she nodded her head and said, 'If you want to go back, you must. If you recite the Shema Israel when you see the light, you will not come to any harm. And when you return, I will offer a malida to Eliyahu Hannabi. I am certain that the prophet will be with you, as you are a good man. You have never broken the law.' Then she smiled at him. The way she looked at him infused him with confidence.

That month, Joseph took long leave and went back to the forest. Simha went to the synagogue and prayed for her husband's well-being.

29

'I KNEW YOU would return.' Raghoji smiled when he saw Joseph.

Joseph went back to the spot where he had seen the light. He left his horse with Raghoji and set off alone on foot with a small bag of food and water in the direction of the light. It took him two days to reach there.

Joseph knew the horse's reaction to the light meant that there was something dangerous there, but he was no longer afraid.

A bend in the forest path brought him to the place where the horse had bolted. The clearing was illuminated with a beam of light so bright that Joseph could not keep his eyes open.

When his eyes grew accustomed to the brilliance, he saw an enormous white king cobra with seven heads and a shining red ruby on its hood. It stood erect, in the stance of attack.

Joseph's first instinct was to run. He thought about how its venom would kill him in a second. But he did not move.

The distance between him and the serpent was only seven feet. He stood like one hypnotized. The cobra's eyes seemed to look into his soul. Joseph did not blink. The intensity of the light increased and seemed to come closer. For a split second Joseph's eyes closed. He folded his hands and said the Shema Israel. When he opened his eyes, he was standing in darkness. There was no more light. The serpent had disappeared.

Joseph was sure that it was an illusion, or perhaps it was a dream. He was certain that it was the effect of Raghoji's stories. Stumbling over rocks, thickets and bushes, Joseph returned to Raghoji's hut. Bleeding and bruised he fell into a deep sleep.

He slept for twelve dreamless hours before he woke up. When he told his story to Raghoji, Raghoji fell on the ground and touched Joseph's feet. He was convinced that Joseph had seen Shesh Nag, the divinity who lived in the forest and protected them. Raghoji had many stories and beliefs about Shesh Nag. It was seen only once in a hundred years, and the one who saw Shesh Nag was sure to be blessed. A child born to such a family would be nature's miracle man.

From that day, Raghoji and his people believed that Joseph was a holy man and Shesha had led him to them. He said to Joseph, 'The divine Shesha has appeared to you. We are worshippers of Naga—sons of Kadru, the principal wife of the sage Kashyap. The Nagas were appointed the powerful rulers or guardians of the nether regions or Patala. Their hoods vary in number from one, five to seven. They are known to possess the best jewels in the universe, and it .is said that the gems they wear give light to Patala.

'Shesha is the rare Naga with seven hoods. He is divine, as he is associated with the gods and is a companion of the supreme god Vishnu. He curls his body in such a way that it becomes Vishnu's throne. For us Vishnu is the symbol of mercy, goodness, cosmic order and dharma. Shesha is also known as Ananta, who forms the raft on which Vishnu reclines with his wife Laxmi at his feet. With Ananta, he floats endlessly in the cosmic waters of the universe. Shesha is the symbol of eternity. When he makes a full circle by sucking his tail, he supports the universe.'

When Joseph returned to Poona, unharmed and radiant, Simha started the preparations for the Eliyahu Hannabi. His return was a good omen.

As a child, Simha had often asked Bathsheba about the village deity—Nagdeva. Bathsheba had told her that she need not fear it because it resembled the staff of the prophet Moses which had transformed into a snake in the Pharaoh's court. That was when the Jews had been slaves in Egypt. The miracles of the prophet had led them out of Egypt. He had parted the Red Sea with the same staff, leading them to freedom, in the direction of Mount Sinai.

But when Simha had asked her about the small silver image of the village deity in her box of jewels, Bathsheba had stared at her in stony silence. The subject was taboo.

30

AFTER HIS GRANDFATHER'S death Joseph asked for a transfer to Ahmedabad. His wife Simha followed him without protest, and brought all their belongings, including her paintings, to the Delhi Darwaza house.

The room upstairs was allotted to them. Simha decorated it with her bird paintings and placed Keya's foot mark next to the mezuzah. It was her talisman for happiness. She also brought Keya to Ahmedabad. Keya had aged and lost most of his plumage, and limped more than before. He romped in the back garden during the day, and spent his nights in a small cage in the courtyard. Simha had brought everything she valued from Poona, and had no reason to complain.

Joseph was now the head of the family. The group photo shows that there were more than forty people living in the house at that time. Joseph is the only one who looks robust and fit. The others look too old or too young.

Joseph was known as Dr Isabjidada. I do not know how Joseph became Isabji. Perhaps after coming to Gujarat, when people had found it hard to pronounce his name, he may have made some changes.

Isabji was famous for his home-made medicines and remedies which worked miracles. The house at Delhi Darwaza was transformed into a laboratory with grinding stones, vats and bottles. Isabji collected herbs and made his concoctions. Everyone in the house was put to work in the pharmacy. His patients loved him. He had a sympathetic nature and a sense of humour.

According to my grandmother, after finishing his duties at the hospital in the cantonment, Isabji opened the back door of the clinic room and attended to his patients. He wore white pyjamas and a long white shirt, over which he wore a long black flowing cloak, a jamah and a huge turban. He gave medicines to anybody who came to him. He charged a small fee which he collected in a green velvet purse. He handed this to Simha every night. He did not want to be bothered with maintaining accounts. On Sunday mornings, he worked with

Menashe at the family clinic.

Those years appear to have been calm. There were no major events or incidents, till David married the thirteen-year-old Shebabeth while he was still a medical student.

Grandmother Shebabeth always started laughing when she talked of her wedding day. She would blush a deep red and say that she had almost lost David because of a coat.

31

DAVID HAD CHOSEN that particular black coat at the cantonment army store because he had liked the big gold buttons. But the salesman had told him apologetically that he could not sell it to him as it had a small oil mark under the left pocket. David bought it nevertheless, and decided to get it cleaned at the newly opened Victoria Laundry. They promised to remove the stain completely. 'Wait and see. Your coat will look first class for your wedding!' the owner assured David.

There was so much to do for the wedding that David forgot to collect the coat. He was reminded of it only on the morning of the wedding, which was to be solemnized at five in the evening, followed by a reception for non-Jewish friends and a dinner for the Jewish community at the prayer hall.

Nobody else was free so he decided to send his orderly Poonja to collect the coat. Poonja was sitting on the floor, bent over a basket of asopalav leaves. Simha had asked him to make torans and decorate the front gate and all the doors of the house.

David quickly wrote a letter in Gujarati on his wedding card to the laundry owner.

It said:

Dear Shri Kantibhai and friends of Victoria Laundry,
I am sending my orderly Poonjabhai to collect the coat,
as today is my wedding day. Please forgive me for
forgetting to send you a wedding card. But with this
invitation, I invite you and all the workers of the
laundry to my wedding reception. It will be held at
6.30 p.m. at our house at Salatwada, near Delhi
Darwaza.

With warm regards,

David Joseph

P.S. Could you please give my wedding coat to
Poonjabhai. Thank you.

At 4.30 everybody was ready to leave for the Bene Israel prayer
hall. The hired carriages were standing at the door. But there
was no sign of David. Worried that he had changed his mind,
Simha went back into the house. Looking troubled, David was
standing in the middle of the room, fully dressed except for his
coat. Poonja had not returned with it.

At five minutes to five, David sent Alibhai to fetch the coat
and also look for Poonja. He returned with a message from the
manager of Victoria Laundry that he had given the coat to
Poonja in the afternoon itself.

Worried that perhaps Poonja had had an accident, David
suggested that they postpone the wedding. He refused to wear
a suit. But Isabji thought it was ridiculous to cancel a wedding
because of a coat! His mother finally persuaded David to wear
another coat, though it did not quite match with the black
trousers. Shebabeth was already at the prayer hall. She saw
that her groom looked upset and wondered why.

The previous night Shebabeth had been dressed in a grass-
green sari and bangles to match for the mehendi ceremony.

Sitting awkwardly with a coconut in his hand, David had looked at her longingly through the sehra tied on his forehead. She ignored his look. She could not possibly smile at him while the women were laughing and applying henna on her wedding-ring finger.

Now, on the wedding day, he looked preoccupied. Not once did he look at her like the night before. Even when he recited the song to welcome the bride, he seemed to be looking through her. She wondered if he had had a change of heart because she had not looked at him during the mehendi ceremony. The mystery was revealed only several unhappy hours later that night, when David told her about the coat. She was relieved that that was all there was to it.

For years the disappearance of Poonja and the coat remained a mystery. David had the police records checked, but there was no accident on that particular afternoon.

Simha had told Shebabeth that David could not accept that Poonja was imbalanced. It was a mistake to have sent him to the laundry on the day of the wedding. This was a delicate subject with David. He did not like to talk about Poonja.

He was hard-working and did all the work allotted to him neatly and correctly, but could appear moody at times. Simha did not trust him entirely but over time Poonja gave no reason for worry. When he disappeared on the day of David's wedding, Simha was certain that he had lost his head. It was only ten years later, when David had returned to Ahmedabad with his family, that the mystery of the coat was solved.

When she heard a knock at the front door in the morning, she was a little surprised, wondering who had come so early, as the milkman and others came at the back door. Shebabeth asked the cook to open the door. The cook returned to say that a beggar was at the door and was asking for David. Brought up on stories of Eliyahu Hannabi who was said to visit Jewish homes dressed as an old mendicant, Shebabeth went to the bedroom on the first floor and woke up David. When David came down, the beggar rushed in and fell at his feet, crying and apologizing. It was Poonja, dressed in a tattered black suit with gold buttons—David's wedding coat.

32

WHEN DAVID BECAME a doctor following family tradition and was posted to Poona Joseph was overjoyed. He gave David the keys to the house in Poona which still belonged to the Dandekars. Before she left, Simha gave Shebabeth the terracotta footprint of Keya. She wanted Shebabeth to fix it next to the mezuzah in their home. It was a talisman for good health and prosperity.

Shebabeth kept herself busy with cleaning the old house and making a garden. The papaya and banana groves were laden with fruit and the fragrance of guava filled the air. Simha had described the house in detail, and when the young Shebabeth entered it, she felt she had come home.

David was of medium height, fair and good looking. He had a mop of dark black hair and dressed well. He was posted at the Yerwada jail, where the political leaders of the freedom struggle were held prisoner.

A photograph of Shebabeth from those days shows an exceptionally beautiful woman with very long hair and a transparent, mother-of-pearl complexion. She was quite short and compared to her body, her feet were enormous, the heels large and fleshy.

Grandmother Shebabeth liked to tell us about her wedding

mojdis. They had come all the way from Baluchistan, on the empire's new frontier, for the wedding. They hurt her so much that she was limping around the house for a month. When she described her marriage, I was just seven, and I regret that I did not ask her for more details.

By the time I was born in 1945, Shebabeth had given up wearing nine-yard saris and wore white saris six yards long, as expected of a widow. To me she always appeared uncomfortable wrapped in six-yard saris. My mother Naomi and aunt Hannah dressed in six-yard saris like all educated women of independent India. Naomi preferred starched cottons and Aunt Hannah loved silk. All the elder women of our house made buns. But that is for later. Let me go back to David and Shebabeth.

Poona was then in the grip of the freedom movement because of Bal Gangadhar Tilak and his newspapers *Mahratta* and *Kesari*. Besides that the menace of the plague was spreading. It was not easy for David to start a new life, in a new city, in such difficult times.

Following the Dandekar family tradition, when David reached Poona, he subscribed to *The Times of India*. But often he saw Tukaji, his assistant and all-purpose handyman, reading the *Kesari* in his spare moments. *The Times of India* often carried criticism of Tilak. Tilak would answer back with a hard-hitting article in the *Kesari* or the *Mahratta*. David often asked Tukaji about Tilak's opinion on the plague and other matters, and their discussions on the politics of the day became a daily routine.

A favourite family story is that grandfather David Solomon Dandekar met Bal Gangadhar Tilak in 1898, when the latter was imprisoned in Yerwada jail. At the time the British had imposed a ban on giving writing paper to Tilak. But David smuggled in sheets of paper for him in his medicine bag. Under the paper there was always a pouch of supari. Every morning Shebabeth cleaned and chopped supari with her nutcracker— both David and she were in the habit of eating paan after every meal. They knew that Tilak was addicted to supari as much as they were, and Shebabeth bought the best areca nuts from the baadees of the Konkan coast.

David had bought Shebabeth a silver paan box, which came to me when Shebabeth died. I often open it and touch the lime-stained interior. I refuse to clean it. It has a delicious ancient fragrance, which reminds me of my grandmother's breath. The paan box with the nutcracker has stayed with me for a long time. Whenever I am disheartened I open it and feel revived.

It was around this period that our family stopped using Dandekar as a surname. Since then we have been using the names of grandfathers as family names.

When Grandfather David's involvement with Tilak was discovered, he was transferred to Satlasana as a punishment. Before he left Poona, David visited Tilak once more. Tilak wanted to thank Shebabeth with a special gift for the supari she had been sending him. He did not have anything but a ring. So he slipped it from his little finger and gave it to David for Shebabeth. The ring was a thin gold band imbedded with a pearl. It is a family heirloom.

Shebabeth closed the house in Poona and returned to Ahmedabad. The house was eventually sold, and Tukaji went with David to Satlasana. Later, he came back to Ahmedabad with him and worked as his compounder.

Before his new posting David came to Ahmedabad to see his brother Samuel, who was in hospital. Samuel had been treating plague victims and had caught the disease in the process. David was not allowed to meet him. With a cloth tied around his mouth and nose, he stood at the door of Samuel's room and saluted his brother.

There is another story hidden in the recesses of the plague story, that of Yeloji.

When uncle Samuel died in the plague, Isabji had planned to get his widow Hadasha married to a cousin, Yeloji, so that he would settle down and stop creating trouble for himself and the family. Hadasha was somewhat introverted while Yeloji was boisterous and a womanizer. When Isabji told him that according to custom, his marriage was being arranged with Samuel's widow, Yeloji was furious. 'She is my vahini. My bhabhi. My sister. How could you even think that I would agree to marry her? She is a pure and gentle lady. You know very well that I am unreliable where women are concerned. How many times you have tried to trap me. But I do not want to spoil the life of an innocent Bene Israel girl.'

Hadasha remained unmarried and stayed with the family till her death.

Much later, when I was in my thirties, I asked my father about Yeloji. He said that his name was actually Eliyahoo. But as he was not really a believer, he did not want to corrupt the name of the prophet, and had changed it to Yeloji.

Yeloji was apparently a colourful character, a practical joker who could invent a story at the drop of a hat and got away with his pranks because of his ready smile. My father said that Yeloji was an incurable romantic at heart.

There is one particular story my father liked to narrate about Yeloji. During the drought, families from Rajasthan camped in Ahmedabad, looking for work. One such group was stationed in the open plot in front of the Delhi Darwaza house. Yeloji had noticed that the women bathed under a tap. For Yeloji this was a god-sent opportunity. He watched the bathing beauties from the stable which was closest to the common tap.

The women would remove their blouses and ghaghras when they bathed, covering themselves with a chunni and wearing only their petticoats.

Yeloji was enchanted by the scene. He tried to attract the attention of one of the younger women, but the girl ignored him. His ego was hurt. Yeloji planned his revenge.

One evening, when the women were bathing, Yeloji burnt their clothes. The women started screaming when they saw the fire. One of them had seen Yeloji running away, and they called out to their men to chase him. Yeloji rushed into the house from the clinic side.

The door was open, and Isabji was sitting there, treating a patient. He was annoyed when Yeloji rushed past and shocked to see a group of irate men coming towards the house with sticks.

With folded hands, Isabji calmed them down and invited them in. They told Isabji about the incident, their eyes searching for Yeloji meanwhile. Isabji asked their forgiveness on behalf of his nephew and called out to Simha to send sherbet for his guests. He also asked her to bring clothes for the women. He was sure that she knew what had happened because Yeloji had rushed from the clinic to the kitchen and out of the house through the back door.

Isabji was so angry he wanted to hand over Yeloji to the group of furious men. But he knew Yeloji would be nowhere around. He managed eventually to calm the men, and the women were placated when Simha brought down a bundle of skirts, saris and blouses from the storeroom. Both Isabji and Simha heaved a sigh of relief when they left the house on a friendly note.

When Yeloji reappeared after things had cooled down,

Isabji reprimanded him severely. His pranks were bringing a bad name to the family. Much later, when Yeloji refused to marry Samuel's widow, he gained a new status in the family. He was remembered as a man of principle.

Meanwhile after Samuel's burial, David proceeded to the small government clinic in Satlasana, with his Bible, the Gita and a mezuzah. He was dejected and confused.

Satlasana was a small town in a hilly forest of north Gujarat. The hard black rocks here had a special sculptural character. They stood in the lush green landscape like ancient funerary stones. Sitting in the veranda of his staff quarters, David would watch the evening sky and listen to the roars of panthers and tigers in the hills.

As the medical officer of the region, David travelled from village to village on horseback, carrying his medicine box and a rifle. Like a shadow, Tukaji followed him on his horse.

One day, after he had helped a village midwife with a difficult delivery, he simply told Tukaji he was returning to be with his wife for the birth of their first child. 'When I saw the newborn child last night and saw the difficulties of the woman, I decided that I should return.'

When David reached the house at Delhi Darwaza, Shebabeth, who had become big and heavy, asked, 'What happened?' David did not answer. He closed himself in the clinic room, took his quill pen, dipped it in ink and wrote his letter of resignation. He would never again work for the British empire. Like Tilak, he would devote himself to the service of the people. Next to the photographs of the forefathers, he placed a photograph of his mentor.

David went to work in his father's dispensary at Bhanderi Pol near Kalupur Darwaza. Since Isabji was no longer very active, he had more patients than he could manage. In the evenings, he sat in the clinic room at the Delhi Darwaza house and treated patients, free of charge. David felt he was now part of India and its freedom struggle.

33

SOLOMON JOSEPH WAS one of the younger sons of Isabji. Perhaps he was born very late in their life, like our prophets from the Bible. He was named Solomon in memory of great-grandfather Solomon and so was also called Solomon-the-Second. He was a bonesetter, and a very well known one at that.

Every year, according to family tradition, the Ahmedabadi Dandekars visited their Bombay relatives. In return the Bombay relatives came in large numbers to spend their vacations in the Delhi Darwaza house.

Whenever Solomon-the-Second was in Bombay, he spent his afternoons at the pet shops of the bustling Crawford Market.

Soon after the death of his wife Ellisa, on one such trip to Bombay, Solomon-the-Second noticed a cockatoo sitting on a perch in an aluminium cage. It was cramped between the cages of twittering munias, sad-looking monkeys, yelping puppies and chattering lovebirds. It was his first summer without his wife, and although he did not admit it, he was depressed and was missing her.

The shopkeeper at Crawford Market saw his interest in the bird, and told him that it was a talking bird. Impulsively, Solomon-the-Second bought the cockatoo. The bird was sleeping with his beak tucked into his wings but on noticing Solomon-the-Second, unfurled his bright yellow crest and mumbled something which sounded like 'Saala badmash.' Solomon-the-

Second could not stop laughing. The swear words won him over.

He then did something uncharacteristic. Usually a penny-pincher in money matters, he threw all caution to the winds and went to Chor Bazaar looking for the perfect cage to house the bird. After a lot of dithering and bargaining, he bought a brass cage for his spiritual mate.

In Ahmedabad everybody loved the bird. Every day, much to the joy of the children, Solomon-the-Second opened the bird's cage and taking him on his hand, wiped him with a cloth soaked in rose water.

The bird lived with him in one of the rooms next to the open courtyard. Solomon showered all his love on the bird. So much so that he named him Ellis after his wife. Solomon-the-Second kept a diary in a beautiful hand in English. The diary, bound in red cloth like an accounts book, contained Uncle Solomon's poems, remedies for broken bones and ten pages about the rift in the family.

Much later, at the zoo, Joshua experimented with Uncle Solomon's methods for setting the broken leg of a kangaroo. From the diary he also learnt that Solomon-the-Second was very good at setting sprains by cranking, pushing, pulling and the application of a fragrant brown paste. Miraculously, the sprain would be cured.

Gradually, Ellis began to spend more hours outside the cage than inside. He also learnt to ward off the cats and crows. Ellis had discovered that the safest place in the house was the dining table, and much to the annoyance of the women, he was always there. They had to save everything from his inquisitive beak.

There were many fights in the house because of Ellis and his habits. He bit clothes, mattresses, furniture, fresh bread, uncut fruit—the list was endless. Besides that, there was the matter of bird droppings all over the house.

The women blamed Solomon-the-Second for the mess in the house, but he stood his ground like a stubborn cockatoo. They realized that Ellis would have to stay in the house like a family member. Solomon-the-Second also got very angry when the women referred to Ellis as 'Woh Kakakaua.' For him, Ellis was no longer a cockatoo or a kakakaua.

When the family fights became too ferocious because of Ellis, Isabji had a meeting with Solomon-the-Second. He asked him to get a bird stand from the army store. He could leave the bird there. A bird stand made birds feel secure because they had a definite place to themselves, Isabji explained to him. And there would also be peace in the house, though he did not mention this. At first his son demurred, but finally agreed when Isabji said that the bird could stay in the clinic room on its stand. He wrote about this incident in his diary as a postscript, commenting that for some time it worked well as Isabji spoke to the bird while he was there with his patients.

The women too softened towards Ellis after he was installed in the clinic, as he no longer disrupted their lives in the kitchen.

Solomon-the-Second's diary says:

Fate has its own way of intervening with the lives of human beings. On Tuesday evening, when I returned home for lunch, I opened the clinic door to say hello to Ellis. He was lying on the floor. I thought he was dead. When I went closer, I saw that he was gasping and choking on a toy car. Had I reached an hour later, Ellis would have surely died. One of the younger children had tried to feed a toy car to the bird. I was furious. I wanted to wring the neck of the child who had committed the crime. But none of the children, including my grandchildren, admitted that they had tried to feed the car to Ellis. Isabji carefully extracted the car from Ellis's throat. Then with an ink dropper, he fed him some water. The bird revived when Isabji caressed his crest and tickled him. But I was angry and ordered my sons and their wives to pack their belongings. I wanted to leave the Delhi Darwaza house right then, that very minute. I did not want to stay in a house where my sentiments were not respected.

Their bags were packed and the horse carriages were waiting at the door, but the women did not want to leave and started crying. I had no patience with their pleas and appeals. Without looking at my father, I offered my hand to the bird. It was time to leave.

Much to my embarrassment, Ellis did not come to my hand. He hid in Isabji's cloak and watched me.

My father looked at me and said, 'In his own way the bird is trying to tell you not to break up the family.' But I was furious and did not heed his words. To my discomfort, I had to literally grab the bird from Isabji and march out of the house. The last image I have of my father is his sitting sadly in a chair. My mother is standing next to him, tears running down her face. I had a premonition that it was the beginning of the break-up of the family.

34

AFTER THEY LEFT the Delhi Darwaza house, Solomon-the-Second's family lived cramped and crowded in the back room of his clinic at Kalupur.

The bird brought good fortune to the clinic. The queues of limping humanity increased. Solomon had given Ellis a swing, which was tied to the ceiling. From here he had a bird's-eye view of the world around. He whistled, and imitated car horns and the moans of the patients.

Work had increased at the clinic but his sons were not willing to help. They had small jobs at the Saraspur textile mills and when they were not at work, they stood at the paan-bidi shop next door and chatted with their friends. For Solomon-the-Second this was like a curse. He hated the fact that his sons were not professionals and more like blue collar workers. So, much against their will, he forced them to leave their jobs and taught them the art of setting bones.

Hanging upside down from his swing, his golden crest open like a Japanese fan, Ellis would watch patients come and go from the clinic and wait for lunch, when Solomon-the-Second would feed him the choicest fruit from his own mouth. Their romance was so well known that Solomon-the-Second was known as Daktar Solomondada Kakakauwallah.

When Solomon-the-Second died, Ellis was left behind to watch a drama unfold between his sons. The two brothers could not work together. They fought and squabbled and totally ignored the bird. Nobody cleaned his cage and Ellis became as dirty as in his Crawford Market days.

According to the last will and testament of Solomon-the-Second, his eldest son Samuel inherited the clinic and the younger brother, Samson, was given a house in Mirzapur which Isabji had bequeathed to Solomon-the-Second. Nobody had ever lived in it but when the fights between the brothers were at their worst, Samuel went to live there and set up another clinic to spite his brother. Then Samuel and Samson indulged in a long-drawn legal battle for the copyright of the name 'Bonesetter Kakakauwallah.'

Legally the bird belonged to Samuel along with the clinic, but he did not particularly fancy Ellis. Without Solomon-the-Second, Ellis had become insecure and whenever patients came, he covered their heads with his droppings and someone had to help wipe the heads which Ellis had blessed.

Samuel was at his wit's end with the bird, so he offered him to Samson. But Samson too was not keen to keep the cockatoo.

By then, David had a houseful of pets of all kinds, and it was well known that cousin Joshua had a good hand with birds. That year, Joshua, who was then just a boy, received Ellis as a birthday present from Samuel.

That was how Ellis returned to Dilli Darwaza in his brass cage. Ellis lived quietly in Joshua's paradise hanging upside down from his perch and watching what was going on around him.

But every paradise has its drawbacks. Ellis had one bad habit. Whenever there was a disagreement in the house, and if one of the women spoke in a high voice, Ellis listened attentively, his eyes shining, crest wide open. When the quarrel was over, Ellis started screeching loudly, thereby letting the whole neighbourhood know that the Dandekars had had a fight!

During such moments, Grandmother Shebabeth dreaded the bird's shrill tongue. She had come to the conclusion that Ellis with his upside-down view of life had brought bad luck to the house of Solomon-the-Second. She was afraid that Ellis would disrupt her own family with his evil eye.

Joshua built a special cage for Ellis in the backyard with swings, plants, creepers, and a hollow tree trunk.

This became Ellis's love nest once Joshua bought a female

companion for Ellis.

The two brothers Samuel and Samson lost everything they had. As long as they lived, they fought legal battles over the right to use the picture of Ellis as a trademark. They spent so much time in court that they lost both their practice and bank balance. The battle continued even when Ellis had become a grandfather of more than twenty yellow-crested cockatoos.

35

DURING THESE YEARS, David was attracted to Sardar Vallabhbhai Patel. Tilak had already planted the seed in his mind, through a long editorial in the *Kesari*. He had predicted that Patel would be an unshakeable pillar in the freedom struggle. During his last days, in the hospital at Bombay, Tilak Maharaj, as he was called, often asked about Patel.

I imagine this is how David got drawn into the freedom movement, but on his own terms. I am sure he was hesitant in the beginning.

Grandfather David befriended Vallabhbhai, and was influenced by him. When he joined the Congress, late-night meetings were often held at the clinic room of the house in Delhi Darwaza.

David won a prestigious municipal election in 1920 and defeated the prosperous mill owner Sheth Mafat Gagal of Ahmedabad, who was known for his generous donations to educational institutions. Defeating Mafat Gagal was a great achievement for a Jewish doctor in those days. Compared to Mafat Gagal, all he had was a philanthropic clinic in Kalupur.

It was with Chandukaka's efforts that David won the election. Chandukaka lived in Molpol in Dariapur, just behind the house in Delhi Darwaza. He often came to the clinic to discuss politics with David. He introduced David to Vallabhbhai Patel.

Chandukaka was younger than David. He was a militant and had tremendous energy. The Gujarati press described him as a man who had the eyes of a hawk and the skin of a crocodile when it came to fighting against a political opponent. He had been an active worker in maintaining peace during communal riots and earned notoriety with the British when he had criticized General Frazer for imposing martial law in the city.

During the influenza epidemic he had worked like a mobile dispensary, going from house to house with a bag of medicines. David had helped him by giving him his fever medicine—pink, bitter and effective.

David hesitated when it came to plunging into active politics. He was basically a dreamer, an armchair politician and social reformist. Vallabhbhai Patel and Chandukaka had seen immense potential in David and Patel decided that David Joseph was the ideal choice in the municipal elections in the Dariapur-Delhi Darwaza area. At the time, people from several communities lived here. The Dandekar house was in Salatwada—literally meaning the corner where the stone carvers or salats of Shahikot—the walled city—lived from the times of Ahmedshah. In and around Delhi Darwaza, Dariapur and Kalupur, there were Pinjaras, Sidi Badshahs, Syeds, Jains, Patels, Brahmins, Hindu masons, Banias and Jews. Every possible merchant had his shop and house here. It was a self-sufficient community.

Chandukaka, who was then a worker and campaigner with the Congress party, saw that nobody bothered about David's religion or caste. He was the right choice for the elections.

It is said that one night when they were sitting in the courtyard of the Dilli Darwaza house, Daviddada, who was smoking a hookah and reclining on a cot, agreed to contest the elections. Without giving Daviddada time to change his mind, Chandukaka dragged him to the common plot of all the pols and mohallas and made the public announcement, though not before Daviddada had dressed with his usual care. (All his photographs show him in a suit and silk waistcoat, holding a walking stick with a silver knob shaped like the head of a tiger. His thick beard added to his distinguished appearance.)

The common plot of the Pols was between Jamadar No Moholla and Salatwada. A huge neem tree stood there with a clay-plastered platform built around it, which served as a stage.

After Chandukaka had introduced him to the large audience that had collected, David gave a short speech focussing on his prime concerns of maintaining hygiene and a clean environment.

Whatever it was he said, the people gathered there obviously liked it, and he was taken in a procession to Vallabhbhai's Bhajia club at Raipur Darwaza and returned to Delhi Darwaza only when it was daybreak.

When David had left the house that night with Chandukaka, Shebabeth thought that they had gone to meet Vallabhbhai Patel. She did not expect him to return home like a king.

I do not understand why, even after he won the elections, Daviddada kept on wearing western clothes. However committed he was to the cause of the Congress, he never wore khadi, or a Gandhi cap. He preferred to look like King George.

His attitude to Gandhiji is also not clear. He took the children to the public meetings of the Mahatma, but while he respected Gandhi, he perhaps had difficulty in pinning his entire faith on him. Sometimes, after dinner, when the family did not have guests, he regaled them with Gandhi's Gujarati-

English speech, and they would all have a good laugh.

When David got involved with political and public life, the doors were opened to the outside world, and complications followed. His reformist zeal brought him into conflict with the Jewish community of Ahmedabad. David wanted to simplify rituals and make them easy to understand. But he faced opposition in the synagogue. He was disappointed and started distancing himself from the synagogue activities. When he changed the method of religious rituals in his own house, he came under severe criticism. But David did not relent. He also felt differently on some other issues concerning the Jewish community.

This was the beginning of the Dandekars' alienation from their community. Daviddada was a reformist, yet he religiously taught his children the Hebrew prayers on shabath evenings and during the festivals. He saw to it that everybody was present for the shabath prayers which he conducted. With Shebabeth he celebrated all the festivals in the traditional manner. Shebabeth insisted that everybody participate in the preparations, and she allotted duties to everyone.

David also became a great advocate of education. He saw to it that his children were well educated—specially his elder daughter Jerusha and son Menachem. Among the children, Jerusha was a brilliant student and had decided to become a doctor. She was to be one of the first few Indian Jewish women to do so.

In the family photograph of these days the men are dressed formally, like Englishmen, and some like Muslims and Parsis. The girls are in frocks and ribbons. The elder women are still in their nine-yard Maharashtrian saris or Parsi-style Gujarati saris. Only one woman is wearing a Gujarati-style ghaghra-choli with a half sari; the material of her blouse is the cotton and silk mashru which is still woven and worn in Gujarat. They appear not to have stepped out of the house. I wonder how they managed to maintain a balance between tradition and modernity. In the later photographs, the dress code changes. The women are in white chiffon saris, worn in the style of the modern Indian woman, with the pallav draped over the left shoulder. The wedding photographs show a western influence. The brides have a veil along with the sari, gloves over bangles and high-heeled shoes with anklets. They look uncomfortable and stiff.

36

THERE WERE MANY pets in the Delhi Darwaza house and the backyard was enclosed with a wire mesh to house David's menagerie. He also had a greenhouse. It was covered with jui and jasmine creepers and in it David had grown ferns, roses and cacti.

The neighbours watched with amazement therefore when David added a female spotted deer and a young nilgai to his collection. Next to the gate there was a stable for the horses and a garage for the family buggy. Inside the house there were a pair of golden cocker spaniels and a white bull-terrier with a black eye-patch, named Ceaser. Whenever David was at home, Ceaser was like his shadow. He was sensitive to David's feelings and knew all his moods, sometimes better than Shebabeth. David controlled his animal kingdom with a certain amount of strictness, which extended to the family. He used his loud, booming voice to great effect.

David and Ceaser had developed a close relationship. Every morning when David left for the clinic, Ceaser tried to follow him. A sharp 'stay' from David made him stop in his tracks. His black bead-like eyes would look sorrowful as he watched his master's receding back. When he heard David's buggy leave, he would sheepishly return to his cushion and sit there watching the door, with twitching eyebrows. It took him an hour to get used to the idea that David had left for work. He would then take a run around the courtyard, barking and chasing the cats. He hated them. Ceaser knew that David was proud of him, as he did not harm or frighten any bird or animal in David's menagerie.

Then, at the stroke of one, Ceaser would sit at the door waiting for David. As his buggy turned in towards Salatwada from the main road and Ceaser heard the familiar sound of the bells, he would start barking with joy. Although many other carriages passed by, Ceaser knew the sound of David's buggy. And if, for some reason, David was late or had gone on a house visit, Ceaser would rush back to Shebabeth and sit looking at her with pleading eyes. Then Shebabeth would tap the place next to her on the swing, and Ceaser would jump up and sit near her. They would wait for David together.

Ceaser would be at peace only at midnight, when he slept at David's feet. He hated the smell of freshly ironed clothes and David's cologne, which meant that he was leaving the house. He himself never stepped out of the house. He knew the difference between friends, strangers, hawkers, regulars, stray dogs and cats.

David had noticed that Ceaser was not as quick as before but he saw no reason to worry. Ceaser, at fifteen, was in good condition for a dog his age. He barked, ate well, and had his daily cat and squirrel races. David knew that a time would come when like all living beings, Ceaser's term on earth would end. But that appeared to be far away.

But David was wrong. Ceaser left them suddenly and without warning. His end came on a hot summer evening.

Ceaser was waiting for David at the door. He had not eaten that day. He was sitting with his head on the floor. Shebabeth assumed that he was feeling hot and would feel better once it became cooler. She asked one of the maids to sprinkle water in the courtyard. Ceaser watched them with sad eyes, but did not move.

When David returned from the clinic, Ceaser sat up. He did not wag his tail as usual. Giving his bags to Shebabeth, David sat down next to Ceaser and caressed his head. Ceaser turned around and lay on his back, so that David could caress his stomach.

David saw Joshua hovering over them with the thermometer which was kept for the dogs. He found the dog was running a fever. Not sure how to treat him, he went back into the house, while Joshua sat on his haunches and watched Ceaser.

David had a wash and changed into his pyjamas. He could not make up his mind whether to call the British veternary officer or the vet who looked after the elephants at the Jagannath temple. Deciding against both, he went to his clinic and made a mixture for fever and worms.

Joshua held Ceaser's head while David tried to pour the liquid into his mouth. Ceaser refused to swallow it and walked out of the main door into the street.

In a loud voice David commanded Ceaser 'down' and 'come', but he did not obey. He did something he had never done before. He went into the street and curled up next to the stable wall. David's threats had no effect. Ceaser sat there with liquid eyes, the tear lines dark and running across his nose. He was foaming at the mouth. It was then that David realized that Ceaser was really sick, and sent for the vet.

Ceaser who had never stepped out of the house compound, refused to enter the house. David sat on his armchair in the veranda from where he could watch him. The vet said that it was a case of worms and prescribed a medicine. But Ceaser refused to swallow it, and spent the night outside the house. That night, as Menachem and Joshua watched over Ceaser, David went to the army headquarters and requested the British veterinary doctor to check his dog. The vet promised to see the dog the next morning. By then, Ceaser was sleeping on his side and panting. David knew that Ceaser was dying. He locked himself in the clinic room and wept.

The army vet had one look at Ceaser and said that the dog had been poisoned. He gave a list of medicines, and looking strangely at David said, 'Try to take him inside the house and give him a cushion to rest. After all, he is an old dog.' He had assumed that David kept his dogs in the street. David tried to explain that the dog had chosen to stay outside, but the vet did not believe him and said, 'Please keep him indoors. It may help.' There was no way to convince him that it was Ceaser's decision to stay outdoors.

The news spread that Ceaser was sick. The neighbours collected in small groups around the house and discussed his strange malady. In the house everybody waited for the worst. David sat frozen in his armchair. He did not know how he was going to live without Ceaser.

Joshua had been observing Ceaser closely. He told Menachem that he needed to do something important and slipped into the clinic room. He read and made notes from the books there and emerged after an hour. He told Menachem, 'Abba will never believe me, but please tell him that Ceaser has rabies. If by chance he bites someone, it is possible he will also become mad.'

Menachem looked at his little brother. 'How do you know? Both the doctors said that Ceaser would be all right. One said he had worms and the other diagnosed food poisoning. So, Dr Joshua David, how did you decide that it was rabies?' Menachem wanted to laugh, but did not. Joshua did not flinch or take offence at his brother's words. He looked straight into his eyes and said, 'Badebhai, I may not be as clever as you or sister Jerusha, or father or the rest, but I know something you do not know.'

'What?' asked Menachem, and decided to take his brother seriously.

Joshua took a deep breath and said, 'Ceaser is frothing at the mouth and has not had a drop of water for two days. I know he has rabies and so I will not touch him.'

Menachem stared at Ceaser and asked, 'Is that enough evidence to decide that a dog has rabies?'

'Yes,' said Joshua. 'Look at these notes which I copied from some books in the library. They say these are the symptoms of rabies. But I am young, and so Abba will not believe me. Please tell him that he must put Ceaser to sleep.'

When Joshua announced that Ceaser must die, he felt a hand on his shoulder. He froze. It was his father's hand. He was certain that he would be spanked. Menachem also looked at his father apprehensively. He had been chatting to his younger brother just to relieve the tension of Ceaser's condition. The fact that the dog refused to enter the house was making everybody nervous. They were not sure how David would react. They knew how much David loved Ceaser.

Then Menachem's eyes gave the thumbs up sign. And slowly Joshua's shoulders relaxed under the pressure of his father's hand. David was not angry. He had overheard the conversation between the two brothers and realized that Joshua was right. All the indications pointed to the fact that Ceaser had rabies.

Much to Joshua's surprise, his father knelt next to him and, with tears running down his face, asked, 'If you know so much, my son, tell me why Ceaser will not enter the house?'

Joshua felt very awkward seeing his big, strong father break down. Swallowing hard he said, 'Ceaser loves us very much and knows that he is feeling strange. He could harm one of us. So, he does not want to enter the house. He has obeyed you all his life, but when it comes to this, he knows better than us.'

David sat on the chair which Menachem offered him and asked his sons whether it would be correct to kill Ceaser. Menachem did not know what to say, but Joshua replied haltingly, 'Abba, if we don't, he will soon be running around Delhi Darwaza and biting everybody. Then, someone will hit him on his head and kill him. If that happens, we will never forgive ourselves.'

That evening the vet came and gave Ceaser an injection which first made him drowsy and then fall into a deep slumber. David carried Ceaser into the house and laid him in his usual place. The next day, his body was packed in a bag of salt and buried on the banks of the Sabarmati.

Shebabeth lit a candle and said a kaddish for Ceaser: 'Help us to understand O Lord, that grief and love go hand in hand, that sorrow of loss is but a token of the love that is stronger than death . . .'

David looked at Joshua, tapped his knee and gestured that he should sit on his lap. Joshua felt a sob rising in his chest as he climbed on his father's knee. David whispered in his ear, 'Will you help me with the birds and animals every day? How did you gather so much knowledge about dogs? Do you spend

your time reading in the library? From now on, after you
return from school, you can clean the cages, brush the dogs
and feed the birds. But, only after you have finished your
homework. And, yes, you can spend some time in the library
on holidays and every night before you go to bed. Then you
will dream of nice things like dogs and birds. Are you afraid
at night?'

Joshua felt happy and carefree on his father's knee, except
that a small dark cloud passed over him at the mention of
homework. But he did not stop smiling because such moments
were rare and he wanted to make the most of them.

37

NOT ALL OF David and Shebabeth's children survived. Their
daughter Sophie—fair, slim and delicate, died young. There is
one photograph of her with her father David in the back
garden of the house in Dilli Darwaza. Most of the other
photographs are group photographs, but this one is of just
father and daughter. I wonder whether he had a premonition
of her death.

David was depressed and was becoming more and more
irritable. He continued with his civic and synagogue activities,
till the time he had a major confrontation with Bamnolkar,
another Bene Israel Jew, who had been elected Mayor of the
Ahmedabad Sudharak Nagarpalika.

Shebabeth, however, continued going to the synagogue and
meeting the women. In this way she kept her contact with the
community. A woman of foresight, she knew that one needed
the community's support in births, deaths and marriages. And,
except for her eldest, she still had to get all her children
married. She loved celebrations and did not want to be isolated.

On the day he died, David returned home early from the clinic. Shebabeth was surprised and rushed to the door to greet him with a glass of water, then returned to the kitchen to make a cup of nimbu-pani for him. He looked pale and sick. She was worried as he usually drove the buggy himself but on this particular day, had asked the compounder to drive him home.

David slumped down in Abraham's chair at the kitchen door and called out 'Maa' to his wife—a name he used only when he was disturbed. The name stuck to Shebabeth for the rest of her life. When anybody uttered the word Maa, it only meant Shebabeth.

Shebabeth heard a warning in the word 'Maa' and rushed out. She asked, 'What happened? Are you sick?'

'I am not feeling too well. I need to rest,' he said.

She helped him climb the stairs and as he lay down on the bed, he signalled to her to sit down next to him. Taking her hand in his, he played with her fingers and caressed the heart-shaped wedding ring incised with the letter D. He was rarely sentimental, and this brought tears to Shebabeth's eyes. They had been together since they were born.

'Take care of everybody. Keep them together,' David told her.

'Don't talk like that. If you sleep a little, you will feel better,' she replied, now openly crying. While she was still speaking, David leaned over to the side of the bed and to her horror, Shebabeth saw that there was a pool of blood at her feet. He had had a massive heart attack. He had left the family in Shebabeth's care.

After the funeral, Shebabeth had to face the most difficult time of her life. Every day there was someone at the door with a receipt which showed that David had borrowed large sums of money. Shebabeth was shocked and felt cheated. Although they were deep in debt, she had to keep up pretences that they were a well-to-do family. The only person who brought in some income was Jerusha.

Jerusha was a gynaecologist. She took up the responsibility of the house and the payment of their debts. She never complained. Shebabeth, who had never worried about money for running the house, was suddenly anxious about every paisa she spent. At the end of the day, she would ask herself, 'Why didn't David tell me about the debts?'

David had never confided in anybody that his political ambitions had crippled him financially. He had borrowed money from ten or twelve people, without leaving any written document. He had eventually withdrawn from politics but, every night, local leaders still met in his house and the flow of drink and food continued. He never disclosed even to Chandukaka that he could no longer host them.

The snippets of news from Europe he read filled him with disquiet. He read a comment by Adolf Hitler about the resurrection of the Nazi party in which he proclaimed: 'I alone will lead the movement. No one can impose conditions on me, as long as I personally bear the responsibility.'

Heinrich Held, the Prime Minister of Bavaria and the head of the Catholic Bavarian People's Party had lifted the ban on the Nazi party saying: 'The wild beast is checked, we can afford to loosen the chain.' Held was one of the first German politicians to make a fatal error of judgement. His comment filled David with a sense of foreboding. All this combined with his doubts about his identity as a Jewish Indian began to make him feel isolated at the time of his death shortly before the Second World War.

38

VALLABHBHAI PATEL AND Gandhiji had been strong advocates of women's education and David had been influenced by them.

He had seen to it that his daughters were sent to school and college. He was a hard taskmaster and insisted that they did not go to bed unless they had done their homework. Jerusha and Menachem decided to become doctors and David helped make their dreams a reality.

He had seen that sometimes Menachem got diverted from his ambition and inclined towards theatre and music, but Jerusha never allowed anything to distract her. She wanted to be first in everything. But when one looks closely at her photograph, one can see a certain anger in her eyes. She wore dresses made of expensive material, which were cut well and showed her slim waistline and legs to advantage. With these, she wore high heels and stockings. Her hair was made into a braided bun, and she wore a thin gold chain around her neck, and a watch on her wrist. She was the picture of perfection.

By the time her father died, she was already a gynaecologist and practising in a private hospital in Ahmedabad. With his death, she was faced with a situation she had never envisaged. She became the only earning member of the family. Moreover, when her father was alive, she had assumed that her parents would look for a suitable Jewish boy for her. Someone as educated as she was.

After her father died, it was certain that nobody would find a groom for her. She was highly educated; her brothers, younger than her, did not know how to find a match for someone as formidable as their sister Jerusha. She was young, but she had already missed the boat.

As she grew older, she lived with her mother in the Saraspur Maternity Home quarters, where she was a superintendent. Once gramophones became popular, she built up a collection of her favourite records and would sit and listen to these in the evenings.

Aunt Jerusha had given me a wine-red sari when she was in one of her affectionate moods. There are many stories hidden within its folds. At that point, nobody wore such colours in the family. Everybody wore pastels and so did I. It was a secret that I was attracted to reds, yellows—all the bright colours. Aunt Jerusha had given me the sari sensing that I liked that particular colour. She had never worn the sari. The folds had formed deep gashes in the cloth. Holding the sari, one could feel Aunt Jerusha's secret hurts.

I often asked grandmother why Aunt Jerusha had never married. I never got a clear answer. She would look a little thoughtful, as though she was looking into the past and searching for an answer. Perhaps, she felt guilty that she had not been able to find a groom for the beautiful Jerusha. Till then the only single women in the house were widows and virgins.

There may have been one other reason why she remained single. This secret was revealed after her seventh-day death ceremony.

After the funeral, when everyone had left, Menachem and Joshua narrated the story of Aunt Jerusha's love life, trying, perhaps, to assuage their guilt, to which I have added a few details.

Jerusha was studying medicine in Bombay. She greatly admired her professor, Dr Ezra. Jerusha must have been in her twenties. He was older than her. He had told her that he was a widower. They were friendly, and Ezra took a personal interest in Jerusha, first as a hard-working and bright student, and later as a woman. Jerusha was flattered that the handsome doctor was interested in her. This was when she was in her final year of college.

Ezra often invited Jerusha for tea in his office. She saw

nothing wrong in it. They spoke about work and shared hospital jokes. For this harmless companionship that Jerusha shared with Ezra, she would pay a heavy price.

Jerusha was due to finish her studies, and Ezra must have felt that he was going to lose her forever. One day, he asked her, 'Miss David, what is your opinion about marriage?'

Jerusha must have been waiting for this moment. But she did not look up and kept pouring the tea, as though she had not heard his question. This was the first time that something like this had happened, and her face was flushed and hot. After what seemed to be ages, she looked up and said, 'Excuse me, doctor, I do not understand your question.'

He laughed and said, 'This is not a question I would ever ask you in class. It is a personal question.'

She was just a little angry and shocked. 'Doctor, I respect you. How can you speak to me like this?'

He insisted, 'I just want to know your views on marriage.'

He had caught her hand and withdrawing it she answered severely, 'According to Bene Israel custom, these things are decided by our elders. We have been brought up to understand that we do not take decisions in this matter. It may be different with the Bagdadis.'

He heard the sarcasm in her voice. Ezra was amused. 'But it is your life,' he said. 'Don't you think that you should take your own decisions?'

'No. I do not even think about such things.'

'If that is the case,' Ezra said, 'why are you still unmarried? According to the norms of your community you are past the age of marriage. By now you should have been the mother of two children.'

'Well, I am studying. Where is the time for marriage? I will be the first woman doctor in my family,' she announced proudly.

Quietly he asked, 'Has your father found a suitor for you?'

Jerusha carefully framed her answer. 'No. I do not discuss such matters with my father. But my mother did tell me that they cannot find a suitor for me as I am highly educated. The suitors who ask for my hand are not worth talking about.'

'What are the possibilities of their finding a suitor for you? I am sure that by now most of the young men in your community are married. I have many Bene Israel friends and I know that it is very difficult for them to find partners after a certain age and education.'

They discussed the problem of marriage in minority communities at length. Jerusha relaxed, assuming that the personal moment had passed. But Ezra continued undeterred, 'Dr Jerusha David. Sounds good. Soon you will be a doctor. Dr Miss Jerusha David, will you marry me? I like you very much. I think I am in love with you.'

With shaking hands, Jerusha placed her cup back on the table and asked, 'Doctor, sir, do you want me to be your second wife?' She must have then pointed towards the photograph of Dr Ezra, his deceased wife and their six-year-old daughter.

Ezra turned pale. 'Do you believe in me? Trust me?' he asked.

'Yes, or do you think I would ever be in a closed room with a man?'

'Then please believe me when I tell you that my wife is no longer alive. She died of tuberculosis. Although I am a doctor, I could not save her. It was my greatest failure. I was married young, and have not yet passed the age of getting married again. I need a wife. In fact, I want you to be my wife.'

Jerusha was moved, yet she heard herself saying, 'These decisions are never taken by women in our families. Please give me time. I must ask my parents.'

Ezra agreed with a sinking heart, knowing that they would never allow her to marry him. He asked, 'Can I please ask your father for your hand?'

Jerusha refused. She stopped herself from saying, 'If I allow you to meet my father, he will kill, me.' Instead she said, 'We know about the differences that exist between your community and mine. There have been two major incidents recently. One the move by the Bagdadis to build a dividing wall in the Bene Israel graveyard, so that your community can have a separate cemetery. When my father read about it, he was furious. He said that the Bagdadis were trying to prove that they were superior and we inferior, because our lineage is impure. I am sure you also know about the Sefer Torah incident. The Bagdadis had issued a statement that we were not clean enough to touch them. My father would never accept our marriage.'

Ezra smiled. 'My dear Miss David, I am not answerable to anybody. Mine was an arranged marriage. Now, at my age and status, I am not going to take permission from my family in Calcutta. If you say yes, I am going to invite them to meet my beautiful bride.' Jerusha blushed, as Ezra continued, 'Are we going to allow walls to stand between us? If we like each other the problems of the two communities should not stand between us. To tell you the truth, I am ashamed that the Bagdadi Jews wanted a separate graveyard. I agree some of them think that they are superior to the Bene Israel Jews. I was disturbed when the British referred to the Bagdadis and the white Cochini Jews as proper Jews—as though the Bene Israel belonged to a lower caste. Fortunately, it was just a passing episode. The British government refused to accept a separate amendment on the grounds that all Indian Jews are of Asian origin. I know many Bagdadis ridicule the fact that Marathi is your mother tongue. You will be surprised, Miss David, that I speak Marathi because I live in Bombay. I also speak Gujarati, because when my grandfather came to India from Aden, he first landed in Surat. Then he moved to Bombay and after that to Calcutta. So we also know Bengali. Let us forget everything and just accept that we are both Jews. That is more important than anything else. I do not understand why your father should have a problem with me. Will you speak to him? Or shall I?'

Jerusha smiled and agreed to speak to her father. She did not want Ezra to meet her father. Jerusha did not tell Ezra that David was known for his ferocious temper, and that he used the cane freely. She did not know how she was going to handle the situation. Yet, she was in love with Dr Ezra sir.

Jerusha returned to Ahmedabad with a degree, and the house rejoiced. She smiled politely and participated in the celebrations. She did not know how to broach the subject of her marriage. David Joseph gave a special blessing for his daughter Jerusha. She was his pride and joy. The first woman who would become a doctor in the Dandekar clan. She felt beholden to her father who had done so much for her. Jerusha knew that although he believed in social reform, in this instance, rather than accept her getting married outside the Bene Israel community, even if the suitor was a Bagdadi Jew, he would kill her.

Jerusha found a quiet moment with her mother Shebabeth, and told her that Dr Ezra was a Bagdadi widower, and wanted to marry her. Shebabeth was shocked.

'Marriage to a Bagdadi? Are you blind to the fact that the Bagdadi Jews have been insulting us since the time they arrived in India? If you marry this Dr Ezra sir of yours, nobody will accept your marriage. Neither the Bagdadis nor the Bene Israel.

Your children will suffer. They will not find acceptance in either community, and will be considered unfit to enter the assembly of the Lord for seven generations. Don't get carried away by this man and his clever words. If you go against our wishes and marry this Bagdadi, you will bring the curse upon yourself. You will never see our faces again. None of our sons or daughters have married a Bagdadi or a Cochini—leave aside other castes. It has never happened in our family, and your father will never agree to it. You know how proud he is of you. Just the other day he was telling me you are the ideal Jewish woman. He has so many plans for you. You cannot possibly disappoint him.'

Jerusha asked her mother, 'Do you have another suitor for me in our community? I accept that Dr Ezra is a Bagdadi, but can you deny that he is a Jew? A doctor at that. Aren't these qualifications enough?' Shebabeth was in a dilemma. They had received three mangas or proposals for Jerusha, but David had rejected them as the suitors were unsuitable for Jerusha.

Shebabeth was embarassed.

That night, when he was about to fall asleep, she told David about Jerusha and Dr Ezra sir. Shebabeth hoped against hope that he had not heard her and had fallen asleep. But he had, and she heard what sounded like a growl. Her husband was looking at her, his eyes wide open. 'Call Jerusha,' he said.

Dressed in a frilly nightgown, Jerusha was downstairs with the other children. Her long hair hung loose and she looked so beautiful that Shebabeth was for a moment tempted to tell David that she was sleeping. With a look of warning, she told Jerusha to tie her hair and go to her father who was waiting for her upstairs. Shebabeth herself lingered downstairs.

Jerusha braided her hair as she went up. David wanted to know every detail about Dr Ezra's proposal of marriage.

Jerusha told him exactly what had happened. He listened with eyes lowered and did not seem to react. But Jerusha was shocked by his final question. 'Has he touched you? After all, he is a married man and knows about life. And you are still a virgin—I hope. It is something precious that you keep for your husband. Are you . . .?'

Jerusha looked angrily at her father, and tore open her braid, knowing that he did not like to see her hair open in front of him, daring him to touch her. With her hair flowing behind her like a bridal veil, she said defiantly, 'No, I am not spoilt. I am a virgin.' Then she stomped down the staircase and buried herself in her quilt. Shebabeth did not have the courage to touch her or console her. She went back upstairs. As she lay down next to her husband he asked her, 'Do you know the dates of Jerusha's cycle? Inform me if she does not get her periods this month.' After that he never spoke to Jerusha, although she had informed Dr Ezra sir that she could not accept his proposal.

When David died, his will was read aloud by his lawyer. There was nothing for Jerusha. It simply mentioned that as she was earning and self-sufficient, he had decided that she should not be given a part of his property. Jerusha went through the ordeal without a change of expression.

In her later years, Jerusha often went to Bombay for conferences or to buy expensive dress material but nobody knows whether she ever met Dr Ezra. Nothing is known about what happened to the Dr Ezra sir love story.

After my eleventh birthday, when I had my first period, Aunt Jerusha was summoned to the house. My mother thought it was too early. Aunt Jerusha scolded her for treating it as an illness. In those days, Dr Jerusha David was a famous gynaecologist of Gujarat. Women travelled long distances to have their babies delivered by Jerushabaidaktar. Yet she was a prisoner of the family.

Shebabeth left the comforts of the Delhi Darwaza house, and set up home with her daughter at her hospital quarters. She wanted to look after Jerusha and protect her from the big bad world. Shebabeth never returned to the ancestral house. Much later, she died in Aunt Jerusha's house. Perhaps Jerusha also needed Shebabeth, but for her own reasons. They felt secure with each other and slept together in a double bed. I cannot think of one without the other.

When Shebabeth died, Jerusha had retired from the maternity hospital. She locked herself in her apartment. And, to give meaning to her long empty hours, she fell in love with General Moshe Dayan. She made a scrapbook of his photographs, and spent hours meticulously cutting them out from newspapers and magazines. The black eye-patch fascinated her and she said that she had fallen in love with a real man for the first time. Had she gone to Israel she was sure that she would have married him.

She had left instructions saying that when she died she did not want the ritualistic coconut milk bath. While we were sponging her nude body and preparing it for the funeral, there was great speculation about whether Aunt Jerusha had died a virgin.

39

MY FATHER JOSHUA was the misfit of the family. He was poor at studies and hid behind his mother. She protected him from everybody, and concealed from her husband that Joshua rarely went to school. He aroused all her motherly instincts as he was weak as a child.

But Grandmother Shebabeth had great hopes for him. When David referred to him as 'Nikamma'—the useless one—Shebabeth would reprimand him, 'One day, my son Joshua will rule the world. Just wait and see.' David would laugh at her saying, 'That's impossible. I would be surprised if he even makes it as a millworker!'

Shebabeth was sure that Joshua would be the one to realize the family prophecy—that one of them was blessed by the gods to be nature's miracle man. She hoped and prayed that the Shesh Nag which Joseph had seen would cast its benevolent eyes on Joshua and protect him, specially after Albert's death.

There was a year's difference between Albert and Joshua. From the family photograph it is obvious that they resembled each other. In fact, they looked like twins. Menachem and Jerusha have an expression of hope on their faces, but Joshua looks frightened. In the photograph he is wearing a cap, and watching the photographer with intense eyes. Albert's eyes are closed and he is under a blanket. Perhaps he died soon afterwards.

Albert and Joshua were playing cricket with their friends, in the open plot in front of the house, where there was a lime mill and the stables. The ball fell into the pit of the mill. The man who turned the mill had gone for lunch, leaving the bullocks tied to the yoke.

Albert jumped inside the mill to get the ball. He wanted to make as many runs as possible. With the sudden commotion, the sleepy bullocks started moving, and Albert was crushed under the wheels of the lime mill. Joshua stood screaming helplessly. He was to feel guilty all his life. Perhaps, it was his ball which had fallen into the press. Shebabeth rushed out and was shocked to see her Albert being crushed to death. She was screaming when David lifted Albert out of the mill with the help of the neighbours. Everybody knew that it was too late, though David tried everything possible to save his son.

After the funeral, David woke up in the middle of the night and saw that Shebabeth was sitting on Abraham's chair at the kitchen door. When he went up to her, he saw that although it was very hot, she was as cold as a block of ice. He took her in his arms and led her back to their room. She whispered, 'Albert has come back to me. His soul has entered Joshua. They are now one.'

Till she could move around, every year on 23 May grandmother Shebabeth made a kaddish for Albert. She would make sweet puris, omelettes and poha with coconut. Sometimes she did not remember the date of the death of a family member, including her husband, but she never forgot the day Albert had died. In the evening, dressed in white, we would wait for Uncle Menacham to recite the kaddish. Then grandmother Shebabeth would pour a stiff peg of whisky for herself, and recount the entire episode of Albert's death with dry eyes and a stony face.

40

SHEBABETH WAS KEEN to send Joshua to school, but if he was late by five minutes, she stood on the balcony watching the road, expecting the worst. When he went out to play, she made sure that he was not far from the house, and that she could see him from Abraham's chair.

At night, in bed, Shebabeth held him to her chest. Joshua was a light sleeper and was afraid of the faintest sound. The kitchen was covered by terracotta tiles and had a slanting roof.

From here he heard strange sounds. Once Joshua woke up
screaming, saying that Albert was calling out to him from the
rooftop. He said that he could see Albert standing there
dressed in a white shroud. Joshua looked pale and sick.

Shebabeth assured him that there was nobody on the roof.
Nobody believed her, but Shebabeth said that she saw Albert
in him. Since Albert had died, Joshua walked like Albert and
shook his head in the same way. When Albert was alive he
walked differently and never shook his head in that particular
Albert-like manner. He was a two-in-one image of both Albert
and Joshua.

Shebabeth enjoyed telling us family stories and her
interpretations of dreams. We believed all she said. She may
not have had a regular education like Aunt Jerusha, but she
was gifted with the art of storytelling, an understanding of life,
and the ability to bond and tie the family together. Perhaps
Book of Esther would not have been possible if I had not sat
on her lap, nervously chewing the end of her sari and listening
to her stories. Perhaps she saw the restless streak in me and did
not like it. So, she kept me confined to the house, spellbound
by her words.

Gradually Shebabeth realized that her son Joshua had a
bee on his bottom. It was impossible to keep his attention or
focus on anything for more than five minutes. The only things
that fascinated him were guns, dogs, deer, canaries and forests.
But he had confided in his mother that when his elder brother
Menachem had taken him to the hillocks around the Kankaria
lake for a midnight picnic on a full-moon night, he had been
terrified. Although there were others around, he had controlled
his fear of the dark with great difficulty.

Upon returning, Menachem did not want to disturb their
mother. He asked Joshua to sleep with him in the clinic room.

Menachem saw Joshua's hesitation. Joshua would have preferred to creep into their mother's bed. Menachem assured him that he would be safe without Shebabeth. Joshua agreed to sleep with him. When Menachem woke up in the morning, he saw that Joshua had snuggled very close to him. Menachem, who was much older, did not like it that Joshua still slept with their mother. He had often tried speaking to Shebabeth about it but she insisted that her son needed her.

When Joshua stirred, Menachem smiled and asked, 'Scared?' Joshua nodded.

'About what?' asked Menachem.

'Every night I see Albert standing on the roof and calling me.'

'Albert is dead. We buried him—remember?'

'Yes, we lowered him into the grave.'

'Albert is dead and cannot return. Everything finishes with death.'

'No, not Albert. We played cricket together. We ate together. We made pee pee together.' Joshua smiled for the first time after Albert's death.

'Why do you sleep with Maa? You are a big boy.'

'Because she is our mother. Albert's and mine. And when Albert comes to take me to heaven she holds me back.'

'I want to meet Albert. I want to see him on the roof.'

'I don't know how you can. I sleep with Maa and I cannot call out to you, or he will disappear.'

'OK, so don't sleep with Maa. We will sleep in our own beds next to each other. When you see him tonight, touch me and I will wake up.'

That night, Menachem insisted that Joshua sleep with him, in his own bed. If Joshua was scared, he would take care of him. Hesitantly Shebabeth retired to her room. Menachem watched Joshua as he reluctantly tried to sleep in his own bed. Menachem covered him with a blanket and caressed his forehead. Around two in the morning, Menachem felt Joshua's cold hand in his, and heard him whisper, 'Albert.'

Menachem sat up. He looked at the roof and whispered, 'I do not see him. Where is he?'

'There,' said Joshua and closed his eyes, pointing towards the roof.

Menachem got up and saw that there were two civet cats on the roof. When the civet cats ran around, the tiles moved, and Joshua assumed that Albert was standing on the roof.

Menachem said to Joshua, 'Get up young man. I want to show you something.' When Joshua sat up, Menachem laughed and said, 'Scared of these poor night creatures? They can only see at night and you think it's Albert. It's not Albert. It's civet cats, rats and bats.'

Joshua felt foolish. He started crying. Menachem put his arm around his shoulders, and said, 'Brother you are a man, not a child. Life and death are part of life. It's the cat's eyes that are shining like stars. There are no ghosts. Come . . .' All night, Menachem sat upright holding Joshua in his arms.

The next day Joshua said to Menachem, 'Bade bhai, I am going to sleep in my own bed tonight. But if I wake you up in the middle of the night, don't get angry.'

'No,' laughed Menachem. 'We will pee-pee together.'

Joshua was relieved. This trust was to last the rest of their days.

3

Joshua

41

JOSHUA CONTINUED TO scamper off to the river at Narayan Ghat near Shah Jehan's palace. He hated the red brick building of the RC technical school opposite the Chalte Pir ki Durgah. The stuffy airless rooms made him sick, and the teachers more so. Swimming in the Sabarmati at Narayan Ghat and watching the herons, egrets, dabchicks, ducks, kingfishers and squirrels was much more fun than poring over school books. In the evening, after he had cleaned the cages, brushed the dogs, cleaned their eyes and fed the birds and deer, he browsed through the books in the clinic room. He never read anything in detail. He only looked at the pictures and the captions. Joshua was fascinated with books on nature, dogs, animals, shikar, guns and antiques. He also liked to see pictures of ornately carved furniture, sculpture and painting. He wondered if one could learn art, instead of maths and science. He went to school only when there were English classes. He enjoyed listening to Shakespeare.

Joshua left the house according to school timings. But Shebabeth knew where he had been when she opened his lunch box. If there was sand in the box, she knew that he had bunked school. She felt ashamed that she would again have to lie to her husband and protect her son from his fury. For David, going to school was like a religion, and breaking its rules was an unforgivable sin.

The first bird Joshua killed with his catapult was a common mynah. His marksmanship was perfect with birds, lizards and mice. But when he killed something, he felt both joy and sorrow. This was the beginning of his adventures with wildlife.

When he killed the mynah, he rolled the bird into his handkerchief and put it in his school bag. That night, following a book on basic taxidermy, he stuffed the bird in the backyard. Then, to cleanse his troubled spirit, he decided to take a swim. He removed his clothes and stood at the water's edge watching his reflection. He looked very skinny and small with his ribcage jutting out from his chest. He counted his ribs and was ashamed.

Every Sunday afternoon, when David taught them the Bible, Joshua saw the illustration of the chained Samson breaking the temple pillars. Joshua wanted to become a muscle-man like Samson. His other role model from the Bible was Daniel, who had emerged unharmed from the lions' den.

When Joshua was thirteen, and had received the silk prayer shawl for his bar mitzvah, his father embraced him and accepted him as an adult. David was disturbed when Joshua asked him for an airgun as a gift of adulthood. His father bought it for him with the promise that he would only practise target shooting at the rifle club. He would not kill birds, dogs, cats or monkeys. Joshua promised that he would not kill anything, but if the langurs jumped on the roof or entered the kitchen, he would fire shots at them to scare them away. David gave him permission to kill lizards and mice with a thin cane, a habit which stayed with him.

As he draped the prayer shawl around his shoulders, David

accepted the fact that Joshua was not like the rest of his children. He would not complete school. His reports showed that he was a weak student and often absent. His class teacher, Master Girijashanker, had suggested to David that Joshua be sent to another school. With a heavy heart and without a word he had accepted the decision. He had been ashamed.

That evening when he saw Joshua whistling happily and brushing the dogs, David felt that he was a failure as a father. He had always wanted to be the perfect parent. The education of his children came before everything else. But, he did not know what to do about Joshua.

He saw that Joshua was growing well with regular exercise. Besides push-ups, he had started lifting weights as well. He practised with the Samson brothers, whose father had recently won the title of Mr India. They lived near the Dandekars, in a lane leading to the Delhi Darwaza crossroads. The elder Samson was a hard taskmaster and Joshua spent many hours in their courtyard, fulfilling his dream of becoming a muscle-man.

For two more years Joshua lived an idyllic life. Joshua woke up late, and had his breakfast when lunch was ready. He had a bath, lounged around the clinic room reading magazines or went to the river for a swim. Then, late in the afternoon, he went to the Samsons for his workouts, after which he cleaned and fed the animals and birds of the house. In the evenings, he bathed, dressed in his best clothes and went target shooting, or to the bazaar, or just sat around with friends on Chandola lake. It was here that he started shooting ducks and roasting them on an open fire.

Friday was the only day he was up and dressed before everybody else. That was the day he went to the open market on the river bed.

He would return frustrated because he could not buy an old watch, a sculpture, a piece of woodcarving or a catalogue of antiques or furniture. David had instructed Shebabeth not to give Joshua any pocket money. He had to learn his lesson the hard way. David knew that Joshua had a fascination for everything beautiful and expensive. That he was not going back to school was bad enough, but David definitely did not want to spoil him.

Sometimes, even if David felt like appreciating a bird Joshua had stuffed and left on his desk he did not react, although he knew he should. Instead he asked him, 'Young man, do you think you are going to make a living out of flexing your muscles or killing birds? Do you think teaching the parakeets to whistle tunes and brushing dogs is going to get you anywhere? You will come to nothing. Look around. Your brothers and sisters are excelling at studies and we have been a family of doctors. When it comes to you, how do you see yourself? Perhaps you will follow the footsteps of Mr India?' David's taunts hurt Joshua. He decided that he would prove to his father that he was not useless. He told him, 'Find me a job.'

In those days, Ahmedabad was a city of cloth mills. It was called the Manchester of India. If someone knew a little about textiles or had a letter of recommendation, it was not difficult to find a job. David asked one of his patients to find a job in a mill for his useless son.

Joshua's heart sank. Every morning Ahmedabad woke up to the whistles of the innumerable chimneys which marked the city's skyline. At five in the morning, the streets and lanes of Ahmedabad were flooded with men carrying tiffin boxes going to work or returning, dirty and exhausted, on their bicycles.

David suggested that with Joshua's 'qualifications' and command of the English language, it would not be difficult for him to work in a mill. That is, if he applied his mind to technical matters. A job was fixed for Joshua in The Ahmedabad Fine Spinning and Weaving Company Limited.

It was a drab, dreary existence, a far cry from his peaceful siestas. Every morning when Joshua left for work, the city looked like a forest of mill chimneys, standing tall and threatening. Shebabeth too suffered. She hated to wake him up at four in the morning, as she prepared his tiffin box. Joshua worked in the mill for a year after which he was unceremoniously dismissed as he was never seen at the looms in the afternoon. Joshua wrote his letter of resignation and returned home, after he had made sure that his father had left for the dispensary.

The women were in the kitchen, so nobody noticed when Joshua entered the house. When Shebabeth emerged from the kitchen to get some curry-patta leaves from the tree in the courtyard, she saw Joshua lying face down on the string cot. He was crying soundlessly. She wiped her hands and sat down next to him. Running her fingers through his thick hair, she asked him whether he was sick. He shook his head and told her that he had been sacked. Both mother and son cried. They did not know how they were going to break the news to David. Shebabeth was certain that she would not be able to save Joshua from his father's fury.

When David returned home for lunch and saw Joshua sitting at the dining table with a sheepish look on his face, he understood that something was wrong, but he took his time to change and wash his hands. 'Are you on night duty?' he asked as he sat down at the table.

Joshua shook his head and did not raise his eyes. Shebabeth told David that Joshua had been forced to resign, for no fault of his. David surprised her by not losing his temper. He smiled sarcastically and said, 'No fault of his. I am sure he did something. Nobody asks a worker to leave unless there is a reason.' Then, looking at Joshua he asked, 'Did you damage a machine or something like that?'

Joshua met his father's eye and said, 'It was all because of a bird—an ostrich.'

Joshua held his breath. He was sure that his father would be furious. But David started laughing and the atmosphere eased in the house.

42

THE OSTRICH HAD been a favourite topic of conversation in the family. They had all seen its photograph in the Gujarati newspapers. It was an unusual photograph, as it showed the sheth of The Fine Spinning and Weaving Company Ltd. riding the bird. He was a small, thin man who liked travelling, and he had brought the bird from Africa. This particular sheth always dressed like an Englishman—in a black suit with a waistcoat, bow-tie, shoes and top hat. And as he was short, he looked ridiculous sitting on the ostrich.

David was very interested in the ostrich. 'I cannot believe this. How can a man ride a bird?' he said repeatedly. Menachem had studied the photograph and said, 'Perhaps it is not real, it is a stuffed bird. The sheth is sitting on it just for the photograph.' But Joshua disagreed. 'It is a real bird because its beak is open.' To which their father asked, 'And how can you say that? Did you read it in your book of taxidermy?' 'No,' said Joshua staring at the photograph, 'it has something about it which says that it is a real bird.'

The conversation was forgotten, but Joshua cut out the

picture from the newspaper and pasted it in his scrapbook, next to a portrait of the super-shikari Jim Corbett and ringmaster Damu Dhotre sleeping on a bed of live tigers. 'One day,' he told himself, 'I will ride an ostrich.'

When Joshua had agreed to work in the mill, it was with the hope that he would get to see the ostrich. But when he saw the dull, grey atmosphere of the mill and the way the workers were herded in and out, he thought there was little chance of his seeing the bird. But when he did he wanted to see it again and again.

When Joshua saw the bird for the first time, it was four in the afternoon. He was in the machine room which faced the garden of the sheth's office. Next to the office he saw a cage with a big bird. He went out on some pretext. It was the ostrich.

At close quarters, Joshua was disappointed. The bird in the cage looked more dead than alive. From a distance, it looked like a stuffed bird. But it was real, and sad and lonely.

Explaining to David why he was forced to resign, Joshua said, 'Abba, do you remember the photograph of the ostrich which appeared in the newspapers. You felt it was a stuffed bird? But I told you that it was not. I was right. I saw it. As long as I was there, I never saw the sheth riding it. Perhaps it was a trick photograph. A sweeper entered the cage every alternate day and changed the trays of food and water. They were afraid of each other. I saw the ostrich chase the sweeper. I got really close to the bird and slowly had him eating out of my hand. The ostrich even waited for me. At exactly four in the afternoon, I saw it standing near the wire mesh. He looked sad and sick. So, I spent my afternoons with him. The supervisor was already unhappy with me and when he discovered me there, I lost my job.

'I am sure the bird misses me. And, of course, I miss the bird. I clipped a feather from the bird's wings as a memento. Do you want to see it? Badebhai Menachem has seen it.'

David did not know how to react, but realized that his son was special. He could not help but advise him, 'If you had taken some interest in science and finished your studies, you could have become a veterinary doctor or a taxidermist.' For the first time, Joshua answered with a certain determination in his voice, 'I will.'

43

TO IMPRESS HIS father, Joshua continued to wake up early in the morning for his body-building exercises. The senior Samson was sure that Joshua would win the title of Mr Gujarat that year. His sons were the same age as Joshua, and they all practised together.

Joshua was then just turning seventeen. He had a long face with thin lips, intense black eyes with a tinge of grey, a strong nose and a mane of thick black hair, which he grew long like Samson's, following the illustrations from the Bible. The exercise had given him a taut, muscular body. He picked up weights as though they were toys and pulled cars tied to his hair, bent crowbars and lifted stones to prove his prowess.

But what he liked best was to strike poses in front of the mirror, flexing his muscles. He wanted to look like a Greek god, and he was very close to his ambition.

That year Joshua won two titles—that of Mr Gujarat and Body Beautiful. His photograph appeared in some of the newspapers, posing in the competition. David commented that Joshua appeared to be wearing only briefs and knuckledusters.

He did not know how he was going to face the Bene Israel community. Shebabeth was making his tea and had her back to him. His comments annoyed her, but she smiled when he asked her to say a blessing for their son. 'At least,' he said, 'he is excelling at something. Perhaps he will end up having his own gymnasium. Joshua's Gym or something like that. He will spend a lifetime training young men in the art of body-building.'

Shebabeth retorted, 'It is better to be a pehelvan than a millworker.'

David did not answer. He was distressed and also pleased that Joshua always had something up his sleeve and came up with the unexpected. Not knowing how to guide him to make a meaningful life, David left him alone. Life would take its own course with Joshua.

One morning, when Joshua was at the Samson gym, a buggy arrived at the door. Two men emerged and asked for Joshua. The maid who was sweeping the courtyard asked them to wait and went into the kitchen to inform Shebabeth. Without turning around, she told the maid to tell them that Daktardada was not at home and they should come later. She did not like to entertain guests till she had had her bath. But the maid returned saying that they did not want to meet Daktardada, they were asking for Joshuababa. Shebabeth was surprised and went to the door. Ustad Lalliwallahsaab stood there with another man. This man looked familiar but Shebabeth was not sure where she had seen him.

Ustadsaheb was dressed in a black shervani. The other man, who was dressed in a white suit, was handsome. Ustadsaheb introduced him as Khalil Ahmed. Shebabeth was impressed by his diamond tie-pin. She invited them into the clinic room, asked the maid to inform Joshua that he had guests, and offered them tea and biscuits. She was curious to know why they wanted to meet her son, but she kept her questions to herself and waited till he arrived.

Joshua entered the clinic room from the door which opened into the street. He greeted Ustadsaab and saw that the guest was no other than the famous film star Khalil Ahmed. Joshua was thrilled to see his favourite matinee idol. Ustadsaab told him that Khalilsaab had come to Ahmedabad to attend a wedding. He explained that Khalilsaab had seen his photograph in the newspaper that morning and wanted to meet him.

Joshua was excited, but kept his cool and asked, 'Chacha did you want to meet me or Abba? Did Maa hear properly? Have you really come to meet me? he asked hesitantly.

Ustadsaab smiled at him. 'Yes, of course we have come to meet you. It was Khalilsaab's idea. First of all, let me congratulate you. You have done us proud by winning the title of Mr Gujarat. I am sure your father is proud to have a son like you.' Joshua hastily acknowledged his felicitations with a 'Shukriya' and waited, wondering why they had come. Khalilsaab was studying him, and Joshua felt self-conscious.

Khalilsaab spoke. 'I saw your photograph in the newspaper. I wonder if you have thought of becoming a film star?'

Joshua almost said 'Yes' without thinking. Then his eyes fell on the chair on which his father sat when he attended to the sick. The chair reminded him that he could not say anything unless he had taken his father's permission. So, he smiled graciously and said, 'Yes, but I do not know . . .' and his eyes were fixed on the chair. Ustadsaab understood, and asked, 'Perhaps you need to ask Abbajan?'

Khalilsaab shot a glance at Ustadsaab and looking intently at Joshua said, 'My producer is looking for a young man like you to play my younger brother in our next film. You have everything that we are looking for—a good face, a perfect body, smile, hair. If you agree, I could take you to Bombay tomorrow and you could sign the contract right away. It's very good money, you know! I assure you that you could become very successful. You may need some training in acting, which I could give you. And . . . we may have to change your name.'

Joshua was taken aback. He shivered with both fear and pleasure. He did not know how to react.

Khalilsaab waited a little then said, 'Good, I will wait for your answer at Ustadsaab's house tomorrow morning. Don't disappoint me. You have the makings of a great star.' Then he shook hands with Joshua and they left.

Joshua stood dumbfounded. He even forgot the normal courtesy of accompanying them to the door. His first instinct was to rush to the kitchen and tell his mother, then he thought better of it—she might not approve—and hurried to the Samson gym. He needed to celebrate this happening with his friends. Striking a pose like Khalilsaab he asked, 'Do you think I could become a film star?'

Samson junior was surprised at this sudden change of mood. 'How come you got this bright idea, Mr Gujarat? I thought we were practising for Mr India? Of course we always thought you had star quality. You could be a great hero of the Hindi cinema. The girls will love you. But . . .' Samson junior drummed his fingers on the table, 'How will you get into films? Will you go from studio to studio with your photographs?'

Joshua sat on the edge of the table and lighting a cigarette like a film star, said, 'Well, my dear friend, the mountain has come to Mohammad. You know who came to see me? Khalilsaab himself.' His friends were impressed. Joshua continued, 'He saw my photograph in the papers and there he was sitting in the clinic room with Ustad Lalliwallahsaab! At first I thought I was seeing visions. How could Khalil Ahmed be there. Only last week we had seen him at the cinema. He was terrific. In real life, he is even better looking than on the screen. And he has a great voice. Well, this man whom I have always idealized, wants to cast me as his younger brother in his next film. I want to accept his offer and leave with him for Bombay tomorrow night.' Then he jumped onto the table and said, 'I want to become the greatest star of India.'

His mentor, Samson senior, started laughing. Putting his arm around Joshua's shoulders he told him to come back to earth. He said, 'I am not at all worried about your acting skills. You are terrific—a natural actor. But, if I were you, I would be shit-scared about my father—if he happened to be David Joseph. You know his ideas about education. For him, education comes above everything. I do not know how he is going to react to your wanting to act in films. You may have forgotten that you are supposed to take his permission. Or will you run away to Bombay with Khalilsaab?' They were no longer smiling, and Joshua's face had lost all its colour. How was he going to speak to his father? Then his face lit up. 'Maa will convince him.'

Saying this he went back to the house. His mother was waiting for him at the door. She wanted to know why Lalliwallahsaab had come to meet him, and who the man in the white suit was. Over lunch he convinced his mother that Khalilsaab's visit was a godsend, as acting was his real calling. She would have to convince David.

Shebabeth was in a dilemma. Her life normally ran in a straight line, but with Joshua it always twisted and turned like a serpent. All the children were obedient and listened to their father, studied hard, joined the services or worked in their clinics. They were all interested in music and theatre, but it was just a form of entertainment. Nobody ever dreamt of making it a profession. Joshua convinced her that because he could not do the regular things, he should be allowed to join films. He manipulated her because she believed that he was made for great things. Shebabeth kissed Joshua's forehead and promised that she would speak to David that night. It took her the entire afternoon to work out what she would say to him.

44

WHEN DAVID RETURNED, Shebabeth was waiting for him at the door, smiling. He smiled back, but from experience he knew that she wanted to speak to him about a delicate matter. He tried to guess what it was, but nothing special had happened during the day. Except that Menachem was playing the harmonium very well and could do a decent rendition of various ragas. He had been pleased when Joshua had joined him. It was good to hear the brothers singing together. He did not know that they practised together. To add to that, Joshua had won the title of Mr Gujarat. That month the house had been unusually peaceful. As he unharnessed the horses and led them into the stable, he asked himself, 'Now what?'

Shebabeth had seen to it that dinner was cooked early. Menachem was going to return late, as he had rehearsals for his college play, and the girls had been sent to a neighbour's house where there was a wedding. They had been invited to see the saris and jewellery. Only Joshua was at home, upstairs, waiting for his father's verdict.

After David had washed and changed into his pyjamas, he sat down at the dining table with a brandy. He smiled at Shebabeth and said, 'Bolo.' She liked the way he smiled. The wrinkles around his eyes suited him. David noticed that

Shebabeth looked beautiful. Even after so many years together, she blushed whenever their eyes met. But he was a little weary of her, as he saw that she had her warpaint on. She was wearing a fresh green nine-yard sari with a maroon border and a bright red blouse. It had a low neckline and her mangalsutra of black and gold beads was nestling between her breasts. When she saw his eyes resting on the hexagonal beads of her mangalsutra, she shyly covered herself and giggled girlishly. His eyes moved to her nosering, silver armlets, the green glass bangles, and the heart-shaped wedding ring incised with his initials.

David took Shebabeth's hand in his and played with her katha-stained fingers. He liked the fragrance of her palms—a mixture of paan and the ittar of roses. David felt a great sense of contentment stealing over him. He knew that whatever it was, they would solve it together. He was willing to agree to every demand she made that night. After all they had grown up together.

The moment he heard her words, his sense of contentment fled. The words 'Khalil Ahmed' and 'film star' destroyed all feeling of peace. Trembling with anger, David rasped, 'No son of mine is going to be a nachnewallah.' Shebabeth's heart sank as David reached for his horsewhip.

Not aware of what was happening downstairs, Joshua stood in front of the full-length mirror and combed his hair. He was wearing a red striped shirt, white trousers and brown shoes. He had decided that as soon as his father gave him permission, he would cycle down to Lalliwallahsaab's house and tell Khalil Ahmed that he had accepted his offer. They would leave for Bombay that night. He looked into his cupboard and saw that his clothes were washed and ironed. All he had to do was pack and leave.

He looked again into the mirror and saw that there was something missing in his dress. So, he took a black silk scarf and wound it round his neck. Satisfied with his appearance, he was toying with the idea of changing his name from Joshua to Ravi Kumar or something similar when he heard his father's roar: 'J-O-S-H-U-A.'

Joshua ran for his life. He escaped from a window to the roof of the stables and from there to the neighbour's terrace, from where he jumped into the Samson gym. Even before Samson senior could finish his sentence, 'Trying to save your skin . . .' Joshua had rushed out of the door and was running towards Delhi Chakla. He wanted to take the route from Jordan Road to Rupa Pari and on to Dariapur Darwaza and Kalupur. He would thus avoid turning towards Prem Darwaza, which was in line with Dariapur Darwaza, as he knew that his father would be waiting for him there.

He did not know that his father would outsmart him.

When he reached Delhi Chakla, his father was standing at the crossroads, whip in hand. The traffic had slowed down around him. Joshua quickly turned towards Delhi Darwaza.

Father and son made three circles between Delhi Darwaza and Dariapur Darwaza. The chase attracted attention and a crowd collected to see the otherwise dignified Daviddadadaktarsaab chasing his wayward son.

Feeling helpless in this situation, Shebabeth went back to the kitchen to finish the little tasks she had left unattended. She was not worried. She was smiling. Joshua was like a cheetah. However hard he tried, David would never be able to lay his hands on him.

When she laid the table for dinner that night, she did not lay a place for Joshua. She knew that he would not return home for a week. He would be either at Adi's, Hosang's or at

Madhubhai's house.

David could not find Joshua. Whip in hand, he turned towards the house and saw that someone had sawn off the huge banyan tree which stood next to the stables. He was shocked to see a stump in place of the tree. It stood like a symbol of all his failures. Great sorrow and anger filled his chest, and he whipped the stump till he was exhausted. Then he stood there shouting and screaming and asking no one in particular, 'Who had the guts to cut down this tree without my permission?'

A crowd collected around David. They stood around him as if they had come to attend the tree's funeral. They felt helpless in the face of his fury.

Menachem returned home from his rehearsal and saw his father standing in the dark next to the tree stump. David was in his pyjamas, dishevelled and distraught. As Menachem climbed down from his cycle he heard someone whisper, 'Perhaps Daktardada has lost his mind.' Gently Menachem took the whip from his father's hand and led him into the house.

That night, Joshua did not stay with any of his friends, as he knew that his father would eventually track him down. Exhausted and anguished, he stopped by Adi's house to borrow his rifle. When Adi saw his condition, he did not want to lend it to him. He was afraid that Joshua would kill himself. Joshua snatched the rifle from the cupboard and disappeared into the night. Adi could not stop him. Dreading the worst, he cycled down to Madhubhai's house, and together they looked for Joshua. They were sure that they would find him at his favourite spot—at the Narayan Ghat side of the Sabarmati river. In the lantern's light, they saw his familiar silhouette standing at the water's edge, still and calm. His eyes were bloodshot and the black scarf was tied around his forehead like a bandit's. He had just shot his first animal—a hyena.

45

AFTER A FEW days Joshua returned to the Delhi Darwaza house as though nothing had happened. When he entered, he saw David and Shebabeth sitting in the courtyard—their favourite place. Shebabeth was peeling apples and David was reading the newspaper, his round Gandhi-style spectacles balanced on his nose.

When they saw Joshua at the door, his mother's face flushed a deep crimson, and his father looked up over his glasses and said, 'Why don't you do something with dogs, instead of the cinema?' Joshua did not answer.

Joshua continued working out his problems in the Samson gym. He would then cycle to Narayan Ghat and wonder why he could not find a direction in life. After his first kill, Joshua suffered from guilt. He had killed the harmless hyena for no reason. It was standing on the banks of the river and had just looked up after a drink. But to Joshua, the hyena seemed to be looking at him scornfully with its bright bead-like eyes and funny ears. He was also feeling guilty because he had broken the law—obey thy father. He had promised David that he would not kill birds or animals. But he had. On that particular night, if he wanted to live—he had to kill.

His father's advice kept drumming in his mind, but he did not know how to make a profession out of dogs.

But he could do something with guns. He was fascinated by firearms. He had bought many books and catalogues on guns from the Friday market and spent hours reading them. He joined the Gujarat Rifle Association and became an expert marksman. In a year his photograph again appeared in the Gujarati newspapers. He had won the gold medal in the target shooting competition.

Joshua was desperate to own a rifle. He often tried his shooting skills by killing pigeons with Adi's rifle. This did not satisfy him. His hands itched to hold a real rifle and kill a tiger or a lion.

Whenever he felt frustrated, Joshua confided in Menachem, who spent hours on the harmonium, mastering various ragas. He had taken permission from David to act in the annual college play. He was to play a poet, and was chosen because of his voice and good looks. He was excited and spent hours memorizing his lines. But David had taken a promise from him that he would not join films, nor become a professional actor. He was aware that local theatre groups had approached Menachem, and he was afraid of another incident like Joshua's. Menachem had assured his father that he would become a doctor and that music and theatre were hobbies, not a profession. He was happy with his medical studies, as long as his father did not stop him from going to late-night concerts, plays or poetry recitals.

Besides that, he had other preoccupations. He was already dreaming about his beautiful cousin Hannah. They were to be engaged in a year. Hannah lived with her family in Bombay. David was satisfied. All his children were doing well—except one, Joshua.

Joshua often sang with Menachem on the harmonium. He told him that he needed a rifle—desperately. Menachem looked at him quizzically and said he did not know how he could help him. Funds were meagre. Both brothers received a small allowance from their mother which was just enough for cycle repairs, cigarettes, an occasional bottle of rum, a snack, or a ticket to the theatre or cinema. There was no money to buy guns and rifles.

After several discussions, the brothers decided to sell all the trophies and cups that Joshua had won. Joshua had a large collection of medals from the Gujarat Body Building Association, Gujarat Rifle Club and the All India Kennel Club. Menachem promised that if he received the prize of best actor, he would contribute it for the purchase of the rifle. It was a deal to be kept secret from their father. And when Adi came to know about the plan, he offered to sell his old rifle to Joshua at a reasonable price.

Those were happy days for Joshua and his friends. Madhubhai had joined his father's business and was given a convertible Ford. The four friends went on long drives around Ahmedabad and killed ducks, partridges, hare and spotted deer, roasting them on an open fire. Menachem never joined them. Whenever Joshua was late, he kept the door on the clinic side ajar and waited for him. The next day, when Shebabeth saw that Joshua's plate of food was untouched, she knew that he had been out on a shoot.

Gradually Joshua built up a reputation of being a superb shot. The brothers sold their medals and pooled in to buy Adi's rifle. Joshua became an authority on arms and their maintenance. He bought all sorts of tools to repair guns. It was still a closely guarded secret from their father and the rifle was hidden in the coal room behind the kitchen.

David came to know about it when a langur jumped into the courtyard and tried to snatch a plate of biscuits from Shebabeth. The big male bared its teeth at her. When he heard his mother's screams, Joshua automatically rushed to the coal room, brought out the rifle and aimed it at the langur. Before he could press the trigger, he saw a stone thrown at it. It jumped back on the roof and disappeared. Joshua lowered his rifle. His father was standing at the top of the stairs with a stone in his hand. Joshua's heart stopped beating. David came down the stairs. 'It is not necessary to kill langurs,' he said. 'For situations like these, I always keep stones and sticks. You could use your airgun. But what is this?' he asked, taking the rifle in his hand. 'If you had a rifle, you could have told me. It could come handy sometimes.' There was a smile on his face.

Once the rifle was out of its hiding place, Joshua often sat in the courtyard cleaning it. David saw the look of concentration on Joshua's face and offered him a room above the stables to set up an arms workshop. He knew that Joshua was very serious about arms, and accepted his son's flair for different things. He admired Joshua for having a good hand at repairing and crafting objects. But once in a while David would agonize over the fact that Joshua had not finished school. With a sigh he would confide in Shebabeth, 'Your Joshua will come to nothing.' Shebabeth would give her standard reply—a reply she must have repeated a hundred times. 'Just wait and see. He has a good heart and strong hands. He is made for great things. I know Isabjidada's prophecy will be realized by Joshua. So what if he does not have a school leaving certificate. He may not be good at studies like Jerusha or Menachem, and you feel that he does not have a goal in life. But what he has accomplished without education is much more than the rest. Shesh Nag protects him. He is not ordinary. Isabjidada was a holy man and I believe in him.'

David would scoff, 'Although Abba was a doctor, he was eccentric and a great storyteller. I do not believe in all he used to say. What was that about a snake?'

Shebabeth would flush angrily and say with tears in her eyes, 'Please do not speak like that. It upsets me. Do you have to be rational about everything? There are some things which defy explanation.' To appease her, David would say with a laugh, 'Okay, I will not doubt your Isabjidada and his visions. I promise I will not say a word about your useless son again.'

Slowly, the workshop above the stables—JOSHUA'S RIFLES—became popular. From his armchair, David would often see cars with insignias and fancy carriages at the door. The young man had earned a good reputation with his expertise. David was particularly impressed when British army officers, rajas and nawabs came to him with their guns. Menachem was proud of his little brother and helped him make a price list. He insisted that Joshua also learn the art of making money.

Joshua gave his month's earnings to his mother. Shebabeth showed the money to her husband with a didn't-I-tell-you look. But David would wonder where all this was going to lead Joshua. He would have preferred Joshua to have a salaried job. Menachem, however, was sure that Joshua would do well. His good looks, expertise and humour made him popular with his clients.

These friendships eventually took Joshua to the forests of Gujarat. Here, Joshua came into his own. His love for nature was similar to Isabjidada's. He felt free and totally at home under the sky. He identified with all that was wild and savage. The forest was his new home and he came to terms with the fact that he was a creature of nature. That was his real nature. For the first time in years he felt liberated—he felt light as a feather and powerful as a leopard.

46

JOSHUA WAS A formidable shikari. It was also his profession. He was an expert at organizing a beat, the exact height to place the machan, the shoot, skinning and the cutting of the claws. He had a natural gift for such matters. And he had gathered a wealth of information from books, magazines and manuals. He preferred illustrated books and learnt quickly by looking at drawings or photographs. His rosewood roll-top desk at the stable karkhana was stacked with letters from well-known royal families of Gujarat.

The letters with gold and silver embossed insignias were invitations for shikar. Joshua chose his clients carefully. He did not like ruthless killers or ugly scenes. He chose those who took to shikar as a sport. Joshua was paid handsomely. His rich friends' cars ran regularly between Delhi Darwaza and their mansions and palaces. He was given special rooms and attendants who looked after all his needs when he visited them. With this, there were sumptuous banquets with the best liquor, followed by ghazals and other entertainment.

To enhance his image of being a top shot, he had a special hunting dress made by the master tailors, Parmar Brothers. They had a shop on the second floor of an old house in the cloth market at Ratan Pol. Joshua chose khaki to show off his star status. It gave him a special image. He looked like a brigadier. Across his massive chest he slung his bullet strap, and wore a back-strap for his rifle and a broad leather belt with his revolver and knife. His hunting boots were specially made by the Chinese shoemaker at Relief Road. His hair was well cut, combed with an upward sweep, and kept in place with a good pomade. His moustache was shaped regularly by the family barber Suliemanbhai. Nobody except Suliemanbhai dared touch his hair. No one ever saw him with a tousled head. For special effect he rubbed jasmine ittar on his hands. In his own way, he was a dandy.

Joshua revelled in the royal treatment he received. The

nights at the palaces were long, beautiful and heady. Joshua enjoyed lounging on silk cushions under enormous chandeliers, paintings and marble sculptures. Listening to a raga or shairi with a glass of rum and platters of kebabs, Joshua felt like a king.

Since Albert had died, his mother Shebabeth had stood by him. But when it came to hunting, she told him that she disapproved of the fact that he had made a profession from killing innocent animals. Shebabeth was depressed that Isabji's prophecy seemed to be proving wrong. Yet she maintained her silence, because he gave her a part of his earnings. Besides that, she could now keep up pretences. When people asked her about Joshua, she could tell them, 'My Joshua works as an adviser to the kings and queens of Gujarat!' Instead of making an issue of Joshua's lifestyle, she made it sound like a family joke. Menachem had been responsible for this. He had convinced her that through hunting Joshua was getting over his childhood fears.

When Menachem saw that Joshua was more comfortable with himself, he helped him take up a correspondence course in taxidermy and veterinary sciences. It was a course offered by the British Veterinary Association. At first Joshua objected, despite the promise he had made to his father. He said he would never ever study again. He could not apply his mind to boring exam material.

It took Menachem months to get Joshua to fill the application forms which he had ordered for him.

Finally, Menachem threw him a bait. If Joshua finished the course, he could attach the prefix Doctor to his name, like the rest of the men in the family—even if it meant that he would be a doctor of dogs. Joshua was tempted to give it a try.

When the packets of books arrived from London, Joshua was nervous, but Menachem was undeterred. He spent time with his brother reading out some interesting portions, until he saw that Joshua had begun to enjoy his studies.

Joshua worked hard and posted his test papers and assignments to London regularly. When he received the two precious diplomas in taxidermy and veterinary sciences with a certificate to practise, David was relieved. Perhaps Joshua would do something worthwhile.

The Friday after the certificate arrived, Shebabeth invited the Bene Israel community of Ahmedabad for a malida to Eliyahu Hannabi which was followed by a grand dinner. She had made a secret wish for Joshua to Prophet Elijah, and it had been fulfilled. And, that night, when the family returned from the synagogue, David brought out some cognac that he had kept for special occasions. This was the perfect occasion for a drink, and Shebabeth brought out her special set of crystal. David's gesture warmed their hearts. Menachem beamed with pride and Shebabeth was pleased that David was smiling and looked happy.

That night, Menachem gave a special present to Joshua—a name-plate which read: Dr Joshua David (Fellow of the Royal Veterinary College of London) Salatwada, Delhi Gate, Ahmedabad. It had a floral border with a portrait of Ceaser painted in the centre.

But, all his life, even after he became a famous zoo man, Joshua suffered from guilt. As long as his father was alive, he did not know how to convince him that he had done something worthwhile with his life.

47

JOSHUA WAS LIVING like a gypsy. He was always away, hunting or busy with his friends.

When Joshua stayed home, it was to console his distraught mother. After David's sudden death, his younger sister Sophie had died. A cholera epidemic was then raging in Ahmedabad and the frail Sophie was its first victim. Shebabeth was inconsolable. She sat motionless in Abraham's chair, which was now falling apart.

Joshua was afraid that the chair would break and she would hurt herself. Joshua persuaded her to sit somewhere else. She got up angrily and sat down in the armchair in the courtyard. While repairing the chair, he told her his favourite jungle stories, but she sat unresponsive—frozen and silent—next to David's empty chair.

This continued until Joshua came down with high fever and a terrible pain in his throat. His mother's mood changed. She was sure he was going to die. Taking Joshua in her arms she cried, 'Deva O deva, spare my son. Don't take him away, the way you have snatched away Sophie, Albert and their father.'

When Menachem diagnosed that Joshua had a bad case of tonsillitis, she brushed him aside. 'Menachem, you are just a boy. How can you diagnose Joshua's illness? If your father were alive, he would have known what to do.'

Menachem took a second opinion from his professor, but Shebabeth was not satisfied. She was terrified when he said Joshua would have to be operated immediately. When Menachem tried to convince her that the army hospital was well equipped for such an operation, she refused to accept the doctor's verdict. She would not allow anybody to touch Joshua and spent hours putting cologne-soaked napkins on his forehead.

When the fever did not subside, she ordered Menachem to go to Bombay with Joshua. She had heard of a well-known ENT specialist and wanted the best for Joshua. She told

Menachem to send his fiancé Hannah's father a telegram, asking him to make an appointment, which Menachem reluctantly did. He understood her anguish.

Whatever the reason, Menachem was thrilled that he would see Hannah again. He packed his best clothes for Bombay. The wedding had been postponed because of Sophie's death. He was relieved when Joshua winked at him. For a moment he wondered whether his younger brother was really sick or just play acting.

Menachem and Joshua took the night train to Bombay. When they reached Hannah's house in the morning, Joshua's throat had swollen to the size of a frog's and he had high fever. Hannah's father rushed him to the hospital where he was operated for tonsillitis.

Joshua recovered slowly. When he returned to Menachem's father-in-law's house in Mahim Menachem sent a letter to his mother by express mail that Joshua was out of danger.

Hannah, Joshua's sister-in-law-to-be, looked after him. She was soft-spoken and looked beautiful in her pastel silk saris and gold jewellery. He was impressed that she was studying French at school. She would greet him every morning with a 'Bon jour'! Unlike him, she was good at maths and Joshua dreaded her academic excellence.

The more he saw her, the more he liked her. She was making her own khadi sari for the wedding and would sit at her spinning wheel in true Gandhian fashion. Menachem had written to her that they were different from other Bene Israel families, as they had associated with Tilak, Gandhi, Vallabhbhai and others.

After spinning for an hour, she would help her mother with the cooking and cleaning. After lunch, as Joshua dozed, Hannah would sit on the window sill and work on a piece of embroidery with gold and silver threads.

Joshua knew that she was looking forward to the day when she would come to their house as a bride. She asked a thousand and one questions about Menachem: his likes, dislikes, food habits . . . Whenever Joshua asked her if she loved his brother, she would lower her eyes and change the subject asking, 'And you, Brother, are you in love?'

'Not yet,' he would answer with a smile. 'Anyway, no decent girl would like to marry a vagabond like me.'

'You are different from your brother. He is taller than you. But you are both good looking. How do you keep the girls away? Hasn't some princess fallen in love with you?'

'Princesses are always hidden behind purdah. If occasionally I see one without purdah, the palace rules are strict and it is not easy to talk to them. Anyway, I am there on business—not romance! No, I do not think I am the marrying kind.'

'Would you like to marry one of my friends?'

'Well, I could consider it, if they are Bene Israel,' Joshua answered cautiously. Hannah would then bring out her album and show him her photographs with her girl friends.

They enjoyed teasing each other, as Joshua found some fault or the other with each of her friends. Invariably, he would stop at the photograph of a serious looking but beautiful girl standing arm in arm with Hannah. 'Perhaps I will choose this one.'

Hannah would protest, saying, 'No, this one is no good for you. Can't you see her glasses?'

'But, I can see something behind the glasses. I do not know what.'

'What if she has a squint?'

'Doesn't matter. Anyway, tell me what is her name?'

'Naomi.'

'Where does she live?'

'She is my neighbour.'

'Then why haven't we seen her so far?'

'Do you want to see her?'

'Why not?'

'You cannot.'

'Why?'

'You just cannot.'

'I don't understand. If she is your neighbour's daughter and your best friend, why doesn't she come here to meet you? Is she invisible or something like that?'

Hannah burst out laughing. 'No, she lives in a hostel.'

'Why?'

'Because she is studious and hard-working.'

'That can't be the only reason she lives in a hostel. Anyway, let's forget it. A girl like that could never be interested in someone like me.'

'Why not? After all, she is a girl. And all girls dream about their prince charming.'

'I work for princes but that does not make me a prince.'

Hannah smiled mischievously as she said, 'We will see what happens when you meet her.'

'When?'

'Perhaps at my wedding.'

'In that case we have to get you married to Menachem as soon as possible!' he replied.

Throughout his stay, Joshua saw Hannah working on her embroidery, but despite his pleas she never allowed him to see her handiwork, which was wrapped in a blue satin bag. Joshua was sure she was making a portrait of Menachem.

After Joshua was well and was packing to return to Ahmedabad, Hannah asked him if he could take a small gift for his brother. He agreed. 'But I also want to take a gift for him. That is, if you help me.'

Hannah was all smiles. 'It's four o'clock. Your train is at nine and you will have to leave by eight. Come, let's go shopping and I will help you buy something for your brother. I'll just change my sari. We will take a taxi and be back in time.'

But Joshua did not move. 'My dear sister, there are some gifts which cannot be bought in a shop. The gift I have in mind for my brother is standing right in front of me. Why don't you come with me? I will make sure that you are married to Menachem right away. You know that he loves you, as much as you love him. I will tell you a secret. Every night he writes you a letter, but never posts it.'

Hannah blushed. 'Na,' she said. 'I cannot come with you right now.' Then she opened the satin bag and showed him an embroidered frame. 'Take this for your brother,' she said. 'He will understand. You can have a look.'

She had written to Menachem, asking for his portrait. But he had not sent her one. So, she was sending the frame without a photograph, leaving it to him to decide which photograph he wanted to put there. Joshua was deeply moved by the way in which she had expressed her feelings. His eyes were wet as he held her hands and said, 'Sister, I am going to persuade my mother to arrange the wedding as soon as possible. We need you.'

Menachem did not react when he received the gift, but Joshua could see that he was touched. Menachem took a photograph of their father and sister Sophie from their album and pasted it in the empty circle embroidered with zari threads and inscribed 'To Menachem, from Hannah.'

48

NAOMI CAME INTO his life unexpectedly, as Hannah's bridesmaid, 'karavali', as they said in Marathi.

Naomi was standing behind the bride in a simple, pale blue sari with a gold border. Joshua did not realize that she was the same girl whose photograph he had seen in Hannah's album. She was tall and stately and had a smile which lit up her face. For Joshua it was love at first sight. He did not know whether she liked him or not. But their eyes met often, and they exchanged a few words when Hannah introduced Joshua to her girlfriends from Bombay.

When the marriage party returned to Bombay, Joshua asked Hannah, 'Your friend Naomi, is she engaged to be married or something like that?'

'No,' she giggled. 'Are you interested in her? She is a very nice person.'

'No, no, don't go so fast. At least find out whether she likes me or not. For all I know, I may have scared her?'

'Naomi does not get frightened easily.'

'She sounds like a strong woman.'

'Yes, she had to be. Her mother committed suicide and her father sent them to a boarding school. But she is also gentle.'

'That must have been hard on her. Does she have sisters or brothers?'

'She has two younger sisters.'

'What is the father like?'

'Deva re deva . . .'

Joshua's heart sank.

Menachem and Hannah were given a bedroom on the first floor of the Delhi Darwaza house and Joshua slept alone in the clinic room. For company he had a dilruba on which he occasionally practised. Unlocking the drawer of his table, he would spend the night looking at the album of Menachem's wedding photographs. Naomi was in almost all the photographs, standing next to the bride. Joshua would fall asleep, dreaming that Naomi was sleeping next to him.

Hannah discovered his secret when Joshua came home late one night after a difficult hunt. He had forgotten to latch the door from the inside. Standing at the door with a cup of tea for him in the morning, she saw that the otherwise orderly Joshua was sleeping with his dilruba, and had Naomi's photograph on his chest. The room was littered with crumpled balls of paper—perhaps love letters to her friend Naomi. Naomi had already confided to Hannah that she liked Joshua very much.

That night, after dinner, Menachem asked Joshua if he could send a marriage proposal for Hannah's friend. Joshua was embarrassed but nodded his head. Menachem drafted a letter to Naomi's father, Mr Daniel Navgaokar, and posted it to him.

They did not receive a reply. Joshua was anxious and lost weight. Every evening he cornered Hannah and asked if there was news from Naomi's father. She would shake her head and tease him. But the days passed and there was still no reply from Mr Navgaokar. Joshua was certain that he would never reply. At the end of the second month, he wrote to them. When they saw Daniel Navgaokar's name at the back of the envelope, both Joshua and Hannah were excited. And, Shebabeth giggled happily at the prospect of another wedding in the family.

But Menachem did not like the look of the letter. That evening, he locked himself in the clinic room and read the letter. It took him a full hour to return to the dining table in the kitchen. By then Joshua had gulped down four large pegs of rum and washed them down with eight samosas. He was sweating and nervous. Hannah sat without uttering a word. She recognized the look on her husband's face. She was certain that it was a refusal from Mr Navgaokar.

Slumping down in his chair Menachem said, 'Mr Navgaokar has written a rather stiff letter on his office stationery. He will be coming to Ahmedabad to discuss my proposal. His daughter lives in a hostel. He has not spoken to her, but will take a decision after he has met Joshua. He is arriving on 12 June by Saurashtra Mail. I am to receive him at the Kalupur railway station and take him to his office guest-house. He will come to our house for tea at four o'clock. That same evening, he will leave for Baroda in his office car. This, he says, is an official visit, during which he will consider our proposal.'

Shebabeth busied herself in the kitchen. She did not like the tone of Mr Navgaokar's letter. How could anyone think of interviewing her precious Joshua! He was perfect. Mr Navgaokar had no business to 'consider' her son. What with stories about the mysterious suicide of his wife, his gambling, and the innumerable women in his life. Yet, she would swallow Mr Navgaokar's insult because Joshua was in love with Naomi.

When Mr Navgaokar entered the house, Shebabeth was not as warm as she normally was. She kept sitting in Abraham's chair and allowed Mr Navgaokar to honour her with a hathbosi. She looked dignified and distant. She watched the proceedings with a sinking heart and a disapproving expression.

Daniel Navgaokar was dressed in a stylish grey suit and carried a smart walking stick. Normally, the boy's parents went to 'see' girls. In this case the tables had been turned. Joshua shook hands with his future father-in-law and sat opposite him as Hannah served tea and made small talk with him.

Mr Navgaokar was a squat man with probing eyes that were magnified by the spectacles through which he studied Joshua. Daniel did not show much interest in Joshua. But, while sipping his tea and conversing with Menachem and Jerusha, he studied the house and tried to gauge their financial situation. Menachem could see that he was not listening, because halfway through a sentence, he turned to Joshua and asked, 'What do you do for a living, young man?'

'Nothing,' slipped from Joshua's tongue, unsure how to answer his query.

Daniel Navgaokar stood up as though he had received an electric shock. He prepared to leave and shook hands with everybody. When he stood in front of Menachem, the young doctor would not allow him to go without an answer. His hand was caught in Menachem's grip. 'Sir, when will you inform us of your decision?'

'I will write to you,' he said noncommittally. Slipping his hand out of Menachem's, Daniel Navgaokar left for Baroda without a wave or a backward glance.

After another two agonizing months, Menachem received one more letter from Daniel Navgaokar:

My dear Dr Menachem David,

This refers to the proposal you sent for the hand of my daughter Naomi for your brother Joshua. I had the privilege of meeting him at your house. I am sorry to say that he is an impudent young man. He is proud of the fact that he does NOTHING.

As you know, my daughter Naomi is an educated woman. I have no intention of getting her married to your brother. I have made inquiries about him. I am told he is uneducated and not a proper match for my precious daughter. He is a pehelvan and a shikari by profession whereas my daughter is a cultured lady. I refuse to give her in marriage to a man who has no code of conduct. Please excuse me for this harsh opinion about your brother. My best wishes to you, your respected mother, your gentle wife Hannah and the dignified Dr Jerusha David.

Yours sincerely,
Daniel Navgaokar Esq.

Joshua was furious. Hannah tried to stop him from rushing out of the house with his rifle. Menachem held his wife back and said, 'Let him go, he will feel better.'

When Joshua returned after midnight, exhausted and bloodstained, and carrying, unbelievably, a dead crocodile on his shoulders, the whole family was waiting for him.

Seeing him alive and well Shebabeth lit a candle and thanked the lord for the return of her son. Her face was tear-stained. She asked, 'So you are trying to show us how angry you are, by killing this poor harmless creature. You rush in and out with that bandook of yours, as though we do not matter. Take this dead reptile out of the house, this very minute. I will not tolerate such madness.'

Joshua went out again and returned without the crocodile. Menachem poured him a glass of rum. As the warmth of the drink spread in his chest, he broke down, 'Abba . . . I need my father. If he had been here, I would never have been insulted like this. Why did he have to die?' The rifle fell on the floor, and muscle-man Joshua cried.

For the next ten years, Joshua was on the go—organizing shikar expeditions for royal families, treating their dogs and repairing guns. He never spoke about Naomi, and told his mother that he would not consider another Jewish woman, ever again. But sometimes he found it difficult when he was attracted to some princess or zamindar's daughter. Some of them liked to have long conversations with him. Occasionally, he accompanied one of the bolder princesses on hunting expeditions. He was flattered by their attention but never encouraged them.

49

WHEN MR NAVGAOKAR walked out of the door at Delhi Darwaza, Naomi disappeared from Joshua's life. Every time Hannah tried to talk about her, Joshua made it clear that the subject was taboo. Mr Navgaokar had inflicted a deep wound on his pride.

Yet, for ten long years, between hunts and late nights with friends, Naomi sometimes crept into his dreams. The bespectacled girl was gradually transformed in his dreams—her face became that of his favourite Hollywood actress Lillian Gish. He saw all her films at English Cinema. He wrote innumerable letters to Lillian, which he never posted. Into these letters, he poured his agony and longing for Naomi. Lillian had an understanding face, and in her eyes he saw something of Naomi, a delicate feminity combined with strength.

The letters helped Joshua release the tension in him, but did not help him get back Naomi. The Samson brothers advised Joshua to write a fan letter to Lillian Gish. They had seen her address in one of the American men's magazines. With their help Joshua wrote to her that he liked her acting, had seen all her films, and thought that she was the world's most beautiful woman with her delicate and ethereal looks.

Joshua was certain that he would not receive an answer. The entire exercise was as useless as his desire to marry Naomi. But he felt strangely relieved when he dropped the letter into the postbox.

After three months, Joshua received a crisp envelope from Lillian Gish. Joshua's heart beat with excitement as he pulled out a black-and-white photograph of the actress with her autograph scribbled over it. She had posed with her head thrown back, her curls framing her face like a crown. Her naked shoulders rose out of her lowered fur coat, and her painted rosebud lips were half open. She seemed to be looking straight at Joshua.

Joshua framed the photograph and put it on his table. Hannah was amused. 'Brother, I do not think this is the correct place for this photograph.'

Joshua threw a loving look at Lillian and asked, 'So, tell me, which is the correct place for the woman of my dreams?'

Hannah smiled. 'In your album of crazy cards.'

'No, not there. I want her next to me.'

'But somebody else is already there.'

Joshua tensed. 'I don't know what you are talking about. Somebody I know?'

Hannah sighed. 'Yes, somebody we know.'

'No, I don't know her.'

'Of course, you know her.'

'I do not.'

Sensing that Joshua's temper was rising, Hannah changed her strategy. 'You may not know her but I know her because she is my friend.'

'Are you talking about the lady whose father thinks I am a loafer?'

'Yes.'

'Why do you mention her? By now, I am sure she must be married to a decent Bene Israel engineer or a doctor. A highly educated girl like her must have many suitors.'

'No, she is not married.'

'I do not believe you.'

'Believe me, brother. We have been in touch.'

'So, you knew where she was all these years?'

'Yes.'

'Why did you keep it a secret from me?'

'I tried to speak to you about her many times but you felt there was no hope. Believe me, Brother, there is . . .'

'Where is she?'

To ease the atmosphere, Hannah smiled and said, 'Before I tell you anything about her, you must smile and promise to buy me a sari.'

'Ah! The mauve one with the gold border you have been talking about? All right, it's yours. Now tell me, where is she?'

'Naomi is in Hubli. She is an English teacher in a residential school.'

'And what happened to her father? Where is he?'

'He lives in Bombay with someone. Every year when Naomi returns home, she suffers. Each sister has found her own solution. After graduation, Naomi took up a job in Hubli as a warden-cum-teacher; the second sister is in a medical college in Delhi. The third is still studying in an arts college in Poona.'

'This is really a terrible story. Now what does the lady in question want to do with her life?'

'I do not know, but she wrote to me that she has no intention of getting married.'

'But is she interested in me?'

'She is.'

'I still want to marry her if she does not mind my lack of education.'

'That is not the problem. But I cannot answer for her. Why don't you ask her yourself?'

At last Joshua smiled. 'I will, if you give me her address!'

Hannah teased him. 'I will, when you give me my present.'

Joshua kissed her, jumped onto his cycle and rushed to the sari shop. He was back in an hour with the sari packed in a red box with a bandhani design and tied with a gold thread. It looked like a Gujarati wedding sari. Hannah looked at the box and laughed. 'Achha, so we are already preparing for the wedding.'

'Yes, as soon as you give me the address.'

'I will, but before that, I must see whether the colour suits me or not.'

Exasperated, Joshua waited impatiently, smoking cigarette after cigarette, while Hannah disappeared into her room upstairs. She emerged shortly looking beautiful in her new sari. She gave him the address, kissed his forehead and whispered, 'May the Lord bless you, so that Naomi comes to this house soon.'

Slowly and laboriously, Joshua wrote his first letter to Naomi. It was a marriage proposal. Her answer shocked both Hannah and Joshua. They had assumed that Naomi would rush to Ahmedabad and melt into his arms like the lovelorn Miss Gish.

Naomi's letter was apologetic. She said that she had been disillusioned by life. She was not considering marriage for many reasons, such as her mother's tragic death, the treatment by their stepmother and her father's callous behaviour. Besides that, she felt old at thirty. Having lived alone, she was not sure whether she could adjust to a man.

Joshua was again disillusioned. But Hannah said

persuasively, 'Brother, if you really want her as your wife you must immediately leave for Hubli. I know Naomi. She looks strong but is afraid to take decisions, because it means going against her father. This is never easy for a girl—even if she hates her father. If you go there, she will agree to meet you. I know she loves you.'

'Perhaps she does not love me any more.'

'Believe me, I know Naomi. Just go to Hubli. Everything will be all right.'

'Are you sure?'

'I cannot promise, but I will pray for you.'

Joshua went to Hubli, and brought Naomi back to Ahmedabad by Saurashtra Express. Face-to-face for the first time, they felt they had known each other for years. At the end of three days together, after frequent walks on the seashore, Naomi agreed to marry Joshua. She wanted to start a new life with him as soon as possible. That night, they kissed for the first time. The gathering tide of the independence movement and the frequent riots were making Naomi nervous. She confided in Joshua that she had had enough of being alone and lonely. She needed a husband and a home of her own.

50

WHEN JOSHUA AND Naomi decided to get married, sometime in 1942, the year the Quit India movement began, the Dandekar family shifted to the Laxmi Nivas bungalows in Shahibaüg. Financially, those were hard days for the Dandekar clan. Although Aunt Jerusha sent them more than half her salary from the Janana hospital and Joshua helped by giving a part of what he earned from his dogs and shikar, it was Menachem who was the major support of the family with his earnings from the clinic he had inherited from his father. But even then there was not enough to run a house like theirs and still maintain a certain lifestyle. The family had grown. Menachem and Hannah had two sons and two daughters.

Ignoring Shebabeth's protests, Menachem rented out the ancestral house at Delhi Darwaza. It gave him good returns, while he paid next to nothing for the Laxmi Nivas house. He saved the rent he received from the Delhi Darwaza house, and enforced strict curbs on spending.

They had shifted to the ground floor of Laxmi Nivas Number 2. Laxmi Nivas belonged to Jayantibhai Shanabhai Shah and Laxmi Nivas Number 1 was the main bungalow of Jayantibhai's elder brother, Sheth Kasturbhai Shah. Both bungalows were built in an orchard of chikoo and guava trees with a compound wall along which tamarind, peepal, banyan, green almond, gulmohur and asopalav trees were planted. Between the two houses there were three fountains, two big gates with decorative grills and several outhouses, which the brothers rented out. At the back of Laxmi Nivas Number 1, there was a mill and a chawl for the labourers. This belonged to the elder brother. A third gate separated the chawl from Laxmi Nivas. The main entrance opened towards Shahibaug Road, which led to Shah Jehan's palace on the banks of the river Sabarmati.

Jayantibhai had been looking for a tenant from a good family. Menachem was his family doctor, and when he had confided in him, Menachem had grabbed the opportunity. That was exactly what he was looking for. Jayantibhai was a Jain, and knew that the doctor's family ate meat and eggs, but he was not bothered. All he wanted was a good tenant. Jayantibhai liked Menachem and enjoyed discussing horoscopes with him.

It was here that Joshua gradually became independent of the family. He rented one of the outhouses to keep his antiques, guns, trophies, books and dogs. He started his married life in this little house.

Joshua married Naomi according to civil marriage rites in the courts of Pankor Naka. It was one of the first civil marriages in the Bene Israel community of Ahmedabad. Some elders called a meeting of the executive committee of the Magen Abraham Synagogue and even considered whether to bar Joshua from entering the synagogue.

When Joshua was told about the rumours of a possible excommunication he decided to stay away from the community. This cold war between him and the community would continue for years, right until Joshua received the Padmashree in 1975. It was then that he was invited to the synagogue with Naomi. A special blessing was read out for them and Joshua was reconciled with the community from which he had been alienated for so long.

Menachem, Shebabeth, Jerusha, Hannah and Naomi had come to the conclusion that a civil marriage was the only solution. They could not have a synagogue wedding, as they did not have the consent of the bride's father. When Joshua signed the marriage certificate, he was happy, and did not care what the elders at the synagogue thought of him.

The wedding reception was held amidst the lighted fountains of Laxmi Nivas, which was decorated with lanterns and strings of asopalav leaves and marigold flowers. The guests were greeted at the door by Hannah and Jerusha amid strains of Mustafabhai's shehnai. Jerusha surprised everybody by wearing a strawberry pink sari.

The festivities took place without the knowledge of Mr Daniel Navgaokar. He was shocked when he received a letter from the runaway bride. Naomi wrote:

> My dear Papa,
>
> I have married Joshua David, the man you rejected and
> thought unfit for me. I am very happy with him and his
> family. With this letter, I am inviting you to visit us at
> our house in Ahmedabad. I came here of my own free
> will. Nobody has forced me. My in-laws are very fine
> people, and have given me a real family—at last.
>
> Your loving daughter,
> Naomi Joshua David.

51

MENACHEM SHIFTED TO another house across the river when he
had saved enough to lead a comfortable life. He had mixed
feelings about the move. He was unhappy that he had to leave
behind his younger brother in Laxmi Nivas but was happy that
Joshua was now responsible for his own life. Naomi had taken
a job as a teacher in a school and they appeared to be happy
together.

Even though Joshua was a hardened shikari, his profession
bothered him. He often suffered from depression after a shoot.
He disliked the fact that he killed for sport. Shooting herds of
spotted deer and black buck was becoming a harrowing
experience for him. Once the beaters of the royal shikar party
had tracked down an animal, they chased it, cornered it, and
ultimately shot it. The healthy animals whose skins would
make flawless carpets and handsome trophies were picked up
and stacked in the jeeps and the others were left behind to be
devoured by hyenas, jackals and vultures.

The hunt was followed by a feast either at the camp or the palace. While his friends rejoiced, Joshua felt depressed, and could not swallow the roasted venison. He did not want to kill any more. But he felt trapped. He did not know what else he could do. He was now a married man and had to run his house. The moment of introspection would end when he returned to Ahmedabad.

Slowly he was making his kennels in the gardens around his house at Laxmi Nivas. He had big plans. 'This,' he would tell himself, 'is the end of my shikar days.' But his resolution would weaken as soon as he received a letter from one of his clients. Joshua could not resist the glamour and excitement of planning a shoot.

Naomi had taken time to adjust to her new life. Joshua left suddenly, at odd hours. She worried about Joshua's safety when he was on a hunt. When she spoke to him about it, she made it sound as if she missed him when he was away. She amused herself by knitting sweaters for him and stitching clothes on the Singer machine she had brought from Hubli. Or she spent the day with Hannah and her children.

This situation did not last very long. After three years of marriage Naomi became pregnant and their life changed. That was the time Naomi often fainted in Joshua's arms, just like Lillian Gish. Naomi was no more a woman of strength. Joshua found that she was prone to depression and the sight of Joshua's bags of flesh, blood and pelts made her nauseous.

After consulting Jerusha and Menachem, Joshua decided that Naomi should be shifted to the Saraspur Maternity Home. Jerusha had moved as the superintendent there, and Naomi would be in good hands. Besides medical care from Jerusha, she would receive love, care and attention from Shebabeth. In times like these, a woman needed a mother.

In Shebabeth's care, Naomi felt that she was again with her mother, Leah. She had lost her mother at sixteen. Her mother had locked her room from the inside, poured kerosene over her clothes and burnt to death. The three sisters had stood at the door, screaming. By the time the neighbours had broken the door and covered Leah with old quilts, it was too late.

Naomi was afraid of childbirth. She did not want a daughter. After her mother's suicide, she was convinced that it was a curse to be born a woman. Her mother-in-law did not agree with her. Shebabeth had had eleven pregnancies. She had reached a stage when she could laugh about them and recount stories about her deliveries, miscarriages and abortions.

During her months of confinement, Naomi wrote long letters to her sisters, Julliet and Sinora. They wrote to her that their father was still angry with her because of her elopement.

When they were young, the three sisters had been in the same boarding school but after school they had had to live in different hostels. They wrote long letters to each other and however much they disliked Durga, their stepmother, they returned home to spend time together under one roof. Naomi's sisters were happy that Naomi had decided to make a home with Joshua Pehelvan. They had sent her a beautiful sari from the money they had saved from their hostel mess fees and meagre pocket money.

Julliet had decided not to marry. Once she became a gynaecologist, she would stay in the staff quarters of the hospital. She wanted to prevail upon their father to give up the woman who was responsible for their mother's death. Sinora had written to Naomi that she was in love with Noel. She had met him at a wedding at Poona's Lal Deval Synagogue. Sinora decided that she would not repeat the Joshua–Naomi love story and wait for years to get married. She would marry Noel, even if it meant running away with him.

However, when Noel's family sent the official marriage proposal for Sinora, Mr Navgaokar accepted the proposal without demur. Unlike Joshua, he said, he had no problem with Noel. He was the perfect suitor for Sinora. He was well educated and had a good job with the prestigious Burmah Shell company, just like him. Sinora had a regular synagogue wedding.

Naomi was hurt that he had sent a general invitation card to Dr Menachem David and family. The David family sent a telegram: 'Blessings to the married couple for a long and happy married life.'

Naomi received Sinora's wedding photograph when she was resting, her legs atop a pyramid of pillows. Naomi sighed and opened the envelope. She missed her sisters and told Shebabeth that she would have liked to dress her little sister for the wedding. After all, she had taught her how to wear a sari.

In the photograph, Sinora looked beautiful in a white sequinned sari, a veil with a tiara of satin flowers, and a bouquet of flowers in her hands. She was wearing gloves, gold bangles and high-heeled shoes. Sinora had insisted on going through all the rituals of a Jewish wedding, such as the mehendi ceremony in a grass-green sari on the night before the wedding. One of the women must have applied mehendi on her wedding-ring finger and tied a sehra of beads and flowers on her forehead. For the farewell of the bride, Naomi was sure that Sinora had worn a bright blue sari.

Naomi ached for Sinora. When their mother died, Sinora was still little and Naomi had been like a mother to her. She had only one photograph of the three of them with their father. They would have preferred a photograph of just the three of them and dressed without enthusiasm. But they did not protest. If their father had got to know that they did not want him in the photograph, he would have been furious.

Daniel Navgaokar was ready and dressed in his best suit. He paced the veranda impatiently as the photographer waited with his paraphernalia. Julliet had decided to wear a long dress with a straight cut. Sinora had chosen frills, ribbons and beads. Naomi was wearing a sari, with the pallav on the left shoulder, and a blouse with puffed sleeves. Naomi had tied her hair in a tight chignon at the nape of her neck. When she saw her reflection in the mirror, she thought that her mother was staring back at her. Sinora, who was standing behind her, began to cry. Naomi held her in her arms and Sinora whispered, 'You look like our mother, Aai.' Julliet also came closer. Crying and consoling each other, they looked at their mother's photograph in the family album. It had been taken a year before her suicide. Sinora said, 'Look, doesn't Naomi look like Aai?'

'Yes,' said Julliet. 'Remember how we had forced her to go to the New Bombay Photo Studio. At first she had refused, but we had pulled out her blue Parsi sari and forced her to wear it. She looked so beautiful with her head covered with the embroidered border. And we were in our best dresses.'

'And, you know, Aai changed my hairstyle and tied those funny ribbons over my ears.'

'But the best part was at the studio,' said Naomi. 'Remember, Aai was small, so when she sat on that throne-like chair, her feet were dangling. The photographer had almost clicked but stopped and emerged from the black cloth and said that Aai should do something about her feet. She burst out laughing and asked him to find a solution. He immediately placed a satin pillow at her feet. He looked like a slave sitting at Aai's feet. And, as though it was the most natural thing on earth, she placed her foot on the pillow like a queen. I still remember the cushion was purple silk with black knotted tassels. It was only then that we noticed that Aai was wearing her special velvet pump shoes. When we teased her about them, she laughed so much that she had tears in her eyes. But, then the photographer was back under his black cloth and she warned us, "Nako," she said, "no smiling." So we all have this funny half-smile in the photograph.'

They stopped talking when they heard their father tapping at the door with his walking stick. They quickly put the photograph back in the cupboard, and only opened the door when Julliet had covered Naomi's head with her sari. 'Now,' she said, 'you look exactly like Aai. I want to see how Papa reacts. You know he saw that photograph we took with Aai. He wants to take a similar photograph. He will frame it and put it in the drawing room, so that he can show off to the world that he is a good father . . .'

When they marched out of the room, they saw the look of shock on their father's face. He turned white as though he had seen Leah's ghost. He would have liked to cancel the shoot. But the photographer had been waiting for three hours and he knew from his daughters' defiant faces that he could not scold them, nor could he force Naomi to change into something more English and modern. He hated her for being the spitting image of her mother.

52

IN HER ADVANCED state of pregnancy, Naomi felt sick and miserable. The contractions started early. There was a danger that she would have a miscarriage. Joshua could not stay with Naomi. He had to leave for an expedition. Starting a family

was going to be expensive, and he could not afford to cancel
the hunt.

Joshua was relieved that Naomi was with Shebabeth and
Jerusha. His mother made hot soups for her and knitted
woollens for the newborn. She would laugh looking at the
booties and tunics and wonder why she was making them. The
baby was expected in summer.

Joshua was distracted. He could not concentrate on the
shoot. Yet, he shot a panther in the forests around Palanpur.
He gave instructions for its skinning and transport.

It was midnight. The driver was sleepy and was driving
slowly. At a bend in the forest tracks, Joshua saw a hare,
running in circles. Wild hares normally reacted strangely to
light. When returning from a shikar, they often saw hares
running in front of the car because the lights hypnotized the
animals. They only stopped when the jeep took another route
or switched off its headlights. It was not unusual to see them
flattened out on the road like a paper cut-out.

Joshua told the driver to stop the car. He wanted to see
why the hare was behaving in such a strange way. He assumed
that it was being chased by a fox, but he could not see another
animal nearby. The driver focused the headlights on the thicket
around which the hare was running. For some reason, the light
on the thicket reminded Joshua of the thicket from the Bible.

. . . And Abraham stretched forth his hand and took
the knife to slay his son. And the angel of the lord
called unto him out of heaven, and said, Abraham,
Abraham. And he said, here am I. And He said, lay not
thine hand upon the lad, neither do thou anything unto
him: for now I know that thou fearest God, seeing
thou hast not withheld thy son from me. And Abraham

lifted his eyes and looked, and behold behind him was
a ram caught in a thicket by his horns: and Abraham
went and took the ram, and offered him up for a burnt
offering in the stead of his son.

The driver of the car did not know why Joshua had asked him
to stop and asked whether he should get a rifle. Joshua was
annoyed that the shikar party only thought of killing. He
retorted with an angry 'No' and instructing the driver to keep
the headlights on went towards the hare. When he was close,
he saw that the hare was covered with blood. One of the
hunting party had fired at random and torn its stomach. Its
intestines had spilled out, and were caught in the thicket.

The hare was running round and round like an animal
performing in a circus. The tragic merry-go-round had to stop
sometime, but the hare had a strong desire to live—its young
ones were possibly hidden in a nearby burrow. Joshua did not
know what to do. His first instinct was to shoot the hare and
release it from pain. Then he saw that the hare was desperate.
Joshua sat down and caught it with a quick sweep of his
hands. Gently, he removed the blood-stained intestines from
the thorns. The hare was breathing heavily and Joshua's
fingers were covered with its warm blood. He could feel its
heart beating in his palms and there was a look of relief in its
watery eyes. He recognized the look. He had seen it often in
the eyes of sick dogs. If he had had his veterinary box, perhaps
he could have sewn up the hare and saved it. Joshua felt
helpless and sad as it died in the cup of his palms. Joshua
looked around to see if there was a burrow nearby with the
young ones. But it was dark, and he could not see anything.

With the help of the driver, he buried the hare. As he
wiped the blood by rubbing his hands on the earth, Joshua

experienced the sensation of a different kind of strength. He knew that the hands which killed also had the power to heal.

That night at the palace guest house, he dreamt of Naomi entangled in a thicket. He woke up. It was still dark. He had hardly slept for an hour or two. He dressed quickly and called for the driver. He had to return to Ahmedabad.

53

JOSHUA'S BREAK WITH hunting finally came after a difficult panther shoot in the forests of Balaram near Palanpur. The animal was a man-eater who had attacked the villagers and killed an eleven-year-old boy. Before that it had carried away dogs and cattle from the surrounding villages. While skinning it, they discovered that it had broken teeth, and porcupine quills were imbedded in its paws. It had taken very long to locate the panther. During the wait, they had gunned down a herd of spotted deer which was passing by.

Joshua had stayed back to supervise the skinning of the panther, removing the claws and collecting its fat in a bottle. He had then returned to the scene where they had massacred the deer. He instructed the beaters to collect the heads with the best antlers and skins with the least damage. After which he had pointed out the animals who could be picked up for their flesh. He was pointing to one particularly bloated doe when one of the men said, 'She is alive and with fawn.' His hand froze.

The doe was lying on the ground in a pool of blood, her eyes shining like glass. A fully-formed fawn had spilled out of her womb. The fawn's heart was beating. Joshua quickly cut the umbilical cord and held the slippery newborn in his hands.

He asked one of the shikaris to wrap it in a bag and take it to the camp. He wanted it for himself.

The doe was breathing her last. Joshua saw to his horror that hyenas and foxes were waiting for the men to leave. Joshua fired a shot and drove them away. Then he asked the runners to pack the doe in a gunny bag and take her to the camp although he knew that she would soon be dead. He could not leave her behind, for the hyenas would have feasted on her even while she was alive. He felt anger and sorrow, and hated his rifles.

Joshua returned to Ahmedabad with the fawn. He called out to Moyuddin, his assistant, and as soon as he appeared from his room over the kennels, Joshua gave him his rifle, revolver and knife and said, 'Sell them for a good price. My shikar days are over.'

He carefully laid the fawn on the dining table. It tried to stand up. Moyuddin washed it with warm water. Then Joshua turned to Naomi. 'This is a gift for my daughter.'

Joshua was not unaware that he could not have continued with his shikar days. He had realized that every year there were fewer birds and wild animals in the forests. He was gradually becoming a conservationist, protesting against shikar as a sport. The incidents of the rabbit and the doe were like signals to the path that was destined for him.

Besides, with independence, the rajas and nawabs, his main patrons, gave up their privileges. On the day they signed the merger document, swords, arms, ammunition were put away. They were left with memories of their grand hunts.

Joshua did not know what he was going to do with his life. He could not take up a job again, nor could he become an actor or musician. But he was now a householder and needed to do something for a living. As he fell asleep in Naomi's arms, he decided to set up a veterinary clinic. The kennels would be a good base to buy, sell and breed dogs. The licence to work as a vet would come in handy to treat dogs. With Moyuddin he would continue to repair guns, and if somebody needed to skin or stuff an animal or bird, he would work as a taxidermist.

Menachem offered to help him with his knowledge of medicine. They used the same basis for medicines for dogs that Menachem used for people. They were old formulas which had come down to him from his grandfather Isabji. Once they had put together the ingredients for stomach and skin ailments for canines, Naomi spent her afternoons grinding the medicines. Moyuddin packed the mixtures in bottles and labelled them with a logo of Ceaser.

I have no memory of the independence of India. I must have been about two years old, when India rejoiced on 15 August 1947. I was probably taken to see the lights and fireworks although there were rumours of possible riots. These were to become a tragic reality in Ahmedabad, destroying the social fabric of the city. I am sure our family participated in the celebrations as a khadi flag from those days is still buried in my box of quilts.

The Bene Israel Jews of India had suddenly become aware that they were connected to a larger Jewish community in Europe. More so, since they had been reading and listening to world news on the BBC about the gas chambers, concentration camps and the extermination of six million Jews by Hitler. They were horrified and afraid, and wanted to underplay their Jewishness or leave for Yerushlayem—Jerusalem—the promised land of their prophets. Perhaps on the eve of India's independence they may also have been disturbed by Mahatma Gandhi's views. Gandhi had advised that the Jews offer Satyagraha against Hitler and had written, 'The Jews are a compact and homogeneous community in Germany. And they have organized world opinion behind them. I am convinced that if someone with courage and vision can arise amongst them and lead them in non-violent action, the winter of their despair can disappear in the twinkling of an eye, and be turned into the summer of hope. And, what has today become a degrading man-hunt, can be turned into a calm and determined stand offered by unarmed men and women possessing the strength of suffering given to them by Jehovah . . . The German Jews will score a lasting victory over the German gentiles in the sense that they will have converted the latter to an appreciation of human dignity.'

The Bene Israel did not know where they stood and what should be their reaction when Hindu and Muslim riots erupted with the partition of India. There were harrowing tales of savage killings: stories of men taking a child by the feet and tearing its body in two down the middle. One story like this, bred many more. When they fled their homeland and landed in India after the shipwreck, the Bene Israel had followed the dictum: mix with the people where you have found a new home. Keep your religion a secret. Let nobody know who you are.

54

AFTER MY BIRTH Naomi continued to work as a teacher in a primary school. Joshua's kennels and rifle repair workshop were doing well. To help with the guns, he had employed Moyuddin from the Palanpur palace. Moyuddin had a natural flair for arms of all kinds. He never spoke about it, but Joshua knew that he made bombs and arms for freedom fighters.

There was none to match Joshua in the understanding and repair of guns or taxidermy. People liked him. He was friendly, had a nice smile and a good sense of humour. He had a solution for almost everything and a warm house, where there was food and drink for everybody. He had a small group of friends with whom he spent his evenings, drinking rum and reciting Urdu couplets. Sitting on my father's knee, some of the romance of his life touched mine—unknowingly and unknown to him.

My father was stuffing a dead bird at our house in Shahibaug. With Babu, he had made the form of a bird in plaster and was tying strings around it, to give it a body. On this, he would stitch the feathers and fix the glass eyes. After he had given the finishing touches, it would look like a real bird. He said to his mother, 'I am trying to become a doctor of animals. Not like the ones we always had in our family.'

Shebabeth laughed. 'How can you become a doctor of animals without going to school or college? I have really spoilt you. You are never serious. Look at Naomi, how responsible she is! She works hard so that you can be as eccentric as you want. I think she also spoils you.'

A shadow passed over my father's face and he changed the subject and asked, 'Maa, kya piyegi? Bada peg ya chota? Whisky with soda? Ya phir straight?'

She said, 'Kuch nahin. It's too early for whisky. Tell Moyuddin to make tea.' Then looking at the dead sarus crane on the floor she said, 'Have you become a hunter again?'

My father shook his head. 'This is Uncle Shaul's Sarus, Stella. You remember the last time he invited us for shabath, we had to wait a full twenty minutes before he could lock up Stella and open the door.'

Shebabeth nodded. 'Yes, I remember he had a sarus as a

pet. Deva re deva, has he killed his pet bird? Don't tell me he is so heartless.'

Babu, who was making the armature in metal, started laughing. My father rubbed his hands and said, 'Start preparing the masala, we are going to eat Stella.'

Uncle Shaul often went to shoot ducks, in a lake not far from Ahmedabad. Late one evening, he had seen a shadow in the bulrushes and assuming it was a large duck, had shot it. Much to his amazement, he saw two big grey birds fly out of the grass. One soon fell down, the other flew over his head. It appeared to be very agitated. When Uncle Shaul parted the grass, he saw that he had shot a sarus crane by mistake. Its mate was alive, but injured.

The bird's anguish touched a chord in Uncle's heart. He knew that sarus cranes mated for life. He buried the dead bird and with Rodriques, his Goan cook, managed to capture the injured bird and brought it to his house in the jeep. With my father's help, he nursed the other bird till it was fit to fly. My father advised Uncle Shaul that he should release the bird back into the wild. But Uncle Shaul kept the bird in the house as a pet.

Uncle Shaul lived alone with Rodriques in a big house with a high wall, in a little lane in Mirzapur, not far from the Delhi Darwaza house. He was related to us, but I did not know how. I had once heard my father tell my mother that Uncle Shaul was nursing a broken heart. In his cluttered drawing room there was a painting of an Englishwoman, Stella. It was said that he had been in love with her. He had remained a bachelor because of Stella.

Stella's portrait in pale blues and pinks was in a golden frame. In the painting, she was sitting under a tree with a Persian cat on her lap. There was a feather in her hat, and pink ribbons flowing down her back. The feather had perhaps been taken from an egret or a heron she had shot with Uncle Shaul.

Stella was the wife of Uncle Shaul's boss. They said Stella was fond of hunting birds and Uncle had been instructed by his superior to accompany her. In memory of those days, he always wore a khaki shirt, breeches, gumboots and a solar topee.

Perhaps there was something between them. Perhaps not. But, for Shaul, after he had gone for ten shoots with Stella, no Bene Israel girl was good enough. After Stella returned to England, Shaul's only passions were shikar, guns, and his garage where he repaired cars.

The sarus was named after Stella. But soon Uncle Shaul realized that a bird is not a dog and cannot be house-trained. The floor of his house was covered with droppings—it was like an abstract painting in whites, greys and yellows.

Stella loved Uncle Shaul to distraction, and was also very protective about the house. Except Rodriques nobody could enter the house without permission. Stella would stand on his dancing legs and attack intruders. A visit to the house meant banging on the door and calling out to Uncle Shaul at the top of our voices till he heard us over the din of his gaggle of geese and turkeys. It took him a long time to herd the birds into their coops and lock Stella in the garage.

Stella had convinced Uncle that he was an incarnation of Stella. Every morning as Uncle Shaul sat on the veranda with his cup of tea, Stella twisted his neck and amused him with his ballerina-like mating dance—he flapped his wings, leapt in the air and moved rhythmically around him. He ended his dance by rubbing his body against Uncle Shaul. Not receiving the expected response, Stella sulked and preened his feathers all day.

A month before he died, Stella tried to seduce Uncle by trying to feed him a piece of bread. During that amorous moment, Stella's beak had come so close to Uncle's eyes that he was convinced the bird was going to peck them out of their sockets. He was sure that it was an attack, and misunderstanding the affection of the bird, had pushed Stella back. After this incident, whenever Stella came near him, Uncle thought that Stella was attacking him. He had come to dread Stella's sharp beak. It was then that Uncle Shaul decided to give Stella to the zoo. He thought Stella was the perfect gift for my father. Joshua tried to persuade Uncle Shaul to accept the bird's offerings of food. But he shrugged his shoulders and said, 'Son, I am not like you. I cannot cope with Stella's advances. You have a way with birds and animals. Keep him in the zoo.' That is how Stella came to the zoo.

Joshua gave the bird an open enclosure with other storks and cranes. But Stella was unhappy and homesick. My father told Grandmother Shebabeth, 'It was amazing to see a bird pining for a man!' Uncle Shaul also missed Stella, but he refused to go to the zoo and see the bird. He did not want to break down in a public place. Though he accepted that Stella was his spiritual soulmate, he would not take the bird back, saying he could not live with a bird who had forgotten to live like one.

Stella refused to eat at the zoo. He lay down with his long neck stretched flat on the ground like a dying snake and kept staring at the door, waiting for Uncle Shaul. Babu kept him alive by force-feeding him with morsels of ground gram and papaya.

Joshua was sure that Stella was dying and told Babu to take the bird to Uncle Shaul's house in a rickshaw. Back in the house, Stella kept watching Uncle Shaul—eyes liquid, neck hanging and legs dangling on the floor. That evening, Stella died in Uncle Shaul's arms.

My father suggested that the bird be buried in a bag of salt, but Uncle Shaul held on to Stella as though he had lost a child. Gently Joshua took away the limp body of the bird from him, and gave it to Babu. He then took Uncle Shaul to his room and helped him into bed.

Later that evening, Joshua came to the house at Delhi Darwaza. He, too, looked shaken. 'When Stella died in this dramatic manner, I tried to calm Uncle Shaul,' Joshua told us. 'But he seemed to be in a delirium. I touched his forehead and took his temperature. He was running a high fever, and looked so ill that I thought it advisable to send for Dr Naginbhai Shah. He gave him a tranquillizer.

'Uncle Shaul slept for three hours. I sat next to him reading. When he woke up, he was sweating, and appeared to be better. So I asked Rodriques to make a soup for him. After he had had the soup, he asked Rodriques to close the door and leave us alone. Sitting in bed, he spoke to me as though I was Stella, his lady love. I realized that he had lost his mind. But I allowed him to speak. He said, "Stella, why did you have to kill your cats? When you were leaving, I had told you that I would look after them. They would have been like my children. But you did not trust anybody. Not even me, although you knew how much I loved you. You knew I was devoted to you.

' "Remember the time when you were on the point of leaving, and had baked a cake specially for me. Your husband, Mr Pauline, was out of station. Nobody had ever made a cake for me. I was embarrassed. It was unheard of that an officer's wife should do something like this for a subordinate—a servant of her husband.

' "I do not know how you could stand Mr Pauline. You

are young and beautiful. He was much too old for you. He had the biggest ears of anyone I knew. Whenever I saw you together, he looked like a fat pelican and next to him, you floated like a swan in your beautiful dresses.

' "I felt very awkward that I had accepted your invitation to tea. But you quickly put me at ease—talking, laughing and teasing me. You were always like that on those numerous shoots in your jeep. But it was quite another matter to meet you in your drawing room. You were so prim and proper in your long straight skirt and crisp blouse. The lace curtains were drawn and gave a soft glow to your face. In the half light, I saw that you had expensive Chinese vases and Persian rugs. On the tea table there were paper-thin cheese sandwiches, warm muffins, a cake in an oval platter, a silver teapot and two cups. One for you and one for me.

' "I sat upright on the edge of my chair till you asked me to relax, and offered me some cake and muffins. Then, with a cup of tea, you reclined on the sofa. It was then that I saw your cats. The house was full of cats—of all sizes and shapes. And your hand moved sensuously in the fur of a big blue Persian cat which had curled up near you. For a moment I wished I was your cat.

' "You loved your cats. You told me how you spent your mornings cleaning them, and that they always had the best of tinned English cat food. When you told me that you wanted to kill them, I choked on the cake and almost fell off the chair. 'Next month I am leaving for London,' you said. 'I cannot possibly fly back with fifteen cats. Besides that, Mr Pauline does not want so many cats in a small apartment. He has asked me to get rid of them.' You did not want to give your cats to anybody. They were adorable but spoilt. Not wanting them dead, I hesitatingly offered to look after them. You looked sad,

as you sat thinking about their future. I assured you that I
would take care of them.

' "Suddenly you were on your knees and holding my
hands, asked me if I would also look after you like the cats?
Deeply shocked I sat frozen in my chair. I wanted to say 'Yes'
and take you in my arms, but I did not. I could feel your soft,
warm palms on my cold hands but I could not open my arms
and take you in them. I regret that moment more than
anything else in my life. You were the love of my life but I was
afraid that the family would not accept a runaway English
bride. A married one at that.

' "My beautiful Stella, you were there at my feet. And,
what did I do? Sit as though I was glued to the chair. The
family and my community were like ropes tied around me. I
could not move. When you saw my expressionless face, you
were very angry. You stood up straight and slim and said,
'Shaul, you are a coward. Perhaps you want to leave now. But
come back tomorrow. I have something important for you. I
need your help.' Feeling like a rat, I bowed and left. I heard the
door bang behind me.

' "The next day, when I returned, you were sitting on the
sofa with the corpses of fifteen cats at your feet. It was a
macabre scene. You had put them to sleep with the help of Dr
Shastri, the camp vet. And I was expected to help you put them
in bags of salt and bury them under your rose bushes. At least
you trusted me to do that. You did not want anybody to know
that you had killed your cats. I did exactly as I was told.
Somehow I always thought of myself as your servant, not your
lover. Though in my dreams we were lovers, yet when I was
with you, I felt very brown, low and Jewish.

' "Then you asked if I wanted to wash my hands. You led
me to your fragrant bathroom. I washed my hands, wiped
them and put away the towel. Then I stood at attention for

more instructions. You walked up to me, planted a kiss on my lips and said, 'Shaul, we could have had a lovely life together with the cats. Anyway, goodbye.' Instead of being a man and taking you in my arms, I stood transfixed. It was obvious that you would have left Mr Pauline for me. And, what did I have to worry about? I did not have any direct family, except the Delhi Darwaza cousins. But I was afraid the Jewish community of Ahmedabad would boycott me.

' "Only later did I reproach myself. If Stella was willing to antagonize her people, why was I such a coward. Eventually they would have accepted us. We were fond of the same things and could have had a happy life together.

' "When I did not respond, you turned away, and without a word led me out of the house. I will never understand why I did not have the courage to say, 'Stella I love you.' " '

Joshua paused and poured himself another drink. He said, 'It was obvious that Uncle Shaul was delirious and was seeing Stella in me. With the death of the bird, he had lost his mind.'

When my father finished telling us the story of Uncle Shaul, I slipped off his knees. I was terrified of this python called family and community that could constrict a human being's heart.

That year uncle Shaul died. Whenever I look at Stella in the diorama of stuffed birds at the natural history museum named after my father, I shiver. Head held high, feathers ruffled, and bald in patches on his crumbling armature, Stella still stands there—the legs seeming to move in a dance of sorts, beak wide open, proclaiming his love for Shaul.

55

THE WALLS OF the house were covered with paintings, antiques and trophies from my father's shikar days. A huge stuffed lion filled our house with his presence. I used the space between his legs as my special route to the bathroom. But before that, I had to push aside the great dane, Bruno, who had decided that the lion's plaster pedestal was his bedroom. Bruno slept there all afternoon. In the evenings, he stretched his legs, stood on the veranda and like a prince, surveyed his kingdom. He behaved as though he was very ferocious—neck stretched out, waist pulled in under his chest wall, ramrod straight on his long sportsman legs, muscular front jaw jutting out under his small erect ears and large eyes. His pink butterfly nose was the most delicate part of his body. Except for Joshua, he did not care for anybody and suffered silently as Joshua tweaked his nose.

Bruno watched with a superior air as the other dogs nuzzled, howled, barked and mated. Often the kennels and corners of the house became maternity wards. My father and Moyuddin spent a large part of their time delivering pups and playing peacemakers to the innumerable dog fights.

Faiju had then just joined us and was being trained to look after the dogs. He cooked for them, fed them, washed their kennels, brushed them, cleaned their eyes and ears—in return for their thank you licks.

Our island of dogs had an all-pervading smell of food—of overflowing milk, and mincemeat boiling in huge cauldrons. The aromas mixed with the smell of placenta, blood and the special doggy-body smells. These merged with the ayurvedic canine medicines which Moyuddin made in the garden.

On certain days in winter, Naomi felt crowded in by the dogs. Their fur gave her an allergy, and she did not want any of them to come near her. Moyuddin and Faiju had a hard time keeping the dogs away from her. The cocker spaniels, gun dogs as they were called, had a free run of the house. Barking at imaginary noises, their hunting skills came to the fore in the games they played with the squirrels, who had learnt to dodge them. They were black, white, red or tan, with long curly-haired ears and the most endearing doleful eyes. The long-nosed, moody daschunds kept smelling every nook and corner for cockroaches and mice.

Our straight-limbed sheep dogs, sable, white or tricoloured, had alert ears and china-blue eyes, just like Elizabeth Taylor, the girl we saw in the *Lassie Come Home* films. Lassie films made me cry and I dreaded the day I would lose my own Lassie. She was always at the door, barking at the vendors who stopped there just to tease her. The fashionable dalmatians in black polka dots joined Lassie at the door. How could any kennel be without them? Matching them in terms of fashion, were the black poodles from Roopnagar. They were trimmed and brushed according to the Parisian fashion scene. Though of uncertain temper, they were the pride of Naomi Kennels.

Then there were the lion dogs of China—the Pekinese. They came in all colours—black, bridle, red, fawn and white, with a wealth of heavy coating and large owl eyes and snub noses. They liked to sleep under the couches, divans and chairs. They attacked outsiders, when we least expected them to. To add to this, they hated the pomeranians—orange-coloured, fox-headed, standing on their slim ballerina legs. They fought with them over the right to cushions, pillows and laps. Cushions were the cause of many a dogfight.

But it was the chihuahuas that had a special place in Joshua's heart. They brought to the fore all his protective instincts. He kept them in a special kennel away from the other dogs. When my father was at home, all the dogs were tied up or locked up in their kennels. Then, the tulip-eared, saucy-eyed chihuahuas were brought to the dining-table. Here, they were groomed and given the privilege of sitting in a milk jug. They were very light and as delicate as the chinaware in which they were allowed to play. My father's favourite pastime was taking photographs of the chihuahuas playing in saucers, milk jugs and tea cups.

I was happy in my island of dogs. Those were days of smiles and tears, because there was never a constant number of dogs. Their numbers kept changing as my father sold them to his clients. I dreaded getting attached to any dog. I could not get used to the fact that dogs were my father's business. 'They are here to make ends meet,' explained my mother.

When the zoo began to take up all my father's time, he decided to wind up the kennels. He found homes for all the dogs, except a few like the chihuahuas, Lassie, the pekes and poms. Without the security of my island of dogs, I sat on the steps of the veranda and cried. Gangaram, our parrot, swinging and watching me from his cage above my head, started chattering loudly to distract me. In his own way he was trying to console me—saying that he would be there with us forever.

56

THE OFFER TO make a zoo in Ahmedabad came to Joshua most unexpectedly. 'It is a miracle. Isabji's prophecy has come true,' Shebabeth said. In a way, she was right. Life had been hard for Joshua. His returns from the kennels fluctuated from good, bad to nothing. Yet he had a reputation of being an excellent veterinary doctor. He cured all kinds of canine sicknesses with his homemade remedies. His medicine and advice could make a dead dog stand up and ask for food. And this natural gift extended to other animals and birds. His canaries whistled and the parakeets imitated his voice.

In those days, Roopnagar, a travelling zoo set up on the river bed under Ellis Bridge, was drawing large crowds. It belonged to Professor Chandu Lal. He travelled with his collection from one city to another in four trucks. When he had taken the necessary permissions from the police or the local authorities, he set up a small tent like a mini circus. He had exotic birds, a goat with a long white beard and enormous curled horns, white rats in a cage with a mini-wheel, and a blue Persian cat with large whiskers who sat on a satin cushion and watched the crowds. Aquariums of colourful tropical fish were placed at the entrance, and there was a special tank for sea horses.

The Roopnagar hoardings and advertisements showed a red sea horse. People came to the mini-circus specially to see this strange marine creature floating on its tail. They were fascinated by the fact that the male of the species gave birth to baby sea horses. Another glass tank had a cobra with a spectacled hood.

Professor Chandu Lal supervised his circus by walking around with a python draped around his shoulders. He dared the bravest to touch the reptile. The main attraction of the show was the black toy poodles which Chandu Lal had bought from an army officer who did not want to take them back to London. The poodles were dressed in skirts with ribbons on their topknots and bells on their collars. They amused the crowds by sitting on tripods like monkeys and walking on their hind legs, their front paws folded like dainty ladies. To resounding applause they jumped through rings and danced on their toes like ballerinas.

In 1956, Professor Chandu Lal decided to sell Roopnagar. He was feeling his age, and his sons were not interested in looking after birds and animals. A friend suggested that if he sold his zoo to the Ahmedabad Municipal Corporation, he would get a good price for his collection.

Professor Chandu Lal invited the Mayor of Ahmedabad and the Municipal Commissioner to see his show. He convinced them that Ahmedabad needed a zoo. Every day large crowds visited Roopnagar. Besides the cinema, it had become the major entertainment for the people of Ahmedabad. Professor Chandu Lal was willing to sell his entire collection for ten thousand rupees.

The Mayor liked the idea. He had seen the London zoo as a student and thought that it would be good to have one in Ahmedabad. He introduced the idea on the agenda of the standing committee of the municipality. Professor Chandu Lal's offer was discussed in detail, and accepted. But when the Mayor, the Commissioner, B.P. Parikh and the Chairman, Syedsaab, had a meeting to discuss the matter, they came across a stumbling block. If they bought Roopnagar, how were they going to look after it?

Around this time, the Mayor's Alsatian was being treated by Joshua for a skin infection and Syedsaab's son Munir used to spend his afternoons with Joshua. Munir helped Joshua with the dogs and practised his photographic skills around the house. He had told his father about Joshua and his dogs. In fact, he had forced his father to accompany him to see Joshua's collection. The evening ended with the two becoming friends. Syedsaab had taken an immediate liking to his son's mentor.

Syedsaab suggested to the Mayor that Joshua David would be the ideal choice to look after Roopnagar. Parikh had his reservations. He had not met Joshua, though he had read his articles on wildlife in the *Gujarat Dainik*. Parikh had just returned from London, and would have preferred to appoint a veterinary doctor or someone with a degree in zoology. Syedsaab offered to introduce him to Joshua.

When the grey Dodge of the Ahmedabad Municipal Corporation turned into the gateway of Laxmi Nivas and stopped at the door, Joshua was attending to a daschund who had a stomach ailment and appeared to be breathing his last. Joshua had inserted a thermometer under its tail when Moyuddin opened the door for the guests. Moyuddin recognized both Parikh and Syedsaab and looked at Joshua for further orders. Joshua realized that the dandy Parikh was no ordinary visitor, but he continued treating the dog, only looking up to welcome them. Naomi had seen Syedsaab from the kitchen window. The man in the dark blue suit with him looked important, and she came to the door and invited them into the drawing room. Parikh's face fell, as Joshua asked them to wait till he had attended to the dog. Rather annoyed, he sat at the edge of the divan and refused Naomi's offer of sherbet, but accepted a glass of water.

From their vantage point on the divan, Parikh and Syed could see that Joshua was doing his utmost to save the dog. Parikh turned to Syedsaab and said, 'You have brought me to the right house. This man really loves animals. Only somebody like him could tell us to wait because a dog needed attention.'

Joshua gave the daschund an injection and wrapping him in an old blanket, left him in Moyuddin's care. When he joined them after washing his hands, he explained the details of the dog's malady to Parikh and Syedsaab. Parikh was interested and wanted to know how Joshua was able to diagnose the sickness of animals, and told him about a Labrador he had lost for unknown reasons. Joshua asked him about the symptoms, and when Parikh described them, Joshua was certain that the dog had died of diphtheria. As they discussed dogs, Naomi served them biscuits, which Parikh accepted graciously. He was curious about what Joshua did for a living.

Joshua laughed. 'I am by religion a Jew, but by caste a

Vaghri. Like them I chase anything on four legs. And when my wife goes to school, I look after our little daughter.'

Parikh lit his cigar, crossed his legs and asked, 'What if we offered you a job?'

Joshua laughed again. 'This must be a joke. You mean you are offering me a job in the municipality. Parikhsaab, do I look like someone who could work in an office? Perhaps you want me to become a dogcatcher. But I am afraid I could not even do that, as my heart would melt if a dog looked at me with pleading eyes.' Then, lighting a cigarette, he looked seriously at Parikh and said, 'Excuse me if I am being cynical about taking up a job. But perhaps you have something special for me.'

Parikh smiled and looked at Syedsaab. Syedsaab had not spoken a word so far. He wanted Parikh to make the first move. Syedsaab now said, 'Look Joshua, we have a proposition for you. If you accept, we could work together.'

'I am at your service, if it is something I can do,' Joshua answered. 'But Syedsaab knows that I do not have degrees and have not specialized in any field.'

When Parikh and Syed told him about their plan to buy Professor Chandu Lal's Roopnagar and set it up in Ahmedabad, Joshua felt strangely excited. Even before they had finished talking, Joshua stood up and shaking their hands said, 'I accept your proposal. I will make a zoo in Ahmedabad. You can go ahead and buy Roopnagar. I will set it up for you. When do we start?'

Parikh held his trembling hands and said, 'Tomorrow.'

57

JOSHUA BUILT THE ZOO around the Hauz-i-Kutb or Kankaria lake, a mile-long water body, with an island in the middle, which had been built in 1451 by Sultan Qutb-ud-din. The zoo was named Hill Garden Zoo. The Ahmedabad Municipal Corporation gifted it the collection of birds and animals from Roopnagar. As a beginning, Joshua made a small greenhouse with an aviary on the hillock near the lake. But he dreamt of bringing tigers, lions, panthers and all types of exotic animals and birds to his zoo.

As he stood on the barren hillock amidst mounds of earth Joshua did not know how he was going to fulfil his dream. He wanted to expand from ten aquariums of coloured tropical fish, a python, a cage full of chattering parakeets, ten pairs of lovebirds, ten yellow roller canaries, an African grey, four macaws, a dozen pouter pigeons, a bearded goat, a Persian cat, white rats, a nilgai, a tank of sea horses and a weather cock on the roof. A brood of peafowl also had a free run of the place. The male, a handsome bird with a beautiful long plumage, liked to perch on the weather cock from where he had a grandstand view of the lake.

The Nawabzada of Palanpur, Zabardastkhan saheb, with whom my father had often gone on hunts, wrote encouraging letters to Joshua.

I have received your letter and am happy that you have taken up the cause of wildlife preservation. This means that our shikar days are really over. I thought that it was a passing phase but now I am convinced that you will never load your rifle. I am looking forward to seeing the zoo on my next visit to Ahmedabad. You were made for great things.

As you know, the tribals from the hills often come down to Palanpur and try to sell us some animal or bird. You often said that I should encourage them, so that they stop killing without reason. That is why I buy whatever they bring, and now we have our own little zoo at the palace. Last week, Lakhu came to see me late at night. Remember him? He used to be one of our beaters during our shikar days. He had something in a gunny bag. From the way the bag was moving, I knew he had bought a big cat. When he opened the bag, I saw he had a six-month-old panther cub. It was small but ferocious. I had a plate of kebabs next to me, and gave him some. He swallowed ten kebabs in one gulp, and then almost brought the palace down with his growls.

Lakhu says he found the cub in the forest. But I am sure that he killed the mother. In a few days he will return, and try to sell me the pelt. Allah alone knows the agony of this motherless cub. Crafty and cunning as he is, Lakhu wanted me to buy the cub for Rs 400. I refused to pay him a paisa more than Rs 250. At first I thought I would release the cub into the forests around Palanpur. But I predict sure death for one so small. So I decided to keep him in our palace zoo, under Bashir's care.

Bashir is of the opinion that the cub will be happy with you. He talks about you often, and is very excited that you are making a zoo in Ahmedabad. So, after consultation with him, I agreed to buy the cub. When I gave the money to Lakhu, you were uppermost in my mind. On your last trip to Palanpur, you told me that you wanted to have lions and tigers in the zoo. Why not start with a panther?

I have read in the *Gujarat Dainik* that the Ahmedabad

Municipal Corporation does not want to keep meat-eating animals in the zoo. I suggest you tell the authorities that the panther cub is a gift from me. I am suggesting this because human nature is such that when a gift is given it is never refused. Lakhu and Bashir will reach Ahmedabad with the cub at about four o'clock in the afternoon. Till you resolve the problem with the municipality, you will have to keep the panther at your house. This may be difficult, as I know Naomibhabhi's feelings and respect them. But you are tactful and will find a solution. Your young friend Adi who lives in a big bungalow in Mirzapur could also keep the cub. I wish you success in this project.

May Allah shower you with his blessings.
Your Zabuchacha.

The plan worked. The front page of the *Gujarat Dainik* carried a four-column photograph of Joshua with the panther cub in his arms. There was a big write-up about the cub being gifted to the zoo by the Sahebzada Zabardastkhan saheb of Palanpur state. And, till the standing committee of the Ahmedabad Municipal Corporation took a decision, the cub would stay in a private house for a month. It was the beginning of bigger things.

58

THE ENCLOSURES FOR the big cats had two sections at Hill Garden Zoo. One section had trees, a pond and an artificial waterfall. The other was a room with a trapdoor, where the animals were fed or kept when they had cubs.

One cold January morning, the animal-keeper, Jagan, was drunk and inattentive. He opened and closed the wrong doors and went off to take a nap under a lemon tree.

Babu, my father's aide, saw the tigers Raja and Rani taking a leisurely walk in the zoo. When the funny-nosed otters in the pond nearby started screeching, Raja and Rani became nervous and seemed ready to bolt. The birds and animals of the zoo were frozen with an ancient fear—that of the hunted. Babu stood where he was, and sent a message to Joshua.

Not wanting to come face-to-face with the tigers, Joshua took a dirt road from where he could observe the animals. He knew that one wrong move and the tigers would jump over the fence and crash into the traffic, and he would be forced to shoot them. In those days, he did not have a tranquillizer gun. Raja and Rani had been born in the zoo and did not know their own power. But they were full-grown and could not be expected to behave like pet cats.

The zoo was unusually silent as Joshua started moving towards the tigers. The eerie silence was broken by a pair of spotted owlets sitting in a neem tree. Their siesta had been disturbed. Looking down at the scene below them, they gleefully started moving their heads like marionettes. Babu glanced up at them irritably. Owls were an ill omen.

Babu has often recounted the story. As he relates it, 'Standing behind Joshuasaab, I heard a great roar. It took me some time to realize that it was Joshuasaab's voice. Joshuasaab had transformed into a tiger. The volume of his voice was so immense that I felt the earth shake. Joshuasaab was roaring and walking towards Raja and Rani. You won't believe this, but he hypnotized them. This is a miracle I have seen with my own eyes. They immediately turned tail and walked back into their cage. I ran and closed the door behind them. But

Joshuasaab kept on walking towards them like one in a trance. His face was red and his eyes were dilated. He stopped only when he reached their cage. From that day Joshuasaab was known as the miracle man of Ahmedabad.'

Babu has now retired, but cannot stop talking about his Joshuasaab. He was closest to my father. Raju is Babu's favourite zoo story. He was born to a mother who preferred to eat him up than raise him. This happens often in a zoo. When a mother delivers a cub in captivity, the smell of human beings sometimes disturbs her. It makes her insecure and she can eat her cubs.

Joshua saved Raju from his mother. His mother had a litter of three. The next day, Babu informed Joshua that on his early morning rounds, he had seen only one cub. She had obviously eaten the other two. They separated the mother from the cub and named him Raju. The mantle of surrogate mother fell on a stray bitch who had given birth to five pups in the greenhouse. He survived.

Because he had only known dogs and human beings, Raju could not be kept with the other tigers. When he was six months old, he was put in a cage with a small enclosure of his own. He slept all day on his back and spent his time trying to kill the flies buzzing on his nose.

Raju was a handsome animal but not an entirely happy one, separated as he was from other animals. He instructed Babu to put Raju on a leash and every evening, when the zoo doors were closed, take Raju for a walk in the rose garden. It was then that Raju had his encounter with the colony of crows.

At that point the zoo was like a forest. The trees were tall and their branches spread out like canopies over the cages. Besides the colony of crows, all kinds of birds roosted in the trees, preening and talking to each other in different dialects.

But the crows reigned supreme. At sunset it was a common sight to see groups of them washing themselves in every available puddle. They had decided that the zoo was their home. Baby crows were taught to fly here. For these sessions, the crows cawed so much that the zoo resounded with the din they made.

Catastrophe struck when a baby crow faltered in its flying lesson and fell on Raju's head. The bird broke a wing and lay between Raju's legs with a drop of blood on its chest. Raju's instincts were aroused by the smell of fresh blood. He ate the baby crow in one gulp.

All hell broke loose. The entire colony of crows fell upon Raju. In the ensuing confusion, Babu lost Raju's leash and a maddened tiger began running through a cloud of crows. When Joshua heard what had happened, he grabbed a towel and an airgun and rushed to face the fury of the crows. He fired in the air to scare them, and the cloud thinned over Raju's head.

Joshua saw that the crows were attacking Raju's eyes with their powerful beaks. He fired again and used the towel to scare them away. By then Babu had Raju on the leash and had locked him in the zoo office. Raju's head was covered with blood and he had lost an eye. When Joshua touched Raju's head, he realized that with the taste of blood, Raju had become a wild tiger.

59

I AM REMINDED OF the stuffed lion that stood in the centre of our small drawing room, and with it, of Bashir. For years it stood there watching us with its unblinking eyes. My father and

Zabardastkhan saheb had shot it together. It had been a difficult shoot.

Its presence filled our house. I felt suffocated because we had to live around it. I must have been very small, because I remember crawling under its belly. And when the house was full of guests, I sat between its legs. I remember that its fur was golden, and smelled of dry grass. Sitting there, unnoticed, I often wanted to ask my father whether dead lions ever passed water. From this vantage point, I heard and saw much that was taboo for children. Whenever my mother caught me listening in, she shooed me away.

Babu said that whenever Joshuasaab was worried, he wrote long letters in Gujarati to Zabardastkhan saheb. Joshua felt alone in his efforts to make a zoo. He was not sure whether he would be successful.

Zabardastkhan saheb sensed his distress, and drove down from Palanpur to Ahmedabad. As always he came on a Sunday. I was playing hopscotch with my neighbour's daughter. Balancing on one leg, I moved aside when I saw the silver-coloured car with its gold insignia stop at our door. Bashir jumped out from the front seat and opened the back door.

Bashir was extraordinary. I stared at him, as if he was someone who had come to life from my children's encyclopaedia. He appeared to have been carved out of ebony. He had Negroid features and his tiny black curls looked like black snails glued to his head. He looked as if he belonged to Africa, not India. He did not wear a white turban like the other courtiers. When he said, 'Salaam, babysaab,' I mumbled a salute and looked up at him, tall as a palm tree.

Zabardastkhan saheb had come on a mission. This was obvious from the tension on Bashir's face. Curious to know what was the matter, I followed them into the house. As usual my father annoyed me by signalling that I should salaam Zabuchacha. I touched a limp hand to my forehead and the prince smiled. I then took my place under the lion's scrotum which hung over me like a ripe mango.

Contrary to his name, Zabardastkhan saheb was delicate rather than energetic to look at. He always seemed to be sitting on a throne with his hands resting on his knees, as though posing for a photograph.

Joshua sat next to him. I could see that he was uncomfortable as he was still in his nightclothes. He would have liked to change, but he knew that it would be disrespectful to keep the prince waiting.

The prince had a booming voice. 'I read your letter. I understand how difficult it is for you to build a zoo. It is no small matter to create a forest. Only Allah has the power to create nature. We are only human.' Then putting his arm around Joshua's shoulders, Zabuchacha continued, 'Joshua, my brother, you need help and I want to give you a gift.' His eyes moved to Bashir, sitting on the floor like a black Buddha. Joshua understood that Bashir was to stay behind and work in the zoo.

From my vantage point I saw my mother Naomi enter the room with two glasses of rose sherbet in a silver tray. She wanted me to disappear, but I behaved as though I had not noticed her signal, because I loved to watch the ritual of the poison taster.

Following the tradition of certain royal families, Naomi poured the sherbet in a saucer and offered it to Bashir as if he were a cat or a dog. He closed his eyes and drank it in one gulp. After ten minutes, when Zabuchacha was sure that the sherbet was not poisoned, Bashir offered him the glass and he drank it. In the palace at Palanpur, all food was tasted by poison tasters before the royal family ate or drank anything.

Bashir's devotion to the prince was obvious. Zabardastkhan saheb took a sip of the sherbet out of respect for Naomi and carefully placed the glass back on the table. Then he looked at Bashir, and announced, 'Bashir now belongs to you and the zoo.'

Bashir cried like a child when the prince suddenly walked out of the house without a backward glance at either Bashir or Joshua. Bashir, who always followed the prince like a pet dog, did not move. He looked like a statue sitting cross-legged on the floor.

When the prince had driven away, Naomi saw that there was a velvet purse on the table. Ten notes of hundred rupees were rolled in a piece of paper which read: 'For Bashir's khana-peena.'

At the zoo, Bashir lived in a small wooden cabin which looked just like the one in the illustration of Uncle Tom's cabin. When Naomi went to school, and I had a holiday, Joshua took me to the zoo. It was Bashir's job to take me around and show me the new arrivals. He was showing me a pair of newly arrived barasingha when I suddenly asked him, 'Are you from Africa?'

'What's that?' he asked. I did not want to confuse him, so I changed the subject.

Joshua had told me that many years ago, the royal family of Junagadh had brought African slaves from Ethiopia. They were known as Sidi Badshahs and lived in the villages around the lion sanctuary at Sasan Gir. There were also some settlements in Ahmedabad, Bharuch and Karnataka.

Sidi Bashir's father, who had been the keeper of the Nawab's dogs, had fled to Pakistan with the Nawab of Junagadh. He had left Bashir with Zabardastkhan saheb.

Bashir's mother had died much earlier. His father must have felt that the child would be safe with the prince.

Bashir was trained to be a beater for the shikar shoots. He had become an excellent hunter and had developed a good understanding of forests and animals. Later, he was promoted to official poison taster of Zabardastkhan saheb. Bashir had felt honoured.

A year passed without incident. Bashir appeared to have settled down in Ahmedabad. He was promoted to the post of animal keeper. He rented a small room in Jamalpur and the Nawab sent him a primus stove, some plates, a tea set, a ladle, two pans and a spoon. These household goods arrived in the royal jeep with Bashir's old string cot, mattress, pillow and quilt. The prince also sent him as a gift a small carved table and two chairs.

Whenever I was at the zoo, I insisted that Bashir take me around, because he talked to the birds and animals and they responded to him. One day, when we were standing at the lion enclosure and encouraging Vanraj and Vanrani to come closer, Bashir's wallet slipped out of his pocket and the photograph of a young woman fell out. I was excited. 'Is this your girlfriend?'

He smiled shyly, and sliding the photo back into his wallet, whispered, 'Secret. OK, babysaab!'

I asked him her name.

'Saeeda,' he told me.

Saeeda did not belong to the Sidi community. She was fair and had a long braid which hung over her left shoulder. When I told him that she was beautiful, he was pleased. Then with a serious expression he said, 'Zabardastkhan saheb must never know.'

'Why?'

'Because he has chosen a Sidi bride for me. She is from

Talala. I have never seen her,' he replied.

'What will you do now?'

'I have to tell Joshuasaab.'

I doubted that Joshua would help him, as he always went along with the Nawab's decisions. So I just sighed and hoped that Bashir's story would have a happy ending.

Fifteen months after Bashir had come to us, Zabuchacha died. My father was inconsolable, and Bashir cried so much that he was sick. He lay in bed staring vacantly at the ceiling. Babu told us that Saeeda, his landlord's wife, was looking after him. It was then that I realized that Saeeda was a married woman.

The last part of Bashir's story came to me from Babu. Every morning, my father took a round of the zoo on his bicycle. One day, he stopped in his tracks. Bashir was standing inside the lions' cage. Vanraj and Vanrani were six feet away from Bashir, crouching, ready to pounce on him. Joshua's first instinct was to shout for help. If he had, the lions would have torn Bashir to pieces. Joshua did not want to make a false move so he got off the bicycle, and treading softly, stood behind the bars which were closest to Bashir. By then Babu had arrived. Joshua signalled to him to stand near the trapdoor.

Bashir was standing motionless as though he had turned into a pillar of black granite. At first, he did not respond to my father's instructions: 'Bashir, move backwards. Keep looking into the lions' eyes.' But something in Joshua's voice finally made him move backwards, and as soon as he reached the trapdoor, Babu opened it and Bashir jumped out. Vanraj and Vanrani immediately charged at him, and dashed against the iron bars. There was a hair's breadth between Bashir and the lions.

For Joshua those ten steps were like ten hours, and he slapped Bashir for the first time. 'Why were you inside the lions' cage?' Bashir did not answer. Later, in the office, when Joshua tried to find out the reason for his strange behaviour, Bashir sat on the floor with eyes lowered and refused to utter a word.

The news spread that Sidi Bashir had had a miraculous escape. At the press conference, Joshua told the reporters that Sidi Bashir had forgotten to close the door and had come face to face with Vanraj and Vanrani. Babu informed Joshua that Bashir did not want to live. Saeeda's husband had found out about the love affair, and there had been a fight. Saeeda was locked up in a relative's house, with the threat that if she met the 'immoral Habshi', they would both be killed. Bashir was back in his log cabin at the zoo. He had nothing with him, not even his clothes.

He was even more distressed when Saeeda's husband refused to give him back his belongings, specially the table and chairs he had received from Zabardastkhan saheb. After his brush with death, Bashir was put in charge of the tropical fish—a further humiliation.

The next morning, Bashir was nowhere to be seen. He was found dead, next to the enclosure of Vanraj and Vanrani. In his shirt pocket the police found Saeeda's photograph.

As Babu concluded philosophically, 'Bashir had been brought up as a poison taster. It was the final solution to his problems.'

60

JOSHUA WAS PARTICULARLY fond of panthers. 'Panthers are made of steel,' he used to say. 'They are more intelligent than people think.' His grandmother Simha had told him stories about the panther who had lived in the family house in Danda.

As a teenager Joshua had tried to restore a glass painting he had found in the storeroom of the Delhi Darwaza house. He had glued the broken glass onto an old wooden frame. While scraping the colour, he had discovered another painting hidden under the layer of paint. It was Solomon's portrait with Chitta sitting at his feet.

When he was making the zoo, he wrote a weekly column about his encounters with animals in the Gujarati newsletter *Fauji Talim*. In the article which won him a 'Pranimitra prize for nature stories,' Joshua had written about a mystical moment in the jungle when he faced a panther during a shoot around Mt. Abu.

We were sitting in our deck chairs and waiting for news, when Bashir informed us that a panther had been spotted. I planned the shoot from a machan. We waited all night, but did not see the animal. We had seen its pugs the day before. That night, the animal did not appear. I was tired. Early in the morning, while it was still dark, I climbed down from the machan to relieve myself. The sound of water on the dry leaves was eerie, and I could hear my heart beat. I looked around. The forest was just waking up: I could hear the peafowl and recognized the call of the drongos, bee-eaters and barking deer. Mornings in the forest are fresh and clear. I breathed deeply and lit a cigarette. Suddenly I felt that I was being watched.

I could feel the presence of a big animal stalking me. Without a roar I heard a roar. Without a snarl I heard a snarl. Without a scratch I felt sharp claws on my neck. Without a touch, I felt the hard fur of a big cat. And without turning my head, I could see the spotted golden fur. I could feel its eyes on me. There was a knot of fear in my stomach. Then suddenly, it melted and changed into something else. Fear was taking the form of a roar in my chest. Without moving or turning, I moved my eyes and met those of the panther. Without my noticing the animal had moved away from me with its legendary feline grace. We were watching each other. I heard myself roaring. The panther was puzzled by the sound of my voice. It looked at me and turned tail. In the split of a second it had disappeared into the forest.

The magic of the moment was lost when he heard a shot. Then he saw the panther lying dead at his feet.

A certain understanding had passed between the panther and Joshua. Joshua did not want to kill the animal after he had looked into its eyes. Joshua had forgotten that his friends sitting on the machan would assume that the animal was going to attack him. Moreover, they did not want to forgo the pelt of a fine animal.

This was the beginning of the lessons the jungle was going to teach Joshua. Lessons he would use later in the making of the zoo.

Two years before he died, Joshua had a similar experience. He came face-to-face with a wild lioness in the Gir forest. They looked at each other for five minutes, as Joshua sat still on a rock. The lioness then turned around and disappeared into the bush, as though he was not a man but one of her own kind.

61

THE SABARMATI WAS in spate, and all the rivers and lakes of Gujarat were overflowing, including Kankaria, the lake next to the zoo. Only a road separated the zoo from the lake.

The blocked gutters of factories around the zoo allowed dirty water to flow into the lake. Thousands of fish died and were dumped on the outskirts of Ahmedabad. A poisonous weed spread its tentacles on the surface of the lake choking it, and the lake had to be emptied. Huge mounds of earth, garbage and dead fish were dumped around the lake.

Two crocodiles emerged from the empty lake and walked into the zoo. It was one of those moments that occur rarely in a lifetime. When Grandmother Shebabeth read about it in the newspapers, she sighed and sent a note to Joshua that Isabjidada's prophecy was being realized. Reptiles such as crocodiles did not easily show emotion: that they trusted him was an extraordinary happening. She believed that Joshua was blessed by the Shesh Nag. With time, the memory of the prophecy had faded, but Shebabeth believed in it with a fierce faith.

It was seven in the evening, and my father had just returned home. He had changed into his pyjamas and was feeding the dogs when Babu arrived and rattled the door frantically. He had cycled down from the zoo. He told Joshua that he had seen two crocodiles strolling in the zoo. In the evening light, they had looked like elongated rocks walking on short legs. When he realized that they were crocodiles, he had panicked. Joshua changed quickly, jumped onto his bicycle and raced to the zoo, with Babu following him.

Joshua had to think of how to capture the crocodiles. He planned 'operation crocodile' and called out to Babu to pick up coils of thick rope and poles on the way.

The newspapers reported that Joshua and his men grappled with the crocodiles, caught hold of their lashing tails, tied up their huge jaws and fastened them to poles. Not knowing where to keep the crocodiles, Joshua lowered them into an unused well.

Joshua had rushed off to the zoo without a weapon. My mother waited up for him, restless and afraid for his life. He returned early in the morning the following day, looking fresh, happy and unharmed. It was amazing how nature sustained him and taught him what to do in a crisis. Miraculously, he emerged victorious and unharmed each time.

When Joshua lowered the crocodiles into the well, he did not realize that they would multiply a hundredfold and bring fame to Hill Garden Zoo.

The crocodiles were named Manga and Mangala. They were later shifted to a bigger enclosure with a pond and a fence covered with multi-coloured bougainvillea. Here they basked in the sun with their mouths open. One often saw birds feeding off insects, salt and rotting meat from their teeth.

The lake was cleaned and filled with water and the dumps of garbage cleared, but the crocodiles never returned to the lake. At the zoo they were fed kilos of meat and fish and there was hardly any food in the lake.

In a year they had settled down and Mangala started digging the soft mud in one of the corners. She laid her eggs standing over the burrow she had prepared for her family of baby crocodiles. Once the hole was full of her soft slimy eggs, she covered them with earth and waited. When the eggs hatched, she dug open the burrow, and when the first baby crocodile cracked its shell and opened its eyes in Hill Garden Zoo, Mangala allowed Joshua to stay next to her.

Nobody knew that one crocodile still remained in the lake. Perhaps it had found its way there from the outskirts of Ahmedabad. This particular crocodile had a wounded front paw and was finding it hard to survive. The fish in the lake were insufficient and he was always hungry. It was then that the crocodile learnt to catch its prey from Naginawadi, a little island in the middle of the lake, where King Ahmedshah had built a summer palace for his queens. It was just an open pavilion surrounded by trees and a lawn which sloped into the lake. A palm-lined road connected the pavilion to the road which ran parallel to the zoo.

Hidden in the water, only its eyes bulging over the surface, the crocodile would watch the lawns of Naginawadi and emerge at two in the afternoon when there was nobody around. He had learnt to drag into the lake stray cats, dogs and cows, as they dozed in the cool shadows of the trees.

The crocodile would have remained undetected, but it made one fatal mistake. It had not eaten for more than a fortnight and was desperate when it saw a young boy sleeping under a tree. The crocodile dragged the boy underwater. The next day the sweeper had hysterics when he found a half-eaten human hand on the lawns. The fire brigade was alerted and Joshua informed. He studied the hand and saw that the teeth marks on it were those of a crocodile.

Joshua was amused when the lake was cordoned off by the fire brigade and a shoot-at-sight order issued by the police. At meeting after meeting he tried to pacify the agitated civic authorities and assured them that he would catch the crocodile. Instinctively he felt that the crocodile was related to Manga and Mangala. It must have become a man-eater in unusual circumstances.

For two days and a night Joshua and his men tried to locate the crocodile in the lake. Joshua knew where to look and here he lowered many baits—iron hooks hidden in huge chunks of beef. It did not seem that the crocodile would fall for the bait. But he did. The moment Joshua felt something heavy tugging at one of the baits, he knew that it was the crocodile.

Joshua, his men and the fire brigade pulled the crocodile out of the lake. The police were standing around with enough ammunition to kill a hundred crocodiles. Joshua had warned them that if anybody fired, he would resign.

In pain, the bait stuck in its jaws, the crocodile lashed out fiercely trying to free itself. Joshua saw that it was enormous, bigger than both Manga and Mangala.

When the crocodile was brought to the zoo, tied to bamboo poles, Joshua received a hero's welcome. He was relieved to see that when he released the man-eater into the enclosure with Manga and Mangala, they did not strike each other with their powerful tails. They were calm and it appeared to be a family reunion.

Joshua watched the new crocodile for signs of illness. The bait had sunk deep, and he was sure that the crocodile would not survive. But Joshua was wrong. After a few weeks, this particular crocodile with the injured paw was making a great effort to dig a hole in the soft earth. Joshua realized that the crocodile was a female, and was trying to make a burrow for her eggs. Considering her size, he wondered whether she was Manga and Mangala's mother. She could be the matriarch. He named her Sumangala.

Joshua and Babu helped the new crocodile make a home for her baby crocodiles. She laid her eggs there. After they covered the hole with earth, he often saw her guarding the eggs. When the eggs hatched, Sumangala appeared grateful. She allowed Joshua to come very close to her. When he tugged at her tail so that she would not crush the eggs, she did not lash out at him. Even after he lost his voice, she responded to the sound of his electric larynx and came to greet him, hoping that he would tug her tail and ride on her back. Sumangala's behaviour amazed everybody, including Joshua. She trusted him and he stood by her.

Joshua kept some secrets to himself. He knew that Sumangala had not been alone in the lake. There was possibly another crocodile there, another man-eater. He confided in the chief of the fire brigade department. Together they spent a month combing the lake for some sign of another crocodile. But there was none. All they found were some old bones, chappals, empty bottles, plastic bags and a silver anklet. The possible presence of a lone male in the lake bothered Joshua for years. He never knew when the crocodile would emerge. When they could not find the crocodile, Joshua assumed that he had left a long time ago, abandoning Sumangala in search of fresh waters.

Fifteen years later, Sumangala's mate surfaced in Joshua's life. It was a dark, rainy night. Joshua and Naomi were asleep. The phone was dead. Joshua woke up with a start when he heard the dogs barking. Somebody was rattling the front gate. He switched on the light and asked, 'Kaun hai?' From the kitchen window, he saw four villagers in dhotis, standing under one big black umbrella.

They had come to ask his help. In a lake near Chaloda village, a crocodile had attacked three young boys who had gone for a swim. It had killed the youngest and eaten him. The other two were seriously injured and had been shifted to hospital. My father did not want to go out on a night like this and was contemplating sending them to the forest department, but when he saw the complete faith in their eyes he could not refuse to help. They had a jeep waiting for him.

According to municipal rules, he could leave only with his zoo team, the fire brigade and the police. The crocodile had been sighted in a particular place and after a night-long vigil, Joshua captured it. The villagers wanted to kill the crocodile, as the boy it had killed had been the only child of a poor widow. Joshua calmed the angry crowd and locked the crocodile in the municipal truck. Then he returned to console the mother of the victim. He said to the crowd. 'We human beings have no right to take a life. Do we know how he became a man-eater?'

On the way to Ahmedabad, Joshua was worried about the crocodile, as it did not show any sign of life. Perhaps it had died in the process of being captured. Or it could be injured.

The crocodile lay inert in the zoo hospital for a month. Joshua was sure that it was suffering from an internal haemorrhage. He decided to take a risk. All marsh crocodiles look alike, but this one had a strange resemblance to Sumangala. With his men standing around with long bamboo poles, Joshua released the newcomer into the enclosure with the other crocodiles.

The crocodile lay there inert for a while. Sumangala had noticed him and was looking in his direction. Moving laboriously on her broken paws, she lay down next to him. They stayed like that, their bodies touching. With her touch, the other crocodile opened his eyes and then closed them. Sumangala slid into the pond, and her mate followed.

It became a common sight to see them side by side, basking in the sun. He was slow and appeared to be ill but he lived for two years. After his death the post-mortem report showed that the iron hook from the bait was imbedded deep in his stomach.

After the heavy monsoon that year, the flamingos had followed the crocodiles to Hill Garden Zoo. Joshua often went to Nal Sarovar, a distance of eighty kilometres from Ahmedabad. Nal Sarovar, a shallow lake of more than a hundred square kilometres, attracted migratory birds. The birds lived in huge flocks on the flatlands of Bhal district, next to the villages of the tribal Padhars.

Joshua sent a proposal to the government of Gujarat that Nal Sarovar be declared a waterbird sanctuary. There were large flocks of migratory birds like flamingos, pelicans, common cranes, painted storks, ducks such as pintails, shovellers, mallards, brahminy and common teals, red shanks and ringed plovers, besides others. Even otherwise, some birds had made the lake their permanent home—the whistling teals, spotbill ducks, kingfishers, cormorants, herons, egrets, spoonbills, and the white, black and glossy ibis.

Joshua felt refreshed and happy in open spaces. Occasionally he missed his forest days and wondered what he was doing in a zoo. He would then remind himself that the zoo was his life.

Joshua and Babu always went together to Nal Sarovar. But, some nights Babu stayed back. He drank a local brew and ate roasted birds with the Padhars. This was a secret from Joshua, who would have disapproved.

Babu had discovered that the Padhars were expert bird catchers and he learnt their techniques. On one visit, when Babu was sleeping off six glasses of their brew, he woke up on hearing a soft honk. It sounded like the call of an agonized bird. He sat up and saw to his horror that his Padhar friends were breaking the pink legs of the flamingos as though they were matchsticks. Their white, scarlet-tipped wings were also being torn from their roots as if they were pieces of paper. Legs and wings were being thrown into a clay pot that was on the fire. Babu retched at the thought of eating flamingo curry. The maimed bodies of the flamingos were collected in a sack which the tribal chief took in a boat to sell to tourists camping on the lake. They sold the flesh of waterbirds to tourists for the sum of two rupees a bird. If the tourists paid more, they even cooked for them.

Vigorously washing his face to sober up, Babu offered to

pay the tribals double the amount, if they gave him the birds.
The Padhar chief agreed. There were no flamingos at the Hill
Garden Zoo, and Babu thought that Joshua would be happy
that he had saved the birds from the tribals' knives.

Joshua was shocked to see the condition of the birds. He
wrote several letters to the forest department, the Chief Minister
and the press. He started a campaign to save waterbirds from
poachers and tourists. He could not do anything about the
Padhars as bird and man had been living together for ages and
for them to change their way of life would take time. As a
short-term solution, he sent Babu back to Nal Sarovar with the
message that Joshua of Hill Garden Zoo would buy any bird
the Padhars trapped. He would pay them twice as much as
they usually got, but on the condition that the birds were not
injured or harmed. As an additional precaution, he left one of
his men there to transport the birds to Ahmedabad. The tribals
did not take long to realize that this was a good business
proposition. Gradually Joshua gained their confidence. He
treated them like royalty when they came to the zoo with
sackfuls of birds. And when they killed a bird or two
occasionally, they travelled all the way to Ahmedabad to ask
his forgiveness.

Eventually, Joshua created a world record by his breeding
of marsh crocodiles and flamingos in captivity.

62

HILL GARDEN ZOO soon became known as the best zoo in Asia.
I could never understand how my father had managed to
create it in such a short time.

Those were hectic days. The Governor of Gujarat, Mehdi

Nawaz Jung, visited our house often. He liked my father's 'gulabi mizaz' and they spent many an evening reciting Urdu poetry over glasses of rose sherbet, kebabs and freshly baked cup-cakes from the Italian bakery. The American ambassador to India, John Kenneth Galbraith, spent a couple of hours at the zoo on two consecutive days. The newspapers were full of photographs of my father with the ambassador and the tiger Raju.

In his book *The Ambassador's Journal*, Galbraith mentions his visit to the zoo.

> . . . we were taken in tow by a remarkable zoologist by the name of David. In the last three years he has created one of the most charming zoos in the world on a little hillside by a tank and lives on most intimate and agreeable terms with his animals. The collection includes two or three tigers which charge their cage walls with inspired viciousness and another so gentle that after being further tamed by playing with a favourite dog, he was available for petting and photography. I was duly photographed stroking him with highly tentative affection. The photographs, which were prominently featured in this morning's paper, look a good deal braver than they really were. Everyone was prepared to evacuate at a moment's notice . . . This morning, we went back to visit the tiger again and see if we could get an authentic picture. With some delicacy, he was manoeuvred outside the cage and with more delicacy, a quick picture was snapped in my company alone.

For this particular photograph, there was tremendous tension, because it was taken outside the tiger's cage. The ambassador had ignored security directives after Joshua had assured him that he would come to no harm as long as he was there besides him. Joshua was holding the tiger when Galbraith sat next to Raju. Joshua moved out of the frame as the cameras clicked. He then led Raju back into his cage. Joshua was pleased that Galbraith had trusted him, and more so his animals.

63

SOON AFTER GALBRAITH'S visit, Pandit Jawaharlal Nehru's office confirmed that the PM would inaugurate the children's park Joshua had made facing the zoo on another hillock.

Joshua had innumerable meetings with the police, security staff and municipal authorities. Roads were repaired, cages painted and decorations planned by Mukund Purohit, a young artist. The malis clipped away at the mehendi bushes, sculpting them into animals and birds. They also made ornate bamboo frames for the bouquets which were to be presented to Panditji.

Babu ensured that the cages were clean, water changed in the artificial ponds and that the bigger animals were washed with sprays of water. Sumitra, the zoo elephant, was painted by her mahout. Potted plants and croutons were arranged inside the cages and fresh gravel sprinkled on the paths.

It looked as though preparations were being made for a wedding. Joshua was always tense, smoking cigarette after cigarette and constantly losing his temper. Even when he returned home at night, he would hold meetings with the police and the bureaucrats. Naomi kept a large supply of snacks, tea, coffee and soft drinks ready. The phone never stopped ringing.

I was told to make a sketch of Panditji for the great event. When the dignitaries stopped for refreshments, I was to take his autograph on the sketch. Everybody was so busy they did not give me an opportunity to say anything.

That year, Joshua had given the final touches to Balvatika—the children's paradise. It was constructed on a hillock next to Hill Garden Zoo. The municipality had planned to make it a commercial centre. When my father heard about it, he asked Mukund to make drawings of a fairyland which existed in his mind. Mukund was a self-taught artist and my cousin's best friend. He spent hours with my father with a sketchbook and a box of coloured pencils. He worked in the state transport department as a clerk, but would appear miraculously whenever my father had an idea which he wanted him to put to paper.

Balvatika's entrance was a pagoda, with painted relief sculptures of birds and children. A hundred steps led to the Noah's Ark standing in a pond of white, pink and blue lotus flowers. The boat resembled an illustration from a children's Bible and had photographs of Joshua and his experiments with animals coexisting with man. A tiger, a lion, an Alsatian, a pye-dog and a macaque frolicked together in one enclosure. Joshua was the sixth inmate—the Homo sapien—who spent an hour with them every day. This utopia was planted with gulmohur and peepal trees, on which the big cats sharpened their claws, but otherwise did not harm anyone. Once in a while, my father put them on a leash and took them for a walk in the zoo. He spoke to them in a soft, soothing voice as he controlled them.

Joshua David was becoming famous all over the world for his experiments in co-existence. This was to be the showpiece during Panditji's visit, and it was widely publicized in the national and international press.

I had grown up seeing Pandit Jawaharlal Nehru. Whenever he visited Gujarat, he passed by our house on Shahibaug Road in an open car, and we showered him with garlands and flowers. He looked handsome and important. Like all children of my generation, I was told he was Chacha Nehru and loved children. I, too, was his fan, although I had mixed feelings about making the sketch and asking him for his autograph. Although Joshua was busy, he found time to check my sketches. He rejected all my drawings till I flexed my fingers and moaned that I was suffering from cramp and said I would make a sketch from the photographs which appeared in the newspapers. I would not let my father down.

Nearing D-day, I had nothing in my sketchbook. So, I decided to cheat. I made a tracing of one of his newspaper photographs and filled in the light and shade—a trick I had learnt from Patel sir. The sketch looked good. Joshua was pleased.

Chacha Nehru arrived with the fanfare which goes with dignitaries. As a traditional Gujarati welcome, beautiful Gujarati girls, daughters of municipal councillors, were to welcome Nehru with an arti. Sumitra, the elephant who had been painted and draped in silks and satins, was to ring a bell and announce that the Prime Minister had arrived. After the arti, Sumitra was to shower Nehru with rose petals.

I would have liked to be one of the five girls at the door. I wanted to be dressed like them. I had imagined I would wear a purple chaniya with silver bells stitched at the hem, a red mirror-work backless choli and a shocking-pink tie-and-dye sari. But Naomi opposed my humble request. According to security norms, only five girls were to be present at the Tiger Gate, the main gate of the zoo, and they had already been chosen by the local Congress party leader.

Expecting a melée of Congress workers and their families, Joshua asked me to stand next to the enclosure of Vanraj and Vanrani. Panditji was to pass by their cage, then through an archway towards his car, and onwards to Balvatika.

I stood at the lion cage, gripping my sketchbook. My palms were perspiring and I hated my drawing. Chacha Nehru passed by without a smile or a glance at the hordes of children waving flags at him.

Joshua looked tense and his fists were clenched. He hated not being in control of the situation. Nehru appeared to be engrossed in his own thoughts. Nothing Joshua said could bring a smile to Panditji's tight face. I assumed Joshua looked ill at ease because he had been forced to wear a brown shervani, according to protocol. As a rule, he wore khaki or a white bushshirt, because he felt his animals and birds recognized him in this uniform. He would need that familiarity when he entered the co-existence cage.

Nehru was playing with the strings in his garland. Instead of appreciating that lions, tigers, dogs and monkeys were living peacefully together, he was throwing stern glances at Morarji Desai, who was then his Finance Minister, standing on his right, or asking Jivraj Mehta, the Chief Minister of Gujarat, a terse question or two.

The Prime Minister cut a satin ribbon and inaugurated Balvatika. He did not seem to notice the thousands of little children standing in the sun and shouting slogans. Children from various municipal schools were standing there without food or water because they believed that Nehru loved them. The crowd was still there when Nehru emerged from Balvatika.

Suddenly, before his grand departure, Nehru seemed to wake up from a deep slumber. He smiled at the cameras and showered the children with rose petals to show that he cared. There was a stampede as the children scampered to pick up the valuable mementoes of Nehru's visit—rose petals and broken marigold flowers.

Standing at the railing of the Noah's Ark, from where I had a commanding view of the Prime Minister's welcome, I decided that I did not want to get his autograph on the ghastly portrait I had made. But I was trapped.

My father had steered Nehru through Balvatika. He had been shown the Noah's Ark. Suddenly he asked my father a question about co-existence—he was obviously having difficulties with Morarji Desai. I do not know what my father said. But Panditji appeared a little more relaxed as my father regaled him with his favourite animal jokes.

Panditji had a quick round of the children's library, and the traffic circle built around an ancient banyan tree which was surrounded by chairs carved out of old tree trunks. He raced past mountain goat buggies to Toyland, where remote-controlled cars whizzed past his feet, and he paused for a second in the music room where toddlers were dancing to the tune of a Gujarati folk song. He was amused, and complimented my father.

Pandit Jawaharlal Nehru stood vacant-eyed as Mustaq, the pigeon expert from the Bhavnagar royal family, showed his bird act. With the sound of a whistle, the pigeons flew away. They circled Balvatika and returned with the wave of a flag, and perched on Nehru's shoulders. Nervously Mustaq shooed them away, but Nehru did not react. Joshua saw the glint of anger in his eyes, so he led the Prime Minister to the Hall of Mirrors, where if you were fat, you looked thin, thin became fat, or you just looked like a distorted laughing Buddha. Nobody laughed, because Nehru did not laugh. But he allowed the photographers to take a shot of him in front of the fat mirror.

I was dreading my moment with him, which would come when Pandit Nehru was ushered into the guest room behind the cages of the chatterings munias and lovebirds. I was wearing the dress I hated most—an outdated mauve spangled nylon frock with a high waistline and puffed sleeves, made by our family tailor. I had worn it over a limp satin petticoat and bandage brassieres. My hair was oily and sticky, braided with red ribbons. I wanted to become invisible, so clutching the sketchbook, I hid behind a stuffed kangaroo.

From a gap between the kangaroo's legs, I could see Pandit Nehru sitting regally on a low divan, sipping his soft drink with a straw. The Chief Minister was telling him that Joshua David was no ordinary man. He walked into the cages of lions and tigers and they obeyed him. Suddenly, Nehru was interested in my father, and spoke to him about his encounters with animals and his favourite golden retriever. He often received animals as gifts from heads of countries. The next time he received an animal or bird, he promised to gift it to the Ahmedabad zoo. My father was all smiles. Then Nehru leaned on a cushion and asked him if he had a degree in zoology. He laughed when my father told him he was an illiterate. Nehru smiled when he said, 'Perhaps you are gifted with King Solomon's ring?'

My father felt more comfortable and freer with Nehru. He said, 'I would like to introduce you to my daughter.' I tried to disappear into the kangaroo's pouch, but somebody pushed me forward.

I was in front of the Prime Minister of India. Blushing beetroot red, my heart in my throat, I could hear my heart going thud, thud. I could not speak. My father asked me to show the sketchbook to Nehru. 'This is my daughter, sir. She has spent months making your portrait,' he said. Awkwardly I stretched out my drawing. Cameras clicked.

Nehru looked carefully at the drawing. I was afraid he

would ask me if it was a copy. But he was polite. He did not say anything. He smiled, and when he was about to give it back to me, I whispered, 'Autograph, please.' Somebody offered him a pen. He signed and turned to congratulate my father. I am not sure whether it was for making the zoo and Balvatika, or because he had such a talented daughter!

Then suddenly his mood changed. His face stiffened as Morarji Desai said something he did not like. Morarji was standing like a Roman senator next to him. Fair, with a beak-like nose, Morarji was in a spotless white dhoti-kurta and Gandhi topi. Nehru did not answer, and there was pindrop silence in the room.

One could hear the scratch of Panditji's pen, as he wrote his comments in Joshua's visitors' book:

I am happy to have visited the Balvatika and the zoo about which I had heard so much. It is a delightful place for children and I wish there were many more like it, all over India.

Jawaharlal Nehru, 4-4-61.

I think the co-existence bit may have been difficult for him, considering his strained relations with Morarji Desai. They had difficulty in staying in the same pond!

As soon as Nehru left, my father broke into smiles. The dignitaries who were present congratulated him. Panditji's visit had been a great success. Joshua ordered a hot cup of milky tea for himself and wrote a letter to his mother: 'Dearest Maa, Pandit Jawaharlal Nehru the Prime Minister of India, has just visited Hill Garden Zoo. He was pleased. I love you. Joshua—your useless son.'

The next day he went to see her with the morning papers which carried a close-up of the Prime Minister of India and

Joshua David the zoologist. Shebabeth burst into tears. 'If only your father had lived to see this day. He would have been so proud of you. I am sure he is watching you, wherever he is,' she said. 'But more than your father, I know Isabjidada is happy. I always told your father about Isabji's prophecy, but he never believed me. You know he was educated. Not like me.'

64

HILL GARDEN ZOO attracted wildlife experts from all over the world. One of them was Groves. He liked Joshua and often visited Hill Garden Zoo to study the herd of breeding wild asses. They were facing extinction in the Rann of Kutch.

Groves noticed a solitary pig-like animal in the warthog enclosure who appeared to be different from the others. Joshua told him that he was called Chubby-face and was a gift from one of his ex-ruler friends. He had been given to the prince by an Australian friend. He had been sent to Hill Garden Zoo, because the prince could not manage him any more. Chubby-face would race around the palace and stop a few metres away from the palace elephant. He would charge at him and stand between his pillar-like legs. Chubby-face knew that the elephant was helpless, as he was chained to a tree. Chubby-face enjoyed teasing animals who were larger than him.

The short-sighted elephant had come to dread the fat and provocative Chubby-face with his jingling bells. The prince could not stop the little pig from indulging in his sadistic pleasures. These came to an end when the terrified elephant broke his chains and ran amok in the palace grounds. He uprooted trees, trampled dogs and almost killed his mahout.

Finally he tired himself out, and the palace staff chained him to a tree.

Chubby-face took a long time to get used to the zoo. He liked to scare the other warthogs into believing that he was the boss. Even after the palace elephant had almost trampled him, Chubby-face had not been cured of the habit of charging at any animal larger than himself. To keep him out of mischief, Joshua taught Chubby-face to play with a wooden ball which he pushed around with his nose.

Gradually Chubby-face became the star of the warthog enclosure by teaching his companions to play football with their noses. Crowds thronged to see the warthog football game. Every evening, after a boisterous game, Babu threw buckets of water on Chubby-face, tied a leash around his neck, and took him for a walk in the zoo. During these walks, Chubby-face eyed Sumitra the elephant. Elephants provoked him.

On one such evening walk, Babu was a trifle careless, and the leash slipped from his hand. The next thing he knew was that Chubby-face had rushed towards Sumitra. He stood there snorting as though he was a dragon! Sumitra swayed her trunk and watched the little pig suspiciously. Before Babu could stop him, Chubby-face charged at Sumitra and stood between her legs. And Sumitra did the inevitable. She lifted the tenacious little pig in her trunk and tossed him to the ground. Sumitra would have trampled on Chubby-face if Joshua had not rushed up and dragged him to safety. Joshua was sure that Chubby-face was dead. Surprisingly he survived, and recovered in a week.

Groves decided to study Chubby-face and made detailed notes. When he returned to Australia he found a species similar to Chubby-face, and wrote a scientific paper, 'Ancestors of the pigs'. He named his discovery Sus David Davidi, after Joshua.

When Joshua received the letter asking for his consent he felt uncomfortable. He may not have been a practising Jew, but he had never eaten pork. It was an unspoken law of the house—only animals that possessed the dual characteristics of cloven hoofs and chewing cud were permitted. All others were forbidden such as the camel, hare, rock badger and pig. It was the Jewish dietary law. The pig was considered an unclean animal in the Bible. Joshua was about to write a polite letter of refusal to Groves, saying that he could not allow his name to be associated with a pig. But then, his co-existence theory got the better of him. He checked his favourite passages on Noah, and found that God had not asked him to leave behind the pig.

'. . . And the Lord said unto Noah, come thou and all thy house unto the ark; for thee have seen righteous before me in this generation. Of every clean beast thou shall take to thee by sevens, the male and his female: and of beasts that are not clean by two, the male and his female . . . and Noah did according unto all the lord commanded him . . .'

Joshua wrote a letter of acceptance to Groves.

65

JOSHUA WAS BECOMING frail. The aperture in his throat was constricting him. Yet he never stopped going to the zoo. It was the elixir of his life. Animals and birds sustained him. And, he had a mystical relationship with panthers. This was evident when a wild panther strayed into Ahmedabad.

The panther had been spotted in the garden of Julliet Moses who ran a school in her bungalow, not far from the zoo. Julliet had seen the panther from the kitchen window. It looked like a big stray dog sitting in the shadows of the hibiscus bushes. She called out to the gardener to drive it away. The gardener noticed the spots, ran in and closed the back door of the house, saying it was a tiger. Julliet panicked and woke up her husband. He called Joshua.

Joshua immediately alerted the fire brigade. While he was driving to the residence of Julliet Moses, he saw the panther running wild in the street. The animal had crashed into a four-wheeler and injured three people: he had chased a vendor of bananas, dashed into an old man taking his morning walk, and the third victim was a cyclist. The panther chased him and reached for his neck as he fell on the ground. Nervous in the strange surroundings, however, he abandoned the cyclist and jumped into an open courtyard where an unsuspecting Ushabehn Patel was washing clothes, beating them with a wooden bat.

As the news spread that a panther was running wild in the streets of Maninagar, huge crowds collected. Joshua was furious that people did not understand that the panther could harm them. He knew that he was no saviour and that if he caught the panther alive, it would be a miracle.

The police and fire brigade arrived, and a huge truck with a cage was stationed near the school.

Ushabehn heard something fall into the courtyard and looked up to see a large animal next to her one-year-old son. She threw the bat at him and picked up her child. The bat frightened the animal and it entered the puja room next to the water tap. Ushabehn ran and closed the door. All she wanted was to save her child. She was certain that the goddess installed in the puja room would protect them.

Joshua was impressed by Ushabehn's calmness as she told him how the panther had entered the house, and relieved that she had locked the ferocious animal in the puja room. He admired her courage.

Ushabehn gave a detailed description of the layout of the house to Babu. Standing in the open courtyard, Joshua planned his modus operandi. The problem was how to capture a panther in a closed room. There was only one exit and there were thousands of people standing outside the house. It was a real challenge. Till late afternoon no solution had been found. Joshua was sure he could catch the panther alive. He gave strict instructions to the police not to shoot unless he told them to. They waited, their rifles aimed at the house. The atmosphere was tense.

Joshua could hear the panther dashing against the walls. With a ladder from the fire brigade, Babu climbed up to the ventilator. He saw that the panther had hurt itself and was getting tired. Joshua's throat felt dry but he refused to eat or drink till he had captured the panther. He was annoyed to see that people were giving the police, the fire brigade and the zoo workers soft drinks and snacks. It never stopped surprising him that people could have picnics in dangerous situations like these. The crowd had also doubled. Joshua called the police commissioner. 'Is this a festival or something? Why cannot we disperse the crowd?'

'Joshuadada, there is only one way—lathi charge—and I know you will not like that. So what can I do? Shoot in the air?'

Joshua sighed. 'Leave them, we will manage. If they want to see the greatest show on earth, they will.'

As Joshua stood smoking a cigarette with his foot on the door, he noticed that it had been repaired recently. He called Ushabehn and asked her about it. She told him that the house was old and the door of the puja room had rotted as it was close to the water tap where they washed clothes and dishes. Joshua said that they could capture the panther only if the lower half of the door was broken. For the first time the brave woman looked uncertain. She called out to her husband and they agreed to break the door.

The cage was brought from the municipal van and placed next to the door. As bait a chunk of beef laced with sedatives was placed in the cage. Surrounded by police guards, four carpenters from the zoo worked slowly and carefully on the door. Babu and others kept a watch on the panther from the ventillator. With bamboo poles, Babu kept the panther in a corner, so that he did not go near the door while they were breaking it. Joshua urged the carpenters to hurry. It was already evening and he wanted to capture the animal before nightfall.

As soon as the plank of wood was removed, the cage was placed there. Then operation panther began. From the ventilator, using the poles, Babu and his men pressed the panther towards the cage. Trying to charge at Babu, the panther hit the ventilator and fell. Slowly, methodically, Babu drove him into the cage. As the trapdoor slid down upon the tired, angry animal, the crowd cheered.

The panther was taken to the zoo. Ushabehn touched Joshua's feet in gratitude. He praised her presence of mind in closing the door on the panther. When Joshua emerged from the house, the crowd gave him a hero's welcome. Joshua wanted to relax with the Moses family but there was a press conference he had to address and admirers streaming in to congratulate him, some to touch his feet.

After Joshua's rescue party had left, Ushabehn held her son close and entered the puja room. The first thing she noticed was that the glass frame of the goddess's picture was broken and blood from the panther's head was smeared on the glass. Ushabehn believed that it was a divine message—a spiritual sindoor. Joshua David had been able to capture the panther with the blessings of the goddess. It was a miracle.

The next day's newspapers were full of photographs of the Maninagar panther, my father, Ushabehn and the blood-smeared picture-frame. In the picture of the goddess, there was a serpent with an upright hood and a halo. Signs such as these made me wonder about my grandmother Shebabeth's story of the visions and prophecies of Isabjidada.

The Maningar panther was named Chitta. He was ferocious, but slowly became calmer. A year later, he was joined by Bijli, the Vadnagar panther. She had been captured by Joshua from a mosque in a similar fashion. The difference was that she was captured at midnight with halogen lamps installed by the fire brigade.

On the way back, my father stopped at our house in Vasna. He wanted the children to see the panther before anybody else. When my father lifted the tarpaulin, Bijli charged at us with great force. We fell back in terror.

It always surprised me that Joshua could capture wild animals without tranquillizer guns. Later Jamsaheb Shatrushalyasinhji—the ex-ruler of Jamnagar—gave a tranquillizer gun to Joshua. He used it on an elephant in musth who had escaped from a circus. Joshua studied the dosage, and sometimes used it to capture ferocious langurs or animals who had strayed into the city. There was also the incident of a nilgai who had been caught in a thorny bush in the suburbs of Ahmedabad. She was shot with a tranquillizer and taken to the zoo. Here she was nursed and later introduced back into her natural habitat. But for panthers and crocodiles Joshua had only used his bare hands. Perhaps he was blessed to communicate with the wild and untamed.

66

JOSHUA DID NOT participate in Jewish rituals at the synagogue, but accepted invitations to chair certain ceremonies. He was gradually becoming like a patriarch of the past. He would borrow a kippa and sit on the teva with a serious expression. On such days, he often spoke of his death, and showed me his frayed old silk tsitsit, hidden under his shirts. Joshua had not touched his prayer shawl since he had received it at his bar mitzvah at the age of thirteen. He knew he would need it at his death.

Whenever I saw the tsitsit in its silk cover, I felt scared and got goose pimples. The symbol of our Jewish traditions was waiting in the cupboard for my father's death. It was like a premonition.

Joshua had a brush with death in Bombay. He was invited as chief guest to the Tefereth synagogue for its golden jubilee celebrations. Joshua left for Bombay on Thursday night by Gujarat Mail. He received a warm welcome on his arrival on Friday morning at the railway station from the Bene Israel Jews of Bombay. In Bombay, as always, Joshua stayed at the railway retiring rooms. After breakfast, he went with the welcome committee of the Tefereth to the synagogue.

Four hours of prayers, a small break and another three hours at the synagogue, and Joshua felt the beginning of a fever, headache and nausea. He assumed it was an attack of malaria, and would pass after a peg with friends at the retiring rooms. He did not eat or drink anything, nor did he tell anybody that he was feeling ill. Joshua regretted that Babu was not with him. Joshua liked his strongman image. The man who walked into the cages of lions and tigers could not be cowed down by a female mosquito. So he smiled, talked, gave autographs and shook innumerable hands before asking the president of the committee to drop him back to his room.

On Saturday night, Joshua was admitted to a Bombay hospital by the matron of the retiring rooms. Late at night, I received a phone call from one of the committee members of the Tefereth, informing me that my father was in hospital. I called Babu. We took a bus and reached Bombay on Sunday morning. Joshua was sitting lost and alone in the emergency ward. As soon as he saw us, he said he wanted to return to Ahmedabad. The doctors refused to give him permission to leave. It was his heart, they said. If something happened to him, they would be held responsible. As Joshua dressed, I had to sign some papers, and after the formalities, we took a taxi to the retiring rooms. Joshua had a hot shower and ordered a lunch of chicken curry and rumali roti before we caught the next train to Ahmedabad. In the train, Joshua rested and joked about his death. I was curious to know how he had felt in the hour of death. Joshua stopped smiling. 'I was thinking about Montu. He kept me alive,' he said.

Babu was sleeping on the berth above us, and Joshua told me this story.

'In my life at Hill Garden Zoo, the two animals who were closest to me were Raju the tiger, and Montu the lion. Montu's mother also wanted to eat him like Raju's mother. As I have told you before, animals feel threatened by the smell of human beings. When they give birth, their protective instincts are so strong that the mother often eats her young, assuming they will be safer inside her, than outside. I saved three cubs. Two died of stomach infection, and Montu survived. He was Vanraj and Vanrani's cub. That day, I could not find a lactating bitch, so we had to take Lassie from you. Remember how upset you were. "Why Lassie?" you asked. You were angry with me, but there was no other way of saving Montu. I gave Lassie all the comforts of a home. The only thing I could not give her was your warmth. And for that I will never forgive myself. I know that without Lassie you were lost.

'When we first put Montu's mouth to Lassie's teats, tears welled up in her eyes. She knew that the teeth which suckled her were different from her own pups. I saw in her eyes that she was afraid. She was aware that once Montu grew up, he could eat her in one gulp. Lassie snapped at Montu, intimidating him so that he obeyed her. Lassie wanted Montu to be afraid of her—and he was.

'There was great interest in a lion growing up in our house. But Naomi was disturbed. She was afraid of him and worried that the golden ball of fur would one day become a big full-grown lion. Naomi could not handle a live lion in the house. Montu toppled everything and got his claws entangled in her sari. Naomi suffered silently, till we shifted Lassie to an enclosure in the zoo, much against your wishes. I could not please everybody. So, I must have hurt your feelings.

'Montu was growing fast. Although he played doggy games with Lassie's pups, he sometimes had difficulty in retracting his claws. He was fighting his natural feelings and trying to behave like a dog. Because I wanted Lassie to be Montu's mother, she would give him a lick or two. I suspect that she tolerated Montu just to please me.

'Lassie must have had great difficulty in adjusting to zoo life. And she had the difficult job of convincing Montu that he was not the king of the jungle—that he was just a domesticated little dog. It was funny because he believed her. Even when he was a full-grown lion with a huge mane and ate kilos of beef, he would wag his tail at Lassie as though he was a little puppy.

This posed many problems for me. I could not introduce him to other lions. When he was six months old, I left him for a few hours with a young lioness. He immediately affected the stance of surrender and she mauled him. That left him a bachelor for life. I decided he would never be alone. I walked into his cage and played with him. He never forgot to retract his claws. There was perfect understanding between us. Until the time he did not see me for three months. That was when I was at the Tata Memorial Hospital for my cancer operation.

'Montu had become insecure without me. After the operation, when I returned, the first thing I did was to enter Montu's cage. But I did not realize that I was still shaky on my feet. Besides, I had lost my voice. I did not know how I was going to control him.

'Facing the full-grown Montu, I was a little nervous. I stood still. But Montu had noticed nothing, and jumped to greet me as he always did with his paws resting on my shoulders. I fell down with Montu over me. Montu was terrified. He immediately went and cowered in a corner. I was furious. This had never happened to me before. I stood up, took a stick and thrashed him till I was exhausted.

'Do you think Montu attacked me or hit back? No, he took the beating, knowing full well that he could easily have made mincemeat of me.

'That night I could not sleep. Early next morning, after Naomi had dressed the wound in my throat, I went to the zoo and entered Montu's enclosure. He was cringing in a corner. I was sorry that he had lost his normal lion instincts of self-preservation. I sat down. Montu came and sat next to me. He licked my hand as though to say that he was sorry to have pushed me. I had tears in my eyes. How does one say sorry to a lion?'

67

IN MARCH 1975, my father received the Padmashree from the President of India, Fakhruddin Ali Ahmed. Joshua had by then lost his voice after a laryngectomy operation for cancer of the voice box. He had learnt to speak with an electric larynx—a battery-operated aid. At the tea party, after the awards function, Indira Gandhi, who was the Prime Minister, greeted my father, saying she knew that he was the zooman from Ahmedabad. She also knew that he spoke with an electric larynx, and wanted to know how he communicated with his wards. She listened attentively, then turned to greet somebody saying, 'David, the country is proud of you.'

On his return, my father was all praise for the great lady who had come to speak to him and shown real interest in his work. He felt honoured that she knew everything about him. At the party, he had invited her to see the zoo, and she had agreed. So he wrote a letter inviting her and also mentioning that her father had been full of praise for the zoo complex.

Indira Gandhi's reply stunned him. She wrote back that she could not accept his invitation as she hated to see animals and birds in cages. She preferred to see them free. My father was furious. He wrote back to her, explaining the importance of zoos for the preservation of wildlife. She never answered.

Soon afterwards, she imposed the emergency and caged many people like Jayaprakash Narayan and Morarji Desai.

Joshua was hurt by Indira Gandhi's reply. Over his evening peg, he would relate the Indira Gandhi story to close friends: 'Indira Gandhi knew everything about my work. She even said, "The country is proud of you." Why did they give me a Padmashree, if they did not understand the importance of zoos? Are they aware of what is happening to our wildlife?'

Joshua wrote articles about wildlife preservation and justified the necessity for zoos. Though he was a non-believer and was not a practising Jew, when he wrote articles on wildlife, he invariably quoted from the Old Testament. In an article titled 'Importance of zoos' in the *Animal Citizen* he wrote:

> The innovation of keeping animals, birds and reptiles in captivity comes from the Bible which says, 'Go unto the Ark; you and your household; and take unto the Ark with you from all living creatures, two of every kind—one pair—one male and female. I will save them together with you; so that after the flood they may multiply and grow and fill the earth.'

> Thus God saved with the help of Noah, all the numerous animals and birds from the largest to the smallest, from extinction. Probably the wildlife sanctuaries and the zoological parks carry on the inheritance by being Noah's Arks in a scientific way and help save birds, animals and reptiles. Let this be an allegory, or a fantasy or a myth, but the thought itself is wonderful and full of imagination of the entire background of preservation of wildlife, even though it may have been a million years ago.

> A zoo garden or park is a connecting link between man and wildlife. It is the only place where a city dweller comes in direct contact with wildlife and studies the cultural, scientific, and educational aspects of a zoological garden . . .

> Most people do not understand the difference between a zoo garden and a zoological park. A zoo garden is a place where a number of birds, animals and reptiles are

housed in a small, limited area in cages or in the open with the purpose of exhibiting them to the public for their educational, recreational, cultural and aesthetic need. While a zoological park is a broader term, where the area is comparatively more and maintained in a habitat closer to their natural environment, resembling a sanctuary to some extent.

It is a common feeling among people that zoo animals are miserable and do not have enough space like in the wild state. But, with experience it is observed that some mammals and birds live better in captivity and breed freely in small enclosures and aviaries also. Another common belief is that animals are unhealthy in captivity. In good zoos, the majority of birds and animals are healthier than in their wild state, where it is the survival of the fittest. Here they are regularly fed and looked after properly. In fact a good zoo is judged not merely by the number of different species of animals and birds but by the health and contentment of the inhabitants.

In order to help the feral population of animals propagate easily, a good number of them should be housed in zoos. So that even if their numbers decrease in nature due to accidents or epidemics like foot-and-mouth disease, rinderpest, poaching, shooting, etc . . . they may be saved from extinction by conserving them in captivity.

The captive breeding of these birds and animals will have to be done on strictly scientific lines. It is necessary to take into consideration the laws of genetics, and make the best use of the inheritance pool in building up viable and healthy animals. This calls for cooperation from zoos all over the world.

The destruction of their habitat is undoubtedly the major cause of changes in the animal populations of the world . . . Rampant and indiscriminate shooting with high velocity and modern rifles, jeeps and blinding searchlights, and pollution of different kinds have affected the fauna and created the present grave situation. Conservation is basically the maintenance of our habitat, whether it is a jungle, semi-forest, salt marsh or a private reserve.

Breeding of rare animals and birds in captivity is an important conservation measure. It is even more important that zoos should breed their own stocks of rare and common animals. Although for many years to come, zoos will be able to draw on the natural surplus of most wild animal stocks for their supplies, they cannot assume that this situation will last forever. Particularly with those species like apes and carnivores, where heavy losses are experienced in the process of capture, the early stages of captivity, epidemics and virus infections.

Almost eighty species of birds have become extinct in the last three centuries. Pesticides are also a great threat to wildlife.

The conservation of wildlife has become most important, yet is sorrowfully ignored. If immediate steps are not taken for their proper conservation, the future of wildlife is terribly gloomy and sad. It is high time that the camera should replace the gun.

As was his habit, I am sure that my father posted a copy of this article to all his critics, including Indira Gandhi. Much later, to his distress, the entire zoo complex was named after the Nehru family!

68

IN MY MEMORY, the zoo was a Utopian dream. I could not reach out to it any more. It was no longer part of my world. It was one of the departments of the Ahmedabad Municipal Corporation.

When Joshua had brought Ashoka to the zoo, Ahmedabad had had one of those unseasonal winter rains. The Sabarmati was flooded.

Ashoka belonged to Mahantji. He had inherited the animal from his father. According to family tradition, the eldest son was given to a certain sect with the elephant, and was expected to live on alms. Mahantji earned a neat amount, which he kept hidden, stitched in the pillow over which he sat in the small wooden howdah strapped with bells around Ashoka's enormous stomach. Ashoka was a handsome animal with a pair of magnificent tusks, the tips of which were encased in silver.

Every six months, when Mahantji returned to the village, he left Ashoka with his wife, Nirmala, and her sister-in-law, Shanti, who were very fond of him. The children played with him, using his trunk as a ladder to climb onto his back. In the afternoons, when the women finished their work, they sat on his back and took him to the river, where Ashoka was the centre of attention. The children scrambled all over him and he showered them with jets of water.

One day, as they headed back towards Ahmedabad after a

round of collecting alms, Mahantji perhaps goaded him too much.

Ashoka felt a strange stirring in his brain. Try as he may, Ashoka could not control the burning musth which was flowing into his temples. His body was aflame.

When Mahantji hit Ashoka's head one more time with the goad, he unleashed a fury which nobody had ever seen before. In one sweep of his trunk, Ashoka pulled down Mahantji and trampled him to death. After which Ashoka rushed onto the road, not knowing where to go and what to do. He needed to cool himself, so he slid into the river and swam in the turbulent waters of the Sabarmati.

By then the fire brigade had informed Joshua that a mad elephant had killed his mahout and was moving towards the city. Joshua was past seventy and not as strong as before. But the thought of the police killing an elephant bothered him, and he asked for the municipal jeep. He took his position on Nehru Bridge, from where he could observe Ashoka through his binoculars. Joshua saw that the elephant did not seem to be moving inland. From experience, he knew that in a situation like this, the elephant did not want to encounter human beings. Perhaps his mahout had hurt him. Or he was in musth. This normally made an elephant hyper-sensitive. Had he been on the rampage after killing his mahout, he would have continued running on the road, trampling people and destroying anything that came in his way. Instead, he had stepped into the river. He stood lost and helpless. A victim of the forces of nature.

Joshua's heart went out to the elephant. If he could get him out of the river, he would be the ideal mate for Sumitra, the female elephant at the zoo. Joshua decided that Sumitra was the solution to this strange situation. Sumitra was going through her first menstrual cycle, and would be the right ploy to entice this unknown male. But Joshua did not know how he was going to get Sumitra to the tusker. He also had his own forebodings about the elephant. He had to trust the animal without knowing him. What if he killed Sumitra?

When elephants crossed a river, they held on to each other's tails. When Sumitra stepped into the river, Joshua recited all the Hebrew prayers he could remember. His instinct with animals was being put to test. Joshua did something he had never done before. He took a vow: if Sumitra could calm the mad elephant, he would prepare a table for Passover. It would be the first time in years.

A crowd gathered to watch this play between man and nature. Rifles and tranquillizer guns were aimed at Ashoka, as Sumitra waded towards him with her mahout.

Joshua was apprehensive. He did not know what the tusker would do. To his relief, when Ashoka saw Sumitra, he trumpeted. It was a friendly call. The two animals touched their trunks in salutation. Sumitra's mahout goaded her to turn her back to the male and start walking towards the banks of the river. Sumitra's touch had been soothing. Instinctively Ashoka held her tail with his trunk and followed her to the shore—and to Hill Garden Zoo.

This was Joshua's last miracle. He did not live to see the Passover.

He was not there to break the unleavened bread, pour the third cup of wine for Elijah and open the door for the prophet. The waters had divided for his final exit.

69

MONTHS LATER, JOSHUA died in his sleep. Breakfast was waiting for him, but he did not wake up.

The news spread like wildfire in Ahmedabad. The house filled with people. The Ahmedabad Municipal Corporation cleaned up the ground in front of our house. The zoo staff stood around him in silence, as preparations were made for his funeral. The entire Bene Israel community was there, stitching the shroud, bathing my father, reading the prayers for the dead.

When he was dressed and ready for the grave, in accordance with his will, a vial of ittar was tied to his heart with a small bag of ashes—his love letters to Naomi. And, when his body was brought out from the house and taken to the ambulance, the zoo workers released a hundred birds. The birds would make his flight easier.

In death, my father looked calm and relieved. In the end, the zoo had become a burden. It was a well-guarded secret. He never confided in anybody what was bothering him. When he spoke about Hill Garden Zoo, I felt he was like Atlas carrying the weight of the zoo on his back. They had become one entity. There was no escape. Each animal had come to him in twos and multiplied into twenties. Many of those who had been close to him were now trophies on the wall. Montu and Raju were dead. Raju died of a stomach infection, but Montu died a painful death.

One morning when Joshua entered Montu's cage for their usual bout of wrestling, Montu did not move. Joshua was worried. He remembered Ceaser and hoped Montu had not contacted rabies.

Joshua immediately sent the zoo jeep to Anand to fetch a team of doctors from the government veterinary college. Joshua's heart sank when they said that Montu was paralysed. Complications had set in when they had been forced to operate upon his infected tail that had become full of maggots. Montu suffered from all sorts of problems. He never recovered.

Joshua tried to make Montu as comfortable as possible. He gave him a grass bed, and personally saw that he was regularly given his injections and food. He hoped that one day Montu would stand up and greet him as he earlier had by jumping around him like a puppy. He felt helpless seeing him sleeping on his back, unable to even drive away the flies which collected on his face. Often Joshua wondered whether Montu should be put to sleep. But he could not take the decision. He could not possibly kill a friend.

Day after day, Montu lay on his back, head thrown backwards, facing the door. He was always looking out for Joshua. Every morning when Joshua entered the cage, there would be a look of gratitude in his eyes. Joshua had learnt to recognize this look since his shikar days. He breathed a sigh of relief and shed a tear when Montu died. Montu was lying on his back, his face turned towards the door, his lifeless eyes watching Joshua with a strange brilliance.

I was thinking of Montu's death as I placed the earth from Jerusalem on my Joshua's closed eyes. At the graveyard, the elders did not know what to do. After my father was lowered into his grave, his son was supposed to sprinkle a handful of earth on his body, before the others. Only then could his grave be covered. My son was too young, and I was a woman. I asked the elders' permission that I be allowed to sprinkle the earth upon him—just like a son. The Bene Israel men collected in a corner, discussed the problem and agreed. I felt relieved and strangely victorious in the face of death and our Jewish rituals.

When I sprinkled earth on my father, I was shivering. I needed to sit down and cry. I asked somebody to drive me home. Some more arrangements had to be made. The funeral party would return to the house. I would have to pour water over their hands as they entered the house for a simple meal of rice and vegetables.

When the community members left, having performed all the rituals, I closed the house for the night. I locked the door, and closed my father's room which was aglow with the seven-day light. For the first time in twenty years, I was afraid of the dark.

4

Esther

70

Now, IT CAME to pass on the third day, that Esther put
on her royal apparel, and stood in the inner court of
Ahaseurus, the king of Persia . . . And, it was so when the
king saw her standing in the court, that she obtained favour
in his sight: and the king held out to Esther the golden
sceptre that was in his hand. So Esther drew near, and
touched the top of the sceptre . . .

—*Megillat* (the scrolls of Esther): Torah

The name of my ancestor was Esther.

How does one write about one's own birth?

Naomi had a difficult delivery. Jerusha was suddenly
afraid. She did not want her sister-in-law to die on her hands.
She called for Dr Anklesaria. Hannah sensed that something
was wrong, and rushed to Saraspur in a carriage. She wanted
to be next to Naomi.

It normally took forty-five minutes to reach Saraspur
Maternity Hospital from Delhi Darwaza. But on that day, the
carriage seemed to fly over the traffic and took just ten
minutes. When Hannah reached the hospital and saw Joshua

standing at the door, white as a corpse, she knew that Naomi's life was in danger.

I am told that when I was born I was very underweight and my mother was so sick that she could not feed me. I could have died. In fact, both of us could have died. While Ankleswaria and Jerusha were making efforts to save Naomi, Grandmother Shebabeth kept me alive by holding me to her tired old breasts. Later, Uncle Menachem sent a goat from Delhi Darwaza in a rickshaw. It was tied to a post in the hospital grounds and Shebabeth fed me with sterilized cotton buds soaked in fresh goat milk.

The eighth day naming ceremony was approaching. There was chaos in the three Dandekar homes—Menachem's, Jerusha's and Joshua's. Such a situation had never arisen before. Menachem and Hannah had decided on their children's names even before they were born. They had made a list of boys' and girls' names and as soon as the gender of the child was known, Menachem took Hannah's consent and the child was named. Similarly with the naming ceremony of their sisters Sarah, Ruby and their children.

Usually the men or the elders decided on the name of the child and then one of the elders would check in the Bible to see that the name did not have a negative connotation.

Joshua and Naomi may have discussed a name or two, but not seriously. When Menachem asked Joshua whether they had decided on a name for me he drew a blank. Joshua did not want to admit that they had not expected a daughter. But when he saw me, squirming like a shrimp in his mother's lap, he was happy. Naomi was not in a condition to feel anything but pain. If she was disappointed, she did not show it. I cannot imagine myself with any other name.

I was born on 17 March 1945—well before the

independence of India and just a day before my grandfather David's birthday.

I was born on Holi. Jerusha was annoyed that the staff was in a boisterous mood. She had given strict instructions that they should not play with colour in the hospital grounds and she was irritated by their happy screams while she was attending to Naomi. Moreover, when one of the nurses, ayahs, or ward boys came to the house with a medicine or message, their faces and clothes had dabs of colour. Jerusha gave them a disapproving look. They knew that they were in for trouble. Jerusha disliked the liberty that men and women took with each other on this particular day.

After the delivery, she was relieved when Naomi fell asleep. Shebabeth lit a candle on the dining table and waited for Jerusha with the special Purim dish puran-poli.

Shebabeth had forgotten that it was Purim—the festival of Queen Esther. Late that night, after I was born, two hours before midnight, she remembered it was Purim and that she had forgotten to light the candle or make puran-polis. Shebabeth was pleased that it was Purim—one of the rare festivals of happiness. She wondered whether the child should be named Esther. But she hesitated, as Naomi was a strong-minded woman, and liked to take her own decisions. She waited for two days but Naomi showed no signs of recovery. Her breasts hurt and she had spasms in her uterus.

The day before the naming ceremony, Shebabeth sent for a cradle from Biscuit Gali and spent the afternoon decorating it with silver buntings and flowers.

Naomi was better. She was resting in bed and reading *The Illustrated Weekly of India*. Shebabeth noticed that Naomi was looking at a painting—a landscape in blues with a star and the silhouette of a young girl sitting under a tree. Naomi smiled for the first time in months and said, 'The girl in the painting is so beautiful.' Shebabeth asked curiously, 'What is the title of the painting?'

Naomi took off her spectacles, wiped them with the end of her sari, put them on again and said, 'Esther—the evening star.' For Shebabeth this was apt, a blessing. 'Hold the baby for a second and look at her. Does she look like the girl in the painting?'

Naomi looked at her mother-in-law and asked, 'Esther?'

'Yes,' said Shebabeth. 'This is Esther. She was born on Purim.'

To get their own back, my grandmother forced Menachem to send a telegram to Naomi's father, Daniel Navgaokar: 'Naomi gives birth to baby girl named Esther—greetings from Dr Menachem David and family.'

71

SINCE NAOMI HAD not fed me with her own milk when I was a newborn, she always felt guilty and was overprotective about me. I was very thin and always sick with some illness or the other. She tried to fatten me by force-feeding me. On Saturday afternoons, she made new dresses and panties for me on her Singer machine and knitted sweaters for me and my father. I could never understand why because Ahmedabad had only two months of mild winter.

My early years were spent amidst birds and animals. The zoo happened when I was six years old. I was happy with Joshua and his menagerie.

I faced my first trauma when I was admitted to Mount Carmel Convent High School. That was the end of my utopia.

Life in school was harsh. The tall, severe buildings were clinically clean and colourless. The depressing textbooks all had dog ears and were covered with little doodles. The school uniform was another sort of prison in red checks and layers of clothing, belts, ties, bows, socks, shoes, ribbons and hair-pins—all barriers to the outside world. In this uncomfortable world, I became a poor student. I was told to wear a dunce's cap and made to stand on the last bench in the class.

The only moments of release came on half-holidays, Thursdays and Sundays, when my father took me to the zoo. I felt at home with our wild friends.

I had to face a new trauma when my mother decided to spend a year in Baroda at the Maharaja Jayajirao University to finish her degree in education. According to the new laws of the ministry of education, she needed the degree to become a teacher in a high school, where the salaries were better.

When she left for Baroda, I felt abandoned for the first time. The zoo took up all of Joshua's time. He had no time for me. He often left me with Shebabeth at the Delhi Darwaza house with Uncle Menachem's family. Grandmother Shebabeth sacrificed her concern for Aunt Jerusha for about six months and then went back to live with her at the Saraspur Maternity Home. I was shunted between three houses, the ones at Shahibaug, Delhi Darwaza and Saraspur. I would have liked to stay with my father and Moyuddin at the Shahibaug house but that was no longer possible.

Although my mother put on a great show of strength, she felt helpless. She knew I needed to stay in one place because of my school, homework, etc. but she could not decide where. Finally, when she was in Ahmedabad for the Diwali vacation, she invited Shebabeth for lunch and suggested that she move in with us at Shahibaug.

Shebabeth refused. However much she loved me, or Joshua, or the Delhi Darwaza house, her first concern was her elder daughter Jerusha. She would cover her head with the end of the white widow's sari and hiding her tears say, 'No, no, I cannot leave Jerusha alone.'

My mother would try to argue. 'But, Maa, Jerushasister is a grown-up woman and Esther is small. She needs you.' She would then try to play upon Shebabeth's emotions. 'Remember, it's because of you that she is alive . . .'

Shebabeth would pick me up, hold me to her breasts and still say, 'No.' But Naomi knew that although she became sentimental about Aunt Jerusha, Shebabeth would find a solution for me.

And, that evening, before she left for Aunt Jerusha's house, Shebabeth suggested that the house in Delhi Darwaza would be best for me. It was close to both houses and I could take the school bus with my cousins. Uncle Menachem and Aunt Hannah would take good care of me. As a special treat, I could spend Thursdays and Sundays and the school half-days with her at the maternity home. Smiling reassuringly at Naomi, she said, 'You know I am getting old and cannot run around. I will employ Mani to look after her.'

'Mani?' My mother did not know any woman by that name. She knew most of the women who lived around the Delhi Darwaza house. Almost all of them belonged to the Pinjara community, and worked in our houses.

Shebabeth explained: 'Mani has just come from Palanpur. A young widow. She has a young son and lives with Nathi's family. I will pay her salary. It will be her duty to look after Esther. I think the problem is solved.'

I was happy. I loved the Delhi Darwaza house. It made me feel secure. I scampered off into all the familiar dark recesses of the ancestral house. Besides, I loved the comfort of being with my uncle and aunt. They did not seem to have problems like my parents. My uncle's family was like a huge banyan tree which sheltered and protected me. Uncle warmed my heart when he opened a bank account in my name: Esther David. He gave me an identity of my own. Every month he credited Rs 100 in the Dena Bank, Delhi Darwaza branch.

He was interested in astrology and I often saw him reading my horoscope. I always wondered whether he had seen something untoward in my horoscope and wanted to make sure that I was well looked after. Perhaps he foresaw the difficulties I was to encounter in my adult life. Or he just wanted to do a mitzwah—a good turn. He did many in his lifetime.

If I was happy in the Delhi Darwaza house that year, I was unhappy in the Shahibaug house. I did not see my mother for months. I only received postcards, written in her steady big hand: she hoped I was well and sent best wishes to everybody at Delhi Darwaza and Saraspur. That did not leave space for me. And when she came for the occasional holiday or weekend, she was anxious and in a bad mood as she cleaned the house, and burst into tears as the carriage came to take her to the station. Those were difficult days.

With my father, it was a problem of a different sort. On his way to the zoo, he came often to the Delhi Darwaza house. But the timing was always wrong. As soon as he arrived I was whisked off to the bathroom and dressed for school. Together with my cousins I would say, 'Bye bye, uncle.' One of them would nudge me and say, 'Stupid! He is our uncle, and your daddy.'

On Sundays, my father was more relaxed. But I suffered. He never seemed to look at me. His gaze would stop lovingly on my cousins' faces, but when it came to me, he seemed to stiffen as he asked, 'How are you?' I would nod my head and wait for him to tap his knee so that I could climb on to his lap. But he didn't. Later, I realized that he was under stress because of the zoo, and his wife was not with him. They must also have been short of money. I was an unnecessary burden on them.

I was heartbroken that Joshua, my childhood nanny, did not belong to me any more. I still remember a particular Sunday when he came to Delhi Darwaza with a perforated box. It was winter and he was wearing a sleeveless white sweater my mother had knitted for him. The five of us jumped around him. 'Come children, cool down,' he said. 'Now close your eyes. I am going to show you something you have never seen before.' We closed our eyes and when he told us to open them we saw that he had a huge chameleon sitting on the back of his hand.

My cousins hastily moved back when they saw the scaly creature with its telescopic eyes. It was a dull brown colour, which started changing first to yellow and then to red, and finally it turned a bright green. My father told us about its tongue—how long and sticky it was, and that it worked like a dart when it saw possible prey—that is a fly or other insect.

I was fascinated and moved closer to the chameleon. It was about to come on my palm with its funny frog-like leg when my father noticed me. His eyes dilated with anger. Mani understood the look and pulled me away, saying it would bite. I wanted to cry. Mani's garlic smell soothed me.

After the episode of the chameleon, I started dreading Sunday mornings. I started avoiding my father. I would emerge from my hiding place only when he asked Mani, 'Where is baby?'

I was happiest with my grandmother. She gave me security

and love. And at the maternity hospital where she stayed with Aunt Jerusha there was a big garden, with arched trellises covered by the heady jui and mogra creepers. Women in advanced stages of pregnancy rested under palm trees and green badam trees, while feasting their eyes on cannas and zenias. Dotted around were bushes shaped like peacocks. In the middle of the freshly mown lawn there was a swing. I enjoyed the freedom of flying high and low. Watching me from the balcony of the house, Grandmother Shebabeth would say, 'Slowly, slowly.' But I didn't care.

I enjoyed the freedom she gave me. To run, to dance, to tease, to laugh, to cry, to sleep whenever I wanted and wind the gramophone and listen to bhajans or Hindi film songs as I chose. When she would sit on her huge armchair with her legs stretched out, I knew that it was story time.

She cooked me a huge lunch of every possible Bene Israel delicacy and made the chapatis herself. They were extraordinary. They opened like a fan with seven flaps—the saat padar chi chapati—soft, sweet and full of ghee. Just like the breasts she offered me when I stayed over for the night. It was our secret.

The umbilical cord was severed between my parents and me during the period my father stayed in Laxmi Nivas and my mother in Baroda. I was seven years old.

72

MY GRANDMOTHER RETURNED me to my mother's custody when Naomi came back to Ahmedabad armed with a Master's in education. She got a job right away as an English teacher in a higher secondary school. The day she received the letter of appointment, the three houses of the Dandekars rejoiced.

The next morning, while I was recovering from my hangover of happiness, my parents left for work. My mother went to the school and my father left for the zoo. I had a holiday and the house seemed to be unusually silent. I ached for my parents, grandmother and the ancestral house, where I had left Mani. I missed her, and prayed for a miracle which would bring her to me. A month later Mani joined me in the Shahibaug house as a cook. My mother had confided in Shebabeth how difficult it was to look after a house and a child. My grandmother found the solution—Mani.

This was the beginning of the fairy tale world which Mani created for me. It was our private make-believe world. To all appearances she was cooking and cleaning, but when we were alone, she opened the doors to her treasure house of stories— folk stories, stories about Ahmedabad, Palanpur, Radhanpur and Baroda. These were followed by a series which was taboo in the presence of my parents—ghost stories, crime stories and strange love stories with tragic endings.

It was impossible to associate beauty with Mani. She had a long horsy face, with a soft down of curly hair on her upper lip and one hard, long hair which grew from a mole on her chin. She bathed every day under the garden tap, but managed to look grey, smelly and dark. She could never get rid of the pungent odour of garlic and bidi.

But Mani was an artist. The moment she started weaving her web of stories, she made the most mundane event sound exciting. She crafted her words like a silversmith, and would slowly transform into a houri. Her face glowed with a strange aura and the smell of tobacco from her mouth changed into fragrant perfumes. Her grey sari looked like a velvet robe, her gnarled witch-like hands had the softness of silk and her eyes were like diamonds. When she came to the end of a story, I saw the shadow of sadness as the glow disappeared from her face. I always wondered about the source of her stories and dreaded the day she would leave or turn into a heap of ashes.

Sometimes I woke her up in the middle of the night, when I needed to go to the bathroom. She would take me into the garden gently and while I passed water, she would stand watching the night sky wistfully. When I finished, she went back to her mouldy quilt in the kitchen and lay down, while I drank a glass of water. Curled up on the floor, she looked like a log of wood.

She was full of life but never spoke about herself. I gathered stray bits of information about her: her husband had died suddenly, and she had come to Ahmedabad with her one-year-old son Allah Rakha. As she had to work to keep body and soul together, she had left him with a family in Delhi Darwaza. She went to see him on Saturday afternoons, when Naomi had a half-day at school and did not need her. Mani would return on Sunday mornings, looking sad and depressed. On Sunday nights, she served dinner like a zombie. Then, she gulped down a few morsels of food and sat smoking bidis at the main gate of the Laxmi Nivas compound. Her eyes would be listless and empty. Whenever I asked her why she sat there, she replied in a low voice, with her palm pressed on her stomach, 'To get rid of this gas in my stomach.' I would wonder about Allah Rakha and feel guilty. I was depriving him of his mother's care. The stories which were meant for him, had come to me. Perhaps that is why she had given him the name Allah Rakha—the one who is looked after by Allah. She had left him to the care of God.

Mani's story was something like this: she was the ninth daughter of the chief perfumer of the Nawab of Palanpur. Her real name was Mumtaz Begum. She did not know how she became Mani. She had happy memories of helping her father in making perfume and playing in mounds of roses, jasmine and champa. It was her duty to take the perfume bottles to the princess. On each visit, she was rewarded with a ride in the royal goat-buggy. She sat next to the princess as they rode around the palace grounds. When she prepared to leave and salaamed, the princess always gave her a dupatta either of silk or georgette-embroidered or sprinkled with silver dots.

Life in the perfumed garden ended when she was married as a child and sent to live with her husband, who was ten years older than her. Mani was very unhappy but the marriage ended in a year when her husband suddenly died. Mani could not understand why her life changed abruptly. She did not know how to react to her new status and hated her widowhood. Sometimes when she was alone, she wore her wedding dress and gold earrings.

Nobody knows the details, but at that point, she had an admirer. Perhaps he was her father's young apprentice. Six months later her mother realized that Mani was pregnant. It was too late for an abortion with hot bricks and Mani refused to reveal the name of her lover.

At this time Joshua was in Palanpur and had ordered a bottle of rose ittar from the royal perfumer. Joshua knew him well and they often discussed the finer points of his perfumes.

Mani's father gave the ittar to Joshua and turned to leave without saying a word. Normally he sat on his haunches at Joshua's feet with his box of ittar bottles and would ask Joshua to try out the different fragrances as he told him about how he had prepared them. An expert on ittars, Joshua rubbed the perfume on the back of his hands and breathed deep its fragrance while Mani's father waited for his opinion. His expression was always that of one expecting appreciation. But on that particular day, Mani's father looked sad. He held

Joshua's hands and cried. He told Joshua that Mani was pregnant, and that she was adamant about giving birth to an illegitimate child. It would ruin the izzat of his house.

Jerusha was then at the Janana hospital. Joshua wrote to her explaining the situation and made arrangements for Mani's transport to the hospital. Jerusha offered her loving care and when Allah Rakha was born, Shebabeth took Mani under her wing. She lived with them in their quarters and helped Shebabeth in the kitchen.

When they returned to Ahmedabad, Shebabeth asked the odd-job maid Nathi to rent out one of her rooms to Mani. Nathi took an instant liking to Mani and offered to look after the child while Mani worked as cook and nanny in the Shahibaug house. Shebabeth had circulated a story about Mani having lost her husband before the birth of her son. It worked. Mani never returned to Palanpur.

Mani married again. She married Nathi's brother and lived with him as one of his three wives. She was happy because he liked her better than the others. Mani wore bright saris and did not sleep like a log in our kitchen. She had a small house where she lived with her husband, his eight children and her own Allah Rakha. I did not see Mani often, as she did not stay with us and only worked from ten to two. I was heartbroken and lonely but understood that she was happy in her own house.

One year after their marriage, Mani's husband was stabbed during a communal riot and she became a widow again. Mani returned to our house, leaving Allah Rakha with Nathi. And, we continued with our secret life. It seemed to help both of us.

73

IN THE FIFTIES, when my father was making the zoo, breeding dogs and repairing guns, most of his British clients returned to

England. Joshua had often repaired their guns, rifles, and pistols or cured their dogs. Before leaving, they came with farewell gifts for Joshua. They knew his likes, and besides antiques and arms, they left their pets with him. The hedgehogs, giant squirrels, deer and rabbits were housed in the zoo, and Joshua found good homes for their dogs. He did not want a repetition of the Stella story. He had never forgotten Uncle Shaul's story about the cats.

One of his regulars was the plump and affectionate Mrs Bradley. She had taken a liking to me when she came to our house with her roller canary named Darling. Mrs Bradley kept the bird in very good shape. It whistled for hours and had a bright orange colour. The rules and regulations were such that Mrs Bradley was forced to leave her Darling with my father.

Tears flowed down Mrs Bradley's fat cheeks as she embraced the ornate canary cage. She refused to leave without her Darling. Mr Bradley had to gently lead her towards the car. Before leaving, she gave me a doll.

I named the doll Sofia after Mrs Bradley. She had a pink frilly frock, bloomers to match, a bonnet, ballerina shoes, blonde curls, soft baby hands, big blue eyes with real eyelashes, round pink cheeks, and a half-open rosebud mouth which said, 'Hello Darling!' when I pressed her stomach.

I spoke to Sofia. I told her all my secrets. I played with her and fed her soft puddings. I even consoled Mrs Bradley's canary by holding Sofia up to her and pressing her stomach. I was sure that Darling missed her mistress and felt better when she saw Sofia.

With Sofia, I felt loved and secure. I even slept with her, holding her small baby hands. Whenever I was at home, she was my constant companion. I even took her to meet my grandmother. Instead of clinging to each other, we would sleep with Sofia between us and Shebabeth would lovingly put her palm on her stomach and tell us stories. Sometimes, she would stop and ask Sofia if she understood what she was saying. Shebabeth understood my feelings for Sofia. I told her that we were inseparable and that it broke my heart to leave her alone at home when I went to school. I had instructed Mani to look after her in my absence.

One day when I returned from school, she was not on my chair where I had left her. I started searching for her. The house was quiet and Mani was in the kitchen, sitting bent over on the floor, chopping vegetables in a plate. Normally she waited for me at the door. When I entered the kitchen, she did not even look up. Mani did not answer when I asked her if she had seen Sofia. She looked at me with vacant eyes. The sort of look she had when she came back after she had seen her son. Finally she said without emotion, 'Gone.'

I started shouting and crying as I pulled Mani's sari. 'How? She is a doll. She cannot just walk off. She needs me and I need her.'

Mani held me to her breasts saying, 'Baby, baby.'

I banged my fists on her chest. 'Why didn't you stop her?' She shook her head saying that she was just a servant in the house and could not stop Sofia. We clung to each other and cried.

My eyes were swollen when my parents returned home. I did not smile. I did not ask them anything about Sofia.

My father understood the expression on my face. 'Are you upset about Sofia? What could I do? You know we need money. So I sold the granite sculpture of Surya to Mr Bhandari. He paid me well. He came to pick it up with his daughter. You have seen her. She saw Sofia and wanted her. She threw a tantrum and refused to go unless she had Sofia. Mr Bhandari is a municipal corporator, a very important man. He offered to pay me Rs 500 more. How could I refuse. Listen . . .' He stopped and looked embarrassed as he took out a wad of bank notes from his pocket. 'I can buy another doll for you. It's not a problem.'

Then my mother took me in her arms and said, 'It was just a doll. Not real. And, my dear child, you must learn to share, huh. You are our only child and I do not want a spoilt child on my hands.' I allowed my mother to kiss me, love me, but all I wanted was Sofia.

After that, I never accepted another doll. My parents bought me a big plastic monster with green eyes which stared at me blankly. Some family friends also gave me dolls as gifts. But they stayed in their boxes, untouched, for so long that my parents gave them away to their friends' children. That was the end of my doll days, and I never forgot Sofia Bradley.

Soon after the abduction of Sofia, the Bracewells also left India. My father invited them for tea before they left Ahmedabad.

It was the beginning of the monsoon. Such rains fell once in ten years. It was grey and dark, and one could hear the strong downpour as it hit the ground. Bolts of lightning lit up the sky with a bright blue flourescent light. There was knee-deep water everywhere, and frightening claps of thunder.

Mr Bracewell came alone in a huge raincoat, his orderly running after him with a black umbrella. He was nice and had gifts for everybody. For me there was a huge box of chocolates in red wrapping paper tied with blue ribbons. As long as he stayed, drinking tea and nibbling at the biscuits, I sat ladylike with the box on my knees. I wanted to tear apart the wrapping, but my mother's eyes were on me. I knew I must say thank you and wait for him to depart before I opened the box. I must not behave as though I had never seen chocolates before.

As soon as Mr Bracewell left, I spread a carpet on the floor and sat looking at the 'Made in England' label. I wanted to open the colourful wrapping paper slowly and carefully, then play with the little rocks of chocolate wrapped in silver-and-gold paper. After I had had my tactile satisfaction, I would lovingly open each piece of chocolate, feel its roundness with my tongue and bite into its softness.

The rains had created a desire in me to stuff myself with as many chocolates as possible, though Uncle Menachem had told me not to eat sweets, because of my threadworms. Normally I obeyed him, but the box was in front of me and I only had to open it. But it was not so easy either. There were other barriers. I could not open the box without my parents' permission. My mother was writing the accounts and my father was looking for a place to put the porcelain poodle that Mr Bracewell had given him. My mother had already put away the pearl brooch she had received. She never wore fancy ornaments.

Without making a sound, I opened the first knot of the satin ribbon on the box. My mother turned around. Her eyes widened and she said, 'NO, NO. Don't you open that. These are good English chocolates. They are not for you alone. You must learn to share. I do not want you to become selfish. You are our only child, but I will not spoil you. I am going to ask Mani to take you right now to Menachem brother's house. You will open the chocolates there. Count them and share them equally with your cousins. Your four cousins and you will have an equal number of chocolates.'

My father smiled and said, 'Good idea.'

My heart sank when I saw that the water was rising in the street outside the house. I told my mother that I could not go to Delhi Darwaza in the rain. I would have liked to be able to tell her clearly that I wanted to stay home and eat my chocolates in peace. I had decided to have two every day, and hide the rest in the ice-box. But Naomi would have none of that and soon the buggy was at the door. Mani was to accompany me to uncle's house.

Mani had heard and seen everything. She understood. In the buggy, as the rain lashed and drenched us, I told Mani that I was going to open the box of chocolates and eat them right there. Mani pretended that she was not watching me. She had gone deaf, dumb and blind. She started humming a Gujarati song.

Normally it took us fifteen minutes to reach Uncle Menachem's house, but with the horse wading through water it took much longer. I ate the chocolates, one after another, and threw the wrapping paper into the water. The wrappers looked like stars. I ate so many chocolates that they were no longer delicious.

When we reached Uncle Menachem's house, I threw the box out of the window and kept the last four chocolates in my pocket. I saw the precious box sailing in the water, and I started laughing. Mani started to drag me towards the house as the water had risen up to our heads. The buggy was no longer moving, and I saw the horse's head bobbing in the water.

Inside the house, Mani changed my clothes and gave me a good rub with rum. I told her to take the four chocolates from my pocket and give them to my cousins. Uncle Menachem scolded us: we could have drowned. Died. I was shivering when I told him that I had come to share the chocolates with my cousins. He smiled, but saw that I was looking sick. He quickly covered me with a blanket and gave me his fever medicine, the pink bukhar ki davai.

I was feverish, nauseous and delirious, and had illusions of falling into space. I could have died that night because of eating chocolates.

When I returned to Laxmi Nivas my mother was in a state of shock. She was sitting dry-eyed at the dining table with a telegram in her hand. Her youngest sister Sinora had died in a hospital in Delhi, leaving behind a husband and two small daughters. Naomi did not go for the funeral. She knew her father would be there. She did not want to see him. I was curious about grandfather. I had a happy childhood with my father's family but did not know anything about my mother's family.

74

WHEN I WAS eleven years old, I saw Raphael and felt my heart burn with strange desires. I was at the synagogue to attend a wedding with my grandmother.

The women's gallery on the first floor of the synagogue had a huge stained glass window and I could feel a golden glow falling on my head. The Star of David was carved on the doors. There were menorahs, chandeliers, ancient ceiling fans, lamps shaped like flames and a thunderbolt design in the wrought-iron railing.

The railing gave a commanding view of the teva, the centre point of the synagogue for prayers and marriages. From here, we, the impure women, looked down, pretending that we were not looking at the men. We could see Prophet Elijah's chair with its blue cover next to the circumcision chair. Elaborate lamps or handis were suspended over the chair. In the gallery we sat facing the marble plaque with the ten commandments or daha yagnya written in Marathi. There was also a blue velvet Torah ark curtain with Jewish motifs and Hebrew letters embroidered in silver and gold threads.

The bride looked ethereal in her white chiffon sari, veil, tiara, bouquet, gloves and high-heeled shoes. The groom was in a three-piece suit. I dreamt that one day I too would stand on that teva with my bridegroom.

When the bride and groom had signed the ketubbah, the marriage contract, one of the women filled my palms with confetti. We showered the newly-wed couple with rice and silver confetti. As I bent over the railing to have a good look at the bride, I saw Raphael. I had showered him with silver confetti. Would he be my groom?

Raphael was fair, had big eyes, a strong nose and a generous mouth. He was smiling. I noticed that he was well built and had a rather prominent collarbone which gave a certain heaviness to his chest. But I did not like his hair. It was brown and thin. He had covered it with a velvet star-spangled skullcap, a kippa, like the other men at the synagogue.

I fell in love with Raphael because the situation had all the ingredients of the Mills and Boon romances I had tucked into school books and read.

The next day, I felt something sticky between my thighs. Naomi told me that it was my first menstrual blood. She looked so tense that I felt the blood was something dangerous and dirty.

I suddenly became religious. I said I wanted to know the meaning of being a Bene Israel Jew. Whenever Shebabeth announced that there was a festival, wedding, mehendi ceremony, circumcision, Eliyahu Hannabi or malida, I pestered her to take me with her to the synagogue. Looking at each other became a game between Raphael and me.

Shebabeth was happy with my new-found religiosity but insisted that I cover my head in the synagogue. I hated to cover my head but for Raphael I was willing to accept anything. When we were ready for the synagogue, my grandmother pinned a neatly folded handkerchief on the top of my head. I called it my kippa kerchief. The older women covered their heads with the loose end of their saris.

Shebabeth liked to exchange recipes with the older women and enjoyed advising the younger ones on childbirths and traditions. She left me alone on the bench directly above the teva. My only regret was that my mother did not allow me to wear dresses which showed my figure to advantage. I had to wear long maternity gowns which I hated. But I had to be careful at the synagogue. I did not want uncles and cousins to notice my nazar milanewali game with Raphael.

To my delight, Raphael was always there. If he moved away, I would become desperate—until he appeared again and smiled teasingly.

When Bene Israel meet at the synagogue, the customary greeting is a hathbosi. From early childhood, we are taught to touch each other's fingertips, and then kiss our own fingers.

After a malida, when I was leaving the synagogue with Shebabeth, we came face to face with Raphael and his parents. The elders greeted each other with a hathbosi, and I was left with Raphael. He extended his hand and looked into my eyes. On the way home Shebabeth told me his complicated family history. She also told me that we Dandekars had had a problem with Raphael's grandfather and there was no give and take of brides or any interaction—uthna-bethna—between the families. But whenever she met them she was polite as she did not like tensions in a small community like ours.

Shebabeth gave me a list of the possible Kars I could get married into. She explained that the Bene Israel Jews came from the Konkan coast. Each family had an Indian sounding family surname, as they used the name of the village or Kar of their origin, like Danda, Kehim, Navgaon, etc. It was difficult to determine when the Dandekars stopped using their village name as a last name. Perhaps it was because the family had journeyed far away from Danda that they had dropped Dandekar as a family name. Or, they felt it was too regional and wanted to give themselves a new identity in independent India. She added that if there was a problem between some Bene Israel families, marriages were forbidden. With a certain harshness in her voice she added that marriage was also taboo with Bagdadi and Cochini Jews.

I guessed that she had noticed the way Raphael had looked at me, and wanted to discourage any romantic ideas she suspected me of having for him. I wasn't listening. Raphael's touch had given me goose pimples. It was a delicious and disturbing feeling. I wanted to touch his face, his hands, his lips. I wondered what it would feel like if we got the chance to kiss. He filled my dreams.

I was sick for two days. I couldn't go to school. I had a headache with an unidentifiable fever, and no amount of medicines helped till Uncle Menachem sent me the bukhar ki davai—pink and bitter.

Raphael's mother was the principal of an English-medium primary school. We were invited to the annual school programme at the Town Hall. The invitation card mentioned that Raphael had not only composed the music for the dances and songs, but also had his own orchestra of flute, drums and violins. He played the saxophone.

Raphael's mother greeted us at the door. I hung back and

was relieved that I did not have to sit next to my mother. I did not want her to see my attraction for Raphael. She would have put a ban on my synagogue visits. I sat huddled deep in my chair. I wanted to watch Raphael undisturbed. He was the star of the evening.

Dressed in a white three-piece suit, tap-dance shoes and a white hat, Raphael transported me into another world. He conducted his band like a professional, and played divine tunes on the piano. He danced better than Gene Kelly, and sang the most romantic songs.

I sat mesmerized and dreamt of the day he would welcome me to the teva—to be his bride.

At home, my father listened to classical music and ghazals and I was allowed to listen to Hindi film songs on Radio Ceylon. I was a little depressed that I did not belong to Raphael's world. I was afraid that if and when he discovered that I was a desi Gujju girl, he would stop staring at me.

But I need not have worried, because when I was in the tenth standard, Raphael and his father came to call on my father. As soon as they entered the house, my mother guessed their intentions and shooed me away into the inner room.

Through the curtain I heard all that was being said. I was thrilled. They had come with a proposal of marriage. His father said that his son was in love with me and if Joshua and Naomi agreed, he would like to get us engaged because after a month, Raphael was leaving for the USA to study music. This was just the preliminary manga for marriage. The wedding could take place in two years.

My heart was beating with excitement. I wanted to tear open the curtain and say 'Yes.' I was sure Raphael was watching the curtain. I heard my father's cold denials. When he was not convincing enough, my mother entered the room with a tray of tea and biscuits and said, 'Excuse me, brother, but Esther is still very young and we want to educate her. We have plans for her. After all, she is our only child.'

Raphael's father asked, 'Does that mean you are refusing my proposal? Our family is also into education. She could continue with her studies after the wedding. I know you do not marry into our Kar, but dear sister Naomi, times have changed. Do our children have to suffer because of the differences our elders had?'

My father smiled as he said, 'No, no, brother, please do not misunderstand us. I am not one to be bothered about Kar and things like that.' His voice softened as he added, 'Esther is too young. We can think of her marriage when she grows up.'

By then my mother had poured the tea and she asked, 'How much sugar for you, brother?'

'None,' said Raphael's father. I could sense the disappointment in his voice.

I wanted to rush out of the room but sat frozen. Chained. The poisonous creeper called Family had gripped my feet and I could not move.

As I did not see Raphael again at the synagogue, I lost interest in religion. It was fated that we should never meet again.

75

ALL THROUGH SCHOOL, I made my mother miserable. So was I. She was ashamed that her daughter was a poor student. Someone who just about scraped through from one class to the next.

The crisis came when I was in the eleventh standard and

was preparing for the Board examinations. I had passed the tenth standard with miserable marks.

Mother Superior from the convent called Naomi for a discussion about my future. I waited outside the office, flushed and nervous. Only the blue flowered curtain separated me from them and I could hear muffled sounds—Mother Superior's voice, stern and angry, and the other almost pleading. I felt ashamed.

After Naomi emerged from the room, she dragged me home and told me angrily about how she was humiliated by Mother Superior. She informed me that my drawing classes were to start that very day. Mother Superior had said I was a threat to their annual scores and I should be shifted to another school. If not, I had to drop maths and science and take art.

I may have filled my books with doodles, but I knew that I was no good at art either. Naomi also knew that. Mother Superior suggested that the school drawing teacher, Patel sir, prepare me for the intermediate art exam and also for the final exam; otherwise I was sure to fail.

So instead of Shah sir who used to be my maths-and-science sir in the tenth standard and owing to whose efforts I had passed with the minimum 35 marks, Patel sir came to the house twice a week to teach me drawing and painting.

I could not decide which sir I hated more. Shah sir, from whom I had just been liberated, was balding, looked old and perspired profusely. He was brilliant with numbers and would get exasperated when faced by my lack of intelligence. I am sure he wanted to rap me with a scale but knew that if I told my father, he would be gunned down. So, he would raise the scale and I would shiver. I only relaxed when he took it to his forehead and scratched his head with it. Shah sir's exit ended my dreams of becoming a vet or a psychiatrist. I had wanted to work with hunting cheetahs in Africa like Joy Adamson, but Naomi had pointed out with a raised forefinger that I needed science to become a veterinary doctor. The alternative profession of psychiatrist was based on the fact that I was interested in the inner life of people. But I had never expressed this desire to my parents as I knew that one needed science to enter a medical college.

I was happy to be rid of Shah sir. I did not realize that although Patel sir looked different from Shah sir, neat rather than sloppy, he was equally unbearable.

I knew Patel sir because he always asked me to write the subject on the class board. He said I had a good hand at calligraphy. He had a knack of picking out the dull students, who would eventually drop science and go to him for art tuition. He was always angling for tuitions.

The tuition sirs always came when my parents were not at home, and as instructed by my mother, Mani sat watching over them like a bloodhound. The sirs never made advances, but they did cheat. They did my homework. But Mani did not realize that so my parents did not know what happened during the tuition hour.

From art class at school, Patel sir knew that my handwriting was my only asset, so he taught me some basic skills to pass the exams. Then, for the daily show for my father, who was very interested in art, he painted a still life or portrait in water colours. He left it on the window, with a note praising me and saying that I was doing very well and had the makings of a great artist. I hated his lies, but these little notes made my parents happy and hopeful. For the peace of the house, I did not tell them the truth. I wish I had.

On Sundays, my day off, as I sat in the sun drying my hair, Patel sir would arrive at 10 a.m. He would be dressed in his best dhoti-kurta and would be carrying a bag of sculptures and paintings.

During his tuitions, he had noticed my father's weakness for artefacts. The sculptures were old damaged statues he had picked up from archaeological sites or the river bed. The paintings were poor copies of the Romantics, with some rare illuminated manuscripts and bric-a-brac. He stayed till midday discussing the finer points of the pieces with my father. I heaved a sigh of relief when he stood up to leave, making a large-hearted offer to sell them to my father. He never left the house with an empty wallet. Joshua always bought something, either for the house or the zoo.

The only thing that interested me in the art syllabus was a small, badly written book on the history of art. I became interested in prehistoric art and Egyptian art. In the Indian section I was fascinated by Amrita Sher-Gil's life and paintings. I liked her *Lemon Sellers*.

From my pocket money, I bought a small booklet on Amrita Sher-Gil published by the Lalit Kala Akademi. Secretly, I enjoyed looking at her semi-nude portrait, showing her full red lips, ripe breasts and cherry nipples. There was a sensuousness in her paintings that I liked very much. I wondered whether she had painted herself in front of a mirror. She became a kind of role model, and I saw myself dressed in a red sari, standing in front of an easel and painting. Perhaps I could become a painter? Paint myself—nude?

Whenever I had a holiday, I spent hours looking at my father's collection of art books. There were volumes on the old masters. The one which caught my eye was by Millais of a blind girl sitting under a rainbow. I must have tried copying it a thousand times, but totally unsuccessfully. I identified myself with the blind girl who could not see the rainbow.

I again had this feeling of uselessness when I took a mixture of pili mitti and chikni mitti from Zini, to copy Michelangelo's *Slave*. When I could not make the clay stand or mould it to the shape I wanted, I was dejected. My parents had great expectations of me—that I would get through my admission exam at the Faculty of Fine Arts at the Maharaja Sayajirao University of Baroda. I was sure I would not. I just did not have the gift. Yet, like the blind girl, I still had my dreams. I dreamt of becoming a painter.

At Baroda, we were guests of Yashwantrao, who was related to the ex-ruler of Baroda. He lived in a house in the compound of one of the palaces on Rajmahal Road. He had done some amazing interiors with the dioramas of stuffed exotic birds. The dioramas had birds on branches and trees, against a landscape painted in great detail. The leaves, bark of trees and other objects were not real, but were made with plaster, wire and colour. He also loved to make intricate lampshades from painted ostrich eggs.

Yashwantrao had strong big hands on which the veins stood out like knotted ropes. His wife spent hours cooking and bringing up their four children. The food in their house was delicious, but I was so nervous that I could not swallow anything.

Shivajirao was Yashwantrao's brother-in-law. He drove the family jeep. He took us to the Faculty of Fine Arts at Pushpa Baug on University Road. I would have preferred to go alone for the entrance test but they all came with me, Shivajirao, Yashwantrao, and Naomi in her starched sari.

I spent three harrowing days at the test—from morning to evening, with a lunch break. Food was literally forced down my throat. The jeep was always stuffed with snacks and tiffin boxes. Every time a plate of food was offered to me, I felt cartwheels turning in my stomach. I did not have the courage to tell Naomi that in a situation like this, it was best to leave me alone. I could not even tell her that I was feeling sick. My head throbbed, my stomach churned, making me nauseous and feverish. In the cloud of mosquitoes around our host's house, I was sure I would come down with malaria. To add to this, I had constipation and migraine which had started between two Mother Superiors and two tuition sirs. They seemed to get worse during the test. These ailments were to erupt whenever I was in a difficult situation.

Each department—painting, sculpture, pottery and graphics—was housed in a different building, old and new. There was an enchanting pond in the centre. The canteen was behind the History of Art department under an acacia tree. We sat outside it in the open on seats of brick. That was one place which attracted me, but there were so many boys there that I was scared to go.

On the fourth day, nobody could accompany me for the test. I was relieved. Yashwantrao had some unannounced guests from Kolhapur. Naomi politely suggested that we move to a hotel. But Yashwantrao did not agree, and Naomi stayed on, on the condition that she be allowed to help in the kitchen. Much against her wishes, she left me alone in the jungle called fine arts.

I hoped that somebody would give a task to Shivajirao, but nobody needed him. He was leaning on the jeep, waiting for me. When I saw him, I asked my mother if I could please take a rickshaw to college. After all I had to learn to travel on my own some day. I did not want to be seen with Shivajirao. But Naomi gave me a suspicious look and said, 'Well, you will. But today Shivaji uncle will take you to college.'

Throughout the journey, I prayed that Shivajirao would

leave me at the college gate and disappear. Somebody obviously heard my prayers. Shivajirao dropped me at the gate and giving me a box of batata pohas left, saying that he had to pick up someone from the station. He would be back by five in the evening.

I had mixed feelings about my freedom as I walked towards the library next to the office building. I passed a cluster of lemon trees and inhaled the citrony tang of their leaves. It felt odd to be alone. I was easily frightened. I was like a rhinoceros which bolts at the sound of its own droppings!

Although I had wanted to get rid of Naomi and Yashwantrao and Co., I also missed them. I braced myself and climbed the stairs. I did well in that particular test. I felt better and when I was coming down the stairs, I saw a boy whom I had briefly met standing in the foyer, watching me with his dark, intense eyes. I felt a strange stirring in my body, and a deep desire to cry. I controlled myself and walked past him without looking at him. But he compelled me to turn around when he said in a deep baritone, 'Hello, Esther Williams!' When our eyes met, I bolted and ran towards the parking. Jumping into the jeep, I told Shivajirao, 'Jaldi chalo, ghar jana hai.'

I would have liked to return home to Ahmedabad. Ahmedabad meant protection. But I had one more interview to face the following day.

The boy, whose name was Ahaseures, had disturbed me. I could feel myself trembling for no reason. His face was etched in my mind and I could not erase it.

That night after dinner, Yashwantrao and Naomi prepared me for the interview, making me even more nervous in the process. When I entered the conference room where the interviewing board was sitting, I was certain that I did not stand a chance.

In the room there was a huge painting by the dean, a well-known painter whose work I had seen in *The Illustrated Weekly of India*. The painting was of a woman milking a cow. My eyes were stuck on the udder of the cow. It had the mark of a child's hand. Later, I discovered that it was the imprint of his daughter's palm. He must have been sensitive to have painted something like that, but he was very gruff. Perhaps it was a facade?

The Dean asked me to sit down. The jury was sitting in a half-circle. I felt like a goat facing a firing squad of butchers.

The Dean was a bear-like man who looked as if he never smiled. A lock of salt-and-pepper hair fell over his eye.

I could not take my eyes off the udder. I woke up as though from a trance when I heard him asking, 'Miss David, tell us why you want admission in this college.'

I mumbled, 'Because I want to become a painter.'

'Why do you want to become a painter?'

I stared at him and again mumbled, 'Because I want to be a painter.' I froze as I heard the jury snigger.

'Do you know what it means to become a painter?'

I started crying. Tears flowed down my cheeks. I was angry with myself. I pulled out my handkerchief to wipe the tears when I heard the Dean signal to me rather brusquely and say, 'OK, you can go.'

Instinctively I looked for Ahaseures. I did not even know him, but I needed him. He was not there.

Naomi had one look at my tear-stained face and stiffened. 'Why,' she asked, 'did you have to cry? Does it mean that you couldn't handle it?' I shook my head and cried as though I had lost everything. Yashwantrao was kind. He told me gently to take hold of myself and said to Naomi, 'Reheno do bhabhi.

Choti hai na. Kitne bade artist ke samne dar gayee. Arre admission nahin mila to kya ho gaya, kuch aur kar legee.'

But Naomi would have none of his reasoning. Whether I was young, or intimidated by the interview board, she did not think I could do anything. 'Yeh kuch nahin kar sakti,' she said furiously. We returned to Ahmedabad in silence.

In Ahmedabad Naomi toyed with the idea of my trying for admission in the English department of St Xavier's College, but as there were subjects like statistics in the first year, she said, 'Maths. Esther can never handle it.'

Then she made inquiries at the Gujarat state-run art college, and my heart sank when she forced me to fill the form. I was useless, a no-good. I could not tell her that I was confused and needed to drop a year. As a teacher this would have been the ultimate degradation for her. She was afraid that everybody would ask her why I was sitting at home, when girls my age were in college.

Suddenly, everything changed. I received a letter from the Dean saying that I had passed the admission test, and should pay my fees and arrange for my hostel accommodation, by such and such date. The tension eased. Naomi started packing my clothes in the green tin trunks which she brought down from the storeroom. I was horrified. I wanted neat leather bags which I could carry myself, not heavy trunks which I could hardly push from one corner to another. I always needed coolies or somebody to help me.

I had just celebrated my fifteenth birthday and was unhappy. There were so many conflicts between my parents and me. I felt knotted within myself.

There were hectic preparations around me. I felt that they were for someone else's departure. I was not asked what I wanted. A list of my needs had been made and everything was packed methodically. At every turning point in my life, I felt like the sacrificial lamb. This was one such moment.

76

I WAS HOMESICK in Baroda. I missed the dogs. Lassie, the Pekinese—Rosie, Leo, Tum-Tum—and the pomeranians—Whisky and Frisky. I missed Mani and our secret world.

Then I received a letter from Naomi. Mani had been asked to leave on charges of theft. She had been sent back to Grandmother Shebabeth's house. In a few years grandmother would be a hundred years old and Aunt Jerusha had also grown older. They needed her more than us, she wrote. Instead, she had employed Zini, who had a clean record and a stable family life.

In my room in the girls' hostel, I cried. My room-mates tried to help, but I told them to leave me alone.

The next day, I dragged myself to college. When Ahaseures tried to tease me I burst out crying. He was taken aback and did not know what to do. So he just took my hand in his. We sat in the college canteen under the acacia tree. He understood, as I told him about Mani and my dogs. One was old, the other blind, but they missed me. I missed them. I was homesick. Uncomfortable in the hostel. Hated my classes. In short, I was unhappy. Without a moment's hesitation, he invited me to live with his family. Their house was opposite the hostel grounds. They were seven brothers. I would be one of the first girls to enter their house. His parents were gentle, and his mother baked the best cakes in Baroda. But I sat like a statue, as he stood with his outstretched hand and said, 'Come.' I could not. I had only to cross the road, and I would have been in

Shushan—our heaven.

I failed the exams that year. Mani was not there to console me, and I could not relate to Zini. My mother was ashamed of my marks sheet. She was an educationist. My father could tame tigers and lions. Their prestige was at stake. There were hordes of visitors and officials who came to the zoo. What if somebody politely asked about my studies? Perhaps I should jump into the lake and end my life, I thought. But I did not have the courage, and there were too many people who recognized me as Joshua David's daughter.

I had to return to Baroda to repeat the preparatory class of the Faculty of Fine Arts. At home in Ahmedabad, family and friends had one sutra: 'Failure is a stepping stone to success.'

Ahaseures was happy to see me back. He asked me to live with him and tried to convince me that I would be comfortable in his house. I said nothing. I wanted to tell him that without a commitment of marriage, I could not possibly live with him. In the Jewish community a wedding at the synagogue with a virgin Bene Israel male was a must. This had been drummed into my head and I could not take the bold step of living with Ahaseures. Had I been brave enough, I am sure my parents would have died of shock.

Whenever I saw Ahaseures, I fell into confusion. It was not easy for me to be natural with Ahaseures, or any other boy or man, for that matter. Somebody was always calling on me at odd hours at the college—my local guardians came to see if I was well, or one of the zoo workers came to give me food packets from home, or clothes I did not like. And, my parents missed me and drove down in the car.

According to university rules, repeaters were not given hostel rooms. It would have been ideal if I had had the guts to move in with Ahaseures. But I was diffident. I was ashamed of my doll-like bloomers, sets of home-made bandages for my periods, and the soft growth of hair on my legs and upper lip. I wanted to wear tiny readymade panties, and sanitary pads, and go to the beauty parlour to wax off all that unwanted hair. I was certain Ahaseures wanted somebody who looked like the nude, hairless marble sculptures in the palace museum at Kamati Baug. But Naomi was strict. She said that good Jewish girls do not go to beauty parlours. The beauty within is more important.

I could never really believe that Ahaseures loved me. There were so many beautiful girls around. It took me a long time to believe in him. By then, it was too late.

As a repeater, I lived in an old house on the edge of the Sursagar lake run by a women's organization. I was incarcerated with five girls, and had to make my own tea. Thali lunches and dinners were served on rickety tables in a dirty kitchen. There were two bathrooms and four toilets between fifty girls. The tiles were broken and the building had a strong stench of urine.

Before my mother left me there, I told her that I did not know how to make tea. Pump stoves scared me, and Naomi bought me a wick stove, gave me a quick demonstration of the art of making tea and then left me to the mercy of a rude old matron.

Evenings at this hostel were the hardest. Boys filled our rooms. They were brothers, cousins, relatives and boyfriends of the girls who lived there. They draped themselves on my bed, and I did not know how to protest. I felt like an outsider. They all looked happy—chatting and playing pranks on each other. I stood on the balcony and waited for them to leave.

It was not the same in the university hostel, because boys were not allowed inside. They stood in the porch and the peon called out to the girls who had visitors. There was a regular lounge where one could entertain visitors, listen to the radio or just read magazines.

Then I again got a room in the Sarojini Devi Girls' Hostel. The fine arts quota had a vacancy. I moved in with two senior girls. One of them was kind and helped me with my assignments, and even made tea for me. I trusted her.

That was the year that her boyfriend Haman—an ugly, scary man—tried to rape me. I never understood her fascination for him. He was always chasing her friends and other girls.

My dreams of the first kiss and romance were shattered as he tore at my clothes, pinched my breasts and bruised my lips. I was still a virgin, but something more delicate broke inside me. I will never be able to write the details of the trap and the escape. But I still felt unclean.

I spent a troubled night. I had to escape from my roommate and Haman. Not knowing how to handle the situation, I took a bus to Ahmedabad.

Confiding in my parents was a mistake. They never trusted me again. But what else could I have done? Perhaps I could have gone to Ahaseures. I needed help, and the only people I felt I could turn to were my parents. But I was wrong. Instead of going home, I should have gone to the police station. But I did not have the courage for that. I had heard that the police always held the girl responsible, checked her private parts, made crude jokes and gave information to the press. It would have been intolerable for my parents to see my photograph in the newspapers as a rape victim.

77

WHEN I REACHED home in an autorickshaw, there was a lock on the door. Nobody was at home. In the same auto I went to my mother's school. I thought she would be more understanding than my father.

I asked the peon to call her and waited nervously in the porch. I saw her coming out of the prayer hall. I felt comforted. I needed her as never before. But she did not like my being in her school. It was her sanctum. With her starched sari and strict look, I could see that she did not like being disturbed there. 'Why are you here? You should be in college.'

Disheartened, I just managed to say, 'Mummy, this is urgent.'

Naomi saw the dejection on my face and cancelled her class. We came home together. As we entered the house, for the first time in my life, I kissed the ancient mezuzah on the door. I could see the Shema written in the small aperture. So far, it had just been a Jewish artefact in the house. In this situation, it seemed to give me courage. I needed a god who would help me. I prayed, and hoped that God was a woman. At least she would understand about being a girl and give me the strength to tell my mother about what had happened.

I told Naomi the series of incidents which had led to the near rape. It was the truth. I waited for her to hold me in her arms, but she did not touch me. She made me feel impure and dirty. I needed her soft arms around me. I begged, 'Mummy, I want to sleep in your lap, please ...'

But she was so disturbed and confused that she did not hear what I was saying. Instead of taking me in her arms, she said, 'I must call Joshua.' I heard her calling my father. 'Joshua, can you come home right now?'

'Now? No. What is the problem?'

Naomi whispered into the phone, 'It is Esther.'

'What about her? She is in Baroda. Where are you?'

'At home. With her.'

'What is she doing there? And why are you back home?'

'I can't tell you on the phone. Can you come?'

'I can't. I'm in the middle of a press conference. We have bred scorpions.'

'But this is urgent. I can't handle it alone.'

'It can't be that bad. Don't panic. Go back to school. Tell Zini to stay with Esther and lock the door from inside. I will come back early.'

Naomi sighed, and putting the phone back on the holder, said, 'Are you all right? I must go back to school and Joshua can only come home at six. Zini will stay with you. Lock the door and sleep or read.'

There was nothing I could do but look at her with pleading eyes as she left.

I spread a mat on the floor and slept next to Lassie. Whisky and Frisky ran around me till they were tired and the Pekes snuggled next to me, flat on their stomachs, wagging their tails and watching me with their big brown owl eyes. Lassie looked at me with bloodshot eyes, raised eyebrows and twitching ears. I think she understood.

I woke up when I heard Zini opening the door for Faiju. He salaamed me with a happy 'Babysaab!' and busied himself in the kitchen. With the sounds of chopping, boiling and clanging vessels, the house was no longer cold. It seemed to become warmer with the fragrance of coconut and coriander. I was hungry but suddenly felt like a stranger in my own house. I did not know how to ask for something as simple as food. But Faiju had seen the look in my eyes and brought me a steaming hot cup of masala tea with mint and ginger. Just then Naomi entered the house. She averted her eyes and I could not drink the tea any more.

She washed her feet in the bathroom, wiped them on the

mat, and signalled with her fingers on her lips that I must not speak in Faiju's presence. Zini had made her exit as soon as Naomi entered the house. It was an unspoken understanding. Naomi then went into the kitchen and made herself a chapati roll, while Faiju brought her a cup of weak tea.

As soon as she had finished eating, Joshua arrived with a jam bottle in his hand. He placed it on the table between us. I could see the scorpion inside, black and enormous, her back covered with innumerable baby scorpions. My father carefully tightened the perforated lid of the bottle and slumped down on the divan next to my mother. He looked at me, dreading the worst. In that look, there were a thousand scorpions between us with their poisonous tailtips raised.

Faiju gave my father his evening peg of whisky and soda and as Joshua had his drink, my mother munched an apple. As soon as dinner was ready and the table laid, Faiju was told to leave. Normally, he only left after we had eaten and he had cleared the kitchen. He knew something was wrong and threw a sympathetic glance at me. I felt better.

My mother asked me to repeat the story. There was something beaten and false in the way I told it again. I felt I was talking about somebody I did not know. Lassie, who understood everything, licked me and tried to erase Haman's touch from my body.

When I reached the end of my story, my parents left me with Lassie and locked themselves in the bedroom. Sitting outside, I felt I was in a doctor's waiting room. I was heartbroken that my parents did not realize I was suffering.

When they emerged, I realized that they did not believe me. In fact, they did not trust me any more. My parents were ashamed that I had 'done' something like this, and did not know how to handle it. They stood in the doorway, looking at me like strangers, and asked, Tell us the truth, what are the possibilities of your becoming pregnant?' They seemed to believe that if a drop of cobra venom could kill a human being, a drop of semen could make a girl pregnant.

I was in a state of shock. I felt numb. I picked up the last shreds of my courage and said in a loud, clear voice, 'I am not pregnant!'

Till my periods came, nobody spoke to me. When my parents were away, Zini kept a watch on me. I pretended I was reading, sketching and writing my history of art notes.

Everybody was waiting for something to happen. Pigeon eggs appeared on my breakfast plate. They were supposed to increase body heat and hasten the menstrual cycle. When the welcome red stain was seen on my bloomers, everybody was relieved. Happily, Naomi made a sanitary napkin with soft cloth and gave it to me. I locked myself in the bathroom and cried.

The tension had eased in the house and not knowing what to do with myself, I made an owl in clay. Unlike my earlier efforts, I could at least make it stand. When I gave it a texture of dots with a matchstick, Zini asked, 'Why did you make an evil bird?' Why did I make images at all? It was against the Jewish law. Perhaps, I was paying for my sins. The neighbours were curious. They were asking each other, 'Why is Esther back in mid-term?'

Then Yashwantrao wrote to my father that I should be sent back to Baroda immediately. There were rumours that I was pregnant and Haman was the father of my unborn child.

I was again in the waiting room of my parents' house, and they were locked up in the bedroom for a private discussion.

I was told to return to Baroda. Naomi would accompany me and change my room. I could no longer stay with a roommate who had trapped me into such a situation.

They were taken aback when I refused. I was terrified of facing Haman, the hostel girls and the college rumours. But my parents were adamant. I had to return. My return would prove that I was not pregnant and nothing had happened between Haman and me. My father was prepared to sacrifice me on the altar of prestige.

I had hoped that the hand of God would hold Joshua's hand in mid-air like it had Abraham's and he would not send me back to Baroda. But nothing happened. No Torah, no mezuzah countered my difficulties.

The rickshaw was waiting to take us to the station. We stood at the door—Naomi and me. We were near the mezuzah, but I did not touch it. I felt numb.

A thousand honey bees seemed to block my ears as Naomi said, 'I need a promise from you. I may not be able to say this in front of the warden and your new room-mates.' Then, she took my hand in hers. My first instinct was to pull it away. But, this was not the time and place to show my temper. When I had rushed back to Ahmedabad, I had ached for her touch, but she had not touched my stained body. Now, like a formidable female prophet, her hand was on my head. 'Promise me you will not speak to Haman, Ahaseures or any other boy or man who shows an interest in you. And you will forget that Haman ever tried to . . . Nothing happened. Remember, nothing happened. And, if you ever tell anybody about what happened or speak to these evil creatures—I will die. You will see my dead body.'

I promised. I would never speak about it. I would forget it. But Ahaseures? How was I going to live without him?

I had strange feelings regarding Ahaseures. There was longing mixed with confusion. He made me feel secure and loved.

I went through the shame of changing rooms, and trying to adjust to an impossible situation at the college. Questioning looks, vulgar remarks, evil stories, and Haman always there—leering at me.

Years later, I heard about Haman's death. His death liberated me from innumerable fears.

I survived my return to Baroda because of Ahaseures. With his friends, Ahaseures formed a protective cordon around me. But why was he protecting me? Had he been responsible for what had happened? Was he feeling guilty and trying to make up for his mistake? I did not know what to believe.

Night after night, as I dozed over my books, I decided that suicide was the only solution. Yet in the morning, I dressed carefully and looked forward to seeing Ahaseures at the university crossroads. He was my hope. He would pass me on his bike with a twinkle in his eyes and an abrupt, 'Hello, Esther Williams?'

I drowned myself in a series of charcoal drawings. I drew lines and rubbed them into black masses. They were heavy and empty. I tried to create forms, which I could neither define nor understand. It was hard to become an artist. Once I had learnt the techniques, what did I have to say?

The teachers shook their shaggy manes and demoralized me. 'Why do you want to become a painter? You have no talent. Do something else.'

Defiantly, I said, 'Perhaps there is hope.' Some laughed, others sniggered.

78

IN THE MORNINGS, Ahaseures worked in the graphics studio. I often went there to pick up a tool or two and watch him working. He was making a ten feet long woodcut print—a huge unfolding landscape in muted browns, greens and blues: of forests and rivers, of waterfalls and banyan trees, with birds of paradise flying over naked men built just like him who were grappling with crocodiles. A struggle between the different elements of nature.

I did not speak to Ahaseures because of my promise to my mother. If I did speak to him sometimes it was like Ellis the cockatoo—a little upside down with the grey matter transmitting messages. But Ahaseures was a man and could not catch my upside-down thoughts. If he did he did not show it.

Ahaseures was spread out on the floor of the graphics studio, his lion chest bulging from his midnight-blue teeshirt, his hands stained with colour. I could not accept that I wanted to hold him in my arms and feel his sensuous Parsi lips on mine.

Ahaseures sensed my presence in the studio. His shoulder blades tightened.

I stood watching him. All I had to do was break the shackles of Naomi's promises and call out to him. But I could not. I was muzzled by just one commandment—thou shall obey thy parents.

When Haman had violated me, my parents had suddenly become aware that my girlish clothes hid the nakedness of a woman—and that there was something dangerous between my legs. That something which was precious and of prime importance for a Bene Israel girl—her virginity.

My parents wrote to Solicitor Uncle to find me a groom from a good Bene Israel family. I had to live a correct Jewish life even if Joshua and Naomi had never been religious. Suddenly they had become like all good Jewish parents. A daughter of the house would be safe in another Jewish house. That is how I was engaged to Benjamin.

Benjamin was a distant cousin nobody had seen before. We only had a passport-size black-and-white photograph in which one could see two ears, one nose and eyes that did not say anything. I wondered why he had not sent a more natural photograph of himself. My father collected photographs for his innumerable albums, so I thought he would agree with me. He did not. I suppose he was anxious to sell Benjamin to me. He said, 'Some men don't like to be photographed.'

There was nothing I could do. I had to say yes. Everything was organized with such speed by our Solicitor Uncle in Bombay. I no longer had control over my life.

Solicitor Uncle had written to my father:

Dear brother Joshua,
There comes a time when we have to take decisions about our children as they do not know what is good for them. Besides, we have a greater burden as Bene Israeli Jews of preserving and propagating our small community. This demands that our children find proper Jewish mates so that their children grow in number. It is no easy matter and we have to guide our children when they live in a society which has so many cultures. We must not allow them to be influenced by anything that is not Jewish and for this reason, we must catch them young. That is before they start arguing and demanding their rights.

I have often thought about your only daughter Esther. She is beautiful and artistic. She is in a dangerous place—Baroda, at the Maharaja Sayajirao University. You did not think of the pros and cons before sending her to study art. I suggest that before she goes out of hand, you should consider this manga from a very good Jewish family. They are related to you and me, in about nine blood lines, hence Benjamin will be the perfect groom for your daughter. If you send your approval by express post, I will confirm the alliance and your daughter will always be protected.

I went with my parents to Bombay for the engagement. I had been brought up with: 'We know what is best for you. Do you think we will do something that will harm you? We are your well-wishers. We are your parents after all.' When I saw Benjamin, I was sure that they did not care for my feelings, desires and dreams.

At night, when the train stopped at Baroda on the journey to Bombay, I thought of escaping. Ahaseures was there. He loved me. But I did not go to him. I was confused. I did not know how much I loved Ahaseures. I had no guts. I followed my parents to Bombay.

Solicitor Uncle's house was cleaned up and decorated for the engagement. I was like a mummy. I could neither protest nor accept.

Benjamin's train was four hours late. I kept telling myself, 'Run, run, you still have time to escape.' But I could not possibly do that to my parents. They had bought my engagement ring, boxes of sweets and flowers, and were beaming with pleasure. If I ran away their prestige would suffer.

I did not see Benjamin arrive as he was shorter than the kitchen window, from where I had hoped to catch a glimpse of my groom-to-be. I turned to my cousin and said, 'He hasn't come, has he?' She shattered my hopes by smiling and tweaking my cheek. 'Kya jaldi ho gayi dekhne ko? He is already in the drawing-room.' Benjamin was barely four-eleven. I was five-five. There had been no indication in the photograph that he would be shorter than me.

'Cheated,' I told myself. 'How will I get out of this?'

He was a sports instructor in Matheran. That came as a surprise to me. How could he have a job like that with such a height? I always thought physical instructors were tall and big.

That evening, I was dressed in a pink shot-silk sari that Naomi had bought for me. 'Surprise, surprise!' she said as she pulled out the sari. I hated that colour, yet she kept buying everything in pinks for me—from panties to pyjamas. To add to that, with a silly smile on her face, she slipped gold bangles on my wrists and hooked a gold chain with a floral pendant around my neck. She obviously did not remember that I preferred silver. Or was she trying to make me fit the stereotype of the Jewish girl who would be acceptable to her in-laws.

I asked with a snigger, 'Which Hindi film did you see last week?'

She said, 'None. Don't you know I love to dress you?'

I knew she was recreating a scene from the film she had seen the week before with Aunt Hannah. With tear-filled eyes the mother of the heroine dresses her daughter in a heavy Banarasi silk sari and while arranging the gold necklace around her neck, tells her, 'Tere haath pile kar doo aur tujhe dulhan ke jode me dekhu, phir uske baad meri ankh band ho jaye . . .' Once I see you as a bride I shall die contented . . .

Then, becoming sentimental, she kissed me with tears in her eyes. 'Remember those frilly frocks and tiny skirts I made for you when you were my cute baby?' Even as a child, I had respected her and never told her that I did not like frills. I was happiest in sleeveless shifts, and knots in my hair.

Where was Ahaseures? I had a mad desire to run back to Baroda and search for him in the canteen, under the acacia tree. I was thinking of Ahaseures even while Benjamin was placing the engagement ring in my palm. According to ritual, I had to wear it myself. I could have refused. But I did not. Obediently I slipped it on my finger. It was ugly. A thin gold ring with a triangle of three gems.

Solicitor Uncle was talking to Joshua. I knew exactly what he was saying. 'Congratulations, brother, now your daughter is in safe hands.' They were behaving as if I had a mangalsutra around my neck. The engagement ring was like an iron trap used to capture wild animals and birds. Even if I could unlock the trap, I knew I would be maimed forever.

I looked at Naomi with pleading eyes. I needed a saviour. But she did not respond. I looked at Benjamin and felt a surge of nausea. He was staring at my face and asking, 'Excuse me, sorry to ask a personal question, but are your beauty spots real?' He was talking about the two equidistant moles on my cheeks.

I wanted to reply, 'Are you blind?' But kept quiet. I was expected to behave like a well brought up Jewish girl. My hands instinctively flew to my cheeks and I wanted to hide my face. I did not want compliments.

He told his uncle, 'She is shy.'

I looked at my future bridegroom. He was not only a head shorter than me but his chest caved into his stomach. He looked like a small boy dressed in a suit for a fancy dress party. His face was all chin. The rest of his features were bunched up, too close to his forehead. When he looked at me with curious eyes, I could see his mighty chin jutting out at me like the prow of a ship. I couldn't help thinking of the moose at the zoo as his ancestor.

He sat next to his uncle like a little child holding on to his parent. I froze when Solicitor Uncle suggested we go for a walk. 'A couple must get to know each other,' he said. I did not want to know Benjamin.

Fortunately he chose a crowded ice-cream parlour close to the house. The first thing I noticed there was a technicolour clock, under which there was a plaster plaque of Omar Khayyam, showing the poet with his muse. Under this his famous verse was inscribed: 'A glass of wine and thou . . .' I winced. To my horror there were green tables and pink chairs and I could hear Shammi Kapoor singing loudly, 'Dil deke dekho.' Give your heart and see what happens. No chance, I told myself.

When the waiter came with a dirty grey cloth to clean our table, Benjamin ordered cold coffee and ice-cream for both of us. He did not ask me if I liked coffee, and I did not tell him that it made me sick. I wanted to tell him that I liked to decide what I would drink and eat, but the words remained unspoken. Perhaps I would have ordered a Killer Diller, Double Trouble or something crazy like that.

I drank the coffee and allowed him to hold my hand and tell me about his work and his house in the hills. It struck me that I would have sex with him in the same way that I allowed him to hold my hand. I did not like the idea at all.

I was not interested in what Benjamin was saying. I concentrated on my hand. Caught in the soft pad of his palm, it was steaming and fretting. I hoped it would transform into a bomb and tear him apart.

But nothing happened and my hand stayed where it was. I asked myself, 'What does one think of on a day like this? Is it normal to think of killing your husband-to-be?'

Benjamin's voice broke into my murderous thoughts. 'Do

you like children?' I gave him a tight smile and slipped my hand out of his. Then I held one hand in the other and pressed them between my thighs, so that the well brought up young man could not reach for them. The coffee felt like lava on my tongue. 'Don't like it?' He smiled as I pushed the glass away. It was not clear whether he was asking me a question or making a statement.

The subject had to be changed. 'Do you have brothers and sisters?' I asked.

'Yes,' he said. 'An elder brother who is married. He lives with his family in the south. And my younger sister is engaged. Actually we are planning to have a joint wedding.' At first I did not take in what he was saying. When I realized he was talking about my marriage, I was shocked and frightened. I started thinking of ways of escaping.

His words were hitting me like meteorites. 'They will like you very much,' he said.

I smiled weakly and asked, 'Do you all look alike?'

Pointing his chin at me enthusiastically he smiled. Then the little nitwit who was supposed to be my fiancé, had the audacity to say, 'Can I tell you something?' I looked at him full in the face. I knew that I could never be his wife. He was asking me if he could ask me a question.

I nodded and started cleaning the dirt in my nails with a toothpick. My head was bent as it should be—shy and obedient.

He said, 'My parents have not seen you but they liked your photograph and forced me to come to Bombay. As soon as I saw you I agreed to marry you. But I think my parents will have some difficulty in accepting you. You know how traditional families are. You will have to wear saris, assist my mother and sister in the kitchen, do the shopping and help look after the house. Your mother tells me that you cannot cook. She is a very nice lady, perhaps you could learn from her. But don't worry, my mother is an excellent cook. She will teach you everything. When we get married, the first thing you must learn is her kheema patties. I love them.'

I tried to pay attention to his words. 'Uncle tells me you are studying painting. That is an unusual profession for our community. I hope you know that it is written in the Bible that we cannot make idols . . . Girls either become doctors, teachers or housewives. After our marriage, you may not be able to work. But, yes, if you want to do something, my sister can find you a job as an art teacher in a school. She knows everybody.'

He paused, thought and said, 'I can even ask my principal. Can you paint and work with children? If one works in a school, it is very important to like children. Do you like children?' He wanted an answer.

I could not decide whether to tell him the truth. My mother had told him that she would teach me to become a housewife. Obedient, respectful, cooperative and eventually a loving mother.

It was a heavily guarded family secret that I was not interested in cooking, cleaning, sewing or housekeeping. I could not pass a thread through a needle or boil an egg. Benjamin would have been shocked to know that I could not tell the difference between tur dal and moong dal and that housekeeping bored me. But Naomi had a standard answer, 'Girls learn.'

When he had completed his monologue, my silent stare unnerved Benjamin. He changed the subject and told me how popular he was with the students of his school. I could see him on the sportsfield in his white knickerbockers, standing ramrod straight, giving orders, his chin pointing at his students like a baton. Naked, I am sure he looked like a little boy.

On our way home, as was expected of a young engaged couple, he held my hand in the dark. From a distance we must have looked very romantic. As we reached Solicitor Uncle's house, I felt his breath on my cheeks. I am sure it was meant to be a kiss and I started laughing. He assumed I was happy with my first kiss, and became bolder and asked, 'We will write to each other?' Without giving him an answer, I slid my hand out of his. Escape appeared to be impossible. His family and mine were like pythons—they had taken a firm grip of my body, life, existence.

I went to meet Daniel the day after my engagement to Benjamin. Naomi had suddenly become sentimental and wanted her father to bless me.

Carrying a box of pedas, we took a taxi to Mahim. He lived in an old broken-down house next to the sea. We climbed the stairs. We could see him from the open door with its ancient mezuzah and his name-plate: Daniel Navgaokar. He lay on his bed paralysed, saliva running down his chin.

A woman came up the stairs in a bright green sari. She was Durga. Naomi looked at her. They recognized each other. Durga opened the door and said, 'I had gone next door for a second.' It was clear that Grandfather Daniel was Durga's prisoner.

Naomi sat next to her father. He did not recognize her. She then took his hand, placed it on my head and asked him to bless me. It did not make sense to Daniel, but Naomi was satisfied that she had done her duty. Then, Joshua placed a cigarette between Daniel's lips. And, I saw a glimmer of acceptance in his eyes. There was a moment of peace between the men. The cigarette calmed him.

We left the room with the smell of Bombay duck and the sound of the sea. We never saw Grandfather Daniel again. A year later we received the telegram of his death. Joshua and Naomi flew to Bombay and returned the following day—sad and tired. The telegram had reached them ten days late.

79

EMILY, THE CHIMPANZEE, came to Hill Garden Zoo soon after I got engaged to Benjamin. I met her on weekends or during vacations. She comforted me with her tight hugs. I told her all that was happening in my life and she understood everything. She would twist her lips and look into my eyes dolefully. But she also had her own world of dreams and fantasies.

Unknown to Joshua, she was in love with him, because he shared a cigarette with her. She took a few puffs from his cigarette, then broke the cigarette in two and ate the tobacco. She was hooked on tobacco. Once the ritual of the cigarette was over, she played with Joshua's shirt buttons. She did not dare open them, the way she opened her keeper's shirt. With her keeper, it was a different sort of relationship. She swept her cage and even swabbed the floor, if her keeper sat with her at the table and fed her bananas. She shared a comfortable companionship with him.

It was clear that Emily adored Joshua. Every morning, she waited for his Austen. When his car slowed down near her cage, she beckoned him closer and begged for a puff.

When I entered her cage, she would swing down from her perch on the window, which overlooked the railway yard, and cling to me and kiss me. Then she would snatch my scarf. Emily loved fabrics, colours and designs. She would inspect my scarf closely and imitate me by throwing the scarf around her shoulders, then try to tie it around her head like a turban. On

Sundays and during festivals, turbaned villagers stood around her cage and marvelled at her tricks. While swinging in her cage and showing them her antics, their turbans had not gone unnoticed. Her little head never stopped ticking.

Then, our friendship got strained. Emily was in my arms and I was thinking of how to get out of my engagement to Benjamin. Wanting comfort I hugged her. The close embrace scared her. She must have felt suffocated. I did not realize that I was holding her tighter than usual and that she was trying to free herself from my arms. My thoughts were on Ahaseures.

Emily bit me on my left arm. I screamed. There was blood on my clothes. I let her go but Emily was so unnerved that she began screaming at the top of her voice. Her keeper rushed into the cage and I ran out. Emily became even more hysterical when her keeper spanked her with a broom. I could hear her screaming.

After that all precautions were taken, and her keeper was instructed to enter her cage with an assistant. Meanwhile, I was rushed to the Vadilal Sarabhai Hospital, and given an anti-tetanus shot.

Thereafter I was frightened of Emily and no longer entered her cage. She rolled on the ground and begged me to hug her, but though my heart went out to her, I could not.

Emily had arrived at the zoo through various dealers and exchanges. From the time of her arrival she started to fiddle with the locks and latches of her cage. She wanted her freedom. Locks had become an obsession with her. When she finally managed to open the lock, she did not know where to go. She was nervous, and followed the route of Joshua's car. It brought her to the zoo office. She got stuck between the spring doors.

Joshua looked up from his files and saw Emily. He was

careful not to scare her away. He enticed her with a plate of biscuits. It worked. Emily jumped onto the armrest of his chair. Sitting there, she ate all the biscuits and took a puff from the cigarette Joshua offered her.

After a smoke, Emily climbed onto Joshua's shoulders as though it was the most natural thing on earth and allowed Joshua to carry her to her cage.

But life was never going to be a bed of roses for Emily. Jealousy was her undoing. There was frantic activity in the cage next to hers. A new cage was being made. Soon two straw-coloured hairy creatures arrived from Australia with their anthropologist Rosemary. She wanted to see how they adjusted to a country like India.

Emily's eyes glittered murderously when she first saw the orangutans. Watching them through the bars, she saw Joshua fussing over them with chocolates and glasses of Bournvita. An overwhelming feeling of jealousy filled her heart.

Joshua had not stopped at her cage for a week. Day after day, she saw his car drive past and stop at the orangutans' cage. Emily could not take such an insult. When Joshua did finally visit Emily, she was in a rage, and as soon as he came near, she pulled him by the shirt and slapped him. Joshua pushed her back. He realized that he should not have ignored her when he had introduced the orangutans into their cage. He felt a deep compassion for her. Emily was ashamed of her behaviour and did not eat for three days. She sat at her window, with her back to the door.

On the fourth day, when Emily heard Joshua's car, she climbed down and waited for him to come close. Not sure of her reaction, Joshua stood still in front of her cage. Wearily, Emily caressed Joshua's cheek. Joshua sat down on the edge of the parapet and they shared a cigarette. Joshua had conveyed to Emily that he loved her more than anybody else.

80

SUMMONING AS MUCH feeling as I could in my voice, I whispered, 'Mummy, I want to die. I do not want to live.'

Perhaps my mother was transforming me into the Golem. It was one of my Grandmother Shebabeth's favourite stories about Rabbi Low of Prague, and how he had created the Golem, who was the rabbi's slave.

My parents had made me, so I would be their slave for the rest of my life. They would be masters of my will. Just like the Golem.

I was already obeying their commands.

'Why do you feel like dying? Promise me, you will never talk like that, especially at night. You are young, beautiful and soon you will be married to this nice young Jewish man. You love each other. What is there to be unhappy about? Just the other day you told me that he writes these lovely long love letters. What more does a young girl want? It is a perfect match.'

I didn't tell her that when these so-called love letters arrived in their blue or pink perfumed envelopes, I felt like throwing up. I did not know how she would react, but when she asked, 'You love him, don't you?' I had my chance and didn't want to lose it. I shook my head. She thought I was saying Yes. Tapping my shoulder happily she said, 'That's a good girl.'

Afraid that I would lose this opportunity, I looked at her as though I was going to die that very moment. Tears flowed easily at moments like these. I whispered softly, 'I want to break my engagement. I do not like Benjamin. I think he is not normal. There is something strange in his letters and his behaviour.'

I continued, 'I do not think Benjamin will ever understand me, and I do not wish to be the sort of wife he wants me to be.' To avoid seeing the expression in her eyes, I closed my eyes and waited. My fate depended on how Naomi would react. I heard her say, 'You have become red like a tomato.' Although I knew that Naomi had the knack of saying the strangest things at the most critical moments, I was disappointed. My sobs redoubled. Pulling myself together, I thought, Are you such a coward that you have to wait for Naomi's approval for everything? Just tell her that you are breaking the engagement.

I passed a hand over my unruly hair and patted my dress in place. Feeling stronger, I said in a loud voice, 'Mummy, I am going to break my engagement.'

Naomi's eyes became hard. She sat up straight. 'Don't you think that we must speak to Joshua and ask him what he has to say?'

'No,' I said forcefully. I could see the shock in Naomi's eyes. I continued, 'You speak to Daddy and I will inform Benjamin.'

We sat opposite each other for half an hour without exchanging a word. Finally, she said sharply, 'Do as you please. But you will break the engagement yourself. We will not be part of it. It is never done in the Bene Israel community. An engagement is like marriage. It is forever.'

For a year I kept on answering Benjamin's love letters with the little bouquet of roses on the left corner: 'I hope this letter finds you in the best of health. We are fine here and I hope that uncle and aunty are fine . . . etc. etc. . . . with love—your Benjamin.' I answered him on blue paper in the same style. I was not used to expressing my likes or dislikes.

My parents assumed that I would not have the courage to break the engagement. I did. My mother accompanied me to

Matheran, but would not help me in this extremely difficult situation. Joshua and Naomi said that they would not help, as they did not want to spoil their relations with Benjamin's family. After all, they were cousins. I felt they were being unfair. They had got me into this situation and now they were washing their hands of me. Was I expected to tell Benjamin that I didn't want to marry him because I didn't like his letters? Nor did I like his chin. He was no match for my Parsi painter in whose presence I had a funny fluttery feeling and whose eyes invited me to do things I was not supposed to do.

I was restless. As soon as I could break the engagement, I would return to Baroda and look for Ahaseures.

Naomi had written to Benjamin's family that we were arriving by such and such train. She had not mentioned the reason for our visit to Matheran. In fact she wanted to stay with them, but I insisted on a hotel. I needed time to compose myself and prepare for the confrontation.

The house was built on a hillock. It was old with a sloping roof and an overgrown garden. Grudgingly I agreed that they had a beautiful view. Although Naomi had called them from the station, all the doors and windows were closed. Perhaps they had guessed the reason for our visit. The photographs of the engagement were proof enough that Benjamin and I belonged to different worlds.

There was a nip in the air, and my hand on the doorbell felt ice-cold. A tall, thin woman in a dressing gown opened the door. She had a kind expression and from her profile I knew that she was Benjamin's mother. She embraced us and led us in. The house had bright curtains and ancient furniture which needed a good hand of polish. There was nothing on the walls, except a poster of Eliyahu Hannabi, another of Rabbi Simon and the Ten Commandments embroidered with gold thread on deep blue velvet cloth and framed.

Benjamin's father was standing in the middle of the room, bent, old and small. He was an older version of Benjamin. This was how Benjamin would look at sixty. We would look like copies of his parents—a short husband with a wife a head taller than him.

We shook hands and sat on a sofa. Benjamin's parents sat in front of us. Naomi exchanged pleasantries with them and complimented them on their beautiful house and view of the hills. Benjamin's mother looked at me and said, 'In our house, you need not worry about your daughter. She will be very happy with us.' I gave her a blank stare.

Naomi looked at me with an expression of look what you are going to miss.

I did not know how to broach the topic of the engagement. So I looked into my bag and made sure that I had not forgotten to bring the gifts Benjamin's family had given me. There was a sari with pink flowers which I hated, a gold chain which I had never taken out of its box, and a book, a biography of a saint, which I had not opened.

Just then Benjamin's younger sister entered with cups of tea and plates of biscuits. Smiling, she offered me a cup and irritated me by saying, 'Benjamin is on his way. He will be here in an hour.' When I did not say anything, she asked, 'Are you going to wear a veil for the wedding? That will really look nice. I am going to wear one. You know the boys in Benjamin's class are preparing a special welcome for you. They are going to decorate the gate of our house with an arch of flowers with the words Benjamin marries Esther.'

Again I did not answer, nor did I smile at the suggestion of a double wedding. Sensing that something was wrong, she told me about her job at a nursery school. Then she asked if

I liked children and for the first time I spoke loudly and clearly, 'No.' Everybody turned to look at me, surprised. I looked down at my nails. If this dragged on much longer, I knew I would start feeling sorry for Benjamin, never say what I wanted to and would make a mess of my life.

I could see that Naomi was waiting for some such change of feeling in me. I hardened myself and kept my eyes averted from Benjamin's parents. I knew I had just one chance to escape from an impossible situation.

Benjamin's mother started talking about her days in Bombay's Jacob Circle—the Jewish locality where she had grown up. She liked the hills—'But once a Bombay girl, always a Bombay girl.' Saying that, she sneaked a look at her husband. He suddenly asked Naomi, 'Sister, what are your plans for the wedding?' My mother again gave me a meaningful look. She did not know what to say. Fortunately, at that moment the doorbell rang and Benjamin entered the house.

He smiled at me. I gave him a weak smile and turned my eyes away. Benjamin sat down and nervously picked up a biscuit.

Not wanting to prolong the situation any longer, I stood up suddenly and told Benjamin that I wanted to speak to him. His mother and sister were taken aback. Good Jewish girls never spoke like this. I could see the look of fear in their eyes.

I walked out of the room and waited for him in the veranda. He followed me, eating the biscuit, and tried to hold my hand. I snatched away my hand with such force that he was startled. He leaned against a pillar and watched me. For the first time, I saw a crafty, cunning look in his eyes.

I braced myself, breathed deeply and said, 'Benjamin, I have come to break our engagement.'

Coolly he asked, 'Is there somebody else in your life?' I did not reply. Instead, I removed the engagement ring from my finger and slipped it into the bag of gifts and gave the bag to him. I looked into the room to tell my mother that I would be at the hotel. Then I ran quickly down the hillock, without a backward glance.

At the hotel, I locked myself in the room and packed. I was in a hurry to return to Baroda. I had to find Ahaseures. I knew I was running out of time.

Naomi returned much later. As soon as I opened the door, she slapped me. Th*en she walked past me into the room.

I went back to my bed, curled up and pretended that I was asleep. As she changed for the night, she muttered, 'What a time I had trying to pacify the family. They are in a state of shock. I was afraid his mother would have a heart attack.' Then she shook me and said, 'I did not expect this of you. My daughter could not be so cruel.' I decided to keep silent. When she seemed to have cooled down, I told her that I wanted to return to Ahmedabad as soon as possible. She refused and stayed a day more, going back to Benjamin's house to console them. I spent the day walking and buying trinklets in the bazaar.

On our way back to Ahmedabad she said, 'You are going to ruin your life. Such a nice Jewish family. Love comes after marriage.' After that we hardly spoke and I kept my head buried in my book. I still remember it was Ayn Rand's *Fountainhead*. Naomi commented, 'It is all this reading which spoils your head.'

A month later, we received a wedding invitation card with a picture of a bride and groom. Benjamin was getting married to a distant cousin. I heaved a sigh of relief, but Naomi and Joshua never forgave me. They wrote regularly to Benjamin and referred to him as the son they never had.

Later they heard that he had tried to kill his wife. But they still did not think badly of him. Benjamin looked small and harmless, but he was obviously mad. I had sensed it from the beginning.

When she was almost nine months pregnant, Benjamin's bride ran away because Benjamin had stood over her with a rifle aimed at her enormous belly. She took refuge in a friend's house and later returned to her parents' home and asked for a divorce. She could not take a day more in the house with the beautiful view.

A year after I had broken my engagement to Benjamin I returned to Baroda for my postgraduation. I first went to the painting studios. I did not see Ahaseures. I registered for History of Art and waited, hoping that he would suddenly appear. He never did. He had left for another city, another life with another girl.

The memory of our last meeting was etched deeply in my mind. It was at the college lily pond. I was confused and playing with my engagement ring. He was watching me. I wanted to tell him that I needed time to free myself from my parents and also to convince them. But I did not say anything.

Then he took my hands in his, and said, 'This ring is nothing. It is just a piece of metal. Throw it in the pond. Our life together is more important.'

I wanted to hold on to his big hands and kiss him, but I could not. The ring appeared to be welded to my finger. It was not a piece of metal—it was history, tradition, preservation and family. An asp on my finger. I pulled away my hands and ran back to the studio. At that moment, all I had to do was throw the ring in the water and tell him, 'I love you.'

I never told Ahaseures how I felt about him. Why was I so stupid and shy? I had never spoken to him about my problems or the family, because if I spoke against my parents, it would amount to going against the law. I kept my secrets to myself.

Ahaseures did not know I was in the process of breaking the engagement. How could I break the walls between us and explain everything to him?

How was I going to live without Ahaseures? I was to spend a lifetime pining for him. What was it that stopped me from doing what I wanted to do? The family was like an albatross. I carried the burden of being Esther Joshua David Joseph Dandekar—an Indian Bene Israel Jew.

Night after night I dreamt of him. I saw him naked astride a white stallion galloping on the sands of the Mahabalipuram beach, where we had once gone on a college tour. Hand in hand, we watched the moon rise as the waves lapped our feet. Sometimes I saw him disappearing into a forest of cactus, as tall as towers, his back bruised. I could see his high cheekbones, strong jaw, thick black hair with its upward sweep, the Parsi lips and small eyes piercing my heart.

I hoped to meet him some day, but that was not to be. He died in 1986—or was it 1987—in America. I do not know how and why. I only know that he lives in my dreams.

I was angry with the entire Jewish race. Why was I a Jew? Why were there so many restrictions—on my thoughts, my mind, my freedom, my body, my desires.

I could not bear the college without Ahaseures, and returned to Ahmedabad.

I would return to my parents again and again. I was always on the run. I needed their protection and support. I did not know what I wanted from life.

81

AFTER I BROKE my engagement I had acquired the reputation of someone with a dark past and a fickle mind. I was under family pressure to get married. Since I had lost Ahaseures, it no longer mattered whom I married. To please my mother, I promised that I would get married as soon as possible. I had to prove to my parents that I was a good girl, a virgin, my morals were sound and that I would go through life like a respectable married woman.

The few marriage proposals I received from Jewish suitors were not considered by my parents. Naomi did not tell me, but I understood that she was afraid that the doubt about my virginity would be a hindrance.

My first marriage is a part of my life I want to hide. I want to drop a curtain over it and pretend it never happened. It is like a scar, an open wound that still exists in my body and mind. This unfortunate marriage is connected with the desire to be the good girl I was expected to be. To prove that I was good, I had to find a good man. I had to prove that I was not wild.

There was so much confusion, so many questions when I married Shree. As I sit writing this chapter, I feel a throbbing in my head and my hands and feet become cold with the memory of those years.

Shree was an officer in the forest department, and came often to our house. I was allowed to go to the cinema with him. Naomi said he was safe. So, when Shree proposed, I agreed. My parents were relieved.

Shree was not Jewish, but at that point that did not seem to matter. Besides that, India had just woken up to inter-caste marriages, and my parents wanted to be large-hearted modern Indian citizens. Shree had not informed his parents and my parents showed no interest in meeting their daughter's in-laws. They were in a hurry to be done with the wedding, in case I changed my mind and brought further shame to the family.

They were in such a hurry to marry me off, that they did not bother to try to get to know anything about Shree. All that they knew was that he was soft-spoken, well educated and had a good job. What more could a girl want?

When I married Shree, I had known him for exactly three months, and as usual I had my doubts. As a precaution, Naomi made me promise that I would marry him. Exactly in the way that she had taken a promise from me that I would not meet Ahaseures. She placed my hand on her head and said if I tried to break the engagement during the period of the legal banns in the office of the registrar of marriage, she would kill herself. I promised her that I would get married to Shree come what may.

On the day of the wedding, I had the opportunity to escape from what was to prove a disaster. My friends were applying mehendi on my palms, the hairdresser was making an enormous bouffant with my long black hair, her assistant was checking if I would look better in a pale pink or orange lipstick. A red brocade sari for the civil marriage was ready on the hanger, the blouse was being ironed and I was trying on the embroidered Marwari mojdis. A shamiana had been erected in front of the house, strings of asopalav leaves and marigold were being strung on the doors and my parents were welcoming guests with tense faces. There was the fragrance of flowers and ittar. Although Joshua and Naomi, too, had married according to civil marriage rites, both bride and groom had been Jewish. At their wedding party, there had been as many Jews as non-Jews. For my wedding, the Jewish community was not on the invitation list. Besides that, during my parents' wedding, my grandmother had insisted on the recitation of the Eliyahu Hannabi prayers and the partaking of a malida before the civil ceremony. But in many ways, it was a similar situation. If my mother's father had not been present for her wedding, Shree's parents were not present for his wedding.

Cutting through plaintive shehnai music that was playing on the gramophone, I heard the phone ring. The phone had not stopped ringing since morning. But, this ring was long and I wondered if it was Shree. My father picked up the phone. I heard him say: 'How can you . . .?' Then he called out to me and asked me to close the door. He did not want the girls to know what was happening. With the mehendi still wet, intricate and green on my palms, I gestured to my father that I could not possibly hold the receiver. He called out to my mother. Naomi held the phone to my ear as I spread out my hands and heard Shree speaking at the other end of the line. He said, 'I don't know whether I should come or not.'

I shouted into the receiver, 'What?' and signalled to my mother to turn down the music. She shrugged her shoulders. She could not as she was holding the phone to my ear. I asked him to repeat what he had said. When I heard what he had to say, for a second I was dumbstruck. All I said was, 'Of course you must come. I have mehendi on my palms.'

'No,' he said. 'I am confused.'

Then Naomi took the phone and started cajoling him to go through with the marriage. I dried my palms under the fan. I saw my father lying face down on the divan in the drawing room. He looked dead. When I saw his head move, I realized he was crying. He said, 'My standing will be ruined. What about all these guests I have invited for the reception?' He rubbed his chest and said he was feeling sick. Naomi told Shree exactly what Joshua was saying. At last he agreed to come for the wedding with five officers from his department.

Naomi turned to me and asked, 'What do you want to do?' Tears streamed down my face. The make-up made smudges on my face. 'I don't know,' I said. I felt like a hunted animal, as I saw the doctor arrive to attend to my father. Joshua had a heart problem. My mother hissed in my ear, 'You will kill him.'

I rubbed the dry mehendi from my hands and said, 'Now what did I do? It is Shree. He does not want to come. He need not.' I looked down at my hands. The colour of the mehendi on my palms was not a deep red as it was supposed to be, but a pale orange like a dying winter moon.

She asked, 'What is happening? Is he coming?'

I sobbed. 'How would I know, you spoke to him. I think you convinced him to come.'

'But are you getting married?'

'Yes, Mother, I will get married and go away, don't worry.'

When I returned to the bridal chamber, my friends were surprised to see my tear-stained face. 'What happened?' I mumbled something about becoming emotional, and we hugged each other and cried. At the end of it I felt better. I dressed slowly, not yet sure if Shree would finally turn up for the ceremony. I hoped he would not. At that moment, I wished Ahaseures would rush in and rescue me like a film hero.

At that moment, I should have been stronger and if Shree had doubts, I should have cancelled the marriage. I should have then returned to Baroda and waited for Ahaseures. Perhaps he would have returned.

Shree respected my parents' wishes, saved their izzat and arrived for the wedding. I saw that he was angry and uncomfortable. Much to the embarrassment of the family, he refused to attend the reception and family dinner. He hated being photographed and was suffering from guilt. He was getting married without his parents' consent and blessings, and they would never forgive him.

As soon as we had signed the marriage decree in the presence of the registrar of marriage, without ceremony or a proper farewell, we drove down to the Dangs to start a new life. As we were leaving, Uncle Menachem stood with folded hands, and looking Shree straight in the eyes said, 'She is but a child. Look after her.'

The house in the Dangs was very beautiful. It was set amidst lush green trees, with the occasional flame of the forest, and the garden was a riot of colour. It overlooked a range of hills and serpentine roads and small villages and hamlets dotted the landscape. We almost always had a good monsoon and sometimes peafowl flew over the valley in a splash of blue and green. A lake attracted a family of deer and numerous birds came there for their pre-roosting bath. Panthers called each other at midnight, and we woke to the song of birds. But there was so much discord between us, that we never heard their song.

In the first few months, I tried to cook and take an interest in running a home. Within a week, I discovered that Shree was fussy about small household matters. Agreed, I was careless and was not bothered about the difference between expensive and reasonable, but Shree tried to transform me into the image of the women of his family, women who slogged in the kitchen, washed dishes and clothes, ironed shirts and made sure that collars were not dirty. These women also dressed properly—they covered themselves from head to toe. I could not cook. I liked to dress in jeans and sleeveless blouses and kurtas. I was addicted to the cinema and spoke loudly, saying things that a woman should not think of speaking about. Besides that, I laughed too loudly for his comfort. 'A woman should be seen,' he said, 'not heard.' I was horrified to discover that he was not interested in who I was, or what I liked to do. He made it clear that he should be the centre of my universe, and my life had to revolve around his needs.

Life became even more difficult after I had made a great effort to make chicken curry from a recipe Naomi had sent by post. Shree sat at the table and looked at the curry with distaste. He told me that he was fasting. As I bit into a chicken leg, he informed me that he had become vegetarian. Calmly, he told me that I could no longer eat meat in his house. He said his house was a vegetarian home and that meant neither lamb, chicken nor fish would be cooked in our kitchen. I could not even eat meat outside the house in a restaurant or in my parents' home. If friends invited us for dinner, I had to inform them in advance that we had become vegetarians. He gave no reasons, and I had to keep the questions to myself.

Like a good wife, I agreed. I promised Shree I would not eat meat for the rest of my days. I often floated in imaginary flavours of. chicken curries or fried fish. I also put away my sleeveless clothes and made new blouses with sleeves. I hated my saris, which I wore even when we went to bed.

Bored, exhausted and disillusioned, I returned to Ahmedabad. I was not yet pregnant. I had to leave Shree.

I rattled the door and Lassie and the other dogs fell on me, licking me and wagging their tails. That night, I tried to tell my parents about my problems. I told them, I wanted to end the marriage. I did not love Shree. As we sat at the dining table, the food untouched, Naomi announced, 'No, not again. You cannot leave Shree. Love? What love? It comes later. You promised. You must return to Shree. If you stay here you will see my dead body.'

I was disappointed that Joshua did not take a stand. He sat examining his drink. The look on his face indicated that these matters had to be sorted out between husband and wife. I was defeated.

'All right,' I told myself, 'I will try to make this marriage work.'

When I entered the house, Shree was listening to music on the radio. Tears were flowing down his cheeks. He looked through me. I was shocked, yet I wiped his tears with my sari and kissed him. He was sobbing. 'I should not have married you. My parents are disappointed in me.'

I sat on the floor opposite him, feeling trapped. If I did not know about dals and brinjals, I also did not know anything about sex and babies. In a year, I was pregnant, and to add to my misfortunes, Shree's father died that year, and Joshua lost his voice.

82

THE CANCER HAD first appeared as a white patch. Joshua had a cold which refused to go, followed by bouts of breathlessness and frequent loss of voice. A year's radiotherapy did not help. Joshua was losing his voice. It was becoming increasingly inaudible. The ENT surgeon advised a complete check for cancer. Uncle Menachem accompanied Joshua to Bombay to the Tata Memorial Hospital and the decision to operate was taken.

All those who mattered in Joshua's life were present in Bombay. There was Naomi, Aunt Hannah, my cousin Malkha, Aunt Jerusha, family friend Nagindas Shah and Joshua's aide Babu. The rest of the Bombay cousins, distant or otherwise, filled the corridors of the ward. The family from Ahmedabad stayed at Solicitor Uncle's spacious flat.

The reason I was not there was because I was six months pregnant with my first child and keeping indifferent health. It was Naomi's decision that I should stay back in the house in Ahmedabad. I looked after Lassie, a family of chihuahuas, Gangaram, our plum-headed parakeet, the cockatoo Ellis the Fourth, some lovebirds, a giant squirrel and Joshua's brood of whistling canaries. I also knew the family thought I was best kept far away, even if I fretted about my father's life.

When Naomi called me the night before the operation, I was sick with worry. Perhaps I would never see my father again. When I had seen him off at the Ahmedabad railway station along with the zoo staff, I had waved, feeling lost and abandoned. I was no longer part of the family. I was an outsider. Naomi assured me that she would keep me informed by express letters and Malkha would phone me if necessary. I made one last effort at arguing that I should join them in Bombay. Naomi put her foot down with a terse 'No.' I stayed back in Ahmedabad dreading the worst.

A week after the operation, Joshua woke up to the realization that he would never be able to speak again. When he had gone into the operation theatre he had assumed that after the larynx was removed he would be able to speak a little.

When he woke up from the anaesthesia, Joshua saw that there was a tube hanging from his throat. He felt a terrible pain in his throat, which was bandaged, and blood had collected under his tongue. He tried to call out to Naomi, but could not. His tongue refused to cooperate. His voice seemed to have disappeared. With a sinking heart he realized that he had lost the most important part of his life—that which had been integral in bonding him with nature. He had controlled his lions, tigers, birds with the modulations of his voice. They knew him because of it.

He was under sedation, and between sleep and wakefulness, his conscious mind was full of words, his lips never stopped fluttering. But when he tried to say something, no sound emerged. Joshua saw the surgeon who had operated on him, standing over him and asking him how he was feeling. Face flushed and eyes dilated with anger, Joshua held his hand and pointed to his throat, conveying that he could no longer speak. The doctor looked at him sympathetically and explained that if they had not removed the voice box he would have lost his life. Joshua grappled with himself to say something, but could not.

Seeing his anguish, Uncle Menachem gave him the nurse's notepad and asked him to write down what he wanted to say. Joshua wrote a line and looked at his brother with a question in his eyes. 'I lost my voice, why didn't you tell me? I have become mute like my animals.'

Since Albert's death, Menachem had been a pillar of strength for him. He trusted him and looked up to him. If Menachem had not persuaded him to have the operation and if he had known he would lose his voice, Joshua would not have entered the operation theatre.

Menachem smiled at him reassuringly. 'You had cancer of the voice box. It is lucky that it was detected, or else you would have suffered and died a painful death.'

Joshua wrote: 'Losing my voice is like death,' and shook his head in anger. Then he winced. The jerk hurt his neck as the freshly operated muscles stretched and blood filled the tube inserted in the aperture of his throat. He could not even move like before. He was used to gesticulating and shaking his head while talking. He needed to talk. He was a man of words. He had never been a quiet, reserved person. The actor within was still alive, and if he did not express himself from every pore of his body, he could not live. He wrote: 'I want to die. You betrayed me.'

Menachem asked the family to leave. He wanted to be alone with his brother. Closing the door, he sat down in a chair next to Joshua's bed. He arranged his felt hat on his thick, long mane of hair, stared at his shoes and smiled. 'I am sure these guys think I am weird. I haven't worn socks with shoes in ages. And, this bushshirt and old crumpled pants must be creating quite an effect. When I am introduced as a doctor, do you see the surprise on their faces? A doctor should not look like me. Doctors must be dressed in three-piece suits, with a tie and polished shoes and socks. Look at me,' he said, twirling his long, unkempt moustache. 'I am not like you. Even in a hospital bed, look how your moustache is trimmed. You look good, like a perfumed garden with that English Leather Babu rubs on your chin twice a day.'

Menachem saw Joshua's eyes had softened and he smiled. Then they hardened when his brother said, 'Actually, both of us need a cigarette. According to regulations, nobody can smoke here, otherwise we could have shared a smoke. With a cigarette between us, I could have explained better. Tell me Joshua, little brother, do you really believe I betrayed you?'

Joshua stared at the ceiling. Menachem continued, 'If I was in your place, I would have felt the same.' Joshua shifted his attention from the ceiling and looked at his brother. 'I have been thinking about what I should have told you, and what I should tell you now. If your voice box hadn't been removed in time, you could have died a painful death. I did not want you to die. You are my little brother. We may have become old men, but I will always love you the way I have and I know you can never stop loving me. I am you elder brother and you have to believe in me. You have been living a crazy life in that zoo of yours. How many Panama cigarettes did you smoke a day? Eighty? Was it correct? And you have been inhaling all those tar fumes when the roads were being made in the zoo. You have built the zoo brick by brick and were always there, inhaling all that is harmful to the body. And what about all those birds and animals you keep kissing? You were careless about infections, fatal diseases. You never took my advice. After a time, I stopped saying anything because you were so happy at the zoo. I have never seen you so happy.'

Joshua seemed mollified. Menachem continued, 'When you went inside the operation theatre I knew that something would happen to your voice because there was a white cancerous patch on your larynx. But, believe me, I did not know you would lose your voice.' Menachem's head was bent and Joshua could see the top of his hat and the tears streaming down his cheeks. Joshua scribbled something on the notepad and gave it to him with his handkerchief. Menachem took the handkerchief, wiped his eyes and read: 'English Leather.' Menachem smiled wryly. 'I did not want to lose you. How would I have gone through life without a brother?' Menachem was weeping.

He had not cried when they lost Albert, Sophie, or their father and mother. Sitting in the hospital chair in the sparse, clinical room Menachem cried for all those he had lost. He also cried as he was grateful to the lord that his brother Joshua was alive. Joshua could not afford to become emotional because it would only clog up his aperture, so he again wrote something on the notepad and gave it to his brother. The note said: 'Let us have a drink.' Menachem laughed and the two decided to ask the doctor if he could have just a teaspoon of whisky, to wet his tongue.

Within the week, Joshua had permission to take a sip of whisky and soda as it relaxed him. He was over the worst and aware that life was more precious than the loss of his voice. In a fortnight, in the voice therapy department, he learnt to use his voice through his oesophagus. Like a child he enjoyed using slates, pens and all sorts of fancy children's material to express himself.

Joshua spent three weeks in the hospital. When he was discharged the doctors asked what he would do on his first day out of hospital. Joshua dressed in his neat, well-ironed clothes, combed his hair in his distinctive style parted in the middle, trimmed his moustache and with a handkerchief folded and tied stylishly around the aperture in his enormous bull neck, walked to the door saying, 'Babu is taking me to Crawford Market. I am going to sit in Rafiq's shop and hear the chatter of birds and animals.'

Joshua rested in the retiring room of Bombay Central for a week, then flew back to Ahmedabad. He was touched to see friends, admirers, officials of the Ahmedabad Municipal Corporation and the entire zoo staff at the airport.

The return from the hospital was the beginning of his second life at the zoo. A routine was set. Naomi learnt how to insert and remove the metal tube in his throat. Joshua returned to the zoo with apprehension, but he had underestimated the powers of the wild. The birds and animals did not feel he was a stranger. Familiar with his smell, they did not miss his voice. They welcomed him like an old friend who had returned to them after a long journey.

The zoo again became Joshua's saviour. Every morning, there was a spring in his step as he dressed for the zoo. He had learnt to live with his empty voice box. The voice therapist in Ahmedabad had taught him to speak from the oesophagus by forcing him to drink huge quantities of soda water. When their sessions had started he had shocked her by asking for whisky instead of soda water. She had assumed that he was an alcoholic. Later she had learnt to enjoy his jokes and was pleased to see his progress. The oesophagus speech helped him to express himself, but it was tiring. Three months later he received a new voice in the form of a machine. An admirer from New York sent him a catalogue of electric larynxes. Joshua pored over the catalogue and dreamt of regaining his voice. After consulting Menachem and his doctor friends, Joshua decided to order one.

Joshua was like a child who had received his first toy. The six-inch gadget in fibre glass was shaped like a mini-microphone with a small vibrator. The therapist helped Joshua to use it. At first he emitted a sound like a croak and even joked that he was transforming into a toad. After long hours of practice, Joshua slowly learnt to speak clearly. It was not his voice, more like an echo of it. It reached even his own ears like a whisper. Birds and animals quickly accepted his second voice and reached out to him when he called them with his strange purring machine.

Around that time, my daughter was born. Joshua came to see me at the hospital. He smiled when he saw her little face in Naomi's lap. He pressed the electric larynx on her chest as though it was a stethoscope and he wanted to hear her heartbeats. As the machine purred, she woke up with a start, opened her eyes, smiled and went back to sleep. She had heard her grandfather's voice. She was never to hear his real voice. Like his birds and animals, she recognized him by his second voice.

83

SHREE WENT FOR his father's funeral and returned after two months a changed man. It was then that we fought over the smallest thing. He was restless and angry. One day, he turned violent. Perhaps he believed I was the evil one who had entered his house and was slowly devouring his parents. First his father died, then his mother. She died when I was pregnant for the second time. When his violence was at its worst, I told him that I wanted to leave him and return to Ahmedabad. He locked the door and stared at me fiercely. 'I will give you five more children. That will destroy your beauty and your pride. After that, where will you go? Your parents will not take you back and no man will look at you.'

To all outward appearances, we looked like a happily married couple. I cooked, washed clothes, cleaned floors, looked after babies, even had sex with him. In return, he gave me a roof, food and clothing. Naomi asked, 'What more does a woman want?' But I was restless, unhappy, and his violence increased. Slowly, it rubbed on to me. I became vicious.

One morning, there was a great uproar outside the house. Poachers had killed the deer. The guards had not reached in time to save the animals, whose bullet-ridden bodies were spread out on the ground with deep gashes on their slim long necks. A female deer was stretched out with an extended belly, the foetus of its unborn fawn spilt in the dirt, its eyes open, the umbilical cord still attached to its mother. I remembered the story Joshua had told me about the moment he had laid down his arms and become preserver from destroyer. It was all because of a doe.

My father had not been able to save the doe. I would. But, I was not a vet, nor did I have any training in the treatment of animals. I called out to Shree and asked him to help.

He stood over me and said harshly, 'Please go home. You do not understand these matters. It is better if you do not interfere in my official work.'

I looked up and saw his knitted eyebrows and angry face. I refused to move. Tears flowed down my cheeks as I begged, 'Please understand, she is alive. We must save her.'

Gritting his teeth, he lifted me by my arm, hissing, 'Go home.' I was afraid that if I did not stand up, he would kick me and beat me, right there in front of the workers.

Defeated, I trudged back to the house.

Back in the house, I tried to divert my mind with household tasks. But my heart reached out to the doe and the fawn. From the window, I tried to see what was happening at the scene of the massacre. I was sure I could at least have saved the fawn. I was shivering with fear. I was afraid of Shree. His fury terrified me. I could not even open the door, rush down the hill and save the fawn.

That night, I stood on the balcony. The sky was a midnight blue. There was a full moon and in the distance I could see a forest fire and hear the faint rustlings of nocturnal creatures moving in the orchard. The strains of a tribal song and the beat of a drum floated towards me. The villagers often had nightlong festivities on full-moon nights. High on mahua, men and women danced and sang.

Just then, I smelt something burning. It was the familiar fragrance of meat roasting on a wood fire. They were roasting the deer. My first impulse was to scream and tell them to stop. But I had never ventured out alone. I was not allowed to. That was one of the many rules imposed on me by Shree. He said it was for my own good. But tonight, I felt reckless. I wanted to go down to the village. I hesitated. It was dark, and I knew the grass was infested with snakes. Just the other day, I had almost stepped on a cobra which had just emerged from its egg. I had assumed it was an earthworm and only sidestepped when it had raised its hood. It resembled the small silver idol

I often saw in the temples of Dang. If I dared to go there Shree would punish me. I would return to his kicks, slaps and abuses.

As I stood on the balcony, I made my decision. The marriage was over. I could not live with Shree any longer. I would return to Ahmedabad. I had also discovered that my son had a patch on the brain. The movements on his right side were affected. The children were victims of an unhappy marriage.

I opened the door softly and going into the storeroom, brought out my bags. Slowly, I started getting my things together. The house was silent and I could feel the soft breathing of the children. Suddenly, I was afraid. What was I doing? How would I bring up the children without a father, without a home? What sort of life would I give them? I could not deny that Shree had given us a home. What did it matter, if he had a bad temper or was violent at times. After all, he was a good man. I felt a strange, nameless emotion for him. I stood over him, hoping that he would wake up, take me in his arms, and apologize for not being able to save the fawn for the children.

Shree woke up with a start, sensing my presence. He sat up and asked angrily, 'What are you doing? You are mad. Just go to bed.' Every emotion I had felt for him vanished. I switched on the light and with a steadfast gaze said, 'I am leaving you.'

He rushed for the knife he always kept under his pillow and held the sharp blade to my neck. Usually when he became violent, I cowered. But now I looked at him defiantly. The children woke up crying. When I pushed the knife away, he slumped down in the bed and cried. Then, to vent his frustration, he picked up the glass of water next to his bed and threw it at the wall. It broke into pieces, covering the floor with shards of glass. I took the children in my arms and held them close.

Shree returned to his bed and went to sleep, curled up in the bedsheet like a wounded animal. If I had made a false move, he would have injured one of us. I carried the children to the divan in the drawing room and patted them to sleep. One was sucking his thumb, the other was chewing her fingers and sobbing.

I returned to Ahmedabad, leaving my daughter behind in the house on the hillock, where the flying foxes hit their wings on the ventilators and frightened her. I had no other option. The next day, when I left his house, Shree held on to her, hoping that if he kept her with him, I would change my mind. I looked at her serious eyes boring holes into my heart. I knew that if I weakened at this moment and stopped, I would never be able to leave. I had to leave my daughter. It was impossible to fight. I would have to get her back through legal recourse. I knew that I would get her back at any cost.

In Ahmedabad, on the first night without her, Naomi spoke in praise of my decision to leave my daughter with her father. At least I was concerned about my husband, who also needed a child. A child who would fill his lonely days. The child, she said, would also compel me to return to my husband.

That night, I got my first attack of hysteria. And Joshua, who was sitting tiredly on the sofa, woke up as if from a stupor. He gave me a stiff brandy and tucked me into bed as he used to when I was a child. He then carried my son to his own bed and held him tenderly, till he fell asleep in the crook of his arm.

84

MY DAUGHTER WAS separated from me by more than five hundred kilometres and yet I heard her cries even in my dreams. Sometimes my son held a shell to his ears as though he was listening to the sea and spoke to his sister as if she was sitting next to him. But he was happy at my parents' and loved going to the zoo with my father. He was especially fond of Maya, the ostrich. He loved her long-legged dance and would scream with pleasure when she ate from his little palm. Maya was careful not to hurt him.

When Joshua had seen Maya for the first time, he remembered the ostrich which had intrigued him as a young man at The Fine Spinning and Weaving Co. Ltd. In those days he had dreamt of riding an ostrich, but when Maya arrived at the zoo, Joshua thought it was cruel to ride a bird.

Maya had come to the zoo in exchange for two kangaroos. It was amazing to see her growing into a big bird with powerful legs, short wings, and wide open, curious eyes. Mahesh was Maya's mate and they were often seen with their necks entwined, feeding each other. They made a perfect pair.

But Maya had one drawback. She was very trusting and had lost her natural fear of human beings. Unknown to anyone, a predator was stalking her. Smoking bidi after bidi, this maniac had been watching her. Beguiling her with peanuts, he persuaded Maya to come very close to the fence. He did this day after day during the lunch hour, when there was nobody around her cage.

Then, one day, he torched her feathers with a lighter. When her feathers started smouldering, Maya tried to peck at the flames but could not extinguish them. She ran around the cage with her flaming wings and her mate tried to help by running around her. By the time Joshua heard of it, Maya was dead. Charred, her feathers burnt to ashes.

We were all shattered when Maya died. The memory of her mute cries and burning feathers has always haunted us.

In Maya's womb, Joshua found a huge clutch of eggs. Fresh, large and as big as melons. Ready to be dropped and hatched. In the ostrich aviary, Joshua discovered that Maya's mate had prepared a hidden nest. When Joshua returned without Maya, Mahesh looked at him with questioning eyes.

Babu had taken lessons in taxidermy from Joshua and they stuffed her. Maya found a place in the Joshua David Natural History Museum which was made with the help of Yashwantrao. Maya stood in her famous ballerina stance, her empty eggshells placed next to her.

85

AFTER LONG AND lonely rounds at the city civil court of Ahmedabad, my daughter came back to me. I won the battle of her custody. But she was no longer the bubbly child I had known. She had become like a mute swan, while my son was trapped in a cage of callipers. The black patch on his brain had eclipsed his life. Those were endless days at the doctors, lawyers and the physiotherapist. My finances were low, and I was dependent on my parents. To add to this, Naomi blamed me for my father's health problems.

When the divorce was proclaimed—without alimony—I agreed. Shree expected me to make a written application for money. I refused to accept pity or alms. We never saw him again.

Soon afterwards, I left my parents home and rented a small flat far away. Here I made a cosy home with the children. We made seats out of boxes and steel trunks and covered them with cheap bright bedsheets. At night, we moved our makeshift furniture and spread out the mattresses on the floor. Even with my limited resources, I bought either chicken or mutton on Sundays and taught the children to eat non-vegetarian food. Having grown up only on vegetables, they hesitated at first, then slowly developed a taste for meat. They even had their preferences—my son preferred chicken, my daughter liked liver. And once a month, we scraped up enough money to go to a restaurant, where we ate fried fish and chips and felt like royalty when we returned home licking bars of chocolate ice-cream. We were like children, growing up together.

I took up the chisel and mallet and tried to make a living as a sculptor. In the search to earn a decent income, I taught sculpture at the School of Architecture, and was the art critic for *The Indian Express;* in the evenings, I worked as a telephone operator for a travel agency, and on weekends, I conducted art classes in the Shanker Bhuvan slums for the Majoor Mahajan Sangh.

I wrote long essays on art. I developed my own views and perceptions. The years I had spent in the library of the Maharaja Sayajirao University had not gone waste. These critiques were well received and one afternoon, I received a phone call from Mahadevan, Editor of *The Times of India,* asking me to write for his newspaper. I discovered that I enjoyed writing. I was invited by various institutions to teach sculpture, art history and art appreciation. My occasional art activities in the slums interested Father Erewitti, a Spanish Jesuit working in the St Xavier Social Service Scheme. He offered me a bigger salary and a wider field of work, where I could use art for development in the underprivileged areas of Ahmedabad. The fascinating results I observed in this field became a lifelong obsession. Each aspect of my life was interlinked with the other. I was invited by the West Zone Cultural Centre at Udaipur to coordinate festivals. This was followed by a nomination to the Gujarat State Lalit Kala Akademi, which I eventually chaired for five years.

In the path which I had chosen for myself, I received as many brickbats as flowers. Nobody knew what was happening in my life. I never allowed anybody to see my tears. People hated me for my guts. I was the strange mystery woman. I did not confide in anybody. Life was not easy, but I became a powerful and ambitious woman. I created my own space in the field of art and culture in the city of Ahmedabad.

Naomi refused to speak to me. My father wept in front of friends and strangers about a daughter gone astray. I was the black sheep of the family. At thirty, I was young, beautiful, divorced and carving out my own destiny.

For years, I had kept away from the synagogue—religion had died with Grandmother Shebabeth. She had died three months before the birth of my first child. I saw Shebabeth in my little daughter's smile. When Shebabeth died, I was with Shree. I was not informed about her death.

When I returned to Ahmedabad, enormously pregnant, and asked for Shebabeth, I was told of her death. At that moment I needed her. I knew she was too sick and old to take a stand, but I needed her to touch my stomach and hold me in the softness of her breasts. She had been the centre of my life; her soft saris and her wrinkled, silken skin had comforted me. She had woven a web of stories around me, creating an illusionary family around me.

'Why didn't you tell me?' I was furious.

'We decided,' said Naomi with a certain finality in her tone, 'that you should not attend the funeral in such a condition. It would also have been awkward; the entire Jewish community was here.' I resented that the family had treated me like an outcaste, just because I had married Shree. I was denied the right to touch my grandmother, feel her and see her before she left for her final destination, eyes closed with the earth of Jerusalem and floating towards the bejewelled rocks of Mount Sinai.

The relationship between my parents and me was a bitter one, but I often left my children with them. They went to the zoo with their grandfather and he taught them to recognize birds and animals. Later, at home, he regaled them with animal jokes. Naomi took on the role of the perfect grandmother, looking after and feeding them, buying them new clothes and shoes, and telling them fairy tales. I did not deprive the children of that comfort.

My life with the children had a set but happy routine. Although we were often worried about my meagre income, we were at peace. The children took on the responsibility of running the house, so that I could work and bring in more money. And, whenever they felt like it, they phoned their grandparents to send the car for them. They went to the zoo with Joshua, or Naomi took them shopping, or they just snuggled up together and regaled each other with stories. They told me that whenever they were together, they rolled with laughter and were sad that I was not part of the merriment. But it warmed my heart.

To avoid arguments, I preferred to keep away from my parents. I knew I was slowly melting towards them. I was worried when the children told me that Naomi had been keeping bad health. After retiring from the school she had been teaching English. She had occasional attacks of fever, nausea, or a stomach infection and there were black patches on her body. Naomi refused to have a thorough check-up. Nobody suspected that she had cancer. They came to know only when, after three years of intermittent illness, one evening she collapsed.

My cousin Malkha came to inform me that Naomi was serious and in hospital.

When I reached the hospital with Malkha and the children, my mother had lost consciousness. The otherwise fierce woman was trapped in tubes, drips and blood transfusions. In her few waking moments, she knew we were there. She smiled at the children and called out to them. They were afraid when they saw their grandmother in such a state. I took them closer to her and she caressed them with great tenderness. Whenever she was awake, Naomi gave me sharp disapproving looks, but allowed me to change her blood-soaked clothes, give her a sponge and apply powder in the crevices of her wasted body. We had changed roles. In her sickness, she needed to be mothered.

Naomi was in the emergency ward of the Vadilal Sarabhai Hospital for fifteen days. On the afternoon of the fifteenth day, Naomi died. Five days earlier, she had suddenly seemed better. She stopped bleeding and was allowed to sit up for an hour. Joshua sat next to her, holding her hand. One after the other, the family, friends and the zoo staff went up to Naomi and said how happy they were to see her sitting up. I hesitated to go closer; I wanted to be there for her, but in the background. Not wanting to disturb her I left the room on the pretext of buying aspirin. I walked around the wards looking at the sick and dying, even had tea outside, and was going back to the studio for a bath when I changed my mind. What if she had again become unconscious? I returned to Naomi's room.

I was relieved to see that she was still sitting against the pillows with the children next to her. The children were uncomfortable and climbed down from the bed and ran towards me. Naomi's eyes, with deep dark circles around them, followed the children and stopped at my face. All eyes were on me. I had no alternative but to walk towards her. I held her cold hands, kissed her pale cheeks and felt tears fill my eyes. Naomi was watching me, her eyes expressionless. Then she looked past me, at the people standing outside. The face she was searching for was not there. The room was still and silent. Each pair of eyes in the room watched us with curiosity. Would Naomi forgive me? Would we come closer in her last moments on earth.

I could feel the sorrow within me turn to anger, as she asked just one question. Otherwise she did not utter a single word, not even to Joshua. The question shot through the room at me like an arrow, cold and sharp. It pierced the very core of my being. 'Where is Shree? Go back to him.'

Joshua and his men ran towards the telephone. The groups of people standing in the corridor began whispering. They were probably talking about me. My hand moved away from Naomi's and I walked out of the ward and into the corridor. I told Joshua that if they called Shree to Ahmedabad, I would walk out of the hospital and they would never see me again. Joshua put the receiver of the phone back on the holder. He walked towards me, bent and defeated. Holding me in his arms, he asked me to respect Naomi's last wish.

The children stood next to me, fear on their faces. Their warm hands crept into mine.

I did not respect Naomi's dying wish. I did not invite Shree to her deathbed. I knew she wanted to place my hand in his and die in peace. But I did not want any more movie scenes in my life. She had often annoyed me by saying, 'A daughter's place is in her husband's house.'

I understood how worried she was about me and the children. I may have even agreed with her, if the situation had been different. I tried to explain to her how difficult it was for me to live with Shree. But she had closed her mind and drawn a curtain over the truth. I pitied her, because all she had asked for was a picture-perfect image of a happily married daughter. I could never give her that pleasure. Nor could I give her the peace of mind that I was safe in my husband's house. I was fated to live under the protection of my father's house.

When the dramatic moment ended, I saw from the doorway of Naomi's room that she had again become unconscious. She was lying on her right side, curled up like an embryo, her eyes closed and lips pursed. I went back to my duty of cleaning her as I saw the blood spreading on the bedsheet.

As crowds thronged to comfort Joshua, I stood a little away from my mother's deathbed, tall, erect and adamant, refusing to bend to my mother's will. The crowds moved away from me as if I was a pariah. The only one who supported me was my cousin Malkha. She took charge of my children and left them with a friend. Her love, concern and understanding still connect me to her.

My mother's death came suddenly, a few days later. When the doctors gave up hope, an elder of the Bene Israel community took my father's permission to read a Hebrew prayer for the dying. Religion had entered Naomi's life while she was breathing her last . . . 'God the divine ruler enthroned high, dwells eternal in supreme holiness and also with the contrite and humble spirit to revive the spirit and give life to the heart of the afflicted. May he in his overflowing and ever present mercy towards us and the house of Israel, in pity and compassion send his saving relief and healing to Naomi, lying afflicted on the bed of sickness. She entreats the Lord her God for generous grace and favour, merciful healing and restoration to health and life.'

When Dr Parikh pronounced that my mother was clinically dead, the room suddenly emptied. The visitors went with

Joshua to comfort him and make preparations for the funeral. The drawing room would have to be emptied of furniture, trophies, paintings, carpets, antiques, fish tanks and all the decorative objects.

I was left alone with my mother to watch over her and wait till the funeral arrangements were made. I touched her to make sure she was dead. Naomi's hands were cold. The tubes had been removed. The veins were swollen with the constant transfusion of blood. The catheter was hanging on the side with the last sign of life, her urine. The nurses had not yet emptied it. The lines of tension and pain on her face were changing into the mask of death and the colour of her skin was becoming a pale blue.

There was an eerie silence in the room. Naomi's eyes flew open. My heart missed a beat. I turned to ring the bell for the nurse. I felt a deep love for my mother. Perhaps she was alive. I did not want her to leave this world with a misunderstanding between us. I wanted her to live, so that we could talk and become good friends again.

I was in anguish as I looked into her eyes—dark, angry and reproachful. I was sure I heard her say, 'Go back to Shree.' I was frightened and pressed the emergency button. The nurses and doctors rushed in, and I told them that my mother was alive. They assured me that she was dead.

When I brought my mother's body back to the house for the funeral, the women from the Jewish community were already there, stitching the shroud.

I gave my mother the ritualistic bath in coconut milk and dressed her in the traditional Jewish shroud. The women had already stitched the pantaloons, a long-sleeved blouse, an overcoat, and the headscarf. They had pulled on her socks and had tied a sprig of fragrant catnip in her hands, held together with a white embroidered handkerchief. The shroud was layered with camphor, the eyes were closed with earth brought from Jerusalem and my son, the male child of the family, performed the last rites. An elder had whispered in my ear, 'If the mother is a Jew, the children become Jewish, automatically, so teach your son the law.' I gave him a blank look, not understanding the meaning of his words. I was watching my son. He was still a child, and his fingers smarted from the wax dripping from the candle he was holding. As my mother was lowered into her grave, I threw a fistful of earth on her and knew that I was burying a part of my past with her. Once the earth covered her, I would be released from all the promises I had made to her.

I wrote to Ahaseures. I needed him. He never answered. He had left for another dream—America.

Since the time we had parted in 1965, he had filled my dreams, night after night. Sometimes he spoke. Sometimes he smiled. He always seemed to be riding towards me. But they were just dreams. I woke up sweating in my empty bed.

In the summer of 1986, I saw him again in my dreams. It was unbearably hot and much as I tried, I could not sleep inside the house. Around midnight, I carried my mattress to the open terrace and slept under the borsali tree. It showered me with the fresh fragrance of its star-shaped flowers. Half-asleep, half-awake, I saw Ahaseures again. He was wearing a white shroud and riding a black stallion. He was standing over me, his hand outstretched. I tried to reach out and touch him, but he turned away. He galloped off into a forest of cacti. His massive back was bruised and bleeding as he flew past the web of thorns which closed upon him.

The next day, I heard about his death. He had died in his sleep. I have never been able to come to terms with his death.

When Naomi died, my father wanted to follow her. He

could not live without her. He drowned himself in drink. I often found him sprawled on the floor in the house at Shahibaug—drunk and crying like a child. Naomi had been his anchor. That is when I decided to look after him. I was tired and needed his shelter, and though he would never accept it, he needed my care.

I returned to my father's house with the children. Joshua and I readjusted to each other. The presence of the children calmed him. He enjoyed his status as grandfather, and behaved like an ancient Jewish patriarch. Every day, we made efforts to reconstruct our family.

86

WE HAD ALMOST forgotten that we were living in a rented house. My father had originally rented it for fifteen rupees. The rent was raised to thirty rupees in 1979.

With a lot of scraping and saving, Joshua had built a small farmhouse in Vasna, in the opposite direction to Shahibaug. Joshua wanted to drop a curtain on his life with Naomi but he still had the zoo. After his retirement, when he was fuming and fretting, not knowing how to live without a zoo, the Mayor, Raffiuddin Shaikh, had passed an order in the standing committee that Joshua David would stay with Hill Garden Zoo as an honorary adviser for life.

The house in Vasna was bigger than the one in Shahibaug. When the foundation stone was laid my father had caught more than twenty cobras there. They had been living there for a long time. We had a cobra in the garden once in a while even after shifting, but as long as my father was there, I knew I had no reason to worry.

The house was decorated in the same style as the one in Shahibaug—crammed with trophies, paintings and antiques. There were also racks full of formalin bottles with bizarre objects like a two-headed child, a Cyclopean goat, a bird with four legs, technicoloured bees, tiger whiskers, porcupine quills, the fat of bears, tigers and lions which had medicinal value, the tail of a rattlesnake, and many others. Many people visited us out of curiosity.

My father lived on the ground floor and I on the first floor. We had a common kitchen. I cooked, cleaned, worked as a lecturer in a state-run college of fine arts, and hosted innumerable parties for my father.

My father was always there for my children. Teasing, scolding, playing with them. Unconsciously, he was filling the place of a father. I was relieved.

Every morning, at the stroke of eight, Joshua left for the zoo in our Austen with Ahmedchacha at the wheel. He returned at two, had his gin and bitters before lunch, napped and then waited first for the children, then his guests. Every day between five and seven, that is before friends started dropping in, my father worked with my daughter. He was writing a book on Asiatic lions and albino animals and birds. The book on lions was published by the Government of India; the manuscript on albinos is still lying in his cupboard. At seven he stopped work, and shared his rum with friends and admirers who filled our house. I always had to cook extra food. I never knew who was going to stay for dinner.

But I learnt not to complain, as sometimes I met unusual people, such as Crystal Rogers. She had come to Ahmedabad to meet the man who had dedicated his life to the preservation of wildlife. As a gift she brought him an injured crow she had found on the way to our house. We loved her innumerable stories and experiences with stray animals and birds. The children were in splits when she told them about the macaque with the injured paw who was addicted to Colgate toothpaste.

I also came to know the power of a faith healer. Erica was a faith healer from Holland who often came to India to visit her musician friend Brij Bhushan Kabra. He wanted her to heal my father. He refused saying he would be happy if she healed my son. She gave him energy and taught me to give him some of my own. I cannot explain the experience, but I know that that night, my son felt better, and a few months later he had grown taller, was playing cricket and trying to use his hand. Above all, he was bursting with confidence.

If I had stopped my father from indulging in his natural gift of attracting people, I would have also missed meeting Shlomo. I cannot remember his last name. I can just about decipher his Hebrew signature in the Bible he sent me. Like the many Israelis who visited our house, he had stopped for a day in Ahmedabad to see the zoo and meet Joshua. As always, he was invited to the house. Shlomo was a historian interested in Hindu mythology and wanted to find similarities with the Torah.

That evening, when I returned from college, I saw Shlomo walking in the garden. It was winter and he was wearing a black sweater over his jeans. He looked like a bald-headed crow as he greeted me with a warm 'Shalom.' I shook hands and entered the house, a little annoyed that I would have to cook something interesting for my father's Israeli fan. I gulped my tea and rushed upstairs to change and see that the children had done their homework.

Shlomo sat talking with my father as I busied myself in the kitchen. My father had told me that he was vegetarian. I understood that he only ate kosher meat.

At eight, my father set the table for his evening peg of whisky. But when my father opened the bottle, Shlomo froze. He said rather brusquely, but politely, 'No, I cannot accept this.' I stopped chopping the salad and looked at Shlomo.

He was past eighty and thin, sprightly and strong, with long knotty fingers that were clutching his knees. He looked funny as he sat on the divan, a strip of sticking plaster on his broken nose, over which his bifocals balanced precariously. Before coming to Ahmedabad, he had been to an ashram near the city. There at the guru's feet he had bent his head to make an elaborate namaskar, and hit his beak-like nose on the rim of the pedestal. His nose had been treated, but a deep red dent still remained.

He asked me in his strong East European accent, 'Esther, do you know that today is the shabath?'

I smiled. 'Yes, today is Friday.'

'Then where is the kiddush?'

'Shabath candles?' I was confused, my father more so. The children listened as though we were talking Greek.

'Well, I am sorry, but I can neither eat nor drink, if you do not do the shabath prayers.'

My father said, 'I am sorry, we are not practising Jews. But according to Indian tradition, you cannot leave without eating.'

'If you want to me to eat, then dear friend, do you mind if I do the shabath prayers?'

My father agreed enthusiastically. 'I respect your sentiments, but as far as I am concerned, I do not believe in anything. I only believe in humanity and that everybody is equal. Is our blood any different from that of the man in the street? The colour is the same—red. I gave up religion long back. But I do believe in nature.'

'So, let us pray to nature. Because there is something more

powerful than man which sustains every living thing. Could I please ask your daughter to set the shabath table?'

I was embarrassed. I had never set a shabath table. I remembered helping my grandmother Shebabeth as a child, but it seemed so long ago. I said to Shlomo, 'Can you help me? I do not know how to set the shabath table.'

Shlomo first asked for a clean white cloth to spread on the table. Fortunately I found an unused silk tablecloth hidden under my mother's saris. Then he asked me for the shabath candlestand. I looked questioningly at my father, hoping he would find me one. He just shook his head. So I looked through the cupboard of old dishes and found a brass plate shaped like a pipal leaf. It looked perfect. I washed off the grime and cleaned it till the dull yellow metal showed an intricate tracery of a creeper. Wiping it dry, I gave it to him with a candle and a matchstick. Shlomo smiled and holding my hands in his, asked me to light the shabath candles.

We stood around the table in a half-circle. Shlomo wrote out the Hebrew prayer in the Roman script and asked me to read the words. I lit the shabath candle and read haltingly: 'Barukh ata adonai elohenu melekh ha olam asher kideshanu ba mitswatenu ve tsianu lehadlik ner shel shabath . . . (Blessed art thou, O Lord our God, King of the Universe who has sanctified us by thy laws and commended us to kindle the shabath light)' I looked up in surprise. My father was saying the prayer with his eyes closed. He smiled awkwardly and said that the words had suddenly come back to him.

Shlomo poured a glass of port wine from my father's collection of bottles and filling the kiddush cup, he gave it to my father. They recited together.

With the men, my son was also repeating the words.

Shlomo said, 'I am not religious and I have not taught you

anything. Your father knows everything. One never forgets what one learns as a child. Let your son learn from his grandfather. Wherever I am, I never miss saying the shabath prayers. It makes me feel good. Do you feel different?'

Shlomo also told us the background and meaning of the Bene Israel. He said, 'There are many mysteries surrounding your people. I saw posters of Rabbi Simon in some Bene Israel houses in Bombay. He was known as Simon the Just for his piety and knowledge of the Torah. He was one of the last survivors of the great assembly, which studied the Torah. He was known to say, ". . . Upon three things, the world is based—the Torah, divine worship and acts of benevolence." He died in 270 B.C.'

You are known as the Bene Israel, which means sons of Israel. It is also believed that you are the descendants of the tribe of Zebulum, the sixth son of the prophet Jacob and Leah. His tribe has the symbol of a ship, which signifies that his children were a seafaring people. Perhaps they fled Israel during the reign of Antiochus Epiphanes and came as far as India and were shipwrecked on the Konkan coast. There is no evidence, just assumption.'

Adjusting his bifocals on his nose, he continued, 'I have also discovered that the Bene Israel observe the fast of Gadaliyah in memory of Gadaliyah, the governor of Judah. Actually, it is a minor fast, for a minor hero, but important to Indian Jews. After the destruction of the First Temple in 586 B.C., the Babylonian king Nebuchadnazzer unexpectedly appointed an able Jewish governor, Gadaliyah. He was murdered by his own people and the remaining Jews, who were not part of the conspiracy, fled. They feared that Nebuchadnazzer would execute them, assuming that it was an act of rebellion on their part. It is possible that you are one of them. Otherwise why would you fast for Gadaliyah?' We had no answer.

I was suddenly interested in the meaning of the word Israel and everything Jewish, but did not have anything to turn to—no books, no knowledge. I looked through Joshua's animal books and could not find a Bible. All we had was a mezuzah on the door—a silent reminder of our Jewish heritage.

When Shlomo had reintroduced the shabath prayers in our house, he had opened a small door in the dark corridor of my life as a Jew. I started a family ritual which has never been broken. I realized that with the shabath, a family is bonded together—through a candle, a glass of wine, a loaf of bread and a pinch of salt.

A month later, I received a packet from Israel. Shlomo had sent us two Bibles. In his letter, he wrote: 'I felt it was my duty as a Jew, to send you the Torah. I did not see it in your house.' I was deeply touched and the children experienced a sense of bonding with their religion, as they caressed the leather-bound Bible. It seemed to root us to something which had always been vague and distant. Our religion had only been a word which we filled in in forms where we were expected to do so.

The Bible gave me the strength to return to the synagogue. At first we went for weddings, then for festivals, and later I dared to attend the malida for an Eliyahu Hannabi. Sometimes, my father came as the chief guest to community gatherings. It was awkward in the beginning. We did not know what to do, how to move, how to sit, how to rock the heels. Nor did we know which fruit to start with while participating in the malida. We observed the person sitting next to us and learnt our Jewish rituals.

In those years, my only contribution to the Bene Israel community of Ahmedabad was that I helped the trustees choose a colour scheme for the synagogue—ivory white for the

walls and brown for the old windows, carved with designs of
menorahs and the Star of David.

87

THERE ARE SOME parts of our lives which always remain a
mystery. My desire to start a new life in Israel is one such
mystery. I often caught myself thinking, 'Should I get rid of the
maya of possession, the hassles of running a house, the struggle
to earn a living—live on a kibbutz and return to Israel?'

Even as a child, I was always aware of Israel. Perhaps
Grandmother Shebabeth was responsible for its existence in my
mind.

When Grandmother Shebabeth lay down for her afternoon
siesta, I would snuggle next to her. Nestling in the curve of her
body, I floated in the fragrance of soap, masala, paan and
stories. She never finished her stories and would doze off mid-
sentence, leaving the rest to my imagination. During those fairy
tale afternoons, she often regretted that she had not found a
groom for Aunt Jerusha. Nor had she been successful in
sending her to Israel. I always asked, 'If Aunt Jerusha decides
to go to Israel, will you go with her?' Even if Shebabeth was
dozing, her eyes would fly open and sitting up she would smile
and say, 'Yes, I want to see Mount Sinai, the holy mountain
where the prophet Elijah took shelter when he was pursued by
the evil Baal. I wish I could just touch the rocks, where the
Lord descended in the form of a cloud, to give the law to
Moses. The Lord called from Mount Sinai amidst thunder and
lightning. And the people in the camp trembled, because the
Lord descended upon it in fire and smoke. And the mountain
quaked. 'Then she would lie back exhausted and say, 'Jerusha

will never leave India. If she were to agree, we could both go to Israel.'

In her later years, although she was bedridden, Grandmother noticed that I was always tense. That was during my tumultuous college days. She did not know what was happening, but she sensed that I was troubled. Holding my hands in hers, she would whisper in Marathi, 'There is nothing here. Go to Israel.'

Shebabeth planted the seed of Israel in my mind. Israel was my oasis. It was the place where I could escape to when I was in distress. Year after year I told myself, 'Next year, Jerusalem.'

Israel often impinged on my life through chance encounters. It came to me through tourists like Shlomo the historian, Eli Jacobson the merchant of carpets, and various officials from the Jewish agency who came to meet my father. Israel also came to me through photographs sent by uncles, aunts, cousins. The photographs promised a land that would liberate me from my past.

When Eli Jacobson came to our house, I must have been seven, recovering from possible death as a result of eating too many chocolates.

One Sunday evening, a buggy stopped at the door, someone rattled the latch, and a booming voice greeted us with a 'Shalom.' Joshua went to the door and stared blankly at the stranger standing there who asked, 'Sir, excuse me, I saw the nameplate and stopped. Can I ask you a personal question? Are you a Jew? I guess you are one.'

Suspicious of the stranger, my father said 'Yes' haltingly.

The man smiled. 'I am also a Jew,' he said. 'I come with greetings from Israel. My name is Eli Jacobson. I sell Persian carpets.' He pointed to the rolls of carpets stacked in the carriage. Joshua opened the door and invited him in.

Eli made himself comfortable on the divan and said, 'From your name, I guessed you were a Jew, but I was not sure because you did not respond to my greeting.'

'Greeting?' asked Joshua.

'Shalom!'

'Shalom?'

'That is how we greet each other in Israel.'

'Shalom!' said Joshua savouring the word. 'What does it mean?'

'Peace.' Joshua was impressed.

The men relaxed and exchanged notes about India and Israel. Joshua told Eli how he had made the zoo in Ahmedabad. Eli complimented him, and compared him to King Solomon because he could communicate with birds and animals.

Huddled in a colonial chair in a corner of the room, I was listening to them. I saw that Eli was very fair, short and fat. He had an enormous nose, a receding hairline and pink cheeks like Grandmother Shebabeth. He had a tattoo on his arm. It looked just like the tattoo on the maid's arms but she had birds, flowers, scorpions and her husband's name, while Eli's looked like numbers. I assumed he was a sailor because I had seen a similar drawing of a sailor with tattoos in my cousins' comic books.

Naomi poured tea and offered biscuits. Eli told Joshua that he had grown up in a kibbutz. He was a Jew of Czech descent and had escaped to Israel when Hitler's army had entered the country of his birth. When he had had enough of kibbutz life, he had taken to selling carpets in Asia. He regaled my father with stories of his kibbutz in the Galilee.

To me, dozing under my shawl, the kibbutz sounded like paradise. Green fields. Orchards. The common kitchen. The games. The songs. No personal responsibilities. I turned a deaf ear when Eli explained that for that sort of freedom one had to pay by waking up early and working long hours.

Like the perfect hostess she was, Naomi poured herself a cup of tea, smiled and asked the inevitable question, 'How interesting! Do you have a family?'

Suddenly, there was silence in the room. My father tried to change the subject, saying, 'So, your family comes from Prague?' This question seemed to upset Eli even more. He replied, 'Terezin.' The room seemed to freeze like a morgue. Eli looked pale as a corpse. Eli broke the silence, saying, 'I lost them. I am a survivor . . . arrived alone in Israel.' The room was charged with so much tension that my stomach began to turn somersaults. Throwing off the shawl I walked weakly towards the bathroom without looking at Eli or my parents.

My ghaghra was sweeping the floor and I had to hold on to the string so that it did not fall off. My silver anklets jingled and I kicked myself for wearing them even when I was sick.

Eli made an effort to lighten the atmosphere and asked, 'Is that your charming daughter?'

Proudly Joshua said, 'Yes.'

'What is her name?'

'Esther.'

When I returned to the chair, Eli stared at me. 'How old is she?'

'Seven,' said Naomi with a smile. 'She is sick. Almost died, eating chocolates.'

Eli immediately put his hand in his pockets, pulled out some colourful candies I had never seen before, and offered them to me. I was tempted but Naomi was shaking her head disapprovingly and Joshua was making lip-movements like his favourite chimpanzee and asking me to say, 'Thank you.'

I shook my head and smiled weakly. 'Thank you, uncle. But I cannot eat any more sweets.'

I heard him say, 'Poor child,' as I closed my eyes. Turning
to Joshua, he asked, 'What are you planning to do? Are you
going to stay in India or leave for the Promised Land.'

I heard the horror in Joshua's voice. 'Never. The zoo is my
life.' Naomi was nodding her head in approval.

I opened my eyes and saw Eli staring at me. 'That is your
decision. What about your daughter.'

'What about her? She will live as we have in India.'

'How.'

'We are not religious, but we live like Jews . . .'

'When she grows up she may find it difficult to live like a
Jew. She may be attracted to Indian ways. She has already
absorbed the Indian way of life. I can see it in her choice of
clothes—silver anklets, tassels in her hair . . .'

'So what?' said Joshua, annoyed. 'Look at my wife. She
wears a sari and she is no less a Jew than the women at the
synagogue. My mother and grandmother wore nine-yard saris,
with heavy anklets, toerings, armlets, waist belts and enormous
noserings, but they observed all the Jewish rituals.' Then he
paused for the correct phrase. 'Their clothes were Indian, but
their hearts were Jewish.'

'What about you?' asked Eli.

I opened my eyes and saw my parents exchange
uncomfortable glances. Naomi's voice cut into the conversation.
'My husband believes in nature, humanity . . .'

Joshua did not want Naomi to interrupt his man-to-man
discussion with Eli, so he abruptly explained, 'I believe in
Darwinism.' Then he burst out laughing as he said, 'You
cannot deny that we are civilized apes. We walk on two legs,
instead of four . . .'

Eli laughed politely, but said insistently, 'Joshua have you
thought about her future? Her marriage?'

'She is just a child. We will educate her and after that she will marry one of her cousins, or we will find her a groom from a good Jewish family.'

'What if she does not like the nice young Jewish men?'

'She will grow up like the women of our family. Educated. Professional. Hard-working. Discreet. Well-behaved. She will not disobey us because she is our daughter. Or she may not marry like many women of our community.'

Eli looked sceptical. 'I have my doubts. One can never be sure about young people. Look at what is happening in Europe and America. Jewish youngsters choose partners who are not always Jewish.'

'We will cross that bridge when it comes.'

'Otherwise you could always send her to Israel.'

Years later, in 1992, at the Jewish quarter in Prague, I remembered Eli Jacobson and placed a pebble in his memory at the monument to those that had perished at the Terezin concentration camp.

Joshua did not take Eli seriously, but Naomi was suspicious. She heaved a sigh of relief when she saw him depart, and said rather irritably, 'Joshua, you must not allow strangers into the house. I wonder if he is from the Jewish agency. I read somewhere that these people are all over the place enticing our people to emigrate to Israel, especially young people.' She looked at me, troubled. Joshua had already forgotten Eli and was busy brushing Lassie. 'Don't worry. If he tries to kidnap my daughter, I will feed him to the tigers.' Their laughter scared me.

88

THE YEAR BEFORE he died, Joshua often implored me to leave for Israel. He wanted me to make my aliyah—emigrate to the land of milk and honey. He was certain that I would be happy there and the children would have a bright future, and eventually find Jewish spouses.

Israel is now a distant memory. There was a time when it was real. I tried to uproot myself from my surrogate motherland, and replant myself in the home of my ancestors. I tried to settle there. I could not. Yet, I liked it.

My departure for Israel was like a pilgrimage. It would wipe out my past. Give me a new life. Help me forget India, Ahaseures, Haman, Baroda, Ahmedabad and wagging tongues, suspicious relatives, acquaintances, society. They never seemed to forget my past, nor did they allow me to forget it. I was running away from India.

The flight from Bombay to Tel Aviv, via Cairo, was quick and emotional. On landing in Tel Aviv, after some formalities, we were sent to the immigrants' hostel in Beersheva. In the taxi arranged by the Jewish agency we drove along the sea and then through the desert towards south Israel.

The sea in Israel is a deep turquoise blue. Tall, sculptured Noguchi columns stand on the road running parallel to the sea, connecting Jerusalem, Tel Aviv, Haifa. Flowers bloom all along the road dividers, green fields pierce the desert and there are hillocks spotted with Arab villages.

We were face-to-face with Jews from all over the world. Black, white, brown, yellow skins intermingled. Sturdy bronzed bodies in shorts rubbed shoulders with people in long, flowing robes. There were also the young soldiers carrying automatic rifles. I was in the land of milk, honey and blood.

In the small two-room flat which was allotted to me at the immigrant hostel, I trembled seeing the visuals on television of war, blood, fire, ambulances. I often woke up to the sound of fighter planes. The entire expanse of the sky was spotted with

them. Army trucks and tanks rolled down the road next to my
balcony. I closed the doors and windows, held my children
close and cried. What a heavy price one had to pay to be a
Jew!

. I had given myself many reasons to run away from India.
Gradually, however, I realized that I had lived there as a Jew
without fear. When I heard the stories of other immigrants and
met the Holocaust survivors, I realized that in India we had
never suffered because we were Jews. Perhaps it was the only
country in the world where the Jews had never faced persecution.
Even the Muslim ruler Tipu Sultan had treated our ancestors
with respect.

In Beersheva, I tried to learn Hebrew, sang folk songs with
other immigrant families, learnt to dance the Hora, ate in the
common canteen. Here, I discovered Israeli cuisine—herring,
balls of Gefilet fish, chicken soup and matzo balls, calf's feet
jelly and lamb's tongue in a spicy sauce. Stuffed cabbage, the
delicious schnitzel made with turkey chops, zucchini stuffed
with mince, roast chicken and borscht. A variety of pancakes,
apple strudel, cheese cake and challah, the plaited bread for the
shabath. We took an instant liking to the felafel—spicy and
just right for the Indian tongue. Pitta bread became a good
substitute for chapatis. In a month, my finances were low and
it was time to look for a job.

I could barely speak Hebrew and with my kind of
qualifications, finding work looked impossible. The social
workers at the hostel tried to help. They advised that I settle
deeper in the south, at the Dead Sea salt works, like most Bene
Israel Jews. Or perhaps I could find work as a secretary in an
international company. I soon realized that without Hebrew, it
was impossible to survive in Israel.

Perhaps I could start an Indian restaurant? Plan menus, do

the shopping, make mounds of masala, cook, set tables, wash dishes. What if the restaurant failed? I was not known to be a good cook. Anyway, was that what I wanted to do with my life? No.

I could no longer see myself living in Israel. I needed to speak to somebody like Shlomo. I searched for him. He was not at the phone number he had given me. Perhaps he had changed house. I tried all the Shlomos in the telephone directory. I could not find him. I never saw Shlomo again. He had disappeared after having instilled in me a desire for Israel and the Jewish way of life.

I was confused. Perhaps it would be a good idea to see as much of Israel as possible while I was there. The Diaspora Museum, the Holocaust Museum, the Museum of Modern Art, the Phoenician port and medieval citadel at Acre, ancient synagogues with mosaic floors, the Roman amphitheatre, Greek columns, Mount Carmel and the caves of the prophet Elijah, the grottos, Masada, the last stronghold of the Jews against the Romans, Zubin Mehta at the Israel Philharmonic, Chagall's sparkling stained glass windows in Jerusalem's Hadashha hospital, the last remnant of king Solomon's temple—the Western Wall. Besides noticing things such as the concentration number tattoed on an old woman's arm in the bus. It reminded me of the Eliyahu Hannabi cha tapa in the Konkan. You make a secret wish, write it on a piece of paper, insert it in one of the crevices of the Western Wall—and your wish is granted.

Having seen most of Israel, I still felt that I had forgotten something important. It was only when I saw the annoucement of a cheap tour to Mount Sinai in the *Jerusalem Post* that I remembered Grandmother and her wish to make a pilgrimage to the mountain. A week later, I was standing on Mount Sinai, in the Negev, choked with emotion, my feet covered with the

374 Book of Esther

ancient dust, next to the craggy rocks. I picked up a pebble, scratched an S on it with my hairpin and inserted it in a crevice in a rock. If she had seen these rugged rocks, perhaps Shebabeth would have been disappointed. Unlike the mountain of her imagination, it was not the diamond of the desert.

On my return to my hostel at Beersheva, I tried to sell Indian embroidery which I had brought from Gujarat. I was told that if I could sell it, I could earn those extra shekels which I needed so badly. The social worker in charge of my file found me addresses of prospective buyers. He said Yael in Tel Aviv was the right person. When I called her, I was relieved that she spoke English, though with a heavy Israeli accent. I took a bus to Tel Aviv, then walked a long distance to reach her house with my bags of embroidery. Yael was a sabra of Russian origin, tall, with huge shoulders. She was friendly and kind, and offered me wine and cake. She liked the embroidery, but she did not want to buy it. When she saw the look of disappointment on my face, she suggested that we meet Ruth Dayan, wife of the formidable General Dayan. Ruth was a connoisseur of arts and crafts.

When I met Ruth Dayan, I remembered Aunt Jerusha and her fascination for the one-eyed General. Ruth Dayan was small, energetic and compassionate. She worked with immigrant crafts. After research, she gave them designs and marketed their products in the state-run handicrafts corporation, Maskit.

I wanted to work with her. But she said that my lack of Hebrew was a disadvantage, and the portfolio of photographs of my sculptures and the newspaper cuttings of articles I had written on art were not enough. She could only buy the embroidery if I had made it and could give me work if I was a craftsperson. I was miserable.

Yael and I spent the day together in Tel Aviv, and she took

me to meet potential buyers. Though we were not able to sell anything we became friends, and I discovered the artistic Israel in private homes and art galleries around the cobbled streets of Tel Aviv and Jerusalem. I discovered that contemporary Israeli arts were a mixture of abstract and Biblical themes, and there was a wealth of Arab crafts—basket weaving, leather work, cane furniture and embroidery. Stopping for lunch at a small restaurant, Yael insisted that I try the octopus soup. Unsure, I asked her if one could eat octopus according to the Jewish dietary laws. She laughed, shrugged her shoulders and said, 'Nobody cares. Do you?' 'No,' I said, as I took a spoonful of the soup. I liked it.

Yael worked with Arab craftspeople and had a sizeable collection of Bedouin embroidery. At the end of the day, she took me to her small boutique stocked with embroidered cushions and cane furniture.

Yael drove me to the bus terminus and kissed me. 'I will call you. We will meet again,' she said.

'Yael, I cannot work in the Dead Sea salt works as a clerk. Nor do I want to work as an art teacher in a nursery school. That is all I am being offered,' I cried.

Yael patted my shoulder and said, 'Everything will work out. Till then learn Hebrew, and next week, I will buy your entire collection of embroidery. I will pay you ten thousand shekels. That will solve your problems for the moment.'

Soon afterwards, a cousin invited us to spend the shabath with his family in Dimona. That is one of my most cherished memories of my adventure in Israel. I remember sitting cross-legged in a tent and drinking coffee with a Bedouin. My cousin and he were security guards in an industrial estate in Dimona, the stronghold of Indian Bene Israel Jews—our little India. Everything here looked like India—saris drying in balconies, men in striped pajamas and the strong fragrance of Indian spices and jasmine flowers.

When I returned to my flat in Beersheva, I was offered a house in the suburbs. It was a small house with a huge wooden door which had iron knockers like those we had in the ancestral house at Delhi Darwaza. Inside, the courtyard was covered with mosaic tiles in green, blue and white. There was an orange tree in the centre, laden with ripe fruit. I felt I had walked into a house from the *Arabian Nights*. There were arched doorways and room arranged around the courtyard, almost like in an Indian house. I was not being offered an apartment, as they normally did. The social worker who showed me the house was of Indian origin. He was insistent that I take it without a second thought. The finances would be worked out later. I was being offered this house as I had asked for a studio–residence where I could sculpt.

I was studying the tiles when I noticed that I was standing on a discoloured brown patch. I asked him if the house belonged to an Israeli family. I could see the irritation in his eyes as he said, 'Does it matter as long as you have a roof over your head?'

'I was just curious.'

Abruptly he said, 'It belonged to an Arab family. They left . . .'

Terrified, I moved away from the discoloured patch and said, 'No, I cannot take this house.'

'You are stupid. Too sentimental. If you want to stay here, get used to the life here.'

We drove in silence to the sculptor's studio who had promised to help find me work. She was a huge woman with a round face and close-cropped hair. She was working on an enormous stone sculpture with an electric drill. Sitting on the

formless grey stone, she smiled and said, 'Shalom.' She quickly
gave me a list of agencies I could contact. She realized that she
was not being hospitable when I told her that I could not hear
her and turned off the drill. She jumped down and offered us
wine and cheese. She was willing to help, but at that moment,
I started wondering if I really wanted to continue as a sculptor.

It was one of the many questions that I began to ask myself
while I was in Israel. Was I an artist? What did I want to do
with my life? So far I had been floating aimlessly. Yael and
Ruth had inspired me. Perhaps I could do similar work in the
slums around my house in Ahmedabad. Ahmedabad? Why was
I thinking about working in Ahmedabad? I was in Israel. I had
to make my life here, a new life. How was I going to survive?
Find work? Live?

When I came to Israel, I hoped that a magic wand would
change my life. I was searching for the fairy tale land of my
grandmother's stories. A land which was covered with gold
dust and where pearls grew on trees . . .

If I wished to live like a Jew, I could live anywhere. I did
not have to live in Israel to feel more Jewish than I felt in India.
For me Israel was a discoloured mosaic floor, stained by
images of violence, fire, blood, ambulances. Israel unnerved
me. I was terrified of terrorist attacks, the right to kill for
survival, and the constant tension. I did not have the courage
to make a home in Israel, all alone. I needed some sort of
support. A person. A family. A community. In Israel, I was
restless with my cousins, uncles, aunts, old family friends. We
had nothing in common. I felt the same distance with my
relatives in Bombay, Poona, Ahmedabad, America, Canada,
everywhere, except one—Malkha.

I needed to return to Ahmedabad, to Joshua, my father.
His presence made me feel safe. Escape was impossible. I felt

responsible for Joshua. I could not leave him alone in India. I
could not make my aliyah to Israel. I saw him, old and ailing,
closing windows and locking doors, alone in the big house. I
could see him missing us. I wanted to be present for him, as
long as he lived. I felt at peace only when I had fed him, seen
that he had washed, changed and was tucked into bed. Our
roles had reversed. I felt relieved as I made preparations to
return.

89

WHEN MY FATHER died in 1989, I had no time to grieve. As his
only child, I had inherited all his movable and immovable
property. My father was buried in a grave, and I was buried
under my inheritance. The house was like an antique shop.
There were old marble sculptures, bronze figurines, Chinese
vases, old woodcarvings, dancing dolls, dioramas of birds and
reptiles such as the stuffed king cobra. Trophies of tigers, lions,
panthers and alligators looked down at me from the walls.
With this, there were innumerable files, books and papers.

As long as my father was there, I was never afraid. But
after his death, I would wake up in a cold sweat. I felt that
somebody was watching me. The lions, tigers and panthers
were snarling and staring at me with their glass eyes. In the
play of shadow and light, their eyes shone like fireflies. Terrified,
I lay in bed without moving. I waited for morning. The reptiles
scared me more than the cats—specially the king cobra. Often,
I heard a hiss close to me. And, even when fast asleep, I felt
slithering movements around me. I covered the snake's glass
case with a cloth.

Trying to get some order in my life, I decided that I had to get rid of everything. Even otherwise, with a cook and a daily help, I could not look after my father's belongings. During his lifetime, there was an army of workers from the zoo to help him. I offered his collection to the Ahmedabad Municipal Corporation and Sundarvan, the nature park. They accepted my offer and displayed everything in the natural history museum which was named after him.

Once the house was empty of all the creatures who had lived with us like old relatives, I felt sad. The house looked bare and lifeless. On the first night after their departure, the house was eerily silent. I missed them. I started sorting out my father's papers and photographs. Among them, I came across a photograph that I titled 'The Death of Albert'. It was brittle, torn at the edges, and had a faded sepia tone. At first I thought it was a painting from my father's collection. But on closer study, I recognized Aunt Jerusha and saw that the reclining figure was Uncle Albert. He looked pale, his head was covered with a white cloth, and although it was the height of summer, he was wrapped up in a blanket. Maybe they had covered his crushed body so that nobody could see the damage. The boy sitting at his feet, with the long face and fez cap, was Uncle Menachem. And the little boy in the corner, sitting at his head, was my father Joshua. Albert looked very sick, perhaps he was dying. How strange, I thought, that somebody from our family had wanted to record his death.

90

I WAS STILL shaken by Joshua's death when G came into my life. G because he was my Golem. The one I created because I wanted to lead a Jewish life with a Jewish husband. I was searching for the meaning of being Jewish. And he needed an Indian wife.

Golem had been coming to Ahmedabad for years, first from America, then France. We had met often. We had our own worlds, and did not want to disturb anything. He was artistic, a little bohemian, cheerful, and the children liked him.

We were attracted to each other. At first we wrote to each other. Then, one day, he called from Paris, at 2 a.m. during Navratri in September 1990. Microphones were blaring around the house and all I understood was that he wanted to settle down with me. I kept on saying 'I don't know . . .' till he asked me to write to him. I spent the night in great perturbation. I was forty-six and did not know what I wanted to do with my life. My father was dead. The children had grown up. My daughter was twenty, son seventeen. They had decided to live in Israel on a kibbutz. They liked Israel. I did not. I was planning to follow them, although I did not want to. I had resigned from a lecturership in a local art college. I had started work on my first novel.

Golem wrote telling me he saw in me the woman he was searching for—wife, lover, friend, mother, sister. Together we would construct a new life.

I was undecided for six months. I spent my days sorting out Joshua's things. Until Golem decided to fly to Ahmedabad to meet me. We could then come to some decision. When I received him at the Sardar Vallabhbhai Patel airport, I knew I would marry him.

Golem was not like Ahaseures, but he was comforting and had a nice smile. There was something familiar about him, as though he was a long lost relative. I agreed. I disagreed. Finally I said Yes. My children and I would fly to Paris. I would stay on and the children would continue their journey to Israel. It sounded very simple. But when I started the process of winding up the house in Ahmedabad, I was unhappy. I did not want to be separated from my children. I was distressed about their life and my own. I was experiencing so many emotions that I was in a tangle. The house in Gupta Nagar seemed to be telling me something. I did not know what. It took me ten long years to decipher the message—it was my home.

91

THERE WAS A time when my parents had tried to make me their Golem, with the engagement to Benjamin. If I had become their Golem, I would have led a Jewish life without questions. Now, I had created my own Golem to give myself a Jewish existence.

My Golem was a young boy when Hitler had hoisted the swastika on the Eiffel Tower. His father and brothers had left for America. He was to follow with his mother and join them in New York. They had had to abandon their house and business.

Golem's mother drove them through Portugal. From here, they were to take a ship to New York. Golem noticed that even during such difficult times, his mother wore her favourite hat. The car was packed with valuables and she was nervous and drove frantically. Golem kept an eye on their belongings whenever they stopped for fuel or water. Besides the packages, like all Jewish mothers, she had brought enough food for a month.

His mother's jewels were stolen on the ship. Golem never forgave himself for not being able to guard them. He was also disturbed that his cousins Catherine and Hanna were deported to a concentration camp. He was to be burdened by both these events for the rest of his life. Although he never accepted this, but his nightmares were perhaps connected to these and other such incidents.

Golem read about Dachau and the systematic Nazi killing machines. Many had mushroomed over Europe—Treblinka, Wolzek, Buchenwald, Sachsenhausen, Ravensbrueck, Mauthausen, Belsen and Auschwitz. He was not sure which camps were used for slave workers and which for the extermination of Jews and those who resisted Nazi rule. He had escaped Hitler by a day and he was to wonder for the rest of his life, 'Why am I alive?'

Six million Jews had died. Exterminated. Transported in cattle cars. Gassed in specially built gas chambers. Burnt in specially built ovens. Infants handed over to female Nazi officials—experts in the art of killing babies by applying pressure on the arteries.

In New York, he heard on the radio: Berlin is liberated. He asked his mother, 'Will Hanna return?' No. Her name was not in the newspapers. His head throbbed. He walked down to the toy shop and tried out the guns. He wanted to massacre the entire Nazi army. Wipe them off the face of the earth. His aunt in Strasbourg had already received the notification of Hanna's death. He was like a sleepwalker in New York.

He saw Hanna in a ditch. Face down. Legs drawn up. Arms outstretched. Dead. Mouth open. The yellow Star of David stitched on her breast like a wound.

Hanna could have been one of the two thousand shot at Belsen. At Mittel-Glattbach they found fifteen hundred bodies in a charnel house. Or among the fifty thousand dead, shot before the Allies arrived. Hanna's body must have been still warm. She would never know the meaning of freedom.

He tried to wipe out the image of the doll they had repaired together. She had stitched the clothes and he had fixed the hands.

92

FOR ME, LIVING with Golem was a new understanding of being Jewish. Unlike the Jews in Europe, we in India had never known the meaning of the Holocaust. We had heard about it, read books, seen documentaries and films, but it was something distant. I had never known what he had known. My only problem was the confusion of being Jewish. It was an emotional problem. Never a physical threat to my existence.

I did not know that Golem was fighting his Jewishness. I was trying to preserve mine. I tried to be the perfect Jewish wife. The symbols of which were the mezuzah and the shabath.

When I entered his house for the first time, I noticed that there was no mezuzah on the door. When I asked him, he shrugged his shoulders and said, 'I never felt the need for one.'

'But I need one.'

'Why?'

'Because I have always had one. It makes me feel safe. Protected. The holy name keeps away evil spirits. Haven't you read: and these words which I command you this day ... You shall write them on the doorposts of your house and gates.'

'I do not believe in such things. Does one have to follow rituals blindly?'

'A Jewish house must have a mezuzah. We are going to fix a mezuzah on our door.'

My daughter was then in Israel. When she came to Paris for a short holiday, I asked her to bring a mezuzah. She brought a scroll-shaped ceramic mezuzah. A small parchment was enclosed within: 'Hear O Israel, the Lord is our God, the Lord is one.' Golem was impressed. I wanted to fix the mezuzah on the door while my daughter was there. I suggested we invite at least ten Jews and have a small party. Golem refused. He said he would feel awkward amongst friends and family. If I wanted to fix the mezuzah, it had to be a secret between the three of us.

Golem took measurements and found the right screws to fix it on the upper half of the doorpost. We fixed it exactly as it should be, tilted at an angle, with the upper part slanting towards the house. My daughter whispered a small prayer: 'Blessed art thou, Lord our God, king of the universe who has sanctified us with his commandments and commanded us to afix the mezuzah.'

The shabath was also a significant point of my life when I rejoined Judaism. It was a release from my weekly concerns and stress of living in another country. It was a day of peace, tranquillity, spirituality and cheer. It refreshed my body and soul.

As I lit the shabath candles, with my hands resting over their flames, I asked the Lord to bless our home. Golem standing next to me was awkward. He was deaf to the music of the shabath, which I was beginning to understand: '. . . in six days, the Lord made heaven, earth and sea, and all that is in them . . . and rested on the seventh day . . . therefore God blessed the shabath day, and hallowed it . . . six days shall thou labour and do all your work; but the seventh day is a shabath unto the Lord your God, in it you should not do any manner of work.'

I was not strict about working on the shabath, but I thought it was a good way to spend time with my Golem. He promised that he would try to work less on Saturdays. It was my obligation, as Golem's wife, to fulfil my religious duty— every Friday evening, I felt like the shabath bride of my Golem. I would whisper, 'Come . . . greet thy bride; welcome the coming shabath tide . . .'

The table covered with an embroidered white cloth was laid in the traditional way, with a bowl of salt next to the braided hallah bread I bought from the Rue de Rosier. A silver wineglass for the shabath prayers, filled to the brim with red wine, stood next to casseroles of steaming hot chicken, rice, boiled vegetables. Two slices of apple strudel and a bowl of salad—exactly the way he liked it with the dressing he enjoyed making—ended our shabath dinner.

I tried to celebrate as many festivals as I could. I made puran-polis for Purim. We observed the Passover days by eating matzot breads and I prepared a ceremonial plate with boiled egg, shankbone, a bitter herb, haroset and salt water, followed by an enormous dinner of chicken soup, gefilet fish and lamb. I had bought a special glass for prophet Elijah. For Passover, I filled the glass with wine for Prophet Elijah and opened the door for him and waited: 'Let us sing together the song of Elijah, and pray that we may soon see a happy world. Elijah, the prophet Elijah, soon may he come, bringing with him the Messiah.' We fasted on Yom Kippur—the Day of Atonement.

Then with apples and honey for starters, we cooked for Rosh Hashanah—the New Year. And I always had an elaborate table with latkes and gifts for Hanukah. Golem was more comfortable with Hanukah. He would smile, make a special Hanukah stand for me and go out of the way to buy gifts, and say, 'It's almost like Christmas!'

Soon, our table had become welcoming and bountiful—as

they said in the Bible. It was not uncommon to have thirty
guests at a time. Friends, acquaintances, fellow Jews and
sometimes strangers called, and asked if they could join us.
Our dining table in Paris was being transformed into the
rosewood table in the ancestral house in Delhi Darwaza.
Suddenly, I had a big family of my own.

The Jewish holidays were becoming my way of life. Golem
participated, but not always with enthusiasm. He would annoy
me by questioning the rituals. For me, my Golem was like one
of the patriachs I had lost. I wanted him to behave like one.
Slowly, I realized that he did not believe in all that I was
beginning to understand and love. He was not sure that he
enjoyed the efforts I was making to give our home a Jewish
identity. He would annoy me by asking, 'How can God bring
so much destruction on the Egyptians, just to keep us alive?
Why us?' I had no answers. No space for logic. No patience to
decide whether God was right or wrong. I only had a great
desire to give myself a Jewish heritage, by becoming the perfect
Jewish wife, like my grandmother Shebabeth.

Golem would never understand why I needed Jewish
traditions and rituals, that being Jewish was becoming a life-
saviour for me. He admitted that he was a non-believer but
said he would try just to please me. I did not realize that his
unwilling efforts would weaken the foundation of our
relationship. I painted a rosy picture of my Jewish household.
I did not realize that it was a losing battle.

Golem worked as though he was his own slave. He worked
for more than eighteen hours a day. He said he had to give
back to the world the price of his life. Of being a survivor.

The long and lonely hours were telling on me. I spoke to
him about my loneliness. We were not building a life together,
as he had promised. He tried to work less. But he could not.

He did not know how to live. The only life he knew was over his drawing table and his pen, which invariably made a big smudge on his shirt pocket.

I started giving myself tasks. I shopped, cleaned, wrote, learnt how to use a computer, went to museums, climbed the Eiffel Tower, took boat rides from Pont Neuf on the Seine. Enjoyed window shopping at the fashion houses in the street next to the Champs Elysees. I went to the Louvre to look at the *Mona Lisa,* touch the Carara marble of Michelangelo's *Slave* and Rodin's *Lovers,* and marvelled at Picasso. I spent long hours at the Pompidou Centre and its modern art collection. I walked for hours in the city of light, and tried to be happy with Golem at the end of the day—candlelight dinners and wine in glasses from Morano. This is what I had always wanted. Romance, art, music, dance, theatre and the security of a home with a man of my own.

In many ways, my Golem had come to my rescue. I was unhappy and lost when we met. I was now safe. My daughter and son had been disillusioned with Israel, and had returned to Paris. We were happy to be together under one roof. My daughter decided to stay with me, and my son returned to India. One was safe with me and her fiancé. The other was secure in our ancestral house.

93

I WAS FLYING back to Paris after a short stay with my son. Once I had settled down on the Indian Airlines flight from Ahmedabad to Bombay, I asked the air hostess for *The Times of India.* When she gave it to me with a smile, I did not realize that my smile would freeze in five seconds sharp. Big bold black headlines stared at me: Plague in Surat. It could spread all over Gujarat. That would include Ahmedabad.

A great fear gripped my heart—my son was alone in Ahmedabad.

By the time I landed in Bombay, I was like a rag. My head was reeling and with great difficulty I waited for my baggage at the conveyer belt. As soon as I could find a phone, I called my son. He was as cool as ever. I asked, 'Did you read the *Times*? There is plague.'

In his usual casual manner he answered, 'Fly to Paris peacefully. I will be all right.' He was in his early twenties but like all frantic mothers, I gave him instructions about food and water and asked him to wear a mask. He started laughing. I did not know whether I should return to Ahmedabad or fly to Paris.

I went but in four days, thirty-seven people had died and three hundred and twenty-four cases were admitted to hospital. It was reported that Europe was on 'alert' about the pneumonic plague in India—specifically Surat, which was very close to Ahmedabad. It had revived public memory of an era associated with drought, disaster and pestilence. A commonly used photograph was that of a father carrying his dead child. Travellers from India had to undergo health checks. The authorities were isolating suspect cases to control its spread.

All international flights were cancelled and nobody could fly out of India. I felt exiled from India and my son. I wanted him next to me, in nice, clean Paris where the plague would not touch him. We would walk down the Champs Elyseés and go to see exhibitions of paintings at the Pompidou Centre.

The photograph of the father with the child in his arms made such an impact that I was obsessed by rats and fleas.

One night I woke up screaming. I had had a dream that

our house in Ahmedabad looked silent and haunted. It looked blue, like Van Gogh's *Starry Night*. Beneath the house, there appeared to be tremendous activity. Rats had made a huge labyrinth and I could hear thousands of rats squealing and trying to find a way out through an exit which opened under my son's bed. My son was sleeping with his mouth open, and a huge cobra emerged from his mouth and stood over his head.

Shebabeth would have said that this dream was a good omen. I could not, because my son could not leave India. The next day, I sent him a packet of tetracycline, just in case . . . He was all alone in Ahmedabad with only Aura, our dog, for company. I cried for him. I was always on the verge of tears. My tears would flow anywhere and everywhere.

After a fortnight, at six in the morning, the phone rang. I grabbed the receiver. It was my son. He asked, 'Mummy are you OK? Don't worry, I am fine. The plague is over, and the cities have been cleaned up of the dead rats and dirt. Ahmedabad smells of pesticide.'

I was so sick that I was advised to see a psychoanalyst. But I needed one who spoke English. The first psychoanalyst I went to was the beautiful Eva Rieux. But something went wrong. At first because my daughter had to accompany me as I could no longer take the metro—it made me think I was in a morgue.

While my daughter waited in a bar, I went to the clinic. With shaky hands, I rang the buzzer, and when the analyst said 'Oui' I said my name and the door opened with a click. I was in a dark passage. I fumbled for the light switch. When the light came on, I found the elevator and pressed the button. The door opened. My heart was beating fast. When I stepped out on the fifth floor, Eva with her narrow face and a huge blonde permanent opened the door. She was wearing a short black dress, black net stockings, and heels. She welcomed me with a tight smile and gestured towards what appeared to be an electric chair. Eva sat opposite me in a corner in a tiny chair like the one I had seen in the children's book of Goldilocks. She was so far away that I thought she was afraid to come in contact with me.

She asked me about my problems and I told her about the fear of the subway and the tears. Then suddenly I asked her, 'Are you Jewish?'

She said, 'Yes, does it matter?'

'Perhaps yes. You may understand me better!'

'No, I do not think so. But tell me, do you remember your dreams?'

'No, I do not dream.' I was lying.

After a little more conversation, she looked at her watch and said, 'Well, your forty-five minutes are over. I charge five hundred francs. If you do not want to continue after this session, let me know. But once you come after the second session, you cannot stop.'

Suddenly I started crying. I stood up and said, 'No, I do not think I am coming back. I am scared of elevators.' She did not move and allowed me to rush out of the clinic.

When I met my daughter in the cafe, she gave me a paper napkin to wipe my tears. She was embarrassed as people were looking at me. Holding my hand, she said, 'Mummy, control yourself. Everything will be all right. Come, have some tea.'

I felt better after the tea. She chattered about this and that, until I stopped her and said, 'Ghar jana hai—I want to go home.' We took a subway home and she got off at Nation, while I continued towards Saint Mandé Tourelle. But at Nation, I wanted to hold her back and say, 'This is not the way home.'

When I reached home, the house was dark and on the windows inside were the shadows of dead rats. As usual, my husband was not home.

The second psychoanalyst I went to was Paula from Canada. It took an hour to reach her clinic in the plush sixteenth arondissement. For the first appointment, I got lost and had to ask for directions from a butcher dressed in a blood-stained apron. The entrance to Paula's clinic had a stained glass window and a small garden. It was full of light.

I had to take the first elevator on the left for the fourth floor. As the elevator door opened, she was there with a welcoming smile. She was large, motherly and cuddly with a bespectacled, pleasant face. She gave me a firm handshake.

Her clinic was full of sofas, cushions, sculptures and paintings. Light filtered into the room from the garden. I sank into the sofa and immediately felt at home. I noticed a huge packet of tissue paper. My first question to her was what use was tissue paper in the clinic of a psychoanalyst. She smiled and said, 'You know, sometimes women get emotional and cry. So . . .' I was relieved that she was prepared for my tears.

She leaned back and concentrated on lighting her cigarette as I told her about how I woke up feeling that there was a big rat sitting between my breasts which was growing so large that I would burst any moment.

She asked me, 'Why does the plague in India bother you so much?'

I said, 'Because my grandfather's brother died during the plague. I was afraid for my son. I had read Albert Camus's *The Plague* and the images came back to me on my flight to Paris.'

I had Camus's book in my bag and I read out the parts which had disturbed me. He had written that during the plague, people die in houses and rats die in streets. And that the plague bacillus never dies or disappears for good; that it can lie dormant for years and years in furniture and linen chests, that it bides its time in bedrooms, cellars, trunks and bookshelves.

I was surprised that to just say this, I needed a psychoanalyst. In India, I could have told this to anybody—to the cook, the grocer or the dhobi. I felt relieved. After that, every time I had a session with Paula, I did not tell her anything about myself, nor did I cry. I did not need the box of tissues.

There was a set routine. As soon as I entered her room, Paula would light a cigarette. That was supposed to be the switch that would make me talk. When the first cigarette finished, she would light another. When she stubbed it out, I knew my session was over.

In a week I was moving around, writing and sketching— as I always did. I wanted to stop seeing Paula. But Golem said that I needed her. He was certain that I was mentally sick. There was no way of fighting him. So, I continued till my final showdown with him. When I think of those days, I am surprised that I was such an obedient and loving wife.

It was strange that the ancient memory of the plague had come back to me in Paris, of all places. In a city where people think of romance, wine and roses I was thinking of blood, gore and abcesses.

I had not bothered about my family history till then. I did not even know the name of the grand-uncle who had died during the plague. At that point, I was working on my first novel, *The Walled City*.

Later, in Ahmedabad, at the graveyard, I discovered that my grand-uncle's name was Dr Samuel Joseph Solomon. He was my grandfather David's brother. While looking after the sick and dying in Ahmedabad, he had contacted the bubonic plague. David had come to see his brother Samuel but had not been allowed to meet him. David had felt helpless and angry. It had been a painful death. When Samuel died, David had buried his brother.

94

MY UTOPIA WITH Golem did not last. In six years we discovered that we were not happy together. I was depressed. Life revolved around Golem's office. We had changed places. He was no longer my Golem. I was his Golem. He took all the decisions. I did what he wanted me to do.

I was aware that he had become secretive. I was often annoyed with him. There was less love, more irritation. Yet, I felt secure with him and did not want to face our problems. I was often angry, or in tears. I did not see anything wrong in such behaviour. But Golem forced me to see my psychoanalyst again.

This was to be phase two with my psychoanalyst Paula. When I asked her what was the matter with me, she stretched out her legs on the footrest, lit a cigarette, smiled and said, 'There is nothing wrong with you. Yet when I look at you, I remember the painting of St Sebastian. There are many versions. You are one of them. Hands tied behind the back, pierced by innumerable arrows, but looking up with faith and hope. You trust your husband?'

'Yes.' We slept in the same bed. We made love. And often I could see Golem's feet sticking out of the quilt. But they did not look like a lover's feet. A corpse's feet. Dead.

Why had Paula asked me about trusting Golem and compared me to the painting of St Sebastian? I had seen it, studied it. It was not my favourite painting. There was something beaten about it. Yet, it had a certain strength. A resistance.

Was my Golem killing me, slowly? I would not allow him to. I had to survive. After all, I was also a survivor.

I started a series of drawings. They were like a secret diary. The drawings were about myself. A harsh hard line, dark and vicious cuts through my body. The face looks upwards. There is darkness in the eyes but also a certain defiance. Where are my arms? Perhaps they are tied at the back of the body. Strangely, my shoulders have a certain movement. I close my sketchbook and go to bed.

The next day, I open the sketchbook. I place a mirror on the table and study myself. This version of Esther is unknown to me. Her face is blurred. Her face has no character. I do not like her.

Something happened after I made this drawing. My Golem did not want to eat. It was the fourth day. I was suspicious. Was he seeing another woman?

Golem talks about living in two worlds—India and France. I am shattered.

I abandon my jeans, shirts, coats, shoes. I dress in a sari. With the sari, I am transformed into the Indian woman I was. The one who had left India six years ago. Left everything to make a home in France. I am relieved she is alive and waiting for me. It is time to return to Ahmedabad. India. Home.

PURIM